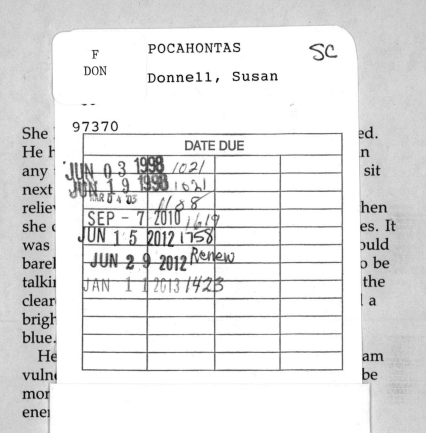

She l   ed.
He h   n
any   sit
next
reliev   hen
she   es. It
was   uld
barel   o be
talki   the
clear   a
brigh
blue.
He   am
vuln   be
mor
ener

POCAHONTAS

SUSAN DONNELL

BERKLEY BOOKS, NEW YORK

POCAHONTAS

A Berkley Book / published by arrangement with
the author

PRINTING HISTORY
Berkley trade paperback edition / March 1991

ISBN: 0-425-12617-X

A BERKLEY BOOK ® TM 757,375
Berkley Books are published by The Berkley Publishing Group,
200 Madison Avenue, New York, New York 10016.
The name ''Berkley'' and the ''B'' logo are
trademarks belonging to Berkley Publishing Corporation.
PRINTED IN THE UNITED STATES OF AMERICA

10 9 8 7 6 5 4 3 2 1

To those who inspired me . . .

Author's Note

THE STORY OF Pocahontas first caught my imagination when I was about ten. In Virginia with my brother and cousins I would play out all sorts of variations of her story, but she always rescued John Smith in his dire moment.

In history there are two schools of thought about whether Pocahontas and John Smith were lovers. I feel sure in my heart that they must have been. History records that Pocahontas was so overpowered with emotion when she saw Smith again in England after several years apart that he could not have been a mere friend. Furthermore, during the early days in Virginia, she would not have risked her life and performed feats of bravery time and again for Smith and his fellow adventurers, who were strangers to her, unless there was a very strong attraction.

Life was so brutal, so immediate, so crammed with adventure during that era. Once in a while my editor would say, "You have so many incidents happening on top of each other, it doesn't seem possible!" But I persisted because these events are historical fact.

Another fact that interested me when I researched the book was the attitude of the English toward the Indians. They were treated as different but equal. The Powhatans were an agricultural people, sophisticated in farming methods (which they taught to the English), who lived in townships of crude houses, adhered to a strong civil code, ate a far better diet than the English, and included a mandatory daily bath in their worship to their gods. They dressed extravagantly in furs, feathers, and doeskins, and their Chief Powhatan (whom the English called the Great King or Emperor, and his favorite daughter Pocahontas, the Princess) ruled with a despot's hand and kept a house for his own use in each of his many townships. They were an immensely healthy people who enjoyed a perfect environment. There was none of the prejudice that built up later after long years of warfare between them.

I forgot about Pocahontas for many years when I was busy living and traveling around the world. Then my deeply loved family home in Virginia burned and for many reasons could not be rebuilt. The family had been on the land for 250 years. I was living in England and suddenly I felt as if I had been badly bruised. I felt an immediate need to reaffirm my background, my family history, which I plan to do in several books. So I sat down and wrote the first words about the remarkable Powhatan princess, of whom I am a direct fourteenth-generation descendant.

CHAPTER

London,
June 1616

"John, look! There must be a church for every family. I never imagined there would be so many."

Pocahontas stood at the railing as the ship worked its way slowly up the Thames, past Gravesend and into the dockland of the city of London. H.M.S. *Treasurer* had arrived at Plymouth the morning before after crossing the ocean from Virginia. There Sir Edwin Sandys, member of parliament, and a small party from the Virginia Company had boarded to escort their protégée, the Indian princess, her husband, John Rolfe, their young son, and a retinue to a formal greeting ceremony in London.

Sir Edwin had been the first up the gangway in Plymouth after their tumultuous crossing from Jamestown, and Pocahontas at once admired his direct and forceful manner and his single-minded attitude. She felt that in his hands her party would fare well. Pocahontas was excited at having been invited by the Virginia Company to promote interest and investment in her beloved country. Sir Edwin had sat down with her and John Rolfe and prepared their itinerary. In doing so, he told her that her old friend and mentor, John Smith, was in Scotland but expected to return to London soon. She felt the familiar sinking sensation at the mention of his name, but she had decided at the beginning of the trip that when Smith was discussed she would not shy away from the conversation. It surprised her that as a result she felt a little more at ease, but the sound of his name still struck her like a blow.

The ship eased past the Traitors' Gate, and Pocahontas frowned as she looked up at the Tower. She knew the Earl of Northumberland, her friend George Percy's brother, had been imprisoned these many years behind the snaggle-toothed iron gate in the grim keep. How barbaric, she thought. They should either kill their prisoners or release them, as my father does. She wondered if that was a Christian thought. She would have to ask.

She reached over to grasp her son's hand. Thomas was dressed in the English manner, a replica of his father in satin doublet and plumed hat. I am as excited as he is, she thought. Tomoco, her sister's husband, had the two-year-old perched on his shoulder so that the boy could see clearly. Pocahontas looked at the riverbank swarming with activity as ships crowded the wharfs. Haulers, buskers, and passengers boarding and disembarking hurried about. It was hard for her to believe there were so many people in the entire world. When he left Virginia, Tomoco had intended to make a notch on his cane to keep count of every tenth person he saw, but had given up long ago.

A crowd of eager faces turned up toward her as the ship was pulled into the dock. She had on her English clothes, but the rest of the Powhatans wore full ceremonial dress, the men adorned with feathers and snarling fox pelts, the women in doeskins and feathered capes, the vivid reds, yellows, and greens a slash of color against the dull English day. There were cries of curiosity and pleasure from the waiting throng as people craned their heads to stare. Sir Edwin had warned her that London waited for her with open arms.

4

As he gestured, Pocahontas saw the Earl of Dorset on the dock. The representative of the king was standing apart with his aides, his beard sharp and pointed in the Spanish style affected at court. Nearby stood a corpulent figure in clerical garb, undoubtedly waiting to greet her on behalf of the lord bishop of London. And talking together in a group were a dozen merchants, her sponsors, their silks and satins attesting to their wealth. The friendly crowd milling in and around these dignitaries was so thick that it took twice the usual time for the visitors and their twenty-strong entourage—the women in sedan chairs, the men on foot—to make their way from the ship to the Belle Sauvage Inn on Ludgate Hill.

Although Sir Edwin had warned her that people would jostle to see her and try to touch her, it was still an ordeal, and the smell, the smell! Pocahontas could see her sister Mehta almost swooning behind her in her sedan chair even though both of them had had oranges pricked with cloves pushed into their hands to hold near their noses. It was hard to know which sense was more deeply offended, hearing or smell. The din of city activity, the cries of the curious as they crowded close, and the yells of hawkers were a painful assault on eardrums accustomed to discerning the subtle sounds of the forest.

Sandys had arranged that the inn would be fully at the disposal of the Virginians for the duration of their visit, and within an hour of their arrival, still staggering on their sea legs, the fastidious Powhatans had the hotel in an uproar of activity. They demanded brooms, mops, and water, and the servants in the entourage swept through the building turning it upside down in their fervor to rout years of accumulated dirt. Sir Edwin took the flustered innkeeper into the shop next door, plied him with wine, and gave him a gold piece, explaining that one had to be patient with the eccentricities of foreigners.

Page boys and apprentices arrived at the door of the inn

bearing baskets of spring flowers, gifts, and thick vellum paper inscribed with invitations to various fetes and functions. By nightfall Pocahontas's head was a whirl of impressions. She wondered if she could possibly keep up this frantic pace and pleaded for time to collect her thoughts for the next day. Although she knew that Smith was in Scotland she couldn't help feeling apprehensive with every knock on the door.

There was a further crisis the next morning. There were not enough tubs in the inn for the Powhatans to take their ritual baths. Tomoco hurried down to the river with four menservants, but they attracted such a crowd it was impossible to offer up their prayers to the river goddess Ahone. They were resigned to forgo sacrifices for the duration of the trip. It was explained to them that this was not a custom of the English and might even frighten them, but baths they had to have. John Rolfe rescued the men by taking them to the Turkish steam baths, a poor substitute until more wooden tubs were collected in the neighborhood.

While Pocahontas rested a dressmaker arrived with two dozen outfits. She marveled at the exotic clothes and their becoming colors—peach and lavender, pale and dark green, red and white, and various shades of yellow and blue. She was enchanted with the range of colors and had no idea such a variety of shades existed in cloth. Sir Edwin explained that the English had had a year to prepare for her visit, and letters across the Atlantic had described every detail of her appearance. She wondered how she would get through the door in such wide farthingales, a fashion that had not yet arrived in Jamestown, and she spent most of the afternoon learning how to maneuver about in hers.

When the Powhatans had settled down, Sir Edwin arranged the princess's first appearance in public—a dinner party at the house of Sir John Smythe, one of the richest merchants in London and a charter member of the Virginia Company. It would be a rather quiet occasion, Sandys explained to John

Rolfe, and would give Pocahontas a taste of things to come.

By the time she had finished the first course of the long meal at Sir John's house, Pocahontas realized how primitive Jamestown was in comparison to London. John Rolfe had tried to describe to her the quality of the things she would find in London—the silver, the gold, the silken cloth, the sparkling glasses they drank from, the rich tapestries on the walls, the fine woods that felt like satin. But no description could have prepared her for the actual luxury. Only the food was not as good. It did not have the freshness, color, texture, and taste of the foods she was used to.

She had also been forewarned about Londoners. Rolfe had advised her to say little and to let others do the talking until she felt sure of herself. But she was astonished by the member of Parliament seated on her right at the table who plied her with question after question about her people, particularly about her father. He wanted to know about the great king's riches and what he needed to buy, while skillfully interweaving compliments into the conversation. He is as clever as one of my father's best river traders, thought Pocahontas.

"You must not take the man seriously, dear Princess," said her host, who was seated on the other side of her. "Parliamentarians are always working. It is the nature of their business."

But she liked the member of Parliament. His barefaced desires struck an honest chord with her.

For the rest of the evening as various people were brought to meet her, Pocahontas made a particular effort with the women. Sir Edwin had told her that they were powerful behind the scenes but ready to be friends in spite of her exoticism if she made the effort. Sandys smiled as he told her the next morning that she had passed her first test with great success. After she left the dinner, all had agreed that she carried herself like a true daughter of a king.

Encouraged, Pocahontas eagerly awaited the activities planned for her. Sandys told her that the aristocrats who surrounded her in Jamestown were now out of favor at court, so he had asked John Smith to write a letter on her behalf requesting that she be received by the king and queen. The monarchs replied that they had every intention of seeing Princess Rebecca, as she was called in the Christian world. She was to be included in a house party at Hampton Court in midsummer. Pocahontas's knees weakened at the thought of being under obligation to John Smith.

At a Lambeth Palace reception given for her at noon by the bishop of London, she had her first taste of ritual and pageantry in England. She wore white, including a white lace ruff and a white hat with a white plume to complement the bishop's barge, which was outfitted in white and gold cushions and which carried them across the Thames to his palace. Boatloads of hawkers and holiday makers waved and clapped as the stately procession of barges—including the Powhatans in flamboyant native clothes of red, green, and yellow, and the only slightly less colorfully attired soldiers of the bishop's guard—moved slowly upstream. No one could remember a woman, other than the old queen, ever being honored at Lambeth in such grand style. But the sumptuousness of the palace and the warmth of her reception gave only a fraction of the pleasure that Pocahontas felt when she saw Virginia honeysuckle, tulip trees, and green creeper vines growing in the palace gardens. She wanted to throw her arms around the new tree heavy with white blossoms and ask how it was that these plants were thriving an ocean away from their native habitat.

"They are the fruits of the work of a father and son, explorer-botanists, the Tradescants," explained a courtier. Pocahontas remembered that she had met the father briefly in Jamestown.

She would have lingered long among the many trees and blossoms whose seedlings had been carried carefully by ship from as far away as India and China—places that she was only just beginning to study about—except that the banquet, the bishop, and the hungry guests awaited.

That night she had chosen to wear a robin's-egg-blue gown made of silk especially dyed in China for her first ball. One of the ladies selected by the queen to accompany and guide Pocahontas, Lady De La Warr, wife of the first governor of Virginia who was a heavy investor in the Virginia Company, produced diamonds to sparkle at her throat and in her hair, explaining that one always wore diamonds with this particular shade of blue and that these were hers to keep until her husband bought her some of her own.

Oh, the dancing, the wine! Pocahontas was intoxicated with every aspect of the Earl of Dorset's hospitality. His Lordship had sent his own sedan, richly embroidered in silks within and heavily scented with musks from Arabia to deflect the smells of the streets they passed through. Footmen in scarlet livery bearing blazing torches lined the stairs leading into his town house, which was furnished in the French manner. She was glad that she had spent hours in Jamestown with John Rolfe perfecting her dance steps, for there were many maneuvers to remember. Seemingly every man there wanted to dance with the foreign princess who so gracefully executed the galliard, branle, and courante to the soft strains of the lute and harpsichord. Pocahontas wished she could wrap the day and evening around her like a silken cloak and wear it forever.

The last days of June raced by in a kaleidoscope of events that dazzled Pocahontas in their variety and interest. King James was intrigued and impatient to see this woman who had captured the imagination of London. He told Sir Edwin to bring her and her husband to Hampton Court a week earlier than planned. He was eager to meet this exotic daughter of a foreign king, this possible rival to his interests in Virginia.

Pocahontas's party decided to take a boat up the river to Hampton Court, for the trip by road was dusty and crowded. Little Thomas enjoyed the river life, with the passing craft carrying produce or people and the various water birds—swans, ducks, and geese—that populated the Thames. Pocahontas was relieved to get away from the inn. She knew that John Smith could return at any time, and a stay at Hampton Court would be a reprieve from the knock at the door that she had half heard now for weeks. She was thrilled with the reception she had received in London. She had talked happily and long about the advantages of Virginia to whoever was interested. Her undertaking to promote the New World was in no way a task and, except for the fear of her encounter with Smith, which she pushed out of her mind by throwing herself even further into her mission, she was content.

On their first evening at Hampton Court the Rolfes were summoned to dine with the king and queen, and Pocahontas wore pink and dressed her hair in roses entwined with pearls, but her hand tightened on John Rolfe's arm when she saw the king. She had been prepared for a man who was strange-looking by all accounts, but this wizened-legged, long-armed man with pendulous lips still surprised her. Nonetheless, she was determined to win him over for Sandys had impressed on her the vital importance of gaining the king's confidence. The queen was plump, but her red-veined face was pleasant, still pretty, and she smiled often. Pocahontas sensed that she was a kindly woman.

In the following days at picnics and tennis, in leisurely walks through the gardens and at the evening entertainments, the king would stop with his entourage of pretty young men and talk for a few minutes and sometimes longer with Pocahontas, who was accompanied by Sir David, the courtier assigned to her, and some of her colorful Powhatans. She used all of her feminine charms and the exoticism of her escorts to entrance the king and, for that matter, everyone else at the pleasure-loving court. As the king later told a gratified Sir Edwin, "She is disarmingly lovely, with a fine mind, every inch an emperor's daughter, but she is not, as you have told me, a threat to me in the colony."

On the morning of the great midsummer ball, Pocahontas was taking her daily walk with callers who had come from London to seek her advice on Virginia. She stopped abruptly near the wide stone doorway leading into the tennis court as the players' voices floated out to her on the summer breeze.

"I hear John Smith is arriving soon."

"Yes, he may even be here tonight."

Her heart seemed to stop and then raced so hard she could barely conclude her business and bid her visitors good-bye. With trembling hands she turned as soon as she decently could and retreated to her rooms in the palace.

Later, in the early evening, the princess walked into the dressing room adjoining her bedroom. She went up to the fireplace and leaned her head against the cool marble, the smoothness comforting her cheek. She did not call her serving maids, not yet; she would dress later for the ball. She relished being alone, a rarity in the palace. She could not get used to having so many people around her all the time. Suddenly she reached behind her back, unhooked her farthingale, let the clumsy garment drop with a soft thud to the floor. Quickly she slipped out of her gown, her two shifts, and her pantalets. Free of clothes she arched her back, flung her arms wide, and walked to the long casement cut into the heavy wall. The mists had cleared and the evening had begun to darken.

She stood, arms at her sides, reveling in the flow of cool air over her body. She felt free, unrestrained, whole again. The large fire in the dressing room fireplace burned warm at her back. The twin sensations flooded her with longing and nostalgia, and again she raised her arms up in futile yearning. Almost in a trance, she started to chant in a low voice. Then her voice rose in a soft wail and dropped again. Words she had not said for a long time flowed from her mouth.

"Ahone, Ahone!" And on she chanted.

Then she stopped abruptly. "No, no," she moaned.

She dropped to her knees and buried her head in her hands. She crossed herself fervently and quickly whispered a Christian prayer of contrition. After a few minutes she sat back cross-legged on the floor nearer the fire, still facing the window. For a long time she remained still, but her mind turned over thoughts that had become worn with time.

Not a word, she thought, not a word in almost six years. I had thought for so long that he was dead. How could he leave and not send back a word? He was my lord, my love. He may attend the revel here tonight. Can I bear to see him? Still she hesitated deep in thought. Then she stood up in one smooth movement and reached for one of her shifts. She walked to the fireplace and pulled the bell rope to summon her maids.

CHAPTER

2

Virginia,
April 30, 1607

The earth was warm from the spring sun. She loved the feel of it against her bare skin. It felt even better than the squirrel and fox furs of her bed. The natural harshness of twigs and pebbles along with the downy softness of moss and the tickle of grass made her feel that she was at one with the earth and the god of earth. She spent hours lying on her back gazing up beyond the high pines to the sky and clouds. Her brothers teased her for being a dreamer, but how else could she find out what messages the gods had for you, she thought, unless you consulted the god of sky and the god of clouds?

Pocahontas rolled over, and her fringed doeskin skirt stuck to the ground. It had rained the night before, and the earth was marked with puddles of clear water. Pocahontas edged over to look down at her reflection in one of the puddles. What she saw pleased her. She twisted her head from side to side to get a better look. Her jaw was firm and rounded with a pointed chin. Her nose was perhaps a little long, but it was straight. Her large brown eyes set wide above her high, smooth cheekbones sparkled with mischief. Because her eyes glinted so often with precocious thoughts and ideas, she had been given the name Pocahontas, which meant Little Mischief or Little Wanton. She was not small, though, and her arms and legs were long and well molded. Her firm, fine skin was the color of sand under water. Pocahontas could see in the eyes of others that she pleased them, and it gave her a feeling of power. Many people said that she looked like her mother, but Pocahontas had never seen her. As soon as she was born her mother was given to one of her father's chieftains on the Rappahannock River. This was his custom. Only her father could afford as many wives as he wanted.

Her father kept a few favored children, who were tended by kindly women in the town. Pocahontas alone had a foster mother all to herself. Wowoca was as fierce and protective of Pocahontas as a mountain cat with her kitten, and caring for the future weroansqua, or chieftainess, was not an easy task. It was a constant battle to try to turn Pocahontas into a properly disciplined Powhatan maiden. Because of her intelligence and spirit, she was the great chief's favorite child. Eventually she would be expected to make a suitable alliance with the son of a neighboring chieftain.

Pocahontas turned over on her back again and gazed at the sky. The blue was deepening, and the day promised to be hot when the sun climbed higher. Now she talked to the god of sky. He was her favorite of the gods and the most comforting. He brought harmony to her being.

This morning she needed harmony. Pocahontas felt her head would burst with curiosity and turmoil about the news she had overheard last night. If only she could have listened longer, but her father's bodyguard had caught her, rapped her sharply on her shoulder, and sent her on her way. How would she ever learn what they were talking about without her father knowing that she was eavesdropping? she wondered.

16

It had been hard to see through the narrow crack in the wall but she had been in the council house many times, so the picture was clear in her mind—the dim light dulled further by the clouds of tobacco smoke that hovered under the ceiling, the walls made of sheets of bark and woven reed matting hung with multicolored feather trophies, the brightly dyed matting on the beaten earth of the floor. She could hear the familiar deep cadence of her uncle Wowincho's voice. What was he doing here? His home village was a day's journey away. He must have arrived secretly. Normally, runners would have come from his town to announce the chieftain's arrival and Powhatan would have sent a delegation out to greet him. Her surprise and curiosity had led her straight to the crack in the wall. Her father, the great chief, was sitting on a small throne covered with furs. If he had been alone with his wives, she would have walked in to bid him good night, but this evening his elder warriors were seated around him talking intensely. She could sense the waves of tension through the bark walls. And there were no black-painted priests present. Straining as hard as she could, she managed to hear snatches of what her uncle was saying.

"Devils who make strange noises . . . The dirty warriors again . . . Hairy . . . Huge canoes!"

Pocahontas was puzzled. What were they talking about? "Warriors" and "devils," Wowincho had said. Had a new tribe come to fight them?

Pocahontas caught a glimpse of her father's face, grim and forbidding. He seemed irritated by what Wowincho was telling him, but she sensed no anxiety. But then, she had never seen her father apprehensive. He was the all-powerful ruler of all the lands, some said as powerful as the gods themselves. Powhatan's word was absolute and unquestioned. Pocahontas was accustomed to his adoring yet fearful subjects who trembled and even fainted in his presence.

It was not fear that she felt now but foreboding. This talk was all too strange, unlike anything she had heard before.

A cloud as flimsy as a spiderweb seemed to film the sun, and Pocahontas shivered. She would just have to wait until they were ready to speak about it. She knew that would not be easy. She had lain awake half the night trying to plot a course that would satisfy her curiosity quickly. In her twelve years, Pocahontas had learned that waiting was hard.

Perhaps she should offer a sacrifice—a bird, a squirrel, maybe a rabbit. It would please the gods and also ward off any trouble from her father for eavesdropping.

Pocahontas lay for a few moments on the warm earth, contemplating her task. She put her ear to the ground. It was a reflex as natural as breathing. It was important to know what might be moving nearby. She was not as proficient as some of the older men in detecting various sounds through the earth, but she knew the basic lore as well as, if not better than, others her age. Did she hear a faint thudding? She wasn't sure. She sometimes found that she imagined sounds. She fingered the sharp flint knife at her waist, a recent gift from her father. Then she put her ear to the ground again. She heard no sound, felt no trace of animal movement. Drawing in her legs, she came to her feet in a single graceful movement. She stood looking toward the forest for a moment, a straight slim figure, her eyes narrowed against the glare of the sun, her long black hair hanging down between her shoulderblades. She began to walk toward the forest, toward the place where the sun would set.

The forest began at the end of the meadow and stretched as far as any of the warriors of the town could ever travel. It was the flowering season, and the dogwood was in full bloom and the forest was bright with its white and pale pink blossoms. Some trees carried great hangings of purple wisteria interspersed with clumps of azalea, brilliant in sharp pinks and reds. The cover was good and the weather clear. It was a perfect day for hunting.

Pocahontas listened again when she reached the first trees. And again after walking a few paces farther. And again. This time she sensed it—a trace of scent on the breeze, a hint of hooves transmitted through the earth. It was faint and indistinct, but she knew it was there, deeper in the forest, away from the town toward the sunset.

She went on slipping from tree to tree, her bare feet moving lightly, checking the ground before each footfall so that she would crunch no twig underfoot. Her mind was now as sharp as the knife at her belt, every sense was fixed on her quarry. She had hunted so often that her movements were instinctive—the pauses to check the wind direction against her skin, the shallow breaths that brought with them the scent of pine, of dogwood blossoms, of deer. Of deer . . .

The scent was clear. She slithered around the thick trunk of an old pine, and stiffened; it was there, a doe, young and pale, a bowshot away, but her weapon was a knife and not an arrow. If only she had been allowed to carry a bow! It was a running feud with her father.

I can't think of that now, she thought. I just have to get her with my knife.

She knew it was going to be the most difficult kill she had ever attempted. She knew that none of the men would even try without wearing their customary mantle of deerskin and antlers to deceive the deer. She would have to wait until the doe came closer, much closer, and then take her by surprise. To drop from a tree would perhaps be best. She would find a low branch and climb up on it.

Her head did not move, but her eyes swiveled as she surveyed the trees around her. There was a maple five or six paces away, with a low-hanging branch that might hold her weight. Cautiously she looked about her, her eyes flickering from doe to earth to tree as she covered the distance. The doe turned away from her, and she seized the moment to run the last couple of paces and leap for the branch and pull herself up.

Her movements were sure and practiced, but even so she had made a succession of faint noises. She held her breath. She could not see the doe now, could not hear her until her breath stilled, could not even smell her. But that was good, if she had alarmed the creature she would have heard the crash and pounding of its retreat.

She waited for a long time. Her left leg was cramped awkwardly, but she dared not move it. She willed away the stabbing pains in her thigh. It would be ecstasy to ease the cramp.

Her senses were focused on the deer. The doe was moving constantly, but never passing under her branch. How would she ever catch this deer if it stubbornly refused to walk beneath her tree? She was beginning to think she had overreached herself. And if she got the deer, how was she going to take it back when it was far too heavy for her to carry alone?

Pocahontas had just about made up her mind to abandon her plan when her skin prickled. A sound, a movement, perhaps just a sensation told her that some living creature other than the deer was close by.

The doe had sensed it, too. There was a rustle, then the thud of the deer's feet. Fully alarmed now, the creature was running away from the intruder and toward Pocahontas and her tree.

Pocahontas had a second to react. There was a blur of movement below and in that same instant she jumped. Her body jarred as it hit the deer's back, but in a moment she recovered and grabbed for the animal's neck. Awkwardly, half astride, one leg trailing the ground, she managed to bring her knife hand to the doe's throat. She dug the point into the base of the neck and thrust her arm up and out. The doe fell instantly,

20

with Pocahontas on top of her. There was a twitch and then the animal lay still at her feet.

Pocahontas let her breath out in a long slow sigh. The first faint feelings of triumph stirred within her, although her body felt drained. Her brain, however, was fully alert. Instinct had brought her down onto the deer, instinct bred in generations of hunters. But instinct also told her she was not alone in the forest. A man was nearby. A different animal would not have frightened the deer in that particular way. She tilted her head and listened.

Clear above the forest sounds came the sharp, distinctive trill of a bobwhite, with one extra half-note, the signal by which her brothers and sisters knew each other. A wave of relief flooded through her. She answered with a similar whistle.

He came slowly, for it was second nature to all of them to move silently in the forest, to keep hidden for as long as possible. But she could see him when he was perhaps twenty paces away for he was tall. It was Pamouic.

Brother and sister stood over the kill and smiled at each other with pleasure. Although the forests teemed with game, it was a moment to savor when another meal was assured. It was part of the ageless ritual. She had pitted her wits and skills against the cunning of the animal world and won.

"It will be good for the feast today," Pamouic said.

For the feast? But she had tracked the deer for a sacrifice to the god of sky to atone for her eavesdropping! Pocahontas thought hard as she leaned up against a tree trunk while Pamouic tied the doe.

It would be dangerous to let her brother know she needed such a large sacrifice. She would have to tell him about her eavesdropping.

To Pamouic she said, "Yes, this doe will be welcome."

All that effort and she still had no offering!

21

The two carried their burden out of the forest through the meadow, across the neat patchwork of fields with the green shoots of corn, the spindly tobacco plants, the rows of shoots and early leaves that showed where by fall there would be pumpkins, tomatoes, peanuts, and squash. A couple of ancient warriors, weak in body but fierce in spirit, jealously guarded the fields by warding off small animals, birds, and children with war calls and brandished spears. Otherwise the land was deserted. Most of the people were in town preparing for the feast.

From the inner field they could see the river, a vast blue expanse of it, so wide that no man could throw a stone across it. And just along the bank was the town of Werowocomoco, the town from which the great Powhatan chose to control his empire.

It was a large village enclosed in a wooden palisade with neat rows of houses along either side of a broad dusty road. The houses were long and gray, measuring from twenty to sixty feet in length. They were shaped like loaves of bread with rounded roofs made of bark and matting. Many of the roofs had been rolled back to let in the clear spring air and to welcome the god of sun.

Inside the palisade brother and sister parted, Pamouic taking the doe. Pocahontas walked slowly toward her father's house, the largest in the town. She wanted to avoid Wowoca if possible until she had changed out of her dirty skirt, otherwise there would be a harangue about disappearing on a feast day when there were so many preparations to be made. Wowoca was not tolerant of hunting expeditions, even on an ordinary day. She thought they were beneath the dignity of the favorite child of the great chief Powhatan.

Pocahontas's latest chore, sternly watched over by Wowoca, had been to learn how to collect taxes. For as Wowoca pointed out, as soon as she was a woman, if she did not marry within the first few months, her father would send her out into his empire. Pocahontas liked the idea. She would travel with a retinue, represent her father's might, and be entertained with feasting and dancing in each of the towns. The journey would be a progression from celebration to celebration. In her father's lands, births, deaths, marriages, sacrifices, torturings, spring, summer, winter, and autumn festivals all had to be celebrated, as did martial victories and martial send-offs. Pocahontas had never heard of a defeat in battle.

When she reached the room she shared with her unmarried sisters in her father's sleeping house she found not only her two sisters but her father's latest bride Sacha. The women were engrossed in the serious business of dressing for the festival. Sacha was a pretty, jolly girl who was readying a feather to trace her ceremonial designs for the festival. Pocahontas wondered how long she would be with Powhatan. She was loath to make friends among the wives and then see them leave and never return. It happened often, but it was impossible not to like Sacha, so Pocahontas could only hope that she could influence her father to keep her in the village. A few of his wives did remain, married off to distinguished warriors. An ex-wife of the great chief was held in high esteem.

Sacha's face was full of laughter as she riffled through feathers and beads. The two sisters, Mehta and Quimca, were having a difficult time making Sacha stand still so that they could trace with fingers and sharpened feathers the full festival pattern on her body. Every line had its place and meaning, the green to celebrate the springtime, red lines down the arms to mark out Sacha as one of Powhatan's wives, the black whorls and circles that traced the meaning of her name, and blue to emphasize her high status.

As Pocahontas watched, she said to herself, By next spring-

23

time I, too, will be a woman and wear a pattern. I will be beautiful, perhaps the most beautiful of all. Little Snow Feather is my private name, the secret of my pattern. I will paint feathers down my arms and across my breasts, soft curling fronds that will cup around my curves and dance down my body. I will ask Pamouic to find the lovely white feathers of an egret for a necklace and to wear in my hair.

"Pocahontas, you are not listening. I have called twice now. Have you not heard?" Mehta turned an eager face to her sister. She was plump and round and not very intelligent, but she was obliging and cheerful.

"Our warriors captured a Monacan yesterday near the river. He was with a large party, but the rest got away."

Captured. Any warrior would rather die in battle than let the enemy seize him. The Monacan must have been taken by surprise. Pocahontas sat back on the clean rushes that were strewn daily about the room. So there would be a sacrifice during the spring festival. She had watched the ritual many times in her short life. It was atonement for a soldier who had made the mistake of being captured alive. It was the chance to show bravery, to die honorably. A sacrifice was interesting because it revealed the true character of a brave. Pocahontas could not recall ever having seen a woman at the stake.

It was a perfect day for the spring festival, warm and dry. The feasting place was only a short walk from the village, a large space where the warriors gathered and sacrifices would be made. Along one side of the clearing Pocahontas saw fires burning steadily under spitted deer, opossum, and beaver. Wild turkeys and other birds were baking in a pit oven. Cooking odors fought with the sweetly pungent scent of honeysuckle and drowned it as she moved nearer.

There were mounds of smoked soft-shell crabs, great woven-weed baskets filled with oysters from the bay, piles of baked corn bread. A row of small silvery fish, each one skewered, waited by the fire. There were onions, greens, squash, and a dozen varieties of berries. Last season's tobacco leaves, dried by the sun, lay ready to be smoked in clay pipes.

On the other side of the clearing stood the warriors, each bright with color for the festival, their oiled bodies glistening in the sun. Their buttocks were painted red, blue, and green and the long plaits that hung down from the unshaven half of their heads mingled with their chestpieces of feathers and furs. Their bows were slung across their backs and full quivers of feather-tipped arrows hung at their sides. Pocahontas saw Pamouic, so tall that he stood out above the crowd, and next to him Secotin, another brother.

Several of the boys who had once hunted with Pocahontas in the woods were there, too. Since that time they had been initiated and had joined the men. She was fond of them, but she knew she could never marry any of them. Her marriage would be an alliance with the son of another chieftain. Powhatan would choose for her a warrior, one who would bring him powerful allies but whom she found agreeable to lie with, too. It was exciting to look at the warriors who were so agile, fit, and strong, and it was pleasant to think of touching or lying with one or two of them. Her body felt warm with longing, but she knew this couldn't happen.

At the other side of the place for feasting, Powhatan's seat stood empty, waiting for the great chief's arrival. On the long wide frame of the bench was heaped a mound of leather—painted deerskin pillows and piles of pelts from soft gray squirrel, golden brown otter, gray, black, and red fox, marten, mink, silver-ringed raccoon, and glistening black moleskin. Behind the great chief's place, against a blurred backdrop of massed white and pink dogwood blossoms, Pocahontas could see the dark outlines of his trophies, row upon row of blackened scalps. Some of Powhatan's wives were already seated there, the young ones with whom he had lain but who had not yet borne him a child. Their bodies were decorated with such a diversity of paints, feathers, flowers, and shells and stone ornaments that no two were at all alike; their lithe, rounded bodies, stained in every shade from pale gold to mulberry, were virtually hidden under the wild extravagance of color. They moved as sinuously as cats as they covertly eyed the warriors.

At the foot of the chief's seat was the special space reserved for Pocahontas. Her place had always been closest to his. She presumed she was placed there so that she could learn from his example. When she was younger she found the sacrifice ceremony strange and tiresome. Now the spectacle interested her; she did not have time to be bored, for her father was far more benevolent than most of his chieftains. Some liked to prolong the ceremonies over several days, but Powhatan preferred a quick sacrifice. His time was precious, taken up with the demanding affairs of his far-flung people.

Pocahontas moved across the clearing and sat down on her mat. Only moments afterward came the hush that announced Powhatan's appearance. All eyes moved to the figure of her father making his stately way to the place of the great chief. She enjoyed seeing him walk in. He looked splendid. His shoulders were broad and straight, and he had the strongest face she had ever seen, sharp-eyed and arrogant. His antler headdress towered high, and ropes of pearls and polished stones hung around his neck. From his shoulders fell a cape of softest white doeskin embroidered in pearls, seed pearls, feathers, and stones; its train stretched along the ground the length of two men behind him. He wore all of his patterns—the patterns of his lands, Werowocomoco and the rest of the five territories he had inherited; the patterns of the eighteen lands he had conquered along

26

the five rivers known as the Appomattox, the Chickahominy, the Pamunkey, the Mattaponi and the Rappahannock; the patterns of his public name and those of his secret private name. All of the patterns were scrolled upon his skin.

Powhatan walked majestically to his place and the line of warriors and medicine men who had attended him dispersed. The great chief lifted his hand to speak.

"My people," he proclaimed in a deep voice resonant with authority, "today we celebrate the spring. We do honor to the gods of spring and to the gods of war. Today we bring a special sacrifice to honor both."

He gestured to the side of the clearing nearest the forest. A group of warriors stood there; eight of them were painted black from head to toe except for their cheeks, which were marked with bright red slashes. Two of them carried a large bundle. Chanting the song of sacrifice, they made their way forward into the field.

The crowd watched in a silence thick with the peculiar quiet of expectation as the men crossed the empty space. They stopped a few paces from the great chieftain and dumped their bundle on the ground. Then they approached Powhatan and knelt before him.

One of the warriors rose and brought forth a thick ceremonial pole, a little taller than a man, painted in jagged stripes of green, red, and black, and surmounted by a grinning carved head. He set this in a hollow in front of Powhatan's place. A low drumbeat began to sound, and the people of Werowocomoco rose to their feet.

"Come," Mehta called, tugging at Pocahontas's arm. "We must dance first."

Pocahontas shook her head, preoccupied. "I'm not dancing today."

Another drum joined in and then another. The notes were

27

deep and echoing, the rhythm insistent. The villagers weaving around the pole picked up the beat and sent it pulsing through the earth, driving through Pocahontas's body.

Sacrifice! the drums demanded. The rattle players joined in, their instruments bright in the sunlight. The flute players caught the rhythm and turned it into a high, swirling melody. Sacrifice!

The music grew louder and louder. It seemed that everyone was dancing except Pocahontas and Powhatan, who was sitting impassively beside her. The ground quivered and groaned, and the dark bundle just beyond the stamping feet seemed to quiver, too. The insistent beat touched a chord deep inside Pocahontas, and her body responded to something ancient within her, some rhythm that had flowed through her people for a millennium. It was sad yet somehow joyous, too.

Then suddenly there was the sign, a sharp nod from the great chief. The music stopped in mid-beat, the dancers an instant later. All dropped to their knees, their arms outstretched. The soft sound of panting filled the air. The great chief waved his hands, and noiselessly all the men, women, and children resumed their earlier positions at the edge of the festival place.

The braves dragged the bundle with grim ceremony until it was only paces from where Powhatan sat. Pocahontas could see the shape now under the black and red blanket. She watched as the head priest reached out to take a corner of the blanket and yank it away.

The man beneath the blanket did not move at first, not even to shield his eyes from the sunlight. The priest kicked him in the side. He jerked and seemed to uncurl, then rose to his feet in one oddly fluid movement. He stood arrow straight before the place of the great chief. He was tall and there was pride in his stance. His nakedness made him vulnerable in dramatic contrast to the festive paints and feathers of the crowd. There was a long slash down his side where blood had dried, but otherwise there was no mark on his lean body.

Someone sighed. Pocahontas looked around. Had the sigh come from her or from Mehta? Or were all of them responding to the young Monacan's beauty and bearing? Something in the firm set of his shoulders, the tilt of his chin, the hard line of his mouth, promised he would die well.

He was not looking at Powhatan or at the warriors who had carried him in the blanket. His eyes seemed to be fixed on the far distance on a point above the horizon. He is praying, Pocahontas thought, her eyes widening. He prays as I do to the god of sky.

Powhatan raised his hand slightly. Two women came forward and took hold of the Monacan by his upper arms. For an instant his gaze wavered. His distant focus changed, and his eyes swept around, evading Powhatan's indifferent stare and settling instead on Pocahontas's upturned face. Their eyes locked. It was only for a moment, an instant of total, stark recognition. But to Pocahontas it seemed an eternity. She knew him; she recognized something essential within him. And he knew her.

The moment was shattered. The Monacan was led to two poles lashed together to form a t-shape that stood permanently at one side of the feasting place. Pocahontas stared at him as the women set about lashing his arms to the horizontal pole, but he did not look at her again.

They were chanting once more, the black-painted warriors, the priests, the people of the village, all joining in a prayer to the gods of war. The great chief looked bored. He had seen it all so many times, and he was irritated that peace could not be negotiated with the Monacans.

But for Pocahontas, suddenly this ceremony was not just another sacrifice. She cared about what happened to the Monacan. It was all so beautiful that it made her ache inside—the lines of the Monacan's body stretched out against the crosspiece, the copper glow of his skin in the afternoon light, the sharp reds, greens, and yellows of the festival paints all around him. She could imagine what he saw: the god of sky so blue today, impassive in the face of human drama; the lush green of the bushes around the festival area; hundreds of faces around him, each painted in the patterns of his enemies; every eye fixed on him, full of anticipation.

He will hold the beauty, she thought. He will keep it clear and cool within him. The glory of the spring day will help him to hold out until the blackness comes.

One of the braves detached himself from the group and stepped up to the prisoner. He tapped the Monacan's chest several times. The chanting continued low and insistent. The brave moved back, giving way to a priest who touched the Monacan firmly along the torso with his magic stick.

The brave returned carrying tools—the thong made of twisted strips of hide affixed to a copper bodkin and a sharpened shell. He used the shell to slash open the prisoner's chest and insert the bodkin. Then he pulled on the thong to make sure it was secure. Taking hold of both ends, the brave turned his back on the Monacan and paced outward with measured ceremonial steps until the thong was taut. The chanting kept pace with him, step after step, its volume rising as the black-painted brave tensed his body and gave a high leap upward and outward.

The second warrior was fixing his thong now, a slow business because the blood gushing down the prisoner's chest impeded him. The chant had become a low dirge, dull and insistent. The Monacan's face was impassive. No sound escaped his lips.

The warrior turned, paced, leapt. The jerk of the tearing muscle and skin seemed to rip through Pocahontas's body. Think blue, she told herself, you must think of blue. You must see the sky. She could feel Mehta and Quimca swaying near her.

Another warrior took his turn and then another. They were all chosen men, the fastest and strongest of the tribe. The Monacan stood straight and silent. His head was lifted to the sky. His chest was one great red wound now. The blood was coursing down his legs, forming a pool in the dust at his feet.

The chant was loud, filling the air. The warriors stepped forward again and again searching the bloody mass for a place to fix their bodkins.

The crowd responded. The drums beat faster, and the people chanted still louder in the cruel insistent rhythm of sacrifice and death.

The head priest moved forward now, and the last warrior retreated. The chant and the drums slowed to a low pounding. The priest's arm moved in time with the beat, knife held high. Off came the fingers of one hand, the fingers of the other. Each time he raised a trophy high the crowd roared. Off came an arm, and a great cry went up. It took many slashes to sever the feet. There was a final cheer, then silence. Behind Pocahontas, Powhatan had raised his hands.

The blood seemed to rush to Pocahontas's head. The cheers, the pounding beat, still echoed there. The thing fixed to the cross was no longer a man. Flies were already starting to settle.

"A good death," Mehta whispered in her ear.

Pocahontas nodded, her eyes as flat as pebbles.

"Come, this time you must dance," her sister said.

It was the dance of celebration. The dance of sacrifice given and accepted. The flutes were wailing, the rattles echoing, the drums pounding out a different undulating rhythm. The people were all on their feet. Pocahontas followed Mehta; at first her feet

31

felt dull and heavy, but suddenly the familiar cadence pounded through her taut body, and in a rush of release Pocahontas threw herself into a frenzy of dancing. Her father saw her and smiled.

Finally she broke away and slipped into the gathering darkness, away from the searching eyes of the men and boys. Couples around her, exhilarated, their passions inflamed by the dark spectacle, wandered off into the woods. She wanted to be alone. She quickly found a favorite spot by the river and sank down onto the cool sands of the bank. She lowered her feet and legs into the soothing water, dipped her hands, and pressed them against her temples. Suddenly it was painful to breathe. Tears streamed down her face. In the water a fish leapt, a silver arc in the twilight, gone in a twinkling. It was a long time before she returned to the festival.

The tension of the day had eased; everyone was relaxed. The women sat over the remaining food gossiping. In one corner of the feasting area a group of young braves performed war dances in a tight circle while others kicked a ball. Up and down the streets of the village the children raced with their dogs, playing games and yelling war chants. Powhatan had retreated to the council house. But the word had spread, the great chief would speak to them that evening. He had important news to tell.

Pocahontas moved back to the place next to her father's before the other villagers returned, relaxed from their break after the tension of the sacrifice. She sat alone as she thought back on the day. It had been a festival, much like the others, but she felt as if something had happened to make her more a woman than she had been when the day began. She had taken a deer. She had endured the sacrifice and not let her father see that she was upset. Surely the god of sky would reward her for this. But it was not these things that made her feel different. It was the moment on the sacrifice ground, that second of total unity when her eyes locked with another person. She knew now she had left her childhood behind forever.

She watched her father approach with his retinue. She could read nothing in his face; he was skilled in masking his feelings. The rest of the village had reassembled and waited patiently. At last Powhatan turned to the crowd and began to speak.

"People of my kingdom," he began. "People of the Five Rivers. Long ago we heard of a strange new threat to our shores, great canoes bringing to these lands the people we call the Tassentasses, the dirty men."

Pocahontas sat up straight, straining her ears to catch every nuance.

"The Tassentasses, the strange ones, came and we sacrificed to our gods, and the gods heard us. The dirty ones died, every one of them. But my brother Wowincho came to us yesterday with a tale brought to him by his braves. Two days ago more Tassentasses arrived on our shore."

There were hisses of indrawn breath around the festival ground, and Powhatan's voice grew louder.

"We banished these invaders once before. We called on the devil god Okeus, and with his help we defeated them. We shall defeat them again. We must be prepared to do battle, to fight a long war if necessary. We must be prepared to make sacrifices to the gods. We must rid ourselves of these invaders. They bring sickness. They speak in strange tongues. They have dirty habits. They steal our land."

Pocahontas listened, astonished. She vaguely remembered hearing stories about strange people on their shores. She couldn't remember if they were myths or dreams. But now they were real, they were here. She was overwhelmed with curiosity about these strange men. She wanted to see them. Every other thought was chased from her mind. Somehow she had to help her father in his struggle.

Powhatan's priests stepped forward at the conclusion of his speech, their black-painted bodies arrogant with authority. The chief priest advanced to the foot of Powhatan's throne and conferred with his ruler. The waiting crowd was aroused now, whispering among themselves in agitation.

Powhatan held up his hand once more and the crowd fell silent.

"My priests tell me that the devil god Okeus must be appeased in the matter of the Tassentasses. We have several moons in which to drive them away. But if we do not send them from our lands soon, we must make an extra sacrifice of our sons."

The crowd groaned and several women sobbed. This was the worst thing that could happen, thought Pocahontas. The special sacrifice would have to be made if the priests demanded it. The regular annual sacrifice was already painful beyond belief. It was necessary, as everyone knew, to keep their nation free of the wasting sickness, ravaged crops, and devastating storms. But to take even more boys would be almost too much for them all to bear.

Any boy could be taken from each of the many towns. Nobody, from the village chieftain down to the simplest farmer, would be free from the fear that his son would be among them. The priests picked the victims; their reasons were secret, and their choice could never be contested.

This must not happen, Pocahontas thought. She would find a way to help her father, to make sure that the Tassentasses left before the priests set a time for the sacrifice.

Her father was leaving the area now, and the crowd was dispersing. All the joy of the spring festival was gone. Pocahontas's heart had turned as dark as the night sky. The morning had held such promise, but now she sensed that the coming of the Tassentasses would change her life, change all their lives.

CHAPTER

3

The New World,
April 1607

John Smith fell hard on his side in the longboat as angry men pushed and shoved him. He could scarcely contain his rage and cursed the sailors who restrained him.

The boat plunged into the water with a splash, dipping and righting itself as the men rowed out into the bay. Three creaking wooden ships, clumsy as washtubs, their sails furled, lay at anchor off Dominica, blown off their course to Virginia. The *Susan Constant* and the *Godspeed* were merchantmen, but the *Discovery* was only a tiny pinnace more suited to river work than to ocean duty. Each ship carried small cannons. They bobbed like large ducks in the calm waters of the tropical bay. These ships had been home to the members of the Virginia Company for the four long months since they had left England, bound for the New World. Tropical heat added to the misery of men whose patience was already sorely tested. The longboat pulled alongside the *Godspeed*. John Smith kicked out in frustration as he hauled himself up onto the deck, where two men grabbed him by the arms and took him down to the brig. The heat there was intolerable. But, Smith reflected, at least the ship's captain was a friend.

He waited an hour before he heard a key turning in the lock of the door to the tiny hold. The door opened, and he was able to make out Bartholomew Gosnold's yellow-haired head through the gloom.

"What the hell happened, John?" Captain Gosnold sat down without lighting the lamp he carried. The heat from it would have turned the little room into a torture chamber.

"The men jumped me and started to string me up. Wingfield ordered me hanged. If Newport hadn't intervened, I'd be swinging."

Edward Maria Wingfield was the acting leader of the expedition, and Christopher Newport was admiral of the fleet and in command while they were at sea, until they landed in Virginia. Before they left England, King James and his lord chancellor had written a set of instructions and placed one copy in each of three identical sealed boxes, one for each ship. The king had definite ideas about what he wanted for his colonies as well as a firm notion of who was to be the leader and which gentlemen would be on the ruling council. Until they landed in Virginia and learned what the secret orders were, everyone was tense and competitive. And the raging heat they had found in Dominica did nothing to calm easily inflamed tempers.

"What was your crime?" Gosnold's square open face was devoid of expression. He had studied law at the Inner Temple before privateering beckoned him seductively, and he was well practiced in hiding his emotions.

"That stupid bastard Wingfield thinks I'm challenging him for the leadership of the expedition. Of course we won't know who will be president until we read the king's orders, but I should lead the council. Wingfield is incompetent."

Gosnold looked at his friend in the dim light. The trouble is, he thought, John Smith is a lion, a lion among the many sheep on this voyage, and a young man still, perhaps only twenty-seven. He had a face on which hard living had not destroyed the marks of an ebullient personality full of an intense love for everything that life had to offer. His red-blond curled mustaches and pointed beard were those of a dandy. But he was no fop. The strong planes of his face and his tough muscular body, like that of a boxer, belied that possibility. No. Gosnold said to himself, no one ever thought of John Smith as a pretender, although some men did whisper that some of Smith's exploits sounded incredible. He had spoken of adventures in France, of fighting for the warlords of Hungary. He had told tales of capture and enslavement by the Turks, a hair-raising escape, and a wild ride across the deserts and steppes of Russia, pursued by his captors, a chain still locked around his neck. Many people thought Smith exaggerated for the sake of a good story. But Gosnold had questioned Smith and listened carefully for any sign of lying or evasion; he had found none.

Gosnold chewed his lip reflectively. There was no doubt Smith rubbed some men the wrong way. He could be boastful, argumentative, and impatient with men he thought idle or cowardly. He was too experienced in the ways of the world to suffer fools. Still he had made many friends on the long voyage. But he had powerful enemies, too, who would be delighted to see him dangling at the end of a rope.

"I have got to obey Newport's orders," Gosnold said, "and keep you in confinement until we reach Virginia. Once we reach land and open the king's instructions, I expect Wingfield will take over. Then he will probably want you in chains. But I think the situation will be defused by then."

Gosnold put his hands on his friend's shoulders. "Relax, John, you are among friends on this ship. We have taken on all the fresh supplies we can hold, and when we are under way, come up on deck. There is a great flock of flamingos on the bay, and the palms and greenery are the last you will see for a while."

Within the hour Smith was leaning against the railing of the ship watching the lush vegetation of the tropical island slide away. The heat was still oppressive and the late afternoon sun was harsh. By straining his eyes, Smith could see the spot on the shore where the men had built a gallows for him. Yes, it had been a close shave, and half the problem, Smith thought, was everyone's discomfort. He had been the only one to wear a thin linen shirt in the intense heat. The others in their heavy doublets, leathers, velvets, and lace were half mad with the humidity. Their irritation was aggravated by rashes and severe itching caused by eating exotic fruit. In their torment their tempers had flashed like fire, and all their envy and resentment of Smith had grown into a furnace of emotion. When Smith defied Wingfield—not for the first time—Wingfield had ordered the men to hang him. Only the timely intervention of Newport, hearing the noise of the fracas from the *Susan Constant*, had saved Smith. He had shown no sign of fear—or of relief, for that matter—when Newport ordered that he be led back onto the ship. John Smith was a formidable man. Few men dared to question his bravery.

The incessant noise of the working ship increased as the wind freshened. Smith was not fond of ships; he preferred adventures on land where a man could bathe regularly in fresh water, a habit he had learned from the Turks. But at the moment of setting sail the drama engrossed him.

"They say we will be in Virginia in a matter of days, especially if this wind keeps up." George Percy stood beside Smith as they watched the crew in action.

"None too soon for me," replied Smith. "It has been a hellish journey."

He liked Percy, a younger brother of the disgraced Earl of Northumberland who was jailed in the Tower of London. Percy had proved a good friend on the voyage over.

40

Percy, a slim, dark young man, smiled. "You don't like too many of our fellow passengers, do you?"

"It is not that I don't like them. But here we are, a complement of a hundred men or so, and fifty of them are hopelessly unskilled in any kind of work or trade."

John Smith spoke with the contempt of a man who had broken through the rigid class structure and pulled himself up a rung, from farmer to gentleman adventurer, although not everyone considered him a gentleman.

"But they are shareholders in the Virginia Company, as you and I are. Good or bad, they have put their money into the venture," replied Percy.

Smith grimaced. "They acted like rabble on Dominica—undisciplined, ignorant. They need a leader, and Wingfield is not the man."

Percy sighed. "It didn't help that you knocked him out in a fight and tried to throw him overboard in mid-ocean. Admit you goaded Wingfield unceasingly throughout the entire trip!"

"Wingfield suggested that I was disloyal to the king and that I was trying to take over the leadership of the expedition." It was no use trying to explain to Percy, an aristocrat, that Wingfield had gone one step too far and tried to patronize him as well.

"We're stuck with him, at least until we arrive in Virginia and can open the boxes containing the instructions."

"Those bloody boxes!" Smith growled. "They will probably instruct us in everything including how to relieve ourselves."

"At least it will be better than sitting on a hole in a plank over the side!" Both men laughed. Seafaring life was bitterly hard.

During the following days the three little ships bucked and tossed their way through the seas in a stiff wind. The ships had endured rough weather crossing the Atlantic to the West Indies, but nothing matched the ferocity of the winds now. For Smith it was torture to be locked in the bowels of the ship ankle deep in water. But finally the storm ceased. With the first pale light of dawn the lookouts gazed to the west. With eyes straining they could see a faint gray smudge. Land ho! went up the jubilant cry.

It was land, their land. Not the Indies, hot and humid and thick with iguanas and tortoises and strange fruits and plants, not the settled territories of Spanish America, but Virginia, the land that had been claimed in the name of their Virgin Queen half a century before, but settled only briefly, and disastrously, once in all the ensuing years. Now the Virginia Company, newly formed, well financed, equipped with a charter from King James, would transform that wretched history. The charter, with its roster of shareholders and the three ships full of men, would make Virginia English territory in reality as well as in name. It was also the first shared venture for men of every rank who had capital in the city of London. Common and noble money was all thrown into the same pot. The shareholders had high hopes that the colonists would find raw materials for England, livelihood for the unemployed in overpopulated England, and most important, gold, silver, and an overland passage to the East Indies and even more treasure.

The ships pulled into a huge bay. Men who the night before had been close to despair were now full of expectation. Confined to the ship, John Smith watched as they impatiently took up oars and rowed the longboats across the bay.

The moment their feet felt firm ground, the men's long pent-up emotions exploded into shouts of relief. Their calls tore the great stillness. Sandpipers and gulls wheeled up in alarm from the dunes and scattered in a whirr of wings and raucous cries. The men capered and jumped like children. Relief made them reckless, and they whooped, hollered, and cavorted. Their shaky land legs foundered in the soft sand, but they stumbled on without a backward glance at the boats or a thought of ambush or the

42

possible need for a fast retreat. Their eyes feasted on spring flowers, pink, white, and yellow among the green grass, and did not see a figure flitting from trunk to trunk among the tall pines, or notice an arrow pulled from a doeskin quiver, or a bow tensed. They had no portent of darkness or danger.

The arrow did not fly. Instead the figure moved deeper into the cover of the forest. The afternoon wore on. The first of the Englishmen reached the edge of the pines and cried out to his friends that he could see a stream among the trees and planned to follow it. The men explored, discovering a new bird, a tree they had never seen, their minds expanding into the challenge of virgin land. Through the fringes of the forest the Englishmen blundered and kicked and hacked their way, searching out the glories of the unknown country. And beyond them, unseen eyes watched, hands gestured, minds plotted.

The sun sank and a red glow filled the sky. Weary, exhilarated, the Englishmen finally congregated once more on the beach. The boy who had been left to watch the dories was the only one eager to return to the ships. He felt menaced by the open space, the silence. He was a city lad.

Christopher Newport, one-armed privateer, admiral of the flotilla, captain of the *Susan Constant*, and the leader until the voyage was fully ended, drew the men around him. Remembering his orders, he began to make a speech.

"I claim this land in the name of King James. And I name it after that most mighty and illustrious prince, Henry Frederick, heir apparent to the thrones of Great Britain, France, Ireland, and Virginia. Cape Henry it shall be!"

"Cape Henry!" some thirty men cried out in unison. Most of them were carried away by the occasion and tossed their hats in the air. Gabriel Archer happened to turn from Newport and then glance toward the dunes. He was transfixed by what he saw. He thought at first they were bears, but he realized almost immediately that these were men creeping, bear fashion, on their hands and knees. Their naked bodies gave off a reddish sheen in the sunset. Each carried a bow in his mouth. Archer gave a sharp nudge to Captain Gosnold at his side.

"The naturals!" cried Gosnold, astonished.

At that moment one of the natives rose to his feet, took the bow from his mouth, an arrow from his quiver, and in a single lightning movement set the arrow, aimed, and fired it.

The missile fell short. But a second one, fired an instant afterward, was better aimed. It caught Archer in the arm, and his cry, sharp as a musket shot, echoed in the still air.

"Stand and fire!" Newport shouted. "Return fire!"

Only a couple of men obeyed his order. Most turned immediately to escape. In a mayhem of scuffles and shouts, the small boats were scraped across the sand toward the safety of the water.

"Make way!" Gosnold shouted. "Make way for Captain Archer! Clear a path for the wounded man!"

Fumbling fingers rammed home a musket charge. The first shot rang out across the sand as arrows flew thick and fast. Another scream announced that a second man had been hit. But the first boat was already striking the water and floating free.

The oarsmen rowed furiously as the boats cut across the water toward the safety of the *Susan Constant* and her sister ships.

At twilight the shoreline seemed peaceful. John Smith sat on the bridge of the darkened *Godspeed* and looked out over the water. Gosnold had managed to keep him out of chains, but he was still confined to the ship. He chafed now at his restriction and swore at his sailors. All the early experiences of Virginia would come to him at second hand! This was the most infuriating cut of all. As the sky darkened, so did his thoughts. He watched the candles glow through the portholes of the *Susan Constant*,

rocking gently in the water fifty feet away. There they were, all of them, the captains and the shareholders preparing to open the boxes of instructions from London. Only he had been left behind. It was almost too much to bear.

In his imagination he could see the main cabin of the *Susan Constant*—he had crossed the ocean on her and knew her well. The captain's cabin would be filled with men standing shoulder to shoulder, the shareholders who were empowered to establish the Virginia Company's first colony in the New World. The long oak table would hold the three wooden boxes banded in iron, their captains beside them—Christopher Newport of the *Susan Constant*, Bartholomew Gosnold of the *Godspeed*, and John Ratcliffe of the *Discovery*. Newport would be the first to open his box, using his surviving right hand. It would be difficult. The boxes would undoubtedly have expanded in the damp, and the locks would be slightly rusty. But he would do it alone, thought Smith.

Smith's main concern was who would be appointed to serve on the ruling council. And who would be the president? The wishes of the leaders of the Virginia Company and those of the king in London would be known. No use conjecturing what else was happening on the *Susan Constant*. He would have to wait for Gosnold's return to the *Godspeed*.

As time stretched on, Smith stared at the stars. His thoughts ranged back to his last nights in London. Ordinarily he didn't allow himself the indulgence of thinking of the women in his life. It weakened a man. Besides, in his long campaigns in Europe and western Asia there were always new faces, new possibilities. But now, on the other side of the world, restrained and frustrated, he needed to open a part of his mind that could distract him.

It was pleasant to wonder if the naturals had women as comely as Annie of the Boar's Head Inn. Would they have lips as soft, breasts as round and succulent? And most important, would they be obliging? Smith thought he could manage without a woman, but he was no puritan. He had been reluctant to attach a young woman to himself when his enterprise was so tenuous, so dangerous.

Voices! The gentle spring night was suddenly alive with voices carried across the water from the *Susan Constant*. A boat was lowered with a splash and men rowed toward the *Godspeed*. As Smith watched, his fury returned. By the time Gosnold climbed the ladder and strode across the deck, Smith was standing by the mainsail mast, a hand on one hip, calling without preamble, "What news?"

"You and I have both been appointed to the council by London, but so has Wingfield, who has also been nominated president. He is trying to push you off the council."

"Damn Wingfield!" Smith muttered, rage filling his mouth so that he could taste it. "Who else will be on the council?"

"Ratcliffe, Martin, and Kendall."

"So Percy wasn't named?"

"No, and I am sure he's badly disappointed. Archer must feel the same, and a few others, no doubt."

Smith did not reply. Edward Maria Wingfield was an old soldier from an aristocratic Catholic family, affluent and well connected. His rank secured a place for him. Gosnold was a popular choice. Young and good-natured, he had explored the coast of the New World a few years earlier, and it was largely through his recruiting efforts that many of the men present had been induced to come to Virginia. Captain John Martin came from a family of goldsmiths. He was expected to play a leading part in the search for valuable minerals in this new land. John Ratcliffe and George Kendall were less obvious choices, but both were able captains. Yes, there must have been a lot of disappointed men besides George Percy.

"How did Wingfield try to block my appointment?" Smith's voice was tight.

"He implied you were fomenting rebellion. He plans to write to London."

"Did he have supporters?"

"Martin is Wingfield's man." Gosnold hesitated. "I think Kendall is too."

"What about Ratcliffe? Which way will he jump?"

"You can depend on only two votes, John, yours and mine."

"Damnation, if only Percy had been named."

"Or Archer or any of half a dozen others. You must face it, John: Wingfield is in control."

"I will be confined for months." Smith's voice was hoarse with frustration. "At the very time when I should be with you to plan the defenses against the naturals and keep discipline on our forays. What hell!"

At first light, anchors were hauled up with a thundering rattle magnified in the silence of the early dawn.

After the incident with the natives, both Smith and Gosnold had decided that Newport should sail on immediately, but instead, the captain of the *Susan Constant* insisted on lowering the shallop, a shallow-draft sailing boat in which they were to explore the rivers of Virginia. The men in the shallop finally discovered a suitably deep channel in the river that ran inland from the bay. The captains now agreed to follow this route.

From his vantage point on deck, Smith could see blue skies and deep rivers, tall trees, clear streams, meadows thick with spring flowers, and forests hung with masses of white blossoms. Virginia looked as fair as he had hoped, but there was little joy in his heart. For four months the men had lived plastered to each other's skins in tiny quarters, enduring the constant shift and sway of the ship, the incessant noise of sailors' calls and running feet, sleep broken by the cries of the sick and the howling of the wind, the cold salted meat, the wet clothes, the everlasting cold, and above all, the stench, a stench so thick it was palpable. It had almost broken the health of the colonists. And now when they wished only to land and build fires, to hunt game, and to sleep peacefully in proper beds in the clean fresh air, they faced more problems.

The naturals were the least of these, Smith thought, in spite of the attack that had wounded Archer and killed a sailor. These braves were very likely subjects of the great king, Powhatan. Raleigh had said that there were friendly tribes and warlike ones in Powhatan's kingdom. Proceed cautiously, he had counseled. Learn which were which and then play them off against each other. But the long journey had depleted their supplies; they would have to trade until they could clear ground and plant their own food.

Smith believed wholeheartedly that for the Virginia Company to survive, the members would have to cooperate with one another, regardless of rank or birthright, and work together to establish friendly relations with the naturals.

Wingfield seemed to know nothing about working with others. He cared only for his own supremacy. He had a record as a competent soldier in Ireland and the Lowlands, but he had never explored alien territories outside Europe. He needed the advice of men like Newport and Gosnold, who knew the Indies and the coast of the New World, men like Smith, who had years of practice in dealing with barbarians. He had no concept of the control needed to discipline men in times of exceptional hardship. He was an aristocrat, and John Smith was the son of a small farmer, a point that Wingfield never let Smith forget, for he was a true son of his time and obsessed with social standing, even at the expense of practicality.

John Smith had been an adviser to the gentry and minor nobility on his adventures through Europe and western Asia. He had fought fiercely beside them in battle and shared their women and wine. He was an ambitious man. He had pursued his quests and travels in order to improve his mind and his status in life. He was determined to break the ironclad rules governing the perquisites allotted to high birth and wealth. And he would save the colony.

"Shall we land today, sir?"

Smith turned around to see young Thomas Savage, the cabin boy. "Too early to tell, lad," said Smith. "But there is hope still."

"I heard that we will land at a place called Cape Comfort."

"Don't depend on it, Thomas. The captains have yet to see the place, and they won't take any risks this time. We will land only if there are no trees close to the shoreline and if we can anchor within cannon range of the shore. The naturals will not take us by surprise again."

Smith gazed at the shore. Each cove beckoned seductively, but in some places the forests were too close, the water near the shore too shallow to allow the ships to anchor, or the land too swampy.

And there were natives there, thought Smith, many of them. Newport's men on expedition had found fires abandoned and a canoe, a great hollowed-out tree trunk forty feet long, pulled up on a stretch of bank. There had been other subtle signs, too— a canoe wake fading on the surface of a stream, the faint sound of dipping paddles, a glimpse of figures disappearing into the woods. The naturals were there, and undoubtedly their unseen eyes followed the progress of the great wooden ships throughout every instant of their passage across the mouth of the bay. Smith turned from his study of the shore and met the puzzled glance of the cabin boy.

"Nor should we kill them," he added, "even if we could."

"They shot Captain Archer," said Thomas belligerently.

"That is true, but we came here to trade, lad, not to start a war."

Savage made a sour face. "We can't trade with them. They are naked and ignorant."

Smith gave a snort of disapproval. "I have seen many men in my time, boy, in all types of clothes and no clothes at all, and I wouldn't call any of them stupid. These may be ignorant, but they are cunning and brave. If you think they are beneath you, you will never get their measure."

"Do you think they have gold, sir? And silver and precious jewels, like the Spanish found?"

"I guess so, boy," said Smith.

Gold and silver. Smith's heartbeat quickened. It was for this that they had come to Virginia, but they had known before they set sail that the naturals Sir Walter Raleigh had encountered here were not the same people the Spanish had conquered far to the south.

The Spaniards had found a civilization that was savage and outlandish but complex, with buildings of stone and treasure houses full of gold and silver. The men on the beach at Cape Henry had looked much less sophisticated, and though earlier travelers had reported that they had considerable knowledge of the earth and waters and skills in farming and warring, no European had yet found a native treasure house.

Raleigh and the few survivors from his doomed expeditions had spoken of the powerful and ruthless king, Powhatan, and warned the new colonists to treat him and his men with caution and respect. They had been only too right, thought Smith, remembering Cape Henry. But the colonists had not come to Virginia to trade shots with the natives. However unpromising the naturals appeared, they had to be guided to friendship, they had to agree to trade, and they had to possess goods worth trading for. They had to have gold, simply had to, or all the work and money behind the Virginia Company would have been wasted.

The wind held fair and soon the ships were easing off their canvas and hoving to in the deep channel to which Newport had guided them. The anchors had barely touched the bed of the bay when they saw the naturals. Newport's lookout spied them first, five of them running along the shore. He called out, and soon the deck of the *Susan Constant* was lined with curious colonists made bold by the comfortable realization that they were well out of bowshot range.

The passengers on the *Godspeed* followed suit. Smith kept to his position in the bow, not caring at that point whether Wingfield saw him or not. He had been held close belowdecks too long and nothing would keep him away from the action now.

He could see they were tall men, taller by several inches, even a head, than the English, well built, with long hair on one side of their scalps, which were shaved on the other, and with a pleasing supple grace. He thought of the instructions Gosnold had shown him three days ago. "Judge of the good air by the appearance of the people," Sir Edwin Sandys and his men had exhorted. "If they have blear eyes and swollen bellies, take that for a warning and move on. If they are strong and clean, take that for a sign of a wholesome soil, and look for a place to set your habitation." These natives were strong and clean.

Obviously Christopher Newport thought so, too, for a group of his men were already manning the shallop. Smith craned his neck. It took a brave man to risk confronting the natives this time, he thought, when Gabriel Archer's wounds were still raw and the naturals' bows and arrows were clearly to be seen. Newport was in the shallop, along with George Percy, John Martin and his son John, a carpenter, half a dozen laboring men, and a couple of sailors. There were twenty men, but Edward Maria Wingfield was not among them.

51

Smith peered at the shore for a better look at the naturals, but they had disappeared. The shallop was close in now, and the beach was deserted. He looked carefully at the forest's edge and caught occasional glimpses of them behind the bushes and between the trees.

Newport was the first to wade ashore, with Percy a few steps behind him. The captain waited until all of the men had gathered behind him, then called out. His cry was no more than a faint echo by the time it reached the deck of the *Godspeed*, but there was such silence that John Smith sensed what he could scarcely hear. He saw Newport take a few steps forward, pause, then lift his arms high in the air so that an empty sleeve dangled from the stub of his missing forearm. He waved as if to demonstrate that he held no weapons; and finally he placed his right hand over his heart in the universal gesture of friendship.

Some leaves shook, barely perceptibly. Newport shouted again. Every man on the ships was holding his breath. Newport's bravado was as thrilling as it was frightening. Would an arrow come at him from behind those bushes? Or would the naturals turn and run?

Damn, I wish I were there on the shore, Smith fumed. It is heartening to see Newport's bravery, but even so, I should be there in his place.

The silence hung in the air. The low trees rustled, and from the midst of them stepped one of the naturals. He stood tall and proud against the green of the forest. He took two steps forward, bent down, and carefully placed his bow in front of him on the ground.

Other natives emerged until five stood on the shore. They moved without hurrying until they were close to the Englishmen.

It was torture for John Smith to be no more than a spectator at this scene. Though he could not hear Newport's words, he could make out the captain's gestures and determine their meaning. The movements the naturals made were not familiar, but as he watched, they, too, began to make sense to him. This was no raiding party, he thought, no group of warriors sent to scare away invaders.

Newport was still gesturing his friendship, as if he couldn't make out the natives' response. Was he really unable to interpret their motions? Or was he deliberately appearing dim-witted? Smith's throat pulsed with impatience. He had spoken many times with men whose words others could not follow. He did this better than any man he knew.

Finally Newport seemed to understand. He turned to talk to Percy and the others. There seemed to be some argument among them. Then two men were left to guard the shallop; the rest, with their weapons over their shoulders, set off with the naturals on a path that led into the forest.

Within seconds they were out of sight. The men left behind with the shallop settled themselves against the mast, muskets idle in their hands, as if they were prepared for a long wait. John Smith eased himself from his position at the railing of the *Godspeed* and vowed to have patience.

CHAPTER

To Kecoughtan,
May 1607

Pocahontas waited for her father along his private path. She was fairly certain that he would be in a good humor after his morning duties. The river goddess Ahone did not ask for a sacrifice of tobacco every day, but she did demand daily bathing in her rivers and ocean. Every member of the kingdom had to comply unless he was ill. A clean body was as important to her as a clean spirit.

In summer, when the river waters were warm and lapped tenderly against the body and the sand was soft and inviting, Pocahontas sometimes had to wait for a couple of hours while her father bathed. Depending on his mood, the great chieftain liked to take one or even several of his wives with him to his retreat.

Pocahontas leaned back against a beech tree by the path. She had never dared search for the cove. Certainly her brothers would never look for it, either. Nor would the villagers. It was death to go uninvited to Powhatan's section of the river.

The sun was high now. Lazily she watched a redbird peck at the seeds in the footpath. Its mate flew in, a blaze of color against the trees. Pocahontas watched them dance around each other in a mating ritual. They were so bright in contrast to the pale men who occupied her imagination. Would those men be as white as the devil god Okeus in the temple? Perhaps the foreign men were his apostles. What Nomeh had heard did not make them sound attractive. He said they wore strange clothes and smelled like polecats, but he had not seen them for himself. And I must, thought Pocahontas with determination. I must.

"Little Snow Feather!" It was her brother Secotin, one of her father's guards this morning.

Pocahontas started and moved to her feet. Secotin playfully nudged her with his bow. He had always teased her without provocation. She had never known how far she could trust him. There was something behind his eyes, some expression that she couldn't interpret, yet he appeared to be affectionate. But one day she was going to get even with him for his constant badgering.

"Is he coming now?"

There was no time for Secotin to answer, for at that moment Powhatan rounded the bend and appeared in front of them. His newest bride was at his side; his hand was on her shoulder. Another of his wives trailed after them, picking flowers along the way, and behind her were Powhatan's personal guards.

"Pocahontas, you have been waiting for me?" The great chieftain extended his hand in a gesture of welcome to his daughter.

Pocahontas could see instantly that his strong features were relaxed. Yes, this was a good time to plead her cause. She felt a little surge of affection for her father and smiled. "Yes, Father, I want to ask you some questions about the Tassentasses."

Her father's gesture silenced her. He turned and spoke for a moment to his wives, sending them away with a pat and a smile, then gave his guards orders to keep watch just out of earshot. He sat down in the pool of shade next to Pocahontas and gestured to Pocahontas to join him, then said, "Now, Mischief."

Pocahontas gave him a confident smile. Her father always called her by her given name. He had chosen it for her, and so it was special to them, more intimate by far than Matoax, or Little Snow Feather, her secret name. He liked it when she was just a little bold. She knew now that she could safely ask for this favor and there was a good chance she would get it.

"Father, I would like to see the dirty ones."

"See them, Pocahontas? But they are a day's journey away."

"Then I must go to where they are. I want to know what they are like."

Powhatan frowned. "Curiosity is dangerous, daughter. Many of our people went to see the Tassentasses when they first came to our land. Some never returned, or came back only to sicken and die. The pale men have powerful magic."

"They have been to our lands before. You said so at the Spring festival."

"We do not talk about this often, Pocahontas, but I have seen them many times over the years. The last time they touched our shores you were too young to care; you were interested only in your pets and games. It is not a matter for women and children, in any case."

"But I am no longer a child and I am interested in them now. They must come from a strange place if they are a different color."

"Too much curiosity, Pocahontas."

"You said at the spring feast that you were going to banish them, Father, but if they keep coming back, perhaps it would be better to let them stay. We could absorb them into our tribe as we do other conquered people. They sound as if, with all their magic, they could be useful."

Powhatan gave a good-natured snort. "We have already tried that, and it does not work."

Suddenly Pocahontas felt unsure. She had never thought that

anyone could be more powerful than Powhatan and his mighty army of warriors. The Tassentasses could be more dangerous than she at first imagined. She must change her tactics in order to win her father over to her plan.

"It is not just curiosity, Father. I want to help you. I want to help drive them away before the summer is over and the time comes—"

"For the sacrifices," Powhatan finished for her in a somber voice. "We all want that. But what can you do, my little Mischief? You are not even a woman yet. This is man's business. It is a terrible thing to have to make sacrifices; none of us wants that to happen. But there will be four moons before the priests sit. We must think and observe before we make any move against the dirty ones."

"Then let me watch for you. My eyes are sharp and my ears, too. And it could be an advantage that I am still a girl. I can go places that men could not. The pale ones may say things in front of me they would not talk about if warriors were present. I could reason with them."

"You may not be able to follow their strange sound," Powhatan warned. "True, Mischief, everyone knows of your sharp mind, but you will be dealing with the strange ones as well as Pochins's men." He frowned thoughtfully.

"Pochins's men?" Pochins was her brother, Powhatan's eldest son.

Powhatan looked at her sharply. "Pochins is very much his own man. The Tassentasses came across the sea and landed in Wowincho's territory, but Wowincho's men drove them back to their big canoes. I had word from runners last night that they are now traveling toward Pochins's lands."

"Then let me go to Kecoughtan, Father," Pocahontas's voice rose eagerly. "I can visit with Pochins and his people. I know the way to Kecoughtan; I can find it easily."

"I thought of sending Secotin," her father replied, "along with Pamouic."

"All three of us could go. They will take me if you tell them to."

"It's a lot to ask of them, a journey like that with a younger sister. Also, there may be more Monacans in the area." Powhatan stopped and looked at his daughter thoughtfully. After a long pause he continued. "You are my favorite child, Pocahontas; I make no secret of it. You will soon become a woman, and I have big plans for you. Perhaps this trip would be a first step toward taking on responsibility. I will talk to Pamouic. You will go. But remember, these strangers are vile. I despise them and so must you. You go not to attack but to observe and listen so that you can report back to me. Never, never let your guard fall. Think of them as your enemy. Remember, too, that you will be a chieftainess, and behave accordingly at all times."

"Father, I always do. I will do this well for you. After all, I am your daughter!"

Powhatan, amused, smiled broadly.

Pocahontas slipped along the various paths, past other buildings that led to her father's sleep house. Powhatan's favorite wives and the few unmarried children whom he kept with him also slept there. It was a long building, the length of ten men end to end. She made her way through the boys' section to the girls' quarters in the middle of the house. Beyond that was the wives' place, and farther still, with a private entrance of its own, was her father's area.

There were four who slept in the girls' section, and Pocahontas went directly to her own sleeping place, a pile of her favorite soft squirrel furs, with a mantle of gray marten thrown over it. She loved the feel of the gentle warmth next to her skin. And there against the wall was the large basket that held her special wardrobe. She had many clothes; all the lesser chieftains within the Five Rivers Kingdom had sent her gifts. There were skirts and moccasins in soft leather, mantles embroidered with feathers and tassels, all embellished with the white feather of her rank. There were ropes of pearls and copper jewelry sent to her in hope of pleasing her father. Pocahontas knelt down on the platform by her basket and began to hunt for the things she would need on the trip. Nothing elaborate, for it would be a difficult journey and they would travel light. In any case, her father's house in Kecoughtan would have plenty of clothing. She needed only a tough skirt in strong leather, a mantle of skins against the evening chill, and for her feet plain brown moccasins, clothes that would not give her rank away. Nothing more.

After she had collected her things, she sat on her bed for a moment and wondered why her father had intended sending only Pamouic and Secotin. Normally a party of soldiers would go with an envoy to hold talks with Pochins and the Tassentasses. But this was not the moment to question. She was lucky that she was going on the trip at all. Pamouic and Secotin were her good friends as well as her brothers. At least Pamouic was. Then she chided herself. Secotin had always been kind.

Pocahontas thought of the conversation last night when her brothers had told her how terrible the Tassentasses smelled. And when they went into the river, they wore all their clothes! No scrubbing with shells or drying off afterward with clean feathers. Completely strange creatures! They had arrived in enormous canoes that flew with the wind and with weapons that roared louder than thunder. How did they ambush? Pocahontas was fascinated.

Pocahontas got up at dawn. She was so excited at the thought of the journey that she had slept very little. Silently, moving as gracefully as a young deer, she slipped through the partition and into the boys' section, past her sleeping brothers, and out into the cool of the pale light.

She went first to the back of the house to a clearing where they kept rows of little wicker cages. Hers was tiny, with a brownish green toad inside. It had been the last task of the previous day to find a suitable sacrifice. She unfastened the cage now and reached in to pick up the toad.

How stupid of the Tassentasses, she thought as she made her way along the path to the river, the toad clammy in her hand. They never paid homage to Ahone. How dangerous never to sacrifice to her. And what a sorry thought that they never gave themselves the pleasure of a leisurely swim.

Soon she reached the bank where the river ran swift and deep toward the great Chesapeake Bay, toward the place where the Tassentasses had come ashore. She reached down and snapped off a sharp reed, then knelt in the soft sand.

"Ahone," she whispered, "I offer you this sacrifice to ensure a safe journey for me and my brothers."

She shivered as she made her sacrifice, for she did not like toads. Perhaps Ahone would be all the more grateful for the distaste she had suffered. Then she shrugged out of her skirt, plunged into the water, and scrubbed herself vigorously. Then she dried off with turkey feathers.

She had to hurry; there was another sacrifice to make to the devil god Okeus. Okeus frightened her, she had lost a brother to him, and the thought of more child sacrifices hung over her like a storm cloud. But the ceremony had to be performed; otherwise the trip would be imperiled. She paused to collect three squirrels in a cage and then joined her brothers. All three of them walked rapidly in silence toward Okeus's temple.

It took time to find the priest, and when they finally entered the temple it was dark and musty. The walls were never rolled back to let in sun, and the only light came from a fire the priest had lit. Pocahontas knelt on the earthen floor with a brother on either side and prayed in a low murmur: "Be kind to us, Okeus. Give us a good journey and bring it to a happy ending. We bring you squirrels, Okeus, but if you lead us safely to Kecoughtan and to the dirty invaders, we will find you a large river pearl, larger than any you have around your neck now."

The priest's rattle made a hollow sound when he shook it. He droned a prayer, and the fire seemed to glow brighter with fierce yellow light. Pocahontas's hands trembled. All the evil in the world seemed to be concentrated in this place. Okeus had to be placated constantly or his terrible cold evil would seep out of the temple and into the town.

"See, the god comes to accept your offerings."

She had seen him many times, but the sight of Okeus still made her shudder. The fire lit him from below, throwing black shadows across his face, making him especially menacing. It was a white face, dead white, and it surmounted a stubby, dark body. She imagined he was like the men who had come across the great water to threaten them. The smoke and fumes drifting from the fire made it look as if the god was stirring, as if he was watching them from behind those hollow-socketed eyes that seemed to hold hers for an ageless moment. Then the fire died, and she, Pamouic, and Secotin were alone in the darkness.

They fell as one to the ground, sighing, and lay there together, motionless. Through the ground Pocahontas could sense the movements of the priests beyond the barrier, soft footsteps creeping about in the gloom.

There was a squeal, short and agonized, then another, then a third. Three squirrels for Okeus, three tiny deaths to appease the god of evil. Three pelts for the priests to add to their collection.

They lay there until the priest came back through the outer door and a shaft of sunlight touched their feet. Then they stood.

POCAHONTAS

The priest shook their hands as they filed past him out of the temple.

"Good journey."

At full light the canoes were waiting on the riverbank. As Pocahontas made her way toward them, with the neat bundle of her mantle in her hand, she saw Pamouic and Secotin readying their own gear. The two men were about twenty, born within a month or so of each other, but no two brothers could have been less alike. Pamouic was all lazy charm while Secotin was ever watchful, quick in both reactions and temper. He had the keenest ears of any brave in the tribe; no man ever sensed a deer, an enemy warrior, or even a snake before Secotin. Near the two men, off to the side, were three soldiers equipping themselves for the second canoe. So her father had decided to send a small escort with them after all.

Secotin raised his hand in greeting for the second time that morning: "Pocahontas, you will be between Pamouic and me in the first canoe."

Pocahontas saw that they were heavy dugouts, not the light birchbark vessels that some of the tribes of the kingdom preferred, and they were painted in the red and blue pattern that identified all of Powhatan's boats. He had several hundred, varying in size from two-man to forty-man canoes. She always thrilled to the sight of her father's fleet when it went out in force on a hunting expedition or a war party. It made her tingle with pride.

Pocahontas had asked her father not to mention to others in the village that she was leaving. She wanted to get away quickly without all the farewells and last-minute messages that might delay them. It was not a long journey—perhaps a half-day's paddling to the point where the river opened out into Chesapeake Bay. She presumed that they would make the entire journey by water. But Secotin might choose to march overland, carrying their canoe above their heads. If so, they would travel over Pochins's territory and arrive at Kecoughtan from the landward side.

Pocahontas wondered where the Tassentasses were now. Would they run into their huge canoes in the bay or even up the river? Some of them might be traveling overland. She looked around at the familiar wooded shores of the Pamunkey as they moved ahead with light, regular strokes. Pocahontas fell into a partial daze as she kept her eyes on Secotin's broad back, her mind locked into the rhythm of the paddle strokes. A part of her mind was aware of the second canoe, just ahead. She glanced sideways and saw the absorbed faces of the soldiers as they moved with the same regular cadence as her brothers did.

As the sun rose higher and higher she began to feel light-headed and hungry. Her mouth was so dry she could no longer moisten her lips with her tongue.

"Secotin, when do you plan to stop? I am hungry."

"As soon as we find a good place."

It seemed to Pocahontas that they had passed several suitable spots. As they kept going, she began to wonder if Secotin was telling her that she was not to slow down their trip. Again she wondered why she had doubts about Secotin. She had never felt this way about her other brothers and sisters. What caused her to doubt him?

Then Secotin turned his head and called to the men in the other canoe. He began to paddle the canoe toward a section of the bank where the branches of a big oak and a willow overhung the river. The two brothers steered the canoe under the sheltering leaves, then tied a plaited rope to one of the branches while the second boat bumped in behind them. The water was at least three feet deep right up to the bank. With a small sigh

Pocahontas removed her skirt and slipped over the side of the canoe into the water.

She dipped under the surface, relishing the cool water on her hot head and neck, and began to swim lazily toward the middle of the river. The water was balm to her body and cramped muscles. She treaded water for a moment, shaking it from her ears, then suddenly froze as she heard the crow call, the danger signal among her people. She turned her head and saw Secotin's chopping hand signal telling her to return immediately to the trees and cover. She slipped under the water, swimming powerfully now without rippling the surface. She felt her way under the outer canoe and surfaced between the two boats with barely a movement in the water.

Pocahontas listened, but she could hear nothing. She could see the others straining to hear; only Secotin looked certain.

Was that a strange sound or only her breathing? She listened again, willing to hear. It was faint, very faint, but definite now, the soft swish of paddles. She turned her head to look at her brothers. Their hands were moving, exchanging a series of precise signals. Canoes—several big ones. Many men—fifty, perhaps more. A fishing party? Some of their own people?

Secotin signaled. No such party had left Werowocomoco or the surrounding villages for many days.

Big canoes. Pocahontas gazed upriver, toward the sound, but there was a sharp bend about two hundred feet away. She could see nothing.

Could it possibly be the magic boats of the white men? No, Pochins's man had claimed that they needed no paddles. It must be a group of Five Rivers people going downriver to fish or trade with neighbors. Then her mind jolted with the memory of the tortured brave. It could be a war party of Monacans! She looked at Secotin's face, hard, intent. That was it.

They waited, immobile as the trees. Pocahontas thought she

could feel a faint vibration in the still water around her.

Her eyes were glued to the bend in the river. At last a dark arrow shape appeared, then another. There were two canoes, big dugouts, each carrying twenty men. Their clumsy strokes created a fury in the water that no Five Rivers man would tolerate; the red-painted prows and the patterns of their headdresses signaled they were Monacans.

The canoes were moving slowly, as if the Monacans were pacing themselves in the middle of a long journey. Their homes were in the mountains far to the west. They must have traveled many days to come this close to the sea. But now they were tired and less than cautious. Not one pair of eyes looked around as they came level with the intertwined branches of the oak and willow trees.

Motionless and silent, the six Powhatans under the trees watched the two canoes glide by. The river was wide and the Monacans were fifty feet away in midstream. Pocahontas could see every feature of the enemy fighters. The sun glittered off their shiny bodies and refracted from the water in bursts of light. The bower of leaves moved gently. A stray twig grazed her cheek. The peace and the beauty were terrifyingly fragile. Pocahontas had never felt so threatened. If only one Monacan of the forty were to take a careful look at the water under the trees, the scene would erupt into carnage. The Monacans would spare her nothing if they caught her alive. The torture would be spread out over days, and every detail would be related to her father. Her eyes moved in her motionless head as she tried to find a means to kill herself before she could be captured.

But the canoes moved slowly onward without any break in the rhythm of the paddling. Their wake washed up to the hidden canoes bobbing under the oak tree and curled around Pocahontas's body in a series of ripples that felt seductive in her first release from fear. The canoes grew smaller, disappearing downstream until they were no larger than ants, faint spots on the wide empty expanse of the river.

Slowly the tension drained out of Pocahontas. She realized for the first time that her body was cold under the water and the skin of her fingers was beginning to shrivel. She looked at Secotin, signaling that she wanted to get out of the water.

Secotin signed back: Not yet.

They waited for what seemed like hours to Pocahontas, until finally Secotin said in a low voice, "I think we are safe now."

As the men balanced the canoe, she hauled herself nimbly back into it. She felt cold, very cold in the shadow of the branches.

"Do we turn back?" asked one of the warriors.

"No," said Secotin. "We paddle onward, hugging the riverbank. As soon as we can, we'll leave the river and travel overland."

"What nerve," Pamouic grumbled, "using our river."

Pocahontas suddenly felt a surge of anger. "In broad daylight, too!" she cried.

No one mentioned the possibility that the Monacans were a full war party. No one mentioned the possibility of capture, torture, and death.

"Let's eat now," Pocahontas said, to ease the taut atmosphere. "Pamouic, take some corn bread. And here is some cold turkey. I'll tear a piece off for you."

It was glorious relief to sit in the canoe and feel the rays of sunlight sneaking through the branches, drying the moisture from her body. It was wonderful to eat the fresh corn bread, baked that morning. But the men were still tense. Pocahontas could feel they were wary, listening in case another group of Monacans arrived.

They finished their meal and drank deeply from the clear river, then waited until the sun rode past its highest point. Although no one mentioned it, all of them knew they would not reach

Kecoughtan that night. They would have to make camp on the way.

It was time to move on. Carefully the men parted the branches and maneuvered their craft out into the water. They concentrated on coordinating their strokes as the boats sped downriver.

Suddenly Secotin lifted his paddle out of the water and signaled to Pamouic to do the same. His crow call floated out over the water to the braves in the other dugout, and the two boats glided together and halted. In the silence they all listened. Pocahontas could hear nothing. She could sense Secotin straining to catch a repetition of the sound that had alerted him.

Yes, he did hear something. He signaled to the other boat to follow, and they all paddled as fast as they could back to the arbor of leaves they had just left. Both canoes slid in under the trees, bumping each other in their haste. The ripples around them faded and died. Birds that had twittered up in alarm circled and finally settled down. The river was still.

Pocahontas mouthed the word "Monacans?"

Pamouic nodded sharply and gestured for absolute silence.

Why? Pocahontas wondered. Why are they returning? Did they sense our presence? Or are they escaping from trouble upstream? Every terrible possibility occurred to her as they waited.

With a display of powerful speed, the invaders were suddenly abreast of them. The small band of Powhatans could see determination but no fear on the faces of their enemy. It was obvious that something had happened to alert them and that they had a plan.

The canoes moved on rapidly for a short stretch, then veered toward the bank above them and jolted to a stop. All except two men—left to guard the canoes—disembarked and moved silently in the forest. The Powhatans could smell the Monacans.

70

But the wind was with them and, with luck, would hold.

Secotin gestured to his band and whispered softly, "We have got to leave this place at once. If they circle back they will find us, and if the wind changes we'll be discovered. Listen carefully. Hug the bank and paddle fast downstream. Pocahontas, keep watch. If you think the Monacans see us—"

Pocahontas nodded. Fear had gripped her again. She was the hunted; it was a new sensation. She knew her body gave off the scent of fear, like that of an animal, and she could smell it on the others.

Secotin looked each of the braves in the eye to be sure they understood his orders. The soldiers pulled out first. The men paddled quickly and silently in sharp precise strokes that made no more noise than a dragonfly touching the water.

All of the Monacans had disappeared into the forest except the men guarding the two canoes. The Powhatans could occasionally hear a twig snap or dry grass rustle underfoot. Pocahontas kept her eyes steadily on the guards. They were gesturing and talking, their eyes averted from the escaping canoes.

Then one of them turned and seemed to search the bank. Blind terror stilled the pulse of her blood. Then Pocahontas saw the Monacan's body become suddenly rigid and alert.

"They have seen us," she hissed.

Secotin's body barely responded, but he half turned to the other boat and cried "Hurry!"

The canoe ahead of them moved into full power, skimming over the water like a sea gull. Their own craft leapt forward with a protesting creak. Pocahontas's eyes were glued to the Monacans. The guards were standing up in the canoes, their shouts echoing across the wide expanse of water.

They were calling to the others. It would take time for them to pile back into their canoes, she thought. Also they did not paddle skillfully, but there were twenty strong men to each canoe.

71

Sheer power would give them speed. It would be impossible for the Powhatans to get away.

"Tell me when they set off." Secotin barely spoke aloud.

"Not yet. Not yet . . . . Now!"

" 'Possum!"

A childhood signal. Pocahontas had not expected the sudden roll of the canoe. But Pamouic had, she realized as she hit the water, and all the instincts of her upbringing helped her to control her body. Pamouic was moving as easily as Secotin, and the two braves caught at the canoe and shoved it hard downstream. A single stroke sent them underwater to the reeds that bordered the river there. Pocahontas reached them a moment later. She came to the surface between her two brothers, her head just above the water in the midst of the reeds.

"The other canoe," she whispered.

"Forget about it. Find a reed and duck."

"Pray to Ahone," Pamouic said. He broke off a long thick reed and handed it to her. She put one end of the reed in her mouth and sank down into the shallow water, close to the muddy bottom. Her skin prickled from the coolness of the water, and as she half lay on the bottom she could see the tall reeds around them and the faint swirl of mud as it settled when their movements quieted. The other end of the reed was above the water, and she breathed easily through the hollow stalk. Pamouic was next to her and he reached out and squeezed her hand.

They waited. A water snail crawled along Pocahontas's arm. She watched its painfully slow progress.

The Monacan canoes sped past, dark shadows on the surface of the water. Pocahontas breathed through her reed, deep, careful drafts. One of the Monacan boats returned. It passed and repassed them. Two long sticks came down from the canoe, stabbing at the reed stand at random. One stab hit Pamouic's hand. He did not flinch, did not move. The Monacan boat went on.

72

They continued to wait for what seemed hours. Pocahontas told herself to be patient; her brothers would tell her when it was safe. She watched the underwater world, the sturdy reeds, a waving weed on the riverbed, the fish and insects. A small water snake slithered by. Her breath was coming naturally, and she enjoyed the feeling of being in a new element. I am a river creature, Ahone's child; perhaps this is my element, this quiet coolness.

Finally Secotin reached out to touch her, signaling for her to remain still. She watched as his head broke the surface. After a long pause he gestured for the others to surface quietly. The water streamed down Pocahontas's face. Her ears were full of water, her hair full of reeds and mud. She looked around and saw that Secotin was already in midstream checking up and down the river, his head bobbing on the current. Pamouic was wading downstream, checking the shore. There was no other living creature in sight.

Her brothers returned to her side a few moments later.

"No sign of a canoe or of any Monacans." Secotin squinted as he gazed off into the distance. "We're close to the mouth of the bay. We can either search for the canoe and take our chances by sea or run overland."

"Overland," said Pamouic.

"Now?" asked Secotin.

"It would be safer to hide until dark, better to cross the river and find some good trees to climb."

"I'll stay with Pocahontas."

"No, I will," said Pamouic firmly.

Cautiously, one by one, they swam across the broad river until they reached the far bank, checking for any strange movement as they went. On the other side they crouched low, using the reeds as cover until they reached a narrow space between the bank and the trees. Then at a signal they broke and ran.

Pocahontas was as fast as a mountain cat. She reached the woods first, chose a tall, thick-trunked tree, and scrambled up, with Pamouic right behind her.

"Keep going up," he called, "until you can see around you."

She didn't need to be told. Her burst of speed had aroused every nerve in her waterlogged body. Now the bark of the tree felt rough and warm. And most important, she was moving toward the sky. No, she thought, I am not a river child. Ahone was good to us and answered our prayers, but it is the god of sky who is my favorite. I should be a bird, not a fish, a bird that soars toward the sun. She climbed eagerly until finally she reached the top. The tree was tall, and she could see for miles in all directions. The forest was a carpet of green leaves interspersed with white dogwood, a magical sight. It was broken only by the great waving expanse of the river. She waited for a moment reveling in the sun and the sky, then spread her arms up to the god of sky as the sun beat down fiercely on her.

Pamouic called, "Any sign of men?"

"I see no one." She squinted and thought she could see the glint of sun on the waters of the distant bay. "But I think I see our canoe downstream."

"That's finished. Come on down and we will find a branch to settle on."

Reluctantly Pocahontas descended until she was at his level. She could just make out Secotin's legs through the branches in an adjoining tree. In their own tree Pamouic had found a solid fork that would hold them in sleep.

"Will you keep first watch, Secotin?" he called.

"Get some sleep. I'll call you at dusk."

"Come on, Little Snow Feather." Pamouic reached out to her and she settled close against him in the crook of the fork. He folded his warm body gently around her. Relief flooded through her at the feeling of comfort he gave her. She smiled as she mused to herself that she was probably the only female who was safe with him. Her brother was notoriously quick with his hands and his lips.

It was night. The sounds of the forest—the hoot of an owl, the flutter of a bat's wings, the squeal of a small animal—penetrated her consciousness. A yellow moon, three quarters full, hung over the treetops. Her rumbling stomach woke her. She was ravenously hungry and thought of the corn bread and turkey at the bottom of the river. They would not eat now until they reached Kecoughtan, in Pochins's land.

In the dark they descended from their perches and stretched. "We'll make straight for Kecoughtan," said Secotin as he shook out his leg muscles. "With any luck we should come across a trail soon."

It was not difficult traveling through the forest even before they found the trail. This was Kecoughtan hunting ground; Pochins's men had fired up the undergrowth the previous autumn, as they did every year. There was only scant spring growth underfoot. Secotin led at a steady loping half-trot with Pocahontas right behind him and Pamouic bringing up the rear. The air was cool. Pocahontas wished she had her leather mantle, but it had gone down with the canoe and the food.

Soon they found the trail, a narrow dirt path tramped down by generations of Kecoughtan villagers. The hard surface allowed them to travel even faster. Still, it was a long way, Pocahontas thought, remembering the distant gleam of the sun on the sea. Even if they traveled at a fast pace all night, it would be daylight before they reached Kecoughtan.

Secotin stopped so suddenly that she almost ran into him. Instinctively she bit back her cry and the question that would follow it. Secotin darted behind trees near the trail and the others went after him. He told them to stay while he scouted ahead. He returned a few minutes later, his expression solemn.

"A Monacan campfire?" whispered Pocahontas.

"Far worse. Come."

They were apprehensive, although Secotin had made it clear there was no danger now. The path widened into a small clearing bathed in moonlight. And there, set out in a formal row, lay three torsos, three scalped and severed heads, and three pairs of arms and legs.

"Our guards were outnumbered but not tortured." Secotin's voice was harsh. "The Monacans could not have had the time."

The three stood silent, shocked.

"Well, there are worse deaths. We had better bury our guards." Pamouic moved toward the remains.

"Pocahontas, climb that tree and keep watch."

Pocahontas seemed frozen to the spot. She stared at the three heads. Two of them looked peaceful, but the lips of the third were drawn back in a terrible grimace.

"Move," called Pamouic sharply.

She climbed the tree, but couldn't bring herself to look at the scene in the clearing. She could hear Secotin and Pamouic grunting as they dug in the hard ground with knives and broken-off branches. Although she peered through the trees in all directions, performing her lookout work conscientiously, she knew by the feel of the clearing that the Monacans had left. They would not be coming back this way.

CHAPTER

Kecoughtan,
May 1607

Secotin was polishing his bow with beeswax. It had been sweet last night. The women who lived by the bay were as sensual as the gentle lapping waters. Chiwoya. He curled his tongue around her name.

"You are in another world, brother," teased Pamouic.

Secotin smiled and lowered his head. "We should be moving on soon."

"We can't. Pocahontas is in the women's house."

Secotin looked up sharply, then frowned. "So she has become a woman? Then we certainly can't leave immediately. How long do women remain there?"

"I'm not sure. A few days, I think."

"This changes everything. We must send a message to our father. He will have plans for Pocahontas. Will he still let her travel to observe the Tassentasses? Perhaps he will give her new duties. One thing is sure: We will be commanded to remain with her. Most likely he will want more people to guard her as well. Does Pochins know?"

"Yes, he is planning an offering and lending us a woman to

take care of her needs. Shall I ask for Chiwoya?" Pamouic smiled and gave his brother a jab in the ribs.

"Good idea."

Pamouic watched his brother carefully. Secotin seemed abstracted.

"Maybe the great chief will give Pocahontas an honorary title. Then she could outrank us all. He may also give her lands and townships to rule, like our two aunts," said Pamouic.

"He might. She is the favorite," replied Secotin.

Pamouic was intent now. "Well, she is number one. But you are highly favored yourself, Secotin, even though Pochins outranks you."

"Perhaps. Some say so." Secotin leaned back and looked directly at Pamouic without blinking.

Pocahontas sat up against the wall in the women's house. She was distressed because she was restricted to these four walls for a few days and would be so confined every month until she was either carrying a child or had become an old woman. She had known that her body would change, but why now, when she had just arrived in Kecoughtan, when she was about to learn more about the Tassentasses? She ached to know what her brothers were doing, especially what Pochins was up to, but she got news only when a new woman arrived or food was brought and even then the bearers rarely knew the answers to the questions she asked.

She had known that becoming a woman would bring changes in her life. She was not a girl now; she was a woman, and she would be expected to marry before the next spring. She smiled ruefully when she recalled her thoughts of the day before.

Powhatan would undoubtedly already have the news. As his favorite, she had always been indulged, but now she would have power as well. Everyone would treat her differently. Pocahontas's eyes gleamed at the thought; she could be truly independent. She knew she could never inherit her father's position—in the Powhatan Kingdom the succession passed from the great chief to his eldest sister's children—but she might be given important tasks to carry out for him. She could even participate in political discussions in the council house. Two of her aunts had done so before they were made weroansqua as female chieftains were called, with their own territories.

And she would still be able to help with the Tassentasses. As a woman she would have more authority. Perhaps she should try to talk to the Tassentasses' women. There must be many of them on the floating islands. Pocahontas wondered if they were as hairy as the men. She burst out laughing.

Naha looked up in surprise. She was Pochins's latest wife. Whispers about her were rife, but Pocahontas had met her briefly in Werowocomoco and liked her. Naha had been married to a chieftain up near the Rappannock River. When Naha saw Pochins, who was visiting on a hunting trip, she abandoned her tribe and her husband and followed him back to Kecoughtan. She would not return to her husband and insisted on being the first to warm Pochins's bed, the first to bear his food. The scandal had spread throughout the Five Rivers Kingdom, and the chieftain up the Rappannock was angry. Powhatan had had to intercede. He pointed out to the chieftain that he should have more control over his wives. Perhaps he tried to satisfy too many? At first Pochins had been embarrassed by Naha's attentions, but as everyone noticed, he did not turn away when she frequently rubbed her breasts up against his back or his arm or gently fingered him when she thought no one was looking. Pocahantas moved closer to Naha as she started to relate her story.

"I was thinking about the Tassentasses," said Pocahontas.

"Tell me about them," said Nahar, "I have been here three days now and missed all the gossip."

81

• • •

It had been midmorning before they finally saw the palisades of Kecoughtan in the distance. The town was a large one, made up of about one hundred twenty-five houses standing in neat rows, with planting fields fanning out around them. As soon as they crossed from the forest into the field, the women working there dropped their tools and stared, then walked cautiously toward them until they were close enough to recognize the trio. Several women hurried into the town to notify the men. Shortly it seemed that the entire town was spilling out onto the fields to welcome them.

Pochins stood at the palisades gate with a group of his soldiers, waiting. When she saw him, Pocahontas felt a great wave of relief and ran the last few yards to catch at his arm in greeting.

"We have been worried, Pocahontas," Pochins said. "The noon runner yesterday said that you would arrive last night."

"Our news is sad."

Secotin told of the whole journey from Werowocomoco, of the Monacans, the bravery of the guards, and the dignity with which they met their death. He told of the shallow graves in the forest and the long walk overland.

Pochins listened to their story carefully. He was Powhatan's eldest son. Pochins the Handsome he was called—tall, grave, and broad-shouldered. He wore a black fox pelt thrown over one shoulder, its fanged head snarling behind his back. A long time ago he had been sent to rule Kecoughtan after he had suppressed a rebellion. The rebels had then been assimilated into many of the towns of the Five Rivers Kingdom, and their own villages were repopulated with Powhatan's own people. Powhatan's custom was to conquer and divide.

Now Pocahontas watched Pochins. She knew him well; he often visited Werowocomoco. He had greeted them with great

82

warmth, but Pocahontas noticed he seemed to hold something back, as if he was preoccupied.

Pochins knocked some tobacco from his pipe and frowned. "Are you sure the Monacans did this deed?"

"There is no doubt. We saw their canoes, we heard them looking for us, and they left their signs on the bodies," said Secotin.

"But what are the Monacans up to? They are not fishermen out for new waters. Do they seek revenge? Surely not for the loss of one soldier." Pochins turned to his soldiers, singled out a dozen, and quickly, decisively gave them orders. "We must guard our shore and forests. Also we must bring the slain guards back to our burial ground."

When they were finally seated on red striped mats and women had carried in plates of hot bread and venison, Pochins told his news: "I expect the pale men to arrive in Kecoughtan shortly. My scouts returned just before you came."

The three travelers swiveled to face him.

"They come today," Pochins went on. "Their floating islands are anchored in the river and my men are leading a band of them here."

"Today!" Pocahontas had thought she was so tired nothing could claim her attention. But a wave of excitement and apprehension flooded through her. So that was why Pochins had greeted them with an air of reserve. He knew Powhatan considered the dirty ones enemies, and she and her brothers were expected to return with tales of their visit.

Pochins turned to his brothers and sister. "The white men will not be here until sunset. Rest now."

As she walked toward the house her father kept in Kecoughtan, Pocahontas thanked Ahone and thanked the god of sky that Kecoughtan was a fine large town. In her mind, she thanked her father for being all powerful and for having his own houses waiting for him and his family when they traveled. In fact, she felt fortunate just to be alive.

"But, oh, I am so tired," she said aloud as she slipped into the women's section and lay down on the first bed of furs she saw. She fell immediately into a heavy sleep.

When she awoke abruptly her hands were cold and she suddenly felt alone. It was a warm day, but she shivered slightly. Then she recalled that the Tassentasses were coming. But instead of anticipation she felt oppressed. What was she doing here? Why had she come all this way to see strange creatures who probably would be repellent to her? She looked around the room. There was no old nurse to call to for comfort, no father to whom she could run. Never in her life had she felt so uncertain, and now, now she longed avidly for her familiar bed and people she had always known.

Her entire body felt heavy and her mind dull, as if a huge crow was hovering over her, beating its wings. She remembered the last two days. In a jumble of flashes she saw the doe dying at her feet, the Monacan tied to the stake, the leafy cove as she shrank from the boatload of passing Monacan warriors, the dismembered braves in the forest glen. But she had seen death all her life and it had never bothered her. After all, she had been triumphant. She had sacrificed well, and she had pleased Okeus and Ahone. What was the matter with her?

I am not a strong Powhatan, she thought. How can I have these misgivings? She felt drops of perspiration down her chest. I must dress and bathe in time for the arrival of the Tassentasses.

She moved quickly, hunting rapidly through the room for some clothes that her father's wives might have left behind. As she pulled a basket from behind a hammock she felt some of her anxiety subside. She took out a pale doeskin skirt with thick fringe and a new pair of moccasins intricately sewn with

84

green thread. The sight of the pretty moccasins cheered her a little. She threw her old skirt and moccasins aside with such strength that they made a loud slap as they hit the ground. That made her feel even better.

I am filthy, she thought to herself. I must find a place where I can bathe and see myself. I want to wash away my weak thoughts. I want to look pretty again, as the great chief's daughter should. The Tassentasses must look at me and admire me.

She stood at the door of the house, trying to recall where the pond was. Then she remembered that it was at the end of the palisade. She glanced around, picked up a bunch of turkey feathers that were propped by the door, and hurried to her bath. She didn't bother to put on the clothes she carried.

When she reached the pond, she scrubbed her body and hair, then dried herself with the turkey feather and stepped into her clothes. She felt renewed. Cocking her head, she could hear a stirring in the town. The noise was faint at first, no more than the echo of many footfalls. Then it grew into a murmur and a rumble through the earth. Ah, the strange ones are arriving, she thought. I must hurry. Her dark imaginings had been chased away. Curiosity took their place.

At first she could not see anything through the crowd of townspeople. Pocahontas pushed closer to the edge of the festive throng, with only one thought in her mind, to see the Tassentasses.

"Pocahontas, here, you belong here," somebody shouted.

She moved toward the voices. Pocahontas knew she should be with Pochins, but she wanted to see the dirty ones for the first time without being part of an entourage so that she could observe them objectively. The crowd swept toward the palisade and then slowed down. Pochins wanted the townspeople to pray to Okeus, to ask for his blessing before the strange men were allowed inside the palisades.

The villagers formed a broad circle. At a sign from the town's priests they fell to the ground. Pocahontas wanted to raise her head and steal her first glance at the strange men, but she was afraid of the wrath of the devil god Okeus.

She put her head to the warm earth. I have just finished bathing, she thought with amusement, and here I am down in the dirt! Then the solemnity of the occasion caught her and she reached out her hands and began the prayer with the others. It echoed from the hundreds of throats, low and rhythmic. They were mourning the death that was not, to stop Okeus from causing the death that could be. If he heard them mourning one death that day, surely he would not require another. And there had been death. The sight of the mutilated soldiers swept before her eyes again. It had been painful to lose them, but they had been careless. They had been caught.

At last the prayer came to an end and she raised her head quickly. Now she could see the Tassentasses.

But they were not white! She felt sharp disappointment. They were certainly very strange, but they were not the white of Okeus or the soft white of clouds or even the lustrous white of a river pearl. They are the same color we are, she thought, only dingy, like cooked fish or a wild pig. All she could see was their hands and faces. Why don't they stain their bodies with nut juices or toughen their skin with sun and weather as we do? she thought. The rest of their bodies was covered with clothing, even though it was a sunny, warm day. Pocahontas thought their clothes were ugly as well. They were not made of skins or feathers and were the colors of stones, earth, and rotting leaves in the fall. Their hair was odd, too. They apparently did not shave the side where they drew their bows. But it was cut shorter than the hair of braves, so perhaps it did not tangle in the bowstrings. It was not shiny black hair hanging straight and smooth, but was the color of sea sand or the soil and curled and rippled around their necks and

86

chins. One of them had a red pelt like a fox. All together the Tassentasses were a terrible disappointment.

Pocahontas moved closer, delighted to be able to see without being inhibited by having Pochins at her side. The villagers crowded around, but this time they left a path for their chieftain, who strode up to his strange visitors. There were twenty of them.

"Welcome to Kecoughtan," Pochins said, holding his head high. His headdress of eagle feathers trembled in the spring breeze. He moved closer to the Tassentasses. Pocahontas could see that he was taller by a head than the largest of the strangers. Most of Pochins's men were his size or even bigger. One of the pale men stepped forward and held out his hand. Why? He had no offering. The strange one turned slightly, and Pocahontas saw that he had only one arm. His sleeve hung loose without flesh and bone in it. Then the dirty one spoke, strange sounds unlike any speech Pocahontas had heard before. She listened intently, wanting badly to understand what they were saying, but it was gibberish to her. Another of the Tassentasses said something in the same odd tongue. They interrupted one another in their hurry to speak. How rude they were! Nor did they bow down to Pochins, who was a hundred times more magnificent than any one of them.

She wondered why Pochins was not angry with their bad manners, but he seemed to ignore them. He simply gestured to the opening in the palisade and turned to lead the Tassentasses into the town. The sky was red from the dropping sun, and a cool wind blew in off the bay. Fireflies danced, making hundreds of twinkling lights around the crowd. Wood smoke mingled with the scent of flowers and salt air.

The serving women brought out mats, but the strange men did not seem to understand what they were for. They looked hesitant until they saw Pochins sit down. And the sight of food seemed to reassure them. The Tassentasses devoured the meal as if it had been a long time since they had eaten so well. Pochins's cooks were renowned. Today they provided oysters, crabs, turkey, venison, corn bread, and tiny strawberries and blueberries.

Pocahontas did not take her eyes off the Tassentasses. She had refused the seat next to Pochins that her rank allowed and had gone to the end of the row near her brothers. She wanted to be as close to the Tassentasses as possible but soon regretted her decision.

She could barely control herself and keep a polite, impassive expression. They smelled as bad as Nomeh had said, but it was not a polecat odor. It was heavy and sour, the way people smelled when they were sick and unable to bathe. Pocahontas could remember only a couple of times when she had smelled a Powhatan, for her people were rarely ill. She watched the strangers and thought, I cannot like these men. They are animals.

She could not discern any markings on their clothes to indicate rank. They had strange things attached to their belts. They were not knives or swords; they had a long shiny front, and the rest was bulky and dark. Pocahontas wondered if they were weapons. The men did not display the alert stillness that Powhatan soldiers would have shown in an enemy village. But they ate. They had the serving women around time and again until Pochins finally waved them away, pulled out his own pipe, and offered one to each of the strangers. It was obvious they had never seen a pipe, but from the movements of their hands Pocahontas could tell that they knew about tobacco.

Suddenly she realized she had understood their gestures. Their faces were easy to read, and they showed their thoughts openly. Pocahontas felt a quick sensation of power. She had not expected to learn so quickly, and she seethed with excitement at the possibilities. She wished she could be alone with them, to find out more about them.

Pochins signaled to the townspeople that it was now time for the ceremonies, and the priest began his song. There was to be a dance of welcome. It was not the lively festival dance Pocahontas enjoyed so much, but at least there was not the usual oratory. The Powhatans were voluble. An ordinary speech would take from two to four hours, but since the Tassentasses would not understand it, Pochins had decided to omit it. As she whirled and pranced, Pocahontas could see the strangers watching the performance. They sat quietly, their faces blank, as if they did not know what to make of the festivities. But she sensed that they knew it would be discourteous to be inattentive. Perhaps they were not so primitive after all.

The dancers slowed to a halt. It had been a long dance; they had wanted to show honor to these strange men, but now all eyes turned to the Tassentasses. They had gathered in a tight group and were whispering among themselves. One of them produced a brown bag and showed it to the one-armed man who seemed to be the leader. With his good arm he pulled out a chain strung with some objects that Pocahontas had never seen before. But the firelight had caught these magic things, and they seemed to dance and gleam with light. They were like frozen pellets of air. A long sigh went up from the crowd. The leader walked over to Pochins and handed the chain to him. Pochins hesitated and the crowd was silent. Pocahontas wanted to go over and shake him. Didn't he see that this precious rare thing was a token of friendship? Finally Pochins accepted the offering and the crowd sighed again with relief. The leader went back to the bag and brought up another chain. This time the ornaments were the color of the sky. Pocahontas gasped at the beauty of them. How lucky Pochins was, how wonderfully lucky were his wives!

Pocahontas suddenly realized why Pochins had invited the Tassentasses to come to Kecoughtan. The pale men had been to these shores before. Pochins knew that they had these marvels. Even though he knew, too, that Powhatan called the strangers enemies, he was greedy for these beautiful things. And also, he seemed to like the Tassentasses. Pochins did not want to give in to his father's commands. My brother is daring, thought Pocahontas.

As Pochins and the leader bowed gravely toward each other Pocahontas wondered how she could seize a chance to talk to the dirty ones. Had she been older, she might have been asked to warm one of their beds. Ahone! What an ordeal, with their smell! But surely Pochins would ask the wives to take the strangers down to the river and scrub them. Then the prettiest would be offered for the night to soothe their bodies and satisfy their lust. But she knew she would never be asked because of her rank.

In the fresh spring morning when the circling gulls flew low over the blue sea, Pocahontas hurried back from her bathing to the entrance of the palisade. She was anxious to see the strangers as soon as she could. As she turned the corner she saw them standing in a group talking quietly to one another as Pochins approached with a party of braves.

She could see they were preparing to leave. Her heart sank. She wanted so badly to speak to them, to hear their voices again. Perhaps now she could understand their talk better than the previous night. But she could only read their expressions. It seemed they were seeking directions, but she couldn't be sure. Frustrated, Pocahontas stared at the men. She would talk to them somehow before they left these shores.

One of the Tassentasses turned, the one with the empty sleeve, and for a moment he caught Pocahontas's eye. He raised a dark eyebrow as if the intensity of her stare surprised him, then gave a sudden smile. Pocahontas smiled back as she said to herself, I want him to remember me.

The braves were ready with their canoe. Pocahontas could hear Pochins give them instructions.

"Take the Tassentasses back to their canoe and watch them. Act as their escorts if they want to travel to see Wowincho and his men, but do not go with them to the Rappahannocks. That is important."

Pocahontas listened intently. Pochins was his own man, but she knew that each of her father's chiefs would have his own ideas about the Tassentasses. Each of them would act differently. She had to learn what each intended to do. Then she could take the information back to her father.

The Tassentasses waved cheerfully as they left, a little group in their brown and gray clothing, drab against the bright sunlight. But the visit had apparently been a success for them, judging by their smiles. The people of Kecoughtan were happy, too, as they guided the visitors to the river. But when the strangers had turned the bend, the townspeople walked back to their homes in a sober mood. The excitement was gone. Now they faced again the daily routine of fishing, grinding corn and tending the spring crops.

Pocahontas's shoulders drooped as she asked herself if she should go back to her father now. No, there was not enough news yet, she decided, and she could always send a runner. She would stay in Kecoughtan and watch and listen to Pochins and to his people until she could make a more complete report. Then she would decide how best to see the Tassentasses.

That evening there was more feasting and dancing. The day had been cool, and the colors of the dancers looked bright in the clear evening air. Pocahontas wore red feathers around her neck and in her hair, and she had found a pair of red-stitched moccasins to wear when she danced. She knew the festivities were a greeting for her and her brothers, to make up for Pochins's subdued welcome the day before. Also, the villagers needed a festival of their own to cheer them up and to celebrate without reserve. It was impossible to dance with fervor when strangers were in their midst. It also occurred to Pocahontas that their brother would entertain them lavishly in the hope that they would tell their father only what Pochins wished Powhatan to know. Pochins had already given the three of them some of the sparkling blue things and the icy-looking gifts that could be worn as a necklace.

While the various foods of the feast were passed around, Pamouic sat with a girl who wore a necklace of white shells. Pocahontas noticed he stroked her here, pinched a little there, caressed her constantly; he could never keep his hands to himself. Secotin had found a girl with wide eyes who sat quietly while he gently fed her a morsel of turkey and then another of wild boar. Just watching her brothers with their women made her body feel strange. She was restless and at the same time slow and languid, but she felt warm and alive as well. Her disagreeable thoughts of the day before had vanished.

"Pocahontas, I want you to meet Kokum. He is the son of the chief of the Chickahominies."

She turned, startled. She had not heard Pochins approach until he was standing over her. Next to him was a warrior whose patterns she had never seen before. As she looked up at his face she could feel the force of his body. In a glance she saw that he was tall, not as tall as her brothers but young enough that he probably would be soon. His body was muscular but lean, with broad shoulders and narrow hips. And his face was handsome, his features finely drawn. Although he smiled at her, there was a detachment, almost an arrogance, behind the mobile mouth and white teeth. He was not a happy man like Pamouic, she thought. His eyes held something cool, but there was also something about him that drew her strongly.

92

Instinctively she crossed her arms over her breasts as if to keep him at a distance.

"May I be with you?" His voice had a quality that touched her nerves. It was compelling, but she was not sure whether she liked it or not. He slid down beside her in one fluid motion. Pocahontas felt uneasy. Her body was reacting as if it had nothing to do with her head.

She tried to think clearly. Chickahominy territory was within the land Powhatan controlled inland from Werowocomoco, but its chieftain had always maintained a degree of independence. This did not bother the great chief, but it didn't please him either. He had spoken at times of trying to arrange marriages that would bring the two tribes closer. Was this to be her marriage?

The conch players and drummers started their rhythm. It was to be a dance that was nothing like the polite welcoming affair that greeted the Tassentasses. Kokum held out his hand, and Pocahontas took it, feeling a vibration throughout her body. The beat caught at them both in this dance for warriors and their women. It was one of uninhibited lewdness, of shared village gossip and sexual conjecture translated into tunes. Its rhythm and words were designed to inflame and lead to passion. The dancers' bodies moved in unison, their eyes searching, their hands touching just enough to make the pulse at Pocahontas's throat throb.

Pocahontas had performed this dance many times. She enjoyed dodging the eager hands of men like Pamouic. It made her laugh. But this time she felt engulfed in a trance, and the only reality was the eyes of the man opposite her. She did not like Kokum, not yet, but when she felt his eyes roam over her body she responded as if it were his mouth eagerly searching hers instead. She sensed that he was taking it for granted that she was his, and yet even with the fire along her limbs she did

93

not want to belong to Kokum, not yet. At the same time she felt an unfamiliar sensation in her breasts. She almost stumbled when his hand brushed her for a second. There was a strange warmth at the bottom of her stomach.

Her feelings were almost overpowering. But she knew that if she were to lie with Kokum it would not be just a simple tumble in the woods. She had always thought that becoming a woman would make her free, but this rush of heightened sensation, this loss of control, would be another form of bondage. Oh, Ahone, why was everything always so complicated? She almost skipped a step but regained her balance. I shall never be free from my body again, she thought. There will always be the man and the things we do together.

She thought of her sisters. She wished she had one of them to talk to, someone to tell her how to handle this weakness washing through her. Pochins's people were kind, but they were merely acquaintances.

The dance ended, and she turned away.

Pocahontas did not want to think about Kokum. Suddenly she did not even want to be a woman. At least not yet. She did not want to lie with Kokum, to become his wife. When he came close, the heat from his body made her catch her breath. She moved away, not rudely but decisively, and shook her head to tell him she would be friendly but she would not lie with him even to please Pochins and her father.

Pocahontas leaned back against the wall in the women's house. She had talked for an hour in a low voice that only Naha could hear. She was amazed that she had been so free. But in the absence of her sisters it was a relief to relay her story to the rapt and sympathetic woman who, above all others, would surely understand what she felt. She had prudently omitted the political aspects of the relationship between Powhatan and Pochins.

The boredom of the women's house was insidious for Pocahontas. Most of the women waiting out their time here enjoyed this regular break in their routine. It gave them a chance to rest and gossip. They knew that no one would bother them; their spirits were considered temporarily unclean.

Now they chattered about the Tassentasses. The women who had missed them were anxious to hear all about it from those who had seen them. They were as curious about and frightened of these invaders as Pocahontas was, but none of the others thought of going to see the huge canoes for themselves. They talked of how ugly the Tassentasses were, how bad they smelled, and how rudely they had behaved.

They speculated about Pocahontas's marriage. "Perhaps you will marry a Tassentasse," one of the wittier Kecoughtans said, and they all laughed. It was such an incredible idea.

Someone suggested that perhaps she would marry Kokum. Another added that Kokum was certainly handsome and his father had power, which he might inherit if he was as good a warrior as they had heard. Two of the younger ones told her in detail how well he had pleasured them. If she had been back in Werowocomoco, Pocahontas would have drifted away when the women started to gossip, but in the women's house there was no place to go. Anyway, it interested her. She thought a great deal about Kokum.

CHAPTER

Jamestown,
May 1607

"**J**amestown." He let the name hang on the air for a moment. "After King James himself."

The land was low, the soil sandy, but the three ships were able to drop anchor within a few feet of the shoreline. John Smith let his gaze wander over the fields toward the woods. Then he stared at the ground in disgust; the soil was even damper than he had feared. The last time he had seen earth like this was near the marshes in Anatolia. The men there had sickened and gone down like flies when the weather became hot.

It had taken two weeks of searching up and down the bay to find a place that both Wingfield and Newport liked. The captains of the individual ships and their crews had dropped soundings, marched over the meadows, tested the waters. But the men, overtired, had grown testy and sullen. They were desperate for a stay on land.

But it had been essential to find a bay or river deep enough for the ships to anchor close to shore so that cannon could cover them in case of attack. The shoreline had to drop immediately into deep water. At last, on a day when the wind blew the salt in from the distant sea in soft puffs, the captains had chosen a point jutting into the river a few miles up from the great bay. The fields were low, rolling, and wide, and the tall trees were not too thick and some came down to the water. The promontory held a commanding position toward the bay, and the estuary was wide. Smith judged that it was well over a mile to the opposite shore.

Even so, there had been several spots that John Smith had thought more suitable, but he had not been consulted. Although he was a member of the governing council, he had been released from confinement only two days ago and he was still on probation.

Now at the end of his hard day's work, Smith sat on a newly felled log. He looked around at the eighty-odd men unwinding nearby. Only half had been working. The gentlemen investors had walked around, as they did each day, enjoying the air, talking politics, writing letters. Smith watched them with contempt. He noticed, however, that the laborers had loaded the ships with fine woods and specimens of soil even before they had built shelter for themselves on land. They were not even investors, but had signed on for the yearly pay. If only he could convince the idle that it was not demeaning but essential, even life-saving, to work in this new world.

He looked up to see George Percy, damp and disheveled, his long nose and fine dark eyes pinched with fatigue. Smith gave his log a brisk pat, and Percy sat down next to him.

"We have accomplished a great deal today. The first load of wood is on board; the first sections of the fort have been built." Percy rested his arms on his knees as he stared out to sea.

"We could do more if all these gentlemen would turn a hand." Smith picked a blade of grass and pulled it thoughtfully between his fingers.

Percy's face relaxed into a smile. Smith could not tolerate the idleness of his fellow adventurers, but there was nothing he could do about it. They were all investors in the Virginia Company.

"Wingfield tells me that we have nothing to worry about from the naturals," Percy said. "He thinks they will never attack."

"He is wrong. One feast with one tribe is no true measure of these people. Powhatan is a despot. A fine meal with one of his lesser kings who is disposed to be friendly is no guarantee that others will follow suit. And I am mightily concerned about how the fort is being built. Wingfield thinks we have no need for cannon emplacements, but we must be fortified. We have got to rid ourselves of this man before he gets us all killed."

Both men stared out to sea. The sun had dropped into the forest behind them, and the first stars sparkled tentatively.

"It is a fair land, John. I hope to see four or five townships of our people up and down this bay."

"We will need more than that to diminish the overcrowding back home. We are four million people now." Smith paused. "The government is concerned that the fabric of life is deteriorating—too much violence, too much drink, too many homeless and out of work, too many broken families. They expect us to find sites for more townships, so it is of vital importance that we get along with the naturals." Smith lowered his voice. "I am worried about our dwindling supplies. We must trade for food."

Percy understood the urgency in Smith's voice.

"And somehow we have to get to the great Powhatan," Smith went on. "He is the key to accomplishing our task here. I think Newport will encourage Wingfield to let me go to him. In their eyes I am expendable anyway."

Percy smiled in the dark. "I will go with you. We'll get other volunteers as well."

As Percy rose and walked away, Smith entered the makeshift hut that served as his temporary living quarters. It contained a mattress and the few things he needed—his guns, his fork and spoon. As he settled into bed he found himself thinking of London and his last evenings there, in particular the night he had dined with John Reynolds, the Speaker of the House of Commons, in his private chambers in one of the towers of Westminster Palace. There he had found not only Sir Edwin Sandys, a member of Parliament and his close adviser, among the guests but also Speaker John Reynolds's two blond nieces. During his two-year friendship with Reynolds, he had heard the Speaker talk about the two beautiful, tempestuous girls. Their father complained bitterly that every eligible man in town had beaten his way to their door, but none satisfied Mary and Elizabeth. He despaired of their ever marrying. That night Smith had sat between them at the table and succumbed willingly to the full barrage of the sisters' charms.

Now, as he lay lonely in the night of a savage world, the happenings of that evening seemed more like a dream. The two women, who were not shy, had been dressed in brilliant colors, one in red, the other in purple velvet. Below their white ruffs their full breasts were all but totally exposed, nipples pouting and rouged. And to punctuate the conversation, Mary had rubbed herself against one of his arms and Elizabeth against the other. He smiled in the dark as he remembered that he hadn't known which way to turn.

As soon as the last mouthful of their creamy dessert, a syllabub, had been finished, Elizabeth grabbed his arm and asked—no, demanded—that he let her show him the apartments she had known since childhood. Like the flame from a taper she had swayed first toward him and then away as she led him from room to room. Finally, in the library, she had pressed one of the panels and been swallowed into the blackness of a small secret room, pulling him behind her. With laughter and warm hands she had pushed him down in the dark onto the sweet-

102

smelling rushes on the floor and rubbed her breasts back and forth across his willing mouth. Within seconds they were fused in rocking ecstasy, a tumultuous, driving, thrusting agony of passion. Finally she gave a little cry before he could cover her mouth with his. After a moment she dropped away and soon he heard her striking flint and lighting a candle. As the flame shot up, she adjusted her skirts, brushed off the reeds, and ran to him. "I knew you would be magnificent. Magnificent! Now we must hurry back or they will miss us."

She had kept up a running patter of conversation as they walked casually back into the room where the other guests had seemingly not noticed their absence—except Mary, who approached them with glittering eyes.

"I have asked Father if Captain Smith may escort me home. I am feeling a little unwell."

In his dark hut in the strange land, Smith remembered with a chuckle that he had thought distractedly at the time, I don't think I misunderstand this situation!

With barely enough time to fortify himself with a gulp of wine, he had been whisked down the stairs, through the great court-yards of Westminster Palace, torchlit against the softly falling snow, and into Reynolds's coach. Every lurch of the cobblestones had produced another sensation as Mary professed her ardor in touch as well as in speech in the mile-long journey to her home. He tried to resist, but she had vehemently declared she did not care who had been in his life, even recently. She sent the coach back to Westminster Palace, and led John into the house, past the dozing servants, and up to her bedchamber. She bolted the door and for the remainder of the night they leisurely explored every possible facet of love. He had taught the tall and lissome girl all the secrets he had learned during many hours spent in the harems of Turkey, his adventures in the palaces of Transylvania, the wild nights with the Russians in Kelum—and quite a few secrets of his own. Toward dawn, exhausted but suspended in a cloud of exquisite sensation and with a final shuddering sigh, they had finally disentangled their bodies.

"You are a marvelous lover. I must see you again," she had whispered as she led him on tiptoe down the back stairs.

He had had to tell her gently but with a secret sigh of relief that he was sailing within hours. He knew he could easily be a slave to the tiny mole that guarded the cleavage of her rounded buttocks.

Now as he slapped at a mosquito, he wondered why he was dredging up these memories like an old man. In all his travels in his twenty-seven years he had never indulged in nostalgia, perhaps because there was always a fresh possibility on each new day. Now he thought, I shall probably be a long time without a woman. He punched the mattress into a more comfortable position and tried to sleep.

The next day was sunny with a cool breeze. The fort was beginning to take shape. Within the walls, men were marking out streets and a marketplace in the sandy soil. Several yeomen were hooking two sails between tall pine trees for a makeshift church until a proper one could be built. Another group continued loading wood on the *Susan Constant*.

When the sun was high in the sky and almost directly overhead, the men threw their tools down and lay down to rest on the grass, which still held the sweet scent of spring. Wingfield, Newport, and the ruling council were aboard the *Susan Constant*. Only John Smith among the investors toiled alongside the laborers on shore. It was a quiet moment. A dragonfly whizzed by and bees droned lazily about their business, while gulls, fat as turkeys, wheeled and jockeyed for position overhead.

Thomas Emery, one of the carpenters, sat up, stretched, and gazed out to sea. As he turned to reach for his hammer he caught

104

a movement out of the corner of his eye. For a second his body froze. Along the rim of the forest stood at least one hundred naturals, silent, staring, motionless. In an explosion of breath he yelled as loud as he could.

"Naturals!"

The men around him scrambled and jumped up. Some reached for their weapons, others for their tools as they cursed and jostled. Many started to load their muskets, their fingers clumsy and heavy with haste. The Indians did not move.

"Hold your fire!" John Smith bellowed.

He quickly saw what no one else seemed to notice. Two of the Indians carried a deer, hung feet up on a pole between them. Smith motioned to the men on the field to keep quiet and stay behind him. He stepped forward cautiously toward the silent naturals. Then waited, his musket at his side. One of the Indians stepped out from the rest and extended his arm, then dropped it. Smith did the same. They began to walk slowly toward each other. The only sound was the shallow breathing of the men.

On the deck of the *Susan Constant* sailors stood silently at the rail watching intently. As Smith walked forward, he noticed that the man he approached was not young and bore the stamp of authority. A crown of black feathers encircled his head, and he handed his bow to an underling as he walked with measured steps. When they were within a few feet of each other, the natural motioned and said, "Pasapegh, Pasapegh."

So he is the king of the Pasapegh, ruler of the land we stand on, a kingdom within the Powhatan Empire, Smith thought as he acknowledged the greeting. The Indian then pointed toward the deer and in sign language indicated that he was bringing a feast to share with the English. He put his hand over his heart, then waved to Smith and his people to lay down their muskets. Smith signaled that they too would like to feast but ignored the request to put down their arms. Both their voices were loud, their

105

gestures grand. Every man in the field could follow the invitation to feast, and a loud cheer went up at the prospect of succulent venison for supper.

The response from the settlers seemed to be a signal to the Indians. Moving with their peculiar grace, like stealthy cats, they walked cautiously among the Englishmen. The two groups circled each other warily. The settlers reached out with careful hands to touch the feathers and the bows and arrows of the naturals. The natives gazed with awe and avid curiosity at the tools and muskets of these men who were new to their land. Some felt the Englishmen's clothing, pinching and prodding. One man looked down to see his sleeve torn in two as the naturals inspected the cloth. Others wandered over near the fort to examine the new planks of wood and the iron nails. Another group gathered twigs and logs for a fire large enough to roast the deer. Over all hung the anticipation of a good meal.

Wingfield, Newport, and the rest of the council bustled ashore and hurried over to Smith, the king and his lieutenants, who were standing around the growing fire. The Englishmen seemed small, their colors subdued compared to the tall, brilliantly painted natives. They gesticulated broadly as they tried to convey the friendship they felt for the natives.

"Gold, we look for gold." Smith, with sweat gathering on his forehead, tried hard to describe his needs as he stared into the jaws of a red fox head snarling over the shoulder of a towering native.

Suddenly, down near the water, voices rose sharply. An outraged yell shot across the field.

"He has taken my hatchet. Hey there, give it back, you!"

Sounds of a scuffle reached the men around the fire. Smith picked up his musket and sprinted toward the center of the trouble. As he ran he saw the carpenter deal a hard blow to the arm of the Indian who had taken the hatchet. The Indian dropped the tool to the ground as three yeomen scrambled and pounced on it. Another natural, incensed, drew his wooden sword and swacked it over the head of the nearest Englishman.

Smith's voice cut through the melee.

"Stop it, stop it all of you."

The scufflers hesitated.

"One more move and I will blast you right in your bellies."

For a moment the only sound on the field was the slapping of a sail on the *Godspeed*.

"A fine mess you have caused." Smith's eyes, sharp with scorn, ripped across the English faces. He turned, anger etched on his body, and marched back to the men standing around the fire. The king and his warriors stood with arms folded, a red flush under their tanned skins, wrath gathering on their faces.

"A mistake, a mistake!" Smith tried to explain. He was met with cold stares. The king called to his men. Two of them picked up the deer.

The naturals walked back toward the forest, a hundred strong. The king then turned to Smith and began to speak in a loud voice, indignation and ire falling from every vowel. No mutual language was necessary for Smith to understand his message. Then the king summoned his lieutenants, walked to the woods, and disappeared.

The Englishmen stood nonplussed.

"That is the worst thing that could happen to us," Smith said.

"As usual, you exaggerate. They will be back." Wingfield moved away from the fire as he looked toward the woods.

"Yes, they will be back with a full war party." Smith tried to keep the scorn out of his voice. He had not yet been pardoned and did not want to see the bowels of the ship again.

"It was important to have a good first meeting," Gabriel Archer commented.

"We can't blame Emery for protecting his hatchet," said

George Percy.

"Yes, but it is our fault for not instructing the men on how to behave with the naturals, who were obviously here on a friendly mission," said Smith.

"It is not for you to give your opinion." Edward Maria Wingfield glanced dismissively at Smith. "I think you all are making far too much of the incident."

Smith turned on his heel, picked up an ax and walked away. No one followed as he started to chop furiously around a tree root.

That evening the fire still glowed, and its heat was welcome. The air had a spring chill, which sharpened the outlines of the early stars and carried distinctly the sounds of the ships creaking at anchor and the murmurs of the tired men. Smith's head was clearer, but he was still worried. He couldn't understand; it was impossible for him to fathom a man, a fellow soldier, who refused to protect his own men. Wingfield had agreed to post guards tonight, but he was still adamant against mounting cannon on shore.

Smith looked around at the men. Often, he noticed, they nervously glanced over their shoulders toward the dark forest. They are frightened, he thought, and I too am not exactly easy. He felt the light cat's paw of a breeze that crept and slithered over the grass and touched the trees with a faint rustle. But each sound, muted as it was, rang loud in his ear and he knew it was the same with the others. No one would admit fear, but all of them knew it was there. Smith turned to George Percy, who with Bartholomew Gosnold sat in the warm circle of the fire.

"No matter what Wingfield says, that was a disastrous meeting with the naturals today. We don't know what they will do next. What if they return to attack? They have seen the inside of the fort now." Smith looked at each man.

"I have been counseling Wingfield to put cannon on the three towers of the fort when it is finished," Gosnold said. "But if it is overrun on the first fight for lack of armament . . . " He spread his hands and raised his shoulders in an expression of helplessness.

"We are not going to be able to persuade him to move the cannon. At least we now have guards to alert us. We will just have to rely on the ship's cannon." Percy's voice held a note of finality.

"Then we should concentrate on establishing friendly relations with King Pochins," said Smith. "He is well disposed toward us and may help us if we have troubles with other groups. And, gentlemen, a vital point: We have got to find out whom we can trade with."

"John, it was decided today on the *Susan Constant* that Newport would sail as soon as possible to bring fresh supplies from London," said Gosnold.

"That will take four months, probably longer. We need to trade now. We are dangerously short of supplies," replied Smith.

"Then let us carry out your plan to take one of the shallops and try to establish trade on the morrow or the next day. It is our best course of action for the moment."

Finally Smith stood up and the others followed. On board the three ships candles had been doused, the portholes were dark, and on land the men had settled down for the night. It was getting late. Day would break soon enough with its new problems and challenges.

"Blasted heat, blasted place, blasted work," grumbled one of the yeomen as he hauled a log over to the riverbank.

"They ask us to work after the midday break. I have never worked more than five hours in my life," retorted another.

"In Suffolk I hear tell that some put in six hour days but, it is more common to work the usual four. They will kill us here."

"If it isn't the work it will be the food, or the bloody natives."

The men grumbled in good humor as they stacked the wood neatly on the bank of the river. Others then took the logs to the *Susan Constant*. Already the ship's hold was almost full. A short dock had been built, several temporary shacks had been erected, and the foundations for several houses had been started.

"Naturals!" Suddenly a great bellow went up from the watch at the edge of the forest.

"God on the Cross! They are back!"

"No, look, there are only three of them."

"So there are, and one of them is but a girl."

The laborers on the field stared as the three Indians advanced. No one made a move for his weapon. The men stood with their tools in their hands, curious but uncertain. They stared especially at the girl. They had not seen a female for many months, and she only reminded them of what they did not have. Some eyes turned hard and sullen with resentment. There was a slight murmur here and there, but for the most part the men were quiet as the hot summer sun beat down upon the unfolding scene.

John Smith, engrossed in conversation with Captain Newport, turned suddenly. The two men had been discussing the shallop and supplies for Smith's trip the next day.

"It's a young girl!" cried Smith as he looked over the field toward the woods.

"From here she looks like the one we noticed at Kecoughtan," Newport said, "she seemed particularly curious about us. They said she was Powhatan's daughter, a princess." He peered intently at the nearing natives. "Her name is Pocahontas."

"The emperor's favorite daughter! She is talked about even in London. Gosnold brought back news of her from his trip in 1603. We decided then, after hearing about her, that there must be a reasonable side to Powhatan." Smith and Newport walked slowly across the field toward the naturals.

"Could they be a decoy?" Smith said anxiously. "Is there a chance there is a war party behind them?"

"No. They are not part of the Pasapegh tribe. And she is the sister of King Pochins whom you will be visiting again tomorrow."

Newport strode forward to meet the naturals. He hesitated for a moment, then smiled and put his only hand over his heart. Smith could see that Newport felt at ease. There was no tension in him as he watched the group approach. When the three native Virginians stood a scant twenty yards away, they, too, put their hands over their hearts. They stood with straight backs, and the girl gave a wide smile, showing her bone-white teeth. Their movements were fluid, not stiff with constraint.

Smith saw that the men were younger than he was but taller by several inches. They were proud and handsome. They might be the great king's lieutenants or maybe even his sons, he thought. They were definitely not functionaries. The girl wore a soft doeskin mantle intricately embellished with beads and feathers. Her face was turned up to his, her eyes wide, almost incredulous.

The pupils of her brown eyes looked dilated, and a soft smile hovered around her mouth. Something about her held Smith's attention. It was not just the intensity of her gaze or her obvious intelligence. She seemed steadfast and even regal but at the same time vulnerable. Smith was intrigued. He thought the girl would never take her eyes off him. He thought she was probably thirteen or fourteen. He spoke the one phrase he had learned from Raleigh: "*Ka katorawinos yowo*. The day is fine."

Her eyes opened wider still until they were huge in her face. Then she spoke quickly in a flood of speech. Her hands almost had a life of their own as they moved in quick animation. The two men joined in with her.

111

"Whoa!" Smith smiled as he threw up his hands. "Those are the only words I know. I don't speak your language."

The girl's shoulders slumped in disappointment. She grasped what he said and spoke rapidly to her companions.

She then turned back to Newport and Smith and gesticulated slowly, gracefully, at the same time speaking patiently and carefully. It was clear that she was conveying good wishes from her brother, the ruler of Kecoughtan. Smith was equally slow in returning the courtesies. He thought at the same time that sign language was a dignified way of communicating. But still he felt frustrated; he needed to learn their language. Pocahontas conveyed that her brother, the king, would like to learn about the tools the visitors had. He would also be interested in trading for some of the things that were new to them. Smith replied that the visitors would very much like to barter, especially for food. She smiled. Smith felt triumphant and thought that his meeting was the best thing to happen in months. When she asked if she and her brothers could look around, Newport and Smith indicated that the place was theirs to explore. Both men bowed low in courtesy. All three naturals burst into laughter. They then tried to bow themselves. It was the turn of the two Englishmen to laugh.

Smith watched the girl walk away, closely followed by her companions. He turned to Newport. "If only our meeting with the Pasapegh had been as friendly. The young princess acted with a great deal of authority."

"Yes, we realized that she had a certain presence when we saw her in Kecoughtan. They treat her with great deference there. I will send one of the cabin boys to stay with the Powhatans and watch what they do. And I will have a shallop ready for you tomorrow. It will be a five-hour trip, maybe less, to Kecoughtan. I would take advantage of their offer to trade at once."

"I intend to, Newport. I intend to."

CHAPTER

Jamestown,
May 18, 1607

When they left the fort, as Pocahontas hurried to keep up with her brothers she talked aloud to the trees.

"His eyes! It was the god of sky looking right at me through his eyes! And his hair! Like the early sun on a golden field." She had never dreamed that anyone could look like the Tassentasse. He was not as tall as her brothers and the clothes he wore were ugly and covered too much of his body. She would have liked to see what his chest and his legs looked like. And what was his station? Why didn't these people show their rank? Still, he had an air of command. He was not a farmer or a carrier. "I wonder if the god of sky has sent him as a messenger or as a warning, or perhaps to be our new ruler? But that cannot happen. My father has been a good chief. Surely the gods are pleased with him. But I must watch this Tassentasse. He is so beautiful, so different. When I saw him, everything went out of my head, and that is dangerous. I have to keep my mind on what my father wants me to accomplish. I have to remember that he is the enemy."

It had been two weeks since she arrived in Kecoughtan. During that time, several messages had arrived from her father, the great chief. He had wanted her to join him on a trip to Uttamussack, the small town where he kept his three royal temples. There he stored his vast treasure of pearls, skins, copper, and tools of war. Each house was guarded by forty of his fiercest warriors. Pocahontas realized her father was signaling that if she did not care for Kokum and marriage now, it was time to think of collecting taxes. For it was the income from taxes that filled his treasure houses to the ceilings. She agreed to come home and discuss whatever he felt was right for her. Then she delayed her return. She sent a runner to ask him if it might be best for her first to finish the task she had started: to discover as much as she could about the enemy. Powhatan agreed.

In her new status as a woman and the marriageable daughter of the great chief, she reluctantly agreed to have three women and two extra soldiers, besides Secotin and Pamouic, in her entourage. She had asked Naha to join them because she had grown to like the runaway wife. But Naha said she could not bear to leave Pochins's side. The constant smell of him, rich in her nose, was as necessary as the air she breathed. But Chiwoya, Secotin's new companion, accepted happily. Pocahontas wondered how wise that choice was as the two of them were in love and constantly slipping off to spend an hour deep in soft leaves or in the warm river or cradled in the crook of a tree.

Seeing them together had made the thought of Kokum dangerously attractive to Pocahontas, and she had lain awake at night wondering how he would be next to her. But that was before she had seen the Tassentasse. Now she pushed Kokum to the back of her mind. Not that she wanted to lie with this stranger; he was far too alien, too unknown, but he intrigued her. She wanted to find out everything about him and his companions. There were dozens of questions to ask, and she longed to learn his language.

"Matoax, Snow Feather! You are slow!"

She lagged behind her brothers on the trail to their campsite. "I will be with you soon. The day is beautiful! There is so much to see!"

Her body felt light, her feet felt like feathers. Was it because she had finally met with the Tassentasses or because a new world was opening to her? She shouldn't feel so euphoric, she thought guiltily. But had the enemy come disguised as the god of sky, or someone sent by him? That just couldn't be, she thought. The god of sky would never trick his people. The riddle of it all made the situation doubly fascinating. Oh, yes, the circumstances were difficult, very difficult; the Tassentasses had been so kind to her. How would she explain the warmth of their welcome to her father? Trickery, he would answer, trickery. She would have to be careful with the Tassentasses, careful in her judgment, careful with her father, careful with her people.

"Matoax, Matoax, you will never catch up!"

She broke into a half-run. Her brothers were well ahead of her, within sight and sound. They were not worried now about encountering Monacans. When the great chief heard about their narrow escape on the trip to Kecoughtan, he had sent out two war parties. All of the Monacans had been captured or killed. The great chief had sent the left thumb of each man to the chief of the Monacans and warned that the same fate would befall any other invaders in his lands. In the forests of Powhatan's territory, the paths were now free of danger, at least for the time being.

As Pocahontas ran to catch up, she said a grateful prayer to Akone for freeing them from worry about the enemy from the northwest. Now she could concentrate completely on the Tassentasses.

Her brothers waited for her in the clearing where they had

established a camp. The spot they had chosen provided a fine base from which to visit the Tassentasses, since it was too far to return to Kecoughtan each day. Their goal was to find out as much about the Tassentasses as they could within a couple of weeks. They had with them several soldiers, including two runners Pochins had given them. They also had Chiwoya and two of Pocahontas's sisters, Mehta and Quimca, who had come from Werowocomoco to join Pocahontas soon after she left the women's house. They, too, were eager to visit the Tassentasses. But in a meeting two days before, in a glen near the old wolves' lair by their camp, they had all decided that for the first two or three visits, only three of them should go to the Tassentasses.

They had been at the camp for two nights. The soldiers had set up portable houses made of matting and bark. The flaps on the sides could be rolled up to let in the breeze in warm weather. This was vital because the matting was weatherproof and warm in winter but much too hot in summer. The great chief used these houses for his hunting trips. Sometimes more than half of the residents of the town would carry them when they traveled with him to stalk deer or hunt bear.

Both nights they had sat around the fire after a supper of fresh corn bread and roasted hare, turkey, or venison. Then the storytelling and the singing started. Quimca's voice was finer than the birds'. They sat enthralled until far too late, listening to her under the stars.

This evening her sisters pounced on Pocahontas as soon as she entered the camp. She pushed them off, laughing and protesting. "Let me eat and then we will tell you everything!"

The sisters could barely contain their curiosity, and their enthusiasm inspired her to tell her first story even before she had swallowed her final mouthful. She described in detail the meeting with the two high-ranking Tassentasses, but without giving away her reaction to the handsome one.

118

"I have told you before how awful these people smell, but I had seen only a handful of them. When you are with many, the odor is overpowering. And their floating islands, their great canoes that fly with the wind, they are the worst of all. The smell is so bad I don't see how they can get on them. I suppose I will get used to it in time, but now I find it terrible. Apparently they do not bathe—ever. What strange gods they must have!"

Pocahontas told of the great thundering weapons that made a noise more deafening than the greatest wrath of the god of sky. And she spoke of the miraculous buildings they were putting up, unlike anything she had seen before. And of the friendship she had made with a young Tassentasse about her own age who had introduced her to some of his food.

"It was a terrible soup made of strange things. I think it is all they have to eat. It seems they do not know how to kill game for food or how to plant seeds or catch fish. But the young Tassentasse who lives on one of the great canoes plays a funny game. He throws his hands on the ground and his feet up in the air and twirls over and over like a leaf turning end over end. He did not believe that I could do it, but of course it was easy. I had to show him I could. I slipped out of my mantle and made many, many twirls all up and down the meadow without stopping. He was very impressed. But my brothers were cross with me!" Pocahontas laughed.

"Powhatan would not like to know his daughter entertained the enemy with only half her clothes on," Pamouic reminded her dryly.

"Certainly not a suitable activity for a woman of marriageable age," added Secotin.

"Sometimes I forget my new responsibilities," conceded Pocahontas. "But I will be more restrained in the future, I promise. Now let us have songs and dances. The evening is fine and the gods whisper happy messages in my ears."

119

As Quimca started to sing, Pocahontas looked at them, all seated cozily around the dying embers of the fire. It was wise to have a fire burning, even if low and banked, to frighten away the larger animals, the bears and boar that might otherwise be bold enough to attack. She watched her companions and thought how fine they all looked—strong and handsome with white teeth gleaming, hair shining, a ruddy glow on their skin, their bodies long and well muscled. She couldn't help comparing them with the Tassentasses, so gray, so small, so untidy. She felt sorry for them all, except the golden one, the one who looked like a messenger from the god of sky.

As Pocahontas moved in closer to the firelight, she looked among the soldiers and decided which runner would carry her first impressions to her father the next day. She would not want to ask for a volunteer. Every Powhatan was proud of his memory and took pains to develop and cherish this faculty. There were memory competitions, and a winner would cling tenaciously to his crown until old age addled his brains, but often even the very old possessed formidable memories. Pochins had a couple of runners with memories so keen they could recount word for word a message that took hours to relate. My first report will be short, she thought. I won't have much to say until I know more about the Tassentasses. We will return to see them tomorrow.

Pocahontas and her brothers talked in the fresh dawn about the tools they had seen and the great weapons of the enemy. They wanted to arrange trade between their father and the white men at once so that they, too, could have these tools and weapons to protect themselves and their lands. Pochins would establish trade quickly, they knew, but bartering would not help their father. And would he trade at all? He might prefer to fight an all-out war, using his overwhelming number of warriors to annihilate the enemy. Would he win such a war?

120

"We have many more warriors," Pamouic said.

"Father does not realize their big fire and thunder would wipe out twenty of us at one time," Secotin replied.

"Don't we want to know about their tools? Don't we want to have them for our own, to help our people?" Pocahontas asked.

"Yes, but we don't know how to use them yet," Secotin replied. "I think we should learn as much as we can about everything, keep our father informed, and then return to him in fourteen suns for a complete review. Perhaps in that time we can discover their weakness. Every enemy has one."

Pamouic stood up. "We have to report to the priests as well," he said. "We have to keep them happy or there will be another child sacrifice."

Pocahontas saw the glance her two brothers exchanged. Their faces were suddenly dour and somber. How quickly they change, she thought. She knew they did not like the control the priests had over all of them, but it was a fact of life. The priests were almost as powerful as their father. Her brothers' thoughts were silly, but now they must go to the Tassentasses.

They arrived early at the broad open meadow near the bay, where the Tassentasses had landed.

"Let us separate today and compare what we have learned at the end of the afternoon." Secotin didn't bother to lower his voice as he spoke to his brother and sister. "That way we won't duplicate what we hear and see."

"They were certainly friendly yesterday," Pamouic replied. "But I will stay near Pocahontas anyway in case there is trouble."

"All right, but give the impression she is on her own. They liked her yesterday. They may give her more information that way."

Pocahontas wandered away from her two brothers and walked among the men working in the field. They paid little attention to her. She watched a workman toil and marveled at how easily his spade moved the soil. The strong stuff of which it was made intrigued her. She pointed to the tool and worked her hands in sign language.

The workman smiled and said, "Iron."

She repeated the word. It sounded strange. She ran her hands over the blade. It felt cold and very, very hard, harder than stone and not as warm.

A shadow fell near her, and she looked up quickly. It was the handsome one, the one who seemed to be from the god of sky, and he was smiling at her. She was relieved to see that his teeth were not black like those of the man to whom she had just spoken.

He pointed to her. "Pocahontas?" he said.

She smiled and nodded. He then pointed to himself. "John."

So that was his name! It was easy to say and she repeated it several times.

John Smith looked at her reflectively, then motioned for her to sit on a nearby log and wait. He went away but returned almost immediately, carrying a square, thin, hollowed-out piece of wood with a flat top. As Smith pulled up the top she could see what appeared to be a piece of the sky or water. She sucked in her breath and put her hand across her mouth. It was magic! It must be the work of the devil god Okeus. She looked again— something green moved across the surface. She jumped away. Smith smiled, a kind smile, the corners of his eyes crinkled, and he motioned to her to look down. She was uneasy—she thought the gods might be angry with her—but she knew she must not show fear. The gods despised that kind of weakness. Smith held out the box and she ran her fingers tentatively over the wood. Everything these strange men had was so smooth, so strong.

Slowly she opened the top and looked again. Ahone, it was still there! Slowly she put a finger out and touched the water inside carefully. It was hard, as frozen as the Potomac River during the season of the long nights. Curiosity won over fear. She looked again. God of sky! It showed her face! She looked the way she did when she gazed into a pond or a lake, only her image now was far clearer. She could see her eyes, open wide in wonder, and her mouth forming an O. Smith then took the piece from her and held it in front of his own face and gestured to her to look. Now his face was in the piece. Pocahontas could scarcely believe what she saw. Smith then put the object in front of her again and she smiled. And it smiled back! She tossed her head from side to side and laughed. The hard water did the same! Pocahontas was enchanted. "It's called a mirror," said Smith with a wink and a smile.

She looked at Smith and her heartbeat quickened. He had brought her magic, magic far better than any the priests had ever given her. He came to sit next to her, and when he was close, she was relieved to find he did not smell strongly. But then she could not avoid looking straight into his eyes. It was her first chance to see him well, and she could barely repress a gasp. The god of sky seemed to be talking to her. His eyes were the same color as the clearest sky after a storm, when everything had a brighter, sharper edge. They were a clear deep blue.

Her face became impassive as she thought, I am vulnerable to this man; he weakens me. I must be more controlled. I must remember he is my enemy.

Smith pointed to himself with both his hands and looked questioningly at Pocahontas, his eyebrows raised.

"*Nemarough,*" said Pocahontas.

"Man," replied Smith. They both laughed, then repeated each other's words carefully.

Smith pointed to Pocahontas.

"*Grenepo.*" Pocahontas laughed.

"Woman." Smith smiled.

Smith pointed to the forest.

"*Musses,*" cried Pocahontas.

"Woods," replied Smith.

It was a game Pocahontas could have played all day. Every part of her exulted in the excitement these new words gave her.

Pawcussaks, guns. *Pamesacks*, knives. *Chepsin*, land. They repeated and repeated until they had covered far too many words for Smith but not enough, not nearly enough for Pocahontas. She knew she could remember every word, even if they continued all day.

Finally Smith called a halt. Pocahontas felt a rush of gratitude toward this man, this enemy. It was almost impossible to feel wary of him. But she said to herself, Perhaps that is exactly what he wants to accomplish. He wants to disarm me. He wants to lull me into forgetting that he and his men have come to steal our land and sicken our people. My father has told me to be on guard, and I must obey him. But it is hard. This man is one that I never, in all my dreams on the meadow, thought could exist.

She turned to see Smith watching her. He then said, "Priest." It was one of the words she had learned.

He motioned for her to stay for a moment.

"*Vittapitchewayne*, I wait," called Pocahontas as Smith left her. The day seemed particularly bright. Every tree, every flower, every man working in the field, seemed to be vividly etched.

Across the fields, perhaps sixty yards away, a flicker, a change in the gray-green of the brush caught her eye. Her ears suddenly picked up a noise so faint but so ominous that she jumped to her feet. Didn't those men around the brush hear the snake? The rattle must sound like thunder next to them. She started running toward them, her arms outstretched, her palms pushing downward, telling them to stay quiet, stay quiet.

124

The men seeing the girl running toward them shifted uneasily and gripped their tools; why was she running in their direction? As Pocahontas approached she swooped down, still on the run, and scooped up a large stone. Out of the corner of her eye she could see that Pamouic was also running toward them, but he was still a good distance away. He must have heard the snake too. Suddenly one of the men sitting near the brush let out a surprised howl. He had been bitten. In the abrupt stillness that followed Pocahontas heard a low rattle. It was obvious from their puzzled expressions that the settlers did not know what was happening, they had never heard such a sound before, they had no idea of its danger.

Within a second of the man's howl, Pocahontas, still running, hurled her stone. It landed with a thud by the fellow who by this time had rolled over on the ground writhing in pain. Pocahontas could see the snake lift its head and the hard ugly rattle grew louder still. Two more stones, then a third, whizzed by Pocahontas's shoulder. The last stone was so close to her temple that she was startled, but she kept on running. She could see that the snake had been hit and that Secotin was after the kill. She rushed instead to the bitten man thrashing on the grass, ripped open the pouch on her belt, and took out a razor-sharp shell. The workman screamed as she slashed it across the snakebite and put her mouth on the wound to draw off the poison. The wounded man fought her, but she hung on until she was satisfied that she had done her best. Then she dropped away.

"You are a quick girl, Pocahontas." Pamouic was at her side.

"I have killed the rattler." Secotin returned his tomahawk to his belt and came to stand with them.

"Someone almost killed me too." Pocahontas looked at her brothers. "Could anybody else have thrown a stone?" Pamouic shook his head. Secotin shrugged and looked away. "With all your experience, neither one of you could have possibly thrown that stone that missed my temple by a hair. Someone else must have thrown at the same time."

Pocahontas looked around for a minute and then she too shrugged her shoulders. "I wish I had some wighscan root to lay over the bite or a sweat house where we could put this Tassentasse. But these people don't have one."

The laborers sweated and cursed as they milled around, unhappy and frightened by the rattler. It was almost as if a devil had struck in the heart of their new home. There was so much unknown in this new land, so much that was dangerous. One of the men spat through his fingers. As Pocahontas looked at them she thought she could read their thoughts. They think I am some sort of evil, she said to herself. They associate me with the snake instead of being grateful for my assistance. She noticed that some of the men looked at her in a sullen way. She wondered, were women unwelcome in their society? Did they never have women around?

She saw that John Smith had joined the workingmen and was looking at her and then back at the men. He seemed to be judging the situation. Then he approached and gently touched her hand. She understood that he wanted her to know that he thought she was brave for stoning the snake and that he thanked her for helping the stricken workman. Did she detect concern for her in his voice and manner? Or did he just want to get her away from the muttering workmen? A tall man dressed in black, with a white strip at his throat, joined them. Smith motioned to the man with him and said, "Priest."

Pocahontas was surprised that a priest would consort freely with the people, as this man did. She had noticed him working and talking with the men on her previous visit, but had not understood who he was. None of the Powhatan priests would ever mingle with the people and be a part of their everyday life. As Pocahontas looked at him she felt no fear. He had a kind face and pale hair. He did not look as if he would put a spell on her or demand extra sacrifices, nor did he fix a hard eye on her.

After three or four tries she was able to say his name—the Reverend Mr. Hunt—which Smith repeated for her patiently.

She turned to Pamouic. "They want me to see their gods, and the priest is going to take me to his temple. I think I must go with him. I will find out if their god is stronger or weaker than ours. It could make a difference in a battle."

She listened and tried to grasp some words as Mr. Hunt turned to Smith and said, "She would make an ideal convert. As a princess she would carry the word to her people. I must try to teach her about our Lord."

She followed Hunt across the field, which was a mass of tracks, ruts, tree stumps, and fallen trees from the construction of the fort. They came to a lean-to fashioned from a sail strung up between two trees. It sheltered some rough benches and a long wooden table, like a trestle.

Hunt couldn't believe his luck. A royal princess was the first of the naturals to step inside his temporary chapel. He had listened to the captains argue about whether to build, whether to confront the naturals or placate them, when all along he had known that the only way to conquer the natives was to convert them. Christianity was the key to establishing the English in the New World—not the Christianity of the corrupt popes and Rome but the clear, fine religion of the Church of England. After all, hadn't God kept America hidden until after the Reformation? It was widely believed at home that God had saved North America for Protestant forces. And here in front of him was the first of his new flock, the perfect convert. He had no doubt that she would accept the true God. She was young, impressionable, and ripe to be delivered from original sin.

"We must pray," said Hunt as he knelt facing the makeshift altar.

127

"Pray," Pocahontas repeated. She pressed her palms together as she did when she addressed Ahone or Okeus.

Their God is not impressive, she thought as she looked at the wooden trestle table. But this priest is praying to him. He must be powerful, since he has given the Tassentasses so many fine and wondrous things, so many things that are so much bigger and more powerful than ours. She looked around her. They pray the same way we do, she thought, but where are the sacrifices? There were no fires, no offerings. She knelt when the Reverend Mr. Hunt knelt, pressed her palms together when he did. She closed her eyes when he closed his. She tried to imagine what this strange God could do for her if she offered up sacrifices to him. It was hard to tell anything about him. He had no face.

Hunt was pleased with the way Pocahontas gave him her attention, pleased that she joined her hands and knelt with him so readily. Yes, she was excellent material. The good Lord would take her happily into his flock.

Pocahontas decided to go back to the camp and offer up a special sacrifice to her gods to assure them that she had not strayed. She would find a marten or a mink. And to make her new friend, the priest, happy, she would bring him something small—a sea gull or a rat—to sacrifice in front of his strange God. She looked at the trestle table skeptically. She would pay him a little respect but not enough to make her own gods angry or jealous.

As the Reverend Mr. Hunt's voice droned on and the minutes passed, Pocahontas's mind wandered to something that bothered her. Who had thrown the stone that almost hit her in the temple? If she hadn't moved her head she would have been struck in that most vulnerable spot. She had always been taught to aim at the temple if she intended to kill. Pamouic and Secotin had absolute control over their throws. They never made mistakes, and she was sure neither of them had thrown the stone. Who else had been behind her? She had seen only her brothers, but of course she had been running fast at the time. She gave herself a shake for reassurance. I must pray now to Ahone and thank her that I was not hit.

After a long time, the Reverend Mr. Hunt completed his devotions. As he put his hand on the top of Pocahontas's head and said a quick benediction, he thought about what a fine pupil she was. Then the two of them rose from their knees, refreshed from their prayers and thoughts of God.

CHAPTER

Jamestown,
June 20, 1607

Smith and Archer crouched low among the weeds and waist-high grass. They had left the besieged fort that morning at dawn to hunt for game. Although it was the end of the day, the heat was still intense. The heavy, wet air sang with mosquitoes. Both men slapped at their faces, thankful that their bodies were protected by clothing and armor. The metal skirts, breastplates, and helmets still burned their flesh, but less cruelly than when the sun was high. Even so, each man held his musket gingerly. Overhead the sky was still a metallic blue, burnished and glowing like a gigantic reflection of their breastplates.

"Another hour and we can make a dash for the fort." Archer shifted his weight on the marshy ground.

Smith grunted. He wondered just how many of the Pasapeghs were watching for a chance to aim one of their arrows into his flesh. In all his years of warfare, fought back and forth across the plains of Europe, he had never encountered such an infuriating enemy. Without any warning, a man could be riddled with arrows before he could get powder into his musket,

133

much less ram it home. Armor was some protection if one did not die of heat prostration.

For the hundredth time Smith silently cursed Edward Maria Wingfield for his lack of foresight. Within a week of the aborted deer feast, the Pasapeghs had returned four hundred strong to storm the colonists' fort. Three of the settlers had been killed before the ship's cannon could blast into action. The clamor and thunder of the cannon had done more to rout the savages than had the actual fire. But at least two dozen Englishmen were dead or wounded. Since then, the settlers had been pinned inside the fort. Unseen bows raked arrows across the gatehead if anyone was foolish enough to step out into broad daylight. It was constant warfare, and in Smith's opinion totally unnecessary. If the precautions he had wanted to take had been implemented, he was sure the situation would be entirely different. He ground his teeth in frustration. At least cannon had been brought ashore and placed on the three towers of the fort. But it was no victory, thought Smith, to be proved right at the expense of continuing warfare, and now they faced the specter of starvation as well.

This was the colonists' second attempt to hunt for game. The first time they were not successful, but today they had bagged six hares and four turkeys. It was still not enough, thought Smith. The colonists' supplies were perilously low. Even the corn would last only a short time. The harvest had been poor so far this year, and when he visited Pochins, he had learned that there was not much food to spare for the colonists. He groaned as he thought of the succulent feasts Pochins's women had served him.

On the first hunting trip, all three hunters had been wounded and left to lie bleeding in the burning sun from early dawn until sunset. Only then was it safe to drag the wounded back inside the fort. Those were three of the idle who had volunteered for that mission. Smith had to admit they were brave enough about their misfortune. Most of them were good shots, he thought, or at least said they were.

"Archer, the light is fading," Smith said. "Now we can inch our way slowly through the grass to the open meadow."

A hell of a way to deal with the enemy, Smith thought, on one's belly slithering over damp ground. Can't stand up and fight like a man. But we have to play their game. We have to have food. We must find a way to befriend these naturals so they will help us cultivate this land.

When the first evening star gleamed, the two men made a dash into the fort. Eager hands unloaded the game off their backs; knives were ready to dress it.

"How many men lost today trying to plant corn?" asked Smith.

"Tom Casen, William Tankard, and Richard Simon," replied Gosnold.

"Did they take all precautions?" Wearily Smith unbuckled his breastplate and stepped out of his skirt. His armor fell to the ground with a clank.

Gosnold wiped his brow. "We gave them cover with the cannon, primed and ready to fire. But the ambush was too quick. All three men got arrows in their necks between helmet and breastplate."

Smith was bone tired. Three men now killed in ambush. At this rate, he thought, we will all be dead before December. That damned fool Wingfield. If we had built the fort with a field inside we could have planted by now. We cannot keep sending men out to clear and plant or even to hunt. It is certain death. We are safe only inside the fort.

"Gosnold, do you think the men will work a field at night?" Smith asked.

"They will not. They are too frightened."

Archer offered Smith water. He took a long drink and shud-

135

dered. The water was filthy! He swore under his breath. The men could not get to a clear stream. The damned naturals didn't attack every day, just when the settlers had developed enough confidence to leave the fort. Then they sent a rain of arrows. Smith moved to a nearby tree trunk and sat down. This was not the adventure for profit that he had envisioned, nor had he enjoyed the glory of establishing a colony in the New World, as he had anticipated when he signed up. Here they were, stuck in the middle of a swamp, gold nowhere to be seen, confined to a badly constructed fort, with an enemy outside the walls that could attack at any time, unseen, unheard. We have fifty times the firepower they have and we can't use it, he thought. They melt into air before we can fire our guns.

Wearily, Smith looked around at the palisades in the gathering darkness. "Did the men work on the fort again today, Gosnold? If they did most of the palisade should be strengthened."

"That has been taken care of. We have other problems. Francis Perkins was caught stealing food. And worse, some of the men have been caught robbing graves outside the fort."

"For God's sake, Gosnold, what graves? How?"

"From what I can gather—and only one other man knows about this—two of the men have made friends with one of the naturals. We don't know how this happened, but through this connection they discovered where the naturals' graves are. They also managed to get out of the fort safely. We haven't spoken to the men about it because we want to see how they escape and trap them in the act. One of their fellow workers told us about them."

"And Perkins? He is not a laborer; he should know better than to steal," said Smith.

"The men are hungry. Perkins is now in the brig of the *Godspeed*," replied Gosnold.

"Poor bastard, but we can't have stealing. That will decimate

136

our ranks as fast as fever. Any more men ill today?" asked Smith.

"No, just the five. But with this heat, I fear there will be more."

"What is Wingfield going to do about the thievery?" queried Smith.

"He is angry. And in this matter he will set a harsh penalty, I am sure. The council will have a meeting in the morning. Now I'll get you and Archer some food," said Gosnold.

Smith watched Gosnold walk away. He is a good man, he thought, but overtired and more gaunt every day. Smith ran his hands over his eyes. I cannot get too tired myself. This low land, these mosquitoes—too much like Anatolia. He looked over at Archer slumped against a tree. None of these men had endured real hardship, he reminded himself. The ocean journey had been far from easy, but at least there had been plenty of food and water. He watched Gosnold tramp back with two bowls of watery gruel. Poor stuff, but better than slugs and leaves. He clapped Gosnold on the arm in thanks. A bite of hare or turkey would be the midday meal tomorrow.

They had been in Jamestown now for a month. During that time Smith had been reinstated on the council, and an uneasy truce hung between him and Wingfield. Smith's success in trading with King Pochins for corn had persuaded Wingfield to include him in decision-making. But Smith knew that he was still on probation. Except for Gosnold, the men on the council continued to back Wingfield.

The month had revealed many things about the settlers. Some of the gentlemen, the idle men, had been the coolest under fire and the quickest to volunteer for dangerous duty—but not for manual work. The rest had worked as hard as men could under a sun far fiercer than they had ever experienced in England. And now the fort was almost finished. The buildings within would take a while longer to complete, but the fortification was as solid as it would ever be. It was far from perfect, but it had stood up well under the rain of arrows. The naturals had given up hope of storming the fort.

A bright skein through the first days at Jamestown had been the daily visits of Pocahontas and her retinue. She would arrive each morning shortly after sunrise, with six or seven of her people and with vital gifts of food. She and her companions would move quietly among the workmen like exotic birds, inquisitive and bright with color. They would examine everything—a shovel, pots and pans, an unloaded musket or pistol. Every few days they would inquire about the mirror. They would hover over it, laughing and smiling, and then gravely return it to Smith.

The Englishmen became used to their visits. Their hostility vanished once they learned that Pocahontas was royal and the daughter of the great king they all wanted to meet. They respected her as they would a princess at home, and they were deeply grateful to her for the gifts of food she brought. They even fell into the error of becoming complacent about its arriving regularly. Occasionally the laborers stopped to try to talk to the braves, who stood watchful and solemn under a nearby tree.

Each day Smith would take Pocahontas by the hand and lead her to a log where they would sit together and teach each other more words. He found himself looking forward to their visits with increasing eagerness, and he was baffled when she and her coterie disappeared as suddenly as she had first appeared. It was doubly disconcerting to be deprived of the corn she always brought with her. He knew that none of her father's subjects would hurt a royal princess in any way, so she could not have come to any harm. She had been able to enter and leave the fort without interference from the Pasapeghs. Perhaps because the harvest had been so poor, the Powhatans were running short of corn and she felt she could not arrive at the fort empty-handed.

It amused him that he missed her inquiring eyes, quick intelligence, and gentle manners. She was an authoritative young woman and yet not in any sense demanding or overbearing. Yes, it was easy to see why she was her father's favorite. Smith found that he thought about her occasionally, and that surprised him. She was in no way like the other women he had known.

There was barely a ripple of wind as the men settled down for the night. A snatch of laughter, a raised voice, hung on the air. An occasional cloud wafted across the new moon, adding a deeper tone of darkness. From the distance the muted sounds of the forest—an owl's call, the shrill scream of a small animal, some faint indistinguishable sound—reached every man in the fort.

The time before sleeping was hardest. Then the immensity of the woods behind the fort, and the unseen enemy within, seemed impossible to overcome. It was only late at night that the tautness in their bodies lessened slightly and each man turned for comfort to the reassuring sound of the river water lapping rhythmically against the shoreline. The scent of the water and of the sea beyond held the promise of a return to England and, sensing that promise, they slept.

The council gathered shortly after dawn, when there was still a hint of coolness in the air, but the mosquitoes were already on the attack. They were like the enemy outside the gate, thought Smith, unseen until the moment they struck.

He sat down on a log between Bartholomew Gosnold and John Martin, ignoring the empty spaces on either side of Wingfield. George Kendall and John Ratcliffe completed the council.

Wingfield did not bother to stand up. All of the men moved slowly, conserving their strength against the day's heat. "We are gathered here to decide the best method of dealing with Francis Perkins," said Wingfield.

"Hang him," Smith said as every eye looked at him. They all remembered that Smith himself had been close to dancing at the end of a rope a short time ago, during the voyage to Virginia.

"I have seen the Spaniards use a method of punishment that is effective," volunteered Kendall.

Martin and Ratcliffe exchanged glances. Kendall had spent two years in captivity during the war with Spain.

"They put a bodkin, with a line attached, through a man's tongue and then tie the line to the tree," Kendall said. "The man's hands are secured behind his back."

"And it takes a while for the man to die?" Martin stared at Kendall.

"Yes, a week or so. I should think faster in this heat."

"We need to emphasize the importance of not stealing food. I say we use the bodkin method." Gosnold fingered the knife at his side.

"Are we all agreed?" asked Wingfield. He looked around. There were no dissenting voices. "Well, then, the sooner the better."

"Exactly how many weeks' supply of food do we have left?" Smith changed the subject, but voiced the concern that troubled them all most deeply.

"Four weeks, if we are very careful," replied Martin, who had been delegated to mete out supplies.

"If you sail tomorrow or the next day, as planned, Newport, when do you expect to return with fresh stores?"

"Twenty weeks would be a fair estimate." Newport frowned as he spoke.

"In the meantime the men will just have to go outside the fort to fish and hunt. The forest is teeming with food," said Wingfield. He got up from his tree stump and impatiently stalked around the circle of men.

"I suggest you make a hunting trip with us," Smith said. "We have already lost men to arrows." Smith and Wingfield eyed each other with mutual wariness. "I aim to try and find some tribes that are friendly," Smith continued. "And most important of all I want to find King Powhatan. He can help us trade. I cannot keep going back to Pochins. As soon as Newport sails for England, I want to explore upriver."

"If it is so dangerous, Smith, you are foolhardy," retorted Wingfield.

Smith ignored him. He knew he was being baited, and nothing would please Wingfield more than to lose him to the Pasapeghs.

Wingfield signaled to the sailors on the *Godspeed* to bring Perkins ashore. The meeting was over. The heat was intensifying now as the council men looked toward ship. On deck, four sailors walked their prisoner, his hands securely tied behind his back, toward the gangway and the waiting shallop. Francis Perkins was a tall man, but now his figure was humped over and his feet dragged as the sailors shoved him into the small boat. The men on shore watched as the shallop quickly closed the distance between ship and shore.

As Perkins was being pulled up the bank, Gosnold turned to the other council members. "I suggest we use the central tree by the square. Every man in the fort should have to pass by Perkins at least once a day."

The other men on the council agreed.

"Shall I gather all the able to the tree now?" Ratcliffe asked. As they all nodded, Ratcliffe moved away.

Smith looked at Perkins, now plainly terrified, his face white, his eyes desperate. Bloody fool, thought Smith. And we lose a good man, a first-class farmer.

Wingfield turned to Kendall. "You have seen this method of killing before. The sailors will take him to the tree, then you will insert the bodkin."

Perkins let out a shriek of anguish when he heard the word

"killing." He fell to his knees and begged for mercy as the sailors, their hands slippery in the heat, half frog-marched, half dragged the protesting prisoner across the meadow toward the center of the fort.

The day had been hazy; by now the sun was well up in the sky. The workingmen had left their tools behind, and the idle, too, had gathered around the maple tree. The Reverend Mr. Hunt, his black clothes somber, stood with prayerbook ready as the men shuffled their feet in the dust and wiped away the sweat that rolled off their faces and plastered the clothes to their bodies.

Smith sighed. Perkins was going to be difficult, but after all, he was no soldier or sailor, just a plain farmer. *God in heaven, I wish he would stop pleading and crying.*

Wingfield held up his hand; the men grew quiet. The only sound was Perkins sobbing.

"You all know by now that Francis Perkins has been caught stealing," Wingfield said. "That crime is punished by death. I hope this will be a lesson to you and we will not have to repeat this example." He turned to Hunt. "If you will give the last rites."

When Hunt placed his hands on Perkins's head, there was a flow of screams as the panicked man tried to twist free. The sailors grunted as they tightened his ropes. Hunt spoke a few soothing words to him and made the sign of the cross. Perkins's face had contorted, and saliva was dribbling from the corner of his mouth, but he calmed down slightly as Hunt prayed. When Kendall stepped forward with the bodkin, however, Perkins's pleas for mercy echoed off the walls of the fort.

The waiting men had all seen death by hanging and torture, some many times, but Perkins's agony made them uncomfortable, and they began to move around impatiently. Here was a man who was hungry, just as they were. His theft of food was a crime any one of them could have committed in a moment of weakness. A man in the crowd called out. "For the love of God, get this over with!"

There was one final anguished shriek as Kendall drove the bodkin through Perkins's tongue. The sailors hauled him to his feet, then strung the rope from the bodkin to the tree and tied and hammered it into place.

There was total silence for a long moment. A man slapped at a mosquito. Another spat on the ground. Then the men turned, still not saying a word to one another, and slowly moved toward their appointed tasks.

Smith thought, A clean hanging is the better way to die, but the men will have had a lesson. He sought out Gosnold and put a hand on his shoulder. "Gosnold, you look exhausted. I will make a bargain with you. If you go to one of the ships and sleep for the day, I will join you in tracking down the grave robbers this evening. But tell me now the name of the man who told you about this."

"Edward Plum, one of the yeoman, is the man you want to talk to, and the three of us are the only ones who know about it. Yes, I am tired, but I will join you this evening at sunset."

The three men looked at one another. Their clothes were wet, but the cool was welcome in the warm night. They would dry soon.

"That was an easy way out of the fort—wading into the water just below the ships and then swimming around to land again." Gosnold's voice was barely a whisper.

"Yes, but now we have to be careful. We are lucky the moon is new. The grave robbers are resting just ahead. We have to keep them in sight or sound and at the same time avoid the Pasapeghs." Smith hardly moved his lips. Around them the trees were thick, and the rich, night smells of the forest provided a pleasant aroma.

"Perhaps we should forget the whole thing." It was obvious Plum was not eager to continue.

"Plum, you may return to the fort. You have helped us, but now we will make less noise if there are only two of us." Smith gave the yeoman a kind push on the shoulder and turned back to Gosnold.

Both men tensed as Plum carefully reentered the water and slid away with barely a ripple. The river was as black as ink with only an occasional gleam of pale light on it. As they watched, they saw his blond head silhouetted faintly against the water. In that instant an arrow stuck out of his head. It stood at a right angle from about where the temple would have been. There was not a sound in the night. Astonished, they watched as the head slowly sank below the surface of the shallow water.

Smith and Gosnold looked at each other. It had all happened in a matter of seconds.

Dangerous or not, thought Smith, we have no choice, we must continue. He turned to Gosnold and in a barely discernible whisper said, "We have to go forward. It will be suicide to return by water for the next several hours."

Since it is a dark night, he thought, it must be difficult for the naturals to see us here in the forest. Also the killer might have been only a solitary hunter returning from a foray. If there was only one Indian near them, they were reasonably safe, but if it was a party . . .

Why hadn't the men they were following been shot? They sounded like bears moving around. That was why Smith felt quite certain it was only one Indian out on his own. He thought the settlers were a party and did not dare strike alone. "Come on," he said to Gosnold. "Move close to the trees and stay low."

Smith agonized that every movement they made caused a crescendo of noise. Each step he took seemed to find a mass of leaves and twigs. Yet he knew the sound was magnified in his ears, for the forest ground was clean and well cleared. He and Gosnold could distinctly hear the men ahead of them moving at some speed.

They reached a trail and the going became easier. The grave robbers seemed to take no particular care as they crashed through the forest, for it was obvious they were familiar with the route. Smith felt frustrated that he could not see his quarry, but there was no question about hearing them.

After what seemed like miles of hard walking, Smith heard the men stop. He flung back his arm and indicated to Gosnold that perhaps they had arrived at their destination.

Smith and Gosnold moved forward cautiously until they could just see into a clearing. They could make out the two men moving slowly among neat mounds of earth, perhaps fifty of them. Interspersed among the graves in no regular order were six-foot poles, carved and painted, looking like guardians of the dead. In the distance an owl hooted. Then the forest was silent. Even the grave robbers were still.

The watching men saw the two robbers drop a sack they had been carrying between them. Out of it they pulled several objects, which Smith and Gosnold strained to see. A faint gleam of moonlight in the deep gloom showed them to be swords and muskets, probably from the arsenal in the fort. As they watched, the two men laid them out neatly to one side of the graveyard in what appeared to be a prearranged pattern. They moved with assurance; Smith thought they must have come here often. The men stood for a moment talking to each other, then wandered slowly among the mounds of earth. They seemed to be looking for a sign. From his vantage point, slightly higher than the clearing where the graves were, Smith could not make out what it was they were seeking. Finally they stopped in front of one mound that looked slightly higher than the others, although Smith thought that could be his imagination. The sliver of a new moon above the tree tops gave precious little light.

One of the men knelt and seemed to scrabble around on the forest floor with his hands. Then Smith and Gosnold heard the sound of flint being sparked.

"They are going to light a fire!" mouthed Gosnold, arching his eyebrows.

A low blaze flickered, and each man took a shovel out of the bag and started to dig into the mound. One of them chopped carefully, then reached into the mound and handed the other an object about a foot long. He used a hatchet to chop out another object identical in length and size to the first and handed it over, also. Then both men flung the dirt back onto the mound and smoothed it over so that it resembled the rest of the graves in the burial ground.

Moving quickly now and furtively, they produced two long prongs from their bag, placed the objects on the ends, and thrust them impatiently into the fire. A few moments later they grabbed at the things with their hands, sank their teeth into the charred remains, and ate voraciously. A plume of smoke wafted the aroma over to the watching Smith.

"God almighty, Gosnold, they are eating human flesh from the new graves!"

In the fort the next morning Smith and Gosnold, tired and disheartened, discussed the event of the night before.

"They obviously had arranged to barter weapons with the Pasapeghs, which explains their confidence in the forest. But I am dead certain their agreement did not include raiding the graves."

"They got away fast enough when we surprised them. I don't think they will try to return to the fort to face the death penalty. They will probably try to find a friendly tribe to live with. We will not have to worry about hanging them, at any rate. And we got our weapons back."

Gosnold looks deathly ill, thought Smith, and our excursion last night did not help him. The disgust he feels, we both feel, has made us dispirited. Smith attempted to divert his friend with conversation.

"Newport sails on the morrow. He has put it off for a day. He has plenty of fine wood to sell in London and a good load of sassafras root. At home they are convinced it cures syphilis."

He stood up and prepared to leave. "We are having another council meeting this afternoon, but I am meeting Ratcliffe and Martin beforehand. They have yet another problem to discuss. Try to get some rest, Gosnold."

As Smith walked toward his meeting, he passed Perkins, still tethered by his tongue to the tree. His groans were muffled in the humid air. Each able-bodied man in the fort had to pass him several times a day. His agony would deter others from breaking the rules of the company. Smith was amazed at the mischief a hundred men could get up to when they were restricted to a confined space. We need more disciplinary measures, not fewer, he said to himself.

John Martin, sturdy and dark, waited for Smith by the chapel. His broad face was wrinkled in concern. He did not bother with polite greetings. "John, we think George Kendall is a Spanish spy."

Smith burst into a short laugh. One of the council members! It seemed improbable. But then, after the happenings of the past twenty-four hours . . . Smith sighed.

Ratcliffe, standing next to Martin, looked irritated. "You may laugh, but if the Spanish attack us here while the *Susan Constant* is away, we will be annihilated."

147

Smith fingered his beard. This was a nasty complication. The Spaniards could destroy the fort. Also, they could secretly ally themselves with the naturals, letting them do all of the work but giving them arms and instruction on how to breach the English defenses. The world would never know the Spanish had been involved.

"If what you say is true, it is a very serious problem indeed. Has anyone spotted Spanish ships?" asked Smith.

"No, not yet," replied Martin.

"Does anyone else suspect Kendall?"

"James Read, the blacksmith," said Ratcliffe. "Although several of us have watched Kendall, Read has been particularly observant. Three times Kendall has been seen talking to one of the Pasapegh braves when they approach on their so-called peace missions. No one else has been able to establish a relationship with that tribe."

Smith looked skeptical. Martin was unaware of his mission with Gosnold the night before. The Pasapeghs had been much more active within the fort than Smith and the other members of the council could have imagined possible.

"But that is hardly grounds to suspect Kendall as a spy," Smith said.

"Ah, but Read has found a coded letter among Kendall's effects."

Smith now felt really worried. Kendall had been present at every council meeting and privy to every plan. If there was any basis for Read's suspicion, it meant that the colony would now have to deal with the Spaniards in addition to hostile Indians, hunger, and fever. It was no secret that Spain wanted all of the New World's eastern coast, from Florida to Newfoundland.

Martin continued. "We are sure that Kendall plans to send the letter with Newport on the *Susan Constant* to a Spanish connection in London."

Smith thought for a moment. "If that is the case, when he hands the letter over to Newport, we will read it. If it seems in any way suspicious we will put Kendall in irons and find out the truth."

CHAPTER
❧9❧

The great chief's cove,
August 1607

He was her father's choice. Pocahontas looked at him again. She knew it was important to marry Kokum for political reasons. Certainly her father had chosen a handsome man, a very handsome man. But there was something about his mouth, something she could not quite fathom, that worried her. Did she sense a coldness in him? He had been kindness itself since she had returned to Werowocomoco. He had been gallant and patient, and so had her father. She knew she was expected to lie with him to confirm their betrothal, but she had been loath to take the step. Am I afraid of being trapped? she asked herself. But trapped by what? Will being with this man take something from me? Will my body betray me by yearning for his when our souls are not in harmony? She looked down at her rounded breasts. When he touched her as they danced or walked together, she felt a pleasant sensation. Even now, she thought, as I sit here in the circle of smiling friends and family, my breasts have hardened because he is next to me and I smell him. Oh, Ahone, I wish I were a beast of the forest and did not have all these complicated thoughts to upset me. I wish I could couple with him, fill my body with seed, luxuriate in sensation, and leave my head behind. I have never had such contradictory feelings before.

Kokum's father, the chieftain of the Chickahominies, was a difficult man, the kind who believed that stirring up trouble would add to his power. Whenever a course of action had been decided upon by Powhatan and the other chieftains in the kingdom, Powhatan was forced to send messages, delegations, and sometimes threats to the Chickahominy to keep them in the fold.

Her father, the great chief, gave her his encouraging smile, the smile that said, Get on with it. At least give it a try. Pocahontas smiled back at her father. Was it her imagination or were her brothers and sisters also waiting for her to take Kokum?

Now her father was speaking. "Pocahontas, as a gift I offer you my private cove from noon today until tomorrow morning at sunrise."

Everyone's eyes turned first toward the great chief and then to Pocahontas. So he is giving me a push, she thought. No one has ever seen the cove except my father and his wives. I cannot refuse.

Pocahontas smiled at her father in a manner that hid her inner turmoil. "How kind of you, Father. We will leave now."

They had just finished the noon meal. She turned toward Kokum, and he rose with her. Her body felt heavy and slow but next to her Kokum moved with his usual easy grace. He reached out to touch her arm and she felt even logier. Two guards moved forward to accompany them, to assure their privacy. Pocahontas wished not quite so many people knew that she and Kokum were going off together, but it was the custom to watch them gravely as they walked down the path toward the river waters. She knew that when she and Kokum were gone, there would be many tales, lascivious in the telling, that would amuse and occupy those they left behind. Later there would be music, singing and dancing. Not as much as when the marriage would take place, but the betrothal was a celebration, too. Then the priests would say a few words and pray that she would be filled with seed directly so that at the marriage her body would be protruding and fecund.

She and Kokum walked slowly down the path. It was perhaps a mile to the Great Chief's cove, and the heat was high at this time of the day. Kokum reached over every so often to nuzzle her neck or gently trace a finger between her shoulderblades. She thought that if her body felt any heavier she would be unable to walk. Every once in a while she would reach over to pick a particularly pretty flower, and Kokum would take it and play it against her breast or her mouth. Oh, yes, what they had to say about Kokum in the women's house was quite true.

At the edge of the cove where the waters lapped enticingly ahead of them, the guards dropped behind and out of sight. Kokum turned to her and slowly pulled her down to the still green grass and gently stroked her arms with slow fingers, up one and then down again on the other arm. He barely touched her, but he looked at her breasts and smiled. Pocahontas felt as if she were being pulled through warm water. Her body slowly began to relax but the heaviness remained. Kokum watched her for a little while, then leaned close to her ear.

"Come. The branches of the tree above us are many, comfortable, and cool. Let us rest there until the heat of the day is gone." Kokum climbed up to the lower branches in quick smooth movements. He reached down, and she was soon behind him and then above him, settling comfortably in a three-pronged fork of the tree. She felt his fingers begin to trace around her ankles and up along her leg. Then his mouth was lingering along her back and under her arms. Slowly, languidly he caressed her. She felt as if she were in a cocoon as the warm air circulated below and above them.

155

With each slow touch, her muscles relaxed a little more until her body was no longer heavy but suffused by a long fluid feeling of lassitude. His touch seemed to be everywhere, light, gentle, but beginning now to play on every response within her body. She seemed suspended in air, and the only touchstones were his warm mouth and his gentle fingers. She wished this flowing feeling, this unfolding of her inner body, this yearning, could last and last. There was no place on her body that he did not explore and delicately titillate, so that at times she felt almost as if she were drifting on the borderline of consciousness in undulating waves of feeling. After one long ascending wave of exquisite sensation, she could bear it no longer and her body shuddered into total response. Oh, and this is not even all of him. She turned her face. His eyes glittered near hers, a half-smile hovered on his mouth. The darkness of him was omnipresent.

"There will be more, Little Snow Feather, there will be more," he whispered into her ear. "Now sleep."

Pocahontas slowly regained consciousness and wondered for a moment if she had ever felt anything but this languid, gently rolling desire. Kokum's hands and mouth were again everywhere, but this time he said, "Come, it is cooler now." He carried her, still half asleep, down to the mossy ground and laid her on the moist green carpet, taking one of the feathers she had discarded—was it only a few hours ago? It seemed like a lifetime. He flicked the feather slowly over her body, already warm and receptive, until she reached up and pulled him toward her.

"Please," she whispered, "please." He moved his mouth over her breasts, lingering, lingering, oh, so long, until her body could stand it no longer and release came as a blessing. She seemed to remember as she again drifted into a semi asleep state that she no longer had any will of her own, that this man totally dominated her body.

• • •

Again she slipped back into consciousness. She did not know how long she had been asleep, but her body was still in a heightened state of expectancy. By now this awareness seemed to be a lasting part of her; she would never be free from it. She had been drawn from sleep by the gentle pulling mouth that moved down across her belly and between her legs. Her body was on a plane now where every touch seemed to be magnified, and trembling release was but a tiny touch away.

She slid again into half sleep, and when she awoke, the sky was not blue anymore but a soft velvet black. Part of her mind wondered how it had turned dark so quickly. The rest of her knew only that somewhere the sound of the river waves was now lapping in her ears and the soft sand was under her body, the body that was not hers any longer but belonged to this man who played on it as if it were his flute.

Now with the coolness below her, her limbs felt less febrile, but deep within her there was now a steady yearning, another hunger so strong she did not know if she could stand it. She found herself pleading—Pocahontas who had never pleaded. She felt his presence over her. The dark outline of his head hovered, waited, while his hands again played her body and she felt herself sinking deeper under his power. She heard her voice as if from a distance, moaning and moaning—would she ever stop? Within her mind she cried, begged to Ahone, oh Ahone, until she felt his movement, felt him beginning and thrusting slowly, then moving further, reaching deep within her. The rhythm was slow and deep and gentle, slower than the wash of the river waters that lapped around their legs, and she clung to him as if he were the only reality in a world of sensation and pulsating desire.

In the black night she did not see or hear anymore. There was consciousness and unconsciousness. At times she felt pebbles

157

beneath her, then again grass and moss, and then water up to her breasts. Sometimes there was sand beneath her and these times were quick and thrusting and she cried aloud with her body's rapture. And through it all her senses were enveloped in escalating response, a long rhythm of sensation, yearning, and ecstasy.

With the first fingers of dawn, he finally was not there and everywhere, but apart and waiting. He took her hand and slowly they walked back up the path together. She realized then that she still had not seen the cove.

The great chief looked at his favorite child. Pocahontas could see that he regarded her now in a different light. And he talked to her as a woman, not as a young girl. Is the stamp of womanhood on me already so strong? she wondered.

"Pocahontas, I want you to forget about these Tassentasses. I want you to collect taxes until you are formally Kokum's wife. Then after your first birthing I shall elevate your status. None of my daughters has been made a weroansqua. I consider you the most promising, the most intelligent. After some instruction I feel you will be a capable ruler of your own tribe."

"Thank you, Father. That is a very handsome offer." Pocahontas smiled. But the thought of Kokum and his command of her body made her quail. How could she explain to her father that something about Kokum made her wary, even though he was kind and considerate. How could she explain that Kokum had only to touch her earlobe and she was driven to leap into his lap in a fever of passion? And yet afterward she felt nothing but the swollen satisfaction of her body. Something at the very core of her remained frightened of the way he could separate her from her inner self.

"Father, I feel I should first finish learning about the Tassentasses. The knowledge will be a great help to you."

"But, Pocahontas, don't you want to remain near Kokum? Does he not please you well?"

Yes, thought Pocahontas, when she and Kokum had returned from their betrothal, and after her morning prayers to Ahone and her bath, it was only too obvious that Kokum had earned his reputation as the brave most accomplished with women. She had been changed during that night. She knew it and so did others. Tonight, or whenever he feels like it, Kokum can come and put his hand over my breast and have me as he wants. No, I must get away. I have to. Otherwise I will become his slave.

"Yes," she said to her father, "but I still have much time ahead of me to do the tax collecting and take on my heavy responsibilities. I have already given you valuable information about the strangers, but I am not finished. I want to speak their language better so that I can gather even more knowledge for you. That will also be invaluable when I become a weroansqua."

Powhatan smiled. Pocahontas knew then that the battle was almost won. She waited respectfully.

"Pocahontas, you always have excellent reasons for what you want to do. I cannot fault you on the need to know their language. But I intend to drive these strangers into the sea, for I do not agree with you that they are peaceful people who only want to explore and trade and then return to their land, and I am afraid more will be coming from their distant place. I will continue my instructions to the Pasapeghs to keep them harassed. You may go back to visit them but do it soon and return soon. We have work to do, you and I."

Pocahontas went over to her father to thank him. "Father, I am so grateful to you. I will take the same retinue as before and use the same camp. And I know what it is you want from me. I shall leave as soon as possible."

She was going to get away from Kokum! She could put off the inevitable for a little while longer. She would go back to the

Tassentasses and learn, learn so much more. The learning gave her such power, and she liked that. She was grateful to the one who looked like an emissary of the god of sky. He had been so kind to her. She wanted to see John Smith again, for it was he who taught her so well. Yes, she wanted to see him very much. Looking into his eyes was like looking right into the god of sky. And that gave her confidence.

Only one more night now with Kokum. He will not like that I am going away, for he, too, enjoys power, and especially the power he has over my body. Just thinking about what he will do to me tonight makes my knees tremble. I wish I could discuss this with my sisters or my father, but Powhatan has set his mind to this marriage. He thinks he has found the man who will make me happiest and at the same time strengthen his kingdom. Maybe a child will make the difference. Father leaves his wives the moment they have given birth. Maybe Kokum will want to do the same.

Tonight Kokum will devour me. Oh, I wish I did not have this feeling that he is part devil! Yes, that is it. That is the trouble. She stopped for a minute and her body shivered as she thought, Okeus must be his special god, and Okeus is powerful—so powerful, so evil! Does Kokum have me under the spell of the devil god?

Again they set up camp near the old lair of the wolves. Now the days shimmered under the sun and even the nights closed in as if the god of fire breathed his displeasure on the world.

Pocahontas had brought a little corn with her from Wereowocomoco. She knew the Tassentasses enjoyed it, and she did not want to arrive empty-handed after such a long absence. She would have liked to bring an offering to their strange and ugly god—a long piece of wood with four legs to the ground that did not resemble any god she'd ever seen. But when she was last in Jamestown she had carried in a mole and two toads to be sacrificed. Their priest had responded first with horror and then with something close to despair. He patiently explained that Christians did not sacrifice animals to their God.

Now as she entered the fort with Secotin and Pamouic and several braves bearing the corn, the settlement was strangely quiet. She looked around and saw a familiar face or two, but there were many fewer men going about their tasks. Where were all the people? At last she saw the one they called John Martin. He stopped in surprise at the sight of her and her entourage. She greeted him and asked where John Smith was.

"He is with Bartholomew Gosnold, who is very ill. They are in the meetinghouse. Quite a few other sick men are there."

Pocahontas hurried to the house, but as she entered it the smell of the sick hit her almost like a blow. She had never experienced anything like it. In her father's world, anyone who was ill retired to the sweat house and burned the fever out. She remembered that they did not have a sweat house here.

She saw Smith before he saw her. He was thinner and tanner, his skin tempered now by the sun but his hair was more like golden corn than the sunrise it had been. When he turned and saw her, his eyes were the same, just like the god of sky, and he smiled happily at her. He came to her quickly, past the men lying on the floor, took both her hands, and led her back outside.

He looked at her carefully, and Pocahontas thought that he, too, could see that she was now truly a woman. They went to sit on the tree trunk they always used when they learned each other's language. Pocahontas looked at him again and felt the way she did when she visited her meadow—as if only good things could happen.

They talked quickly in a mixture of English, Powhatan, and sign language, but mostly in English, since Pocahontas's memory had served her well. Smith told her that many of the men were ill with the swamp fevers, that Gosnold looked as if he would not last the day. He told her the men were hungry, terribly hungry. Newport, the man with only one arm, had left for England to bring back food supplies, but they did not expect him until the snow was well on the ground. He talked to her now as her father did; he treated her like an adult.

"I have brought you corn." Pocahontas indicated her soldiers who stood near the gates of the fort. "I did not know your men were so hungry and ill or I would have tried to bring more."

She asked why they did not have a sweat house in the fort to treat the sick. When Smith looked baffled, she explained that it was a closed room with a large fire in it over which water in huge kettles gave off hot clouds of mist. She could see, however, that this method of curing the ill was too alien for him to understand. She then asked which roots they were using as medicine. He said none, but he brightened considerably at the thought. So that method is not strange to him, Pocahontas said to herself.

He took her back into the meetinghouse to see the sick. There were perhaps twenty-five men lying close to one another in the crowded room. Some had thick mats under them. Others lay on the bare floor. Some of them moaned and tossed, but many were too weak to move. Their bodies were swollen and yellow or emaciated and gray. The stench of sickness and unwashed bodies almost made Pocahontas retch, but she made her way to where Smith was leaning over Bartholomew Gosnold. She knew he was one of Smith's true friends. She also sensed as she looked at Gosnold that the man did not have long to live. He lay with his eyes closed and his face was ashen. There was little flesh left of him, and the bones of his face jutted out so that he looked like a caricature of his former self.

She put her hand on Smith's arm. "I will send for my sisters who are at my camp. They may have some Wighsan roots with them. If not, they can find some. We must give the men a solution of that immediately. Also we must wash them and their clothing."

She hurried to instruct Pamouic, who stood outside, to send one of the soldiers for her sisters. Then she asked Secotin if he and two of the other soldiers could make a fire outside the meetinghouse and boil water in a kettle. She tried to remember what remedies to use. She thanked Ahone that she had learned many remedies from the older women outside the sweat house in Werowocomoco several snows ago when two of the villagers had sickened and one had died.

She returned to Smith, who was leaning over his friend. She saw him take Gosnold's hands and cross them over his chest and close his eyes. Smith does for the departed just as we do, thought Pocahontas. And now he prays, just as we do. Perhaps our gods are not so different.

Then Smith turned and she saw how sad he looked. The blue of his eyes was clouded and his shoulders sagged. But only for a moment. He straightened, his jawline hardened, and he looked at one of his lieutenants nearby and give instructions.

Pocahontas and her sisters ignored the heat and burning sun as they toiled among the sick men. They cleaned them, forced a bitter herbal drink down their throats, and boiled their dirty clothes. They wanted to burn them and supply clean skins instead, but Smith stopped them and explained that a man's dress was of great importance to him. It showed his rank and his position in society. Pocahontas looked carefully at the filthy pile and wondered where the rank could possibly show, but by now she had resigned herself to the many odd ways of the Tassentasses.

For several suns Pocahontas and her retinue left their camp early enough to supervise the cooking of the cornmeal at the fort before they nursed the men. Each morning Smith would be waiting for her with news of any happenings during the night. Each day she grew more and more eager to see him again. The boiled drinking water and the Whigsan root along with nourishing cornmeal had a salutary effect. Although the graveyard now had some forty fresh graves, the surviving men began to put flesh on their bones and the desperation faded from their eyes. Every man in the fort now followed Pocahontas and her sisters with grateful eyes. But it was "the little princess," as they called her, to whom they spoke quiet greetings and moved quickly to help in any way they could. She was without doubt the leader of her people, an obvious aristocrat, and in her presence they felt a renewed confidence in the naturals.

Absorbed in hard work, dealing with the many crises among the starving and epidemic-ridden men, Pocahontas had neglected her duties toward her father. She found herself feeling instead a new warmth, almost a kinship, with these strange men who treated her with as much thoughtfulness and courtesy as she enjoyed in her father's kingdom. She looked forward now to their quick smiles. Some of them helped her with new words of English. She was grateful, for there had been no time for her lessons with Smith. In their place, though, something far more important was happening. A communication had developed between Pocahontas and Smith that barely needed words. As hard as she toiled these days, Pocahontas found she had never been happier. This strange man, with his strange ways, was suddenly not strange anymore. In their work together they moved in harmony, almost by instinct. It was something she had never experienced, even when hunting with her brothers.

At first when she returned to her camp in the fading sun, tired but somehow exhilarated, she thanked Ahone for giving her a reprieve from her coming marriage and duties. But as the days passed and her happiness increased, she began to want her life to continue this way. Why couldn't she stay with the Tassentasses and help them and at the same time be loyal to her father, yet not marry Kokum? She knew this was impossible, but in her heart she wanted it, and she found every excuse to give credit to the Tassentasses. Her dispatches to her father were invariably favorable to the strangers, and her father's replies were becoming shorter and more curt.

On a day when there was some respite from the heat, the cook at the fort reminded her that they were running out of corn. Pocahontas called her brothers and sisters, and they decided to tell the Tassentasses about the friendly tribes who would barter with them. Pocahontas agreed with Smith's earlier view that he could not deplete Pochins's supply further.

Secotin reminded Pocahontas that it was time to show the Tassentasses how to hunt and fish. Now that they were becoming well again they needed fresh game to supplement their diet of corn. But Secotin added with a hint of scorn in his voice, "Their hands are so clumsy and their memories so poor that they will have a hard time mastering the fish nets and traps in the river."

"Remember, Secotin, they are from a different sort of land," Pocahontas said. "Also they are not as strong or healthy a people as we are."

Pocahontas waited until the sun had dropped down near the forest behind her. Then she found Smith and together they walked to their usual meeting place on the log by the permanent chapel.

"We are short of corn again. I will tell you which tribes are most likely to be friendly and trade with you. I have asked my father for corn twice. He has given it to me as a favor because he thinks it is mostly for my use, but I cannot ask him again. He is not an easy man, John."

"I realize that."

"Stay away from the Pasapeghs, the Weanocs, and the Chick-ahominies. The Chiskiacks, the Quiyoughcohanocks, and the Warrasqueocs will be friendly. But barter carefully. Do not give them too much. One sword for ten baskets of corn would be fair, or one string of beads for twenty baskets." She hesitated for a moment before she continued. "Let them give you feasts and women for you and your men. It would be an insult to turn them down."

Pocahontas then described the characteristics of the various tribes and told Smith how to distinguish friendly from unfriendly Indians and how to behave without giving unintentional offense.

Smith leaned forward. "Pocahontas, I want to meet your father, the great king."

"This meeting will have to be arranged very carefully. As I said, he is a difficult man. I have been here almost a full cycle of the moon, a month." She smiled at her use of a new word. "I must go back and tell him of my experiences here. Then I will attempt to arrange a meeting. I must tell you that he does not feel kindly toward you and your people, at least not yet."

Smith turned to her, and she saw a new expression in his eyes, an expression that made her stomach tighten and her hands tingle. She felt her breath coming quickly.

"You have saved us here, Pocahontas. I am loath to see you go."

He reached out to touch her hand. She felt her body start to tremble slightly. I can't take my eyes away from his, she thought. I feel as if I am sinking into their blue depths. She opened her mouth to say something, but nothing came out. Her whole being was paralyzed by the look in his eyes.

He reached over and gently stroked her cheek, brushing her hair aside. His touch was so intense that Pocahontas thought for a moment that she might faint.

"Excuse me, Captain. You asked me to speak to you at sunset about the storehouse."

They were startled. Lowery the carpenter stood before them, his big hands clenched at his sides.

Smith gave Lowery a nod and told him he would be with him shortly. As Lowery moved off, Smith turned to Pocahontas. "It is difficult for us to talk privately, but I want you to understand that I am more than grateful to you for rescuing us. In this New World you are a person without parallel. Go to your father, he wants you now, but please return soon. We need you." His voice dropped. "And I want to see you."

Pocahontas found it almost impossible to tear her eyes away from his. I must leave now, she thought, but this is where I am happy—here, next to him. After a long moment, she turned away. Still, she could not speak. It was not as if her throat felt tight. It was as if an unseen hand were pressed gently against her mouth. A cold feeling started between her shoulderblades. Was it a warning from the devil god Okeus?

CHAPTER
10

On the river,
December 1607

T he wavelets broke gently against the shallop as it cut
through the water of the river. Smith sat back as comfortably as he could in the unyielding little vessel. He
decided, as he adjusted the furs over his legs, that he would
barter for a canoe tomorrow if the Indians would part with one.
They were far better constructed and easier to maneuver than
this small boat.

The water was icy. The blue of the sky was now a deep, winter hue. The trees had shed many of their leaves and only the
most hardy had retained a touch of color. Autumn had been
successful for barter; the settlers had been able to deal for food
with several neighboring tribes. Smith found that Pocahontas
had visited each group to whom he had journeyed on her way
home during the late summer. She had prepared the way for
them. But why hadn't she returned? It has been four months
now. Each day he expected her to arrive at the fort and each
evening he was disappointed. He had not kept a conscious,
active vigil, but he was aware of his disappointment every day
she did not come. Not only had he missed seeing her but he also

wanted to talk to her about her father. Finally he had decided to strike out on his own. He needed to find Powhatan's territory and explore the possibility of meeting the great king himself. Also, London wanted him to find the Indian Sea, the western gateway to India. After meeting Powhatan he could proceed up to the Chickahominy River to its headwaters which might lead them into that sea. And there was always the possibility that he could procure corn from the inhabitants, although Pocahontas had warned him the Chickahominy were not particularly friendly. It would be a tedious journey of at least a day. He took with him seven men, including the gentlemen George Cassen, John Robinson, and Thomas Emery. All were excellent marksmen.

Smith shifted his weight carefully in the shallop. Any sudden movement and the little boat with its shallow bottom could dump them all in the cold river. He saw that the frost was still on the ground as he gazed out over the banks on either side of him. The seasons changed so abruptly here, he thought. The trees blazed into color almost overnight and then just as suddenly they were bare. But he had not been sad to see the summer go. It had been the harshest he had yet experienced. Almost half of the settlers had died of starvation or disease. If it had not been for the life-saving ministrations of Pocahontas, they might all be under the ground now. She had saved the colony. He thought for the hundredth time how remarkable she was, how lucky he was to have her as an ally.

He had written to London telling of her exploits on behalf of the colony. It was the one positive report in an otherwise sober letter. He also wrote of George Kendall, the spy. The letter left on the *Godspeed* in October. Newport had opened the Kendall letter the day before he sailed. It was incriminating enough to alert them all, and Kendall was thrown into the brig. The council convened immediately to question him, but to no avail. There was only one recourse—torture. They hung him by his thumbs with weights on his feet. It was not long before Kendall confessed that he had been sending and receiving messages to and from the Spanish in Florida via Pasapegh runners. When the council found out that one of their own had betrayed them so grievously, they decided to hang him, but not before he revealed that he had discovered where the great king Powhatan stored his treasure. He told the skeptical council that it was kept in huge houses in the hamlet of Uttamussack. They hanged him without mercy.

The graveyard is getting full now, reflected Smith. Even his archenemy Wingfield had had a close call just a month ago and had come within a hairbreadth of the gallows. Out of carelessness, Wingfield had contaminated with dirt the two gallons of sack and aqua vitae that Newport had left for the communion table in the chapel. The council was furious, and the rest of the settlers had called for blood. Wingfield was voted out of the presidency and off the council, and Ratcliffe was made the new president. Not only had the remaining members of the council become increasingly disillusioned with Wingfield's leadership, but they later became suspicious that he intended treachery. He, too, had been imprisoned on the *Discovery*. He was still there, thought Smith with satisfaction.

The river was now beginning to narrow into a stream. Smith called to the men to keep a flint close at hand in case they needed to fire their guns suddenly. His warning came not a minute too soon. Two tall braves suddenly stood on the near bank. They appeared, as the naturals so often did, seemingly out of nowhere. They had their bows at their sides and their hands over their hearts in a peaceful gesture. Smith quickly decided to pull to shore. They were Powhatans, they told Smith in their own language, and were on a hunting expedition, but they would be glad to escort the Tassentasses farther upstream if they wished.

Smith turned to his group. "Four of you remain here with the shallop," he told his men. "Emery, Robinson, and I will explore a little farther upstream in the braves' canoe. Give us a flint and keep yours handy. This may be risky, but they seem friendly enough."

After paddling a mile or two upstream with the braves, Smith decided to explore the countryside on foot. He turned to Emery. "You and Robinson stay here with one of the guides and make camp. I will go with the other brave and scout the land. I won't be long. I have a feeling we may be in Powhatan territory at last."

He and his guide had silently made their way a half-mile inland when the trees and rocks around them suddenly seemed to reverberate with a bloodcurdling yell. Smith grabbed his guide, locked an arm around his neck, and jammed the pistol into his back. In that instant, an arrow scraped by Smith's thigh with a whoosh. He looked up. Two natives, their faces tight with concentration, had their bows drawn and arrows aimed straight at him. One part of his mind saw immediately that they were not in war paint. They wore ordinary skins and furs, as if they had been out hunting. Keeping a grip on his guide, Smith fired at both men, missing them. He then released his guide, who was terrified by the noise of the pistol and cowered at his feet. He quickly reloaded his pistol, a French wheel lock. As he did so, four more naturals sprang from the woods. He fired, and three of them staggered down, mortally wounded. Suddenly there were a dozen more Indians where there had been four. He grabbed his guide again. In broken Powhatan he told him that if anything happened to him, or to Emery and Robinson, he would kill him.

The naturals gathered in close around Smith. He was surrounded. The winter sun streamed down through the leafless trees onto the possum, marten, and squirrel furs that hung around the braves' shoulders. The leader of the group barked out an order. The men threw down their bows and arrows, which landed with a clatter on the frozen ground. The leader then motioned to Smith to give up his pistol.

Smith ignored him. When he spoke, his breath came out in puffs of steam in the cold air. "Where are my men?"

"We have killed them all."

"Why don't you try to kill me?" Smith tightened his grip around the neck of his guide.

"You are the captain." The Indians had quickly discerned he was the leader by his air of command.

Smith knew that because of his rank he was to be spared for the moment. I have got to try and get out of here, he said to himself. My only hope is to get back to the canoe. He poked his pistol threateningly into his guide's ribs and began to back away from the hunters. The naturals made no move to stop him. He walked backward for perhaps a quarter of a mile while the braves kept their distance. Now they held their bows in their hands but did not aim them. The light was bright, the air clear, every twig and tree seemed sharply defined. The warm breath of the guide fell rhythmically on his arm.

"God's blood!" Smith's foot suddenly slipped off an embankment into cold mud. Without releasing his grip on the guide, Smith looked helplessly down as they both foundered in the icy muck. His feet were mired in the bog. Every tiny movement sank them even deeper.

The hunters standing on the bank watched impassively as if they had all the time in the world. Smith stared back defiantly. But by the time the icy mud had reached his upper thighs he was nearly dead with the cold. He decided his moments to live were few either way. He tossed his pistol to the nearest natural. The hunters quickly pulled Smith and his guide out of the mud. Half carrying the frozen men, the party went immediately to the campsite that Robinson and Emery had prepared.

As the naturals chafed his legs to restore his circulation, Smith saw that the fire was full of bones—the bones of Cassen, Robinson, and Emery, he thought.

His guide leaned over to him and said with some pleasure, "We tie prisoners to a tree and cut off their hands and legs and throw them in the fire in front of them. Then we cut out their stomachs. While they are still alive we burn them and the tree."

Smith forced his face to remain expressionless. The blood was now coursing normally in his legs and he could stand. He turned to the leader and demanded that his captors take him to their king. If it is Powhatan, I may have a chance, he thought.

But after an hour's tramp though the woods, they led Smith to the king of the Pamunkeys. He was a dour man, a brother of Powhatan. Smith felt instantly that this man would give him no mercy or even fairness should he dislike him. He thought quickly. I could speak to him of my friendship with Pocahontas, but he might disapprove of her visits to us. There must be a way to divert him; if I can just buy some time.

After searching in his pocket he brought out his ivory compass. He rubbed his thumb over the smoothness of the glass. His captors were amazed at the shiny hard substance they could see through. They were fascinated by the play of the needle and by Smith's lecture, spoken in broken Powhatan and sign language, on the roundness of the earth and sky and their relationship to the sun, moon, and stars. The Indians listened, rapt.

But as soon as the king took the compass into his own hand, his men grabbed Smith and tied him to a tree. For the third time that day, he thought he was doomed. He started to say a prayer. The braves seized their bows, readied their arrows, and aimed. And again he was saved.

The king put up his fist, clutched around the compass, and told Smith he would spare him. But he added, "There were crimes committed here by your brothers three winters ago. I will take you on a journey from village to village. If you are recognized as the evil one who did those crimes, you will be killed."

For over a month, Smith was taken from hamlet to town through four kingdoms of the Powhatan federation. He was stared at, poked, and judged. "Monster" he was sometimes called, but his red-gold hair saved him. The man who committed the crimes on Gosnold's expedition in 1604 had had black hair.

Still the Powhatans were not finished with him. Now they wanted to know about Jamestown. They asked question after question. How many men were there? How many guns? What supplies did they have? Smith expected at any time to be deprived of the good food, warm housing, and the occasional warm woman they provided on his odyssey. He expected to be tortured, and when he wasn't, he concluded they were saving him for something. But what?

On a bitter cold day near the new year, his captors woke him from a sleep in a bed of warm furs and announced that after his breakfast of corn bread and dried venison, they would travel to Uttamussack.

Uttamussack, thought Smith, where Powhatan's treasure houses were supposed to be located. Perhaps Kendall was right about the treasure. His hopes soared. Are they taking me to the great king himself?

Smith gladly submitted to his captors' usual manner of marching: three tall warriors on either side of him, two ahead and two behind, with the Pamunkey king's son in command. After five hours of travel they reached the outskirts of Uttamussack. Five of the biggest men Smith had ever seen met them, and after a brief discussion they escorted the party into the village.

There were perhaps ten buildings of a normal size in the hamlet, but dominating the town were three large houses, larger than any Smith had seen in the New World, perhaps eighty feet long.

Around each of the houses paced twenty guards, every one of them nearly six and a half feet tall. They were patterned with red paint and menacing in their manner. Powhatan's treasure houses, said Smith to himself excitedly, containing gold and pearls, rubies, precious stones, and silver. His mind raced. He could barely control his eagerness, but he would not let his captors know what he was thinking. Finally, he thought, finally I have found the riches. Now the Virginia venture will be a success. But I have got to stay alive. I must. What do they have planned for me? Will I see the great king or will I be killed? Maybe I am here to be offered as a sacrifice.

With a prod on his shoulder, he was led into one of the smaller houses in the compound and seated on a black mat. The room was lit by a small fire, but still it had a gloom he associated with churches back home in England. The light flickered over great bunches of dried herbs hung on the wall, which gave off a rich aroma, making him feel relaxed and a little sleepy. But as his eyes adjusted to the dim light he could see in a far corner an idol, a wooden figure with a white-painted face, evil in expression and almost alive in its malevolence. In front of it were offerings of two small, dead animals. Smith said a quick prayer as a prickle of fear started between his shoulderblades. That figure looks like the devil himself, he thought. Just for good measure he spat between his fingers and repeated an incantation against the devil he had been taught as a child.

At that moment a figure burst into the room. Still thinking about the devil, Smith thought, My God, who is this? He started to stand up. A firm hand pushed him back down and left a mark of black coal on his doublet. Smith gave a little sigh and thought, This one is human at least, but he's the most evil-looking man I have ever seen. The huge fellow, painted black from head to toe, moved slowly in a sort of dance around the room. On his head were moss-filled snakes and weasels, their tails twisted into a macabre crown. He moaned an incantation as he circled the fire. Then he produced a rattle, and his voice rose into a wail and then dropped back into moans. He started to sprinkle cornmeal around the fire. Perhaps he is putting the evil eye on me, Smith thought, alarmed. He had confidence in handling every contingency that life had to offer, but he could not hope to best an agent of the devil.

Three more naturals, equally large and equally black, surged into the room. Smith's senses were sharpened by fear. The newcomers joined the dance, their arm and leg movements jerky and slow. They, too, alternately wailed and moaned. Three more entered, and they all sang a song in a low pitch, continually moving in a circle around the fire. Suddenly they stopped dancing and laid corn kernels in a symmetrical pattern around the meal. They dropped to their knees, bowed their heads low, and groaned long and loud. Then they placed little sticks between the corn kernels and repeated the groaning ritual. They must be priests, thought Smith, devil priests. The smoke from the fire, the perfume of the herbs, the constant movement of the priests made the air heavy and close. He felt oppression now as well as fear.

Suddenly the dancers jumped to their feet and threw their hands up high. Then they were back on their knees again. In quick movements they pressed the corn against the sticks, then threw the sticks into the fire. With a great leap they all stood, their limbs trembling.

The first priest turned to Smith and said, spitting the words into his face, "The meal is our country, the corn kernels are our seas, and the sticks are your people. We will crush you and your people and run you into the ocean."

They were gone as quickly as they had come.

Smith sat waiting. The idol in the corner stared at him through the smoke like evil incarnate. Finally two of his guards entered and one of them told him to get up. He had a small smile on his face. "The great chief Powhatan's priests have now prepared you," he said. "We will leave for Werowocomoco tomorrow."

A dozen canoes left the next morning for the day-long trip. Icy rain trickled down Smith's neck. He watched the naturals and noticed yet again that the weather never seemed to affect them. They wore furs around their shoulders, but their deerskin clothing did not fully cover the rest of their bodies. They did not seem to react to either cold rain or hot sun.

It would take a day to reach the core of the Powhatan kingdom, Werowocomoco. Pocahontas would be there, thought Smith. Surely she would intercede with her father. She must help me persuade the king to cooperate with me and the other settlers. After our loss of Roanoke, if this colony does not survive, the English will lose heart, and the perfidious Spanish will take over the coast, from Virginia to Newfoundland and then move west to the East Indies. We have won a great war against them, but we may lose a continent.

Smith realized, as he sat hunched over, clasping his knees to try and gather warmth to his body, that he thought of Pocahontas far too much. In his mind he could see her high cheekbones, the sheen on her black hair, the tilt of her head. He was bold beyond his rank to let her dominate his thoughts. She was the daughter of a great king, and he was a commoner. He would be wise to push these thoughts of her out of his head, but other women seemed dull in comparison to Pocahontas, with her dark vitality.

The gray day made his thoughts gloomy. He had been ebullient at finding Uttamussack last night, but now he thought of the three men he had lost. He had revised his opinion of the gentlemen colonists completely. They were not good at manual labor, it was true, but they had proved to be courageous, resourceful, and dependable in combat. The good blood in their veins stood for something after all. He was sad at losing fine men. The Indians had not even left any of their remains for burial at Jamestown, he thought, as he rubbed his brow.

His guards paddled steadily, silently, with only a brief stop for food at midday. They never seemed to tire, and they didn't talk to each other. After many hours the rain ceased and a mauve tinge filled the sky to the west. Then ahead of them they saw men standing on the bank holding unlit torches.

So this is Werowocomoco at last, thought Smith. He immediately began to look for a slim girlish figure, although his experience traveling through Powhatan towns told him that she would not be standing on a riverbank. Powhatan's favorite child would be waiting for him by her father's side. Each day runners would have reported the progress of his trip through the Powhatans' country.

The waiting men escorted Smith half a mile to a spot where two hundred of Powhatan's attendants stood in groups in front of a long house. The men looked him over carefully. They talked among themselves, and once in a while one of them would give him a poke with a forefinger or peer intently at his beard.

Smith thought, they are a tough, hard-looking group of courtiers. I can expect little mercy from them. I wish I could identify one of equal rank to whom I could talk. He couldn't keep himself from glancing around for Pocahontas, but he could see little in the dark.

After a half hour of waiting, he was led around to the other side of the house where light streamed from an opening. As he was shoved inside, a great shout went up. The room was packed with perhaps three hundred fifty people. After the dark and cold outside, the heat and bright light momentarily stunned him.

His eyes adjusted and intense color assailed his senses. Torches blazed every few feet, illuminating the green, yellow, blue, and red patterns adorning the men's bodies. Brilliant plumage and exotic headdresses decked their shining hair. At the end of the room, on a bedlike dais heavy with lustrous mink, marten, and fox skins sat the great king Powhatan. On either side of him and behind him stood twenty of his women in feather capes of many colors. In contrast to the men they wore their hair loose, dressed with white down and feathers.

Smith heard two sticks being clapped together, and a deafening shout rose up from the crowd. Smith was pushed to a spot in front of Powhatan, but not too close, and he could clearly see the man who controlled his destiny. He did not feel reassured. The king before him had strong features, and his expression was cold, determined, and cunning. He dominated the room, not by his great height or strong body but by the authority of his personality. The king exudes power, thought Smith, more power than any man I have ever seen.

The king turned to speak briefly to a soldier at his side. Smith seized the chance to search the room. His eyes roved in every direction. For a second he thought he had found her, but no, it was not Pocahontas. Where was she? If she is not here, I am finished, he thought, as dread started its corrosive spiral through his body. He looked again, but did not see her. She has abandoned me. Something has happened to change her mind about us. He bowed his head as he thought for a moment. Then he straightened his shoulders and looked at the great king in front of him. Smith knew he would need every bit of his courage to get through the next few minutes.

She heard the great shout ring out from the council house. He has arrived, she said to herself. Her body felt frozen, as if she could not move. For a fleeting moment her face wore a tough cast, like Powhatan's. Her arms were crossed and her hands clenched as she sat in her father's house. They will have the festivities, the feasting, and then the sacrifice. My father and I have made our bargain, but I do not have to witness the happenings tonight. I will not go.

Slowly she stood up and with stiff movements paced the length of the house, then retraced her steps. Earlier, in order to be as inconspicuous as possible, she had changed along with her sisters when they put on their finest clothes. Although she prepared herself, she did not tell them that she was not going to the ceremonies.

Matoaka, Little Snow Feather, is my private name, and I feel as icy in my heart as the first fall of winter snow, she thought. She looked down at her leggings of beautifully dressed white skins. From her neck to her knees she wore an intricately woven mantle of the whitest swans' feathers. It resembles the white silk shirt that John Smith showed me, she thought. Everything reminds me of him all the time. I must control my thinking; I have got to be a stronger person. I have not seen him for three months and yet . . .

She had returned to Werowocomoco from Jamestown when the sun was at its hottest. Her father had greeted her warmly but with a reticence that let her know a lecture would be forthcoming. She had expected it and had her answers prepared.

He had told her how happy he was to see her, but he was disappointed with her dispatches. She had neglected her duty to him and to her people and had been easily influenced by the enemy. He added that he felt she was probably too young after all to take on such an important task and that it was his fault for letting her go in the first place. He said that he did not blame her, but wondered why she felt friendly toward the enemy when her brothers and sisters were still loyal to him.

Pocahontas told him that she had expected his reaction. But, she asked, how could he judge a people when he did not know them? Contrary to what he was thinking, the Tassentasses were

183

friendly people who hoped to get along with the Powhatans. She wanted to continue to study the Tassentasses and learn even more of their ways. They had useful customs and tools from which our people could learn. She was careful not to mention her feelings for John Smith.

Powhatan replied that she was being unreasonable. She must put the Tassentasses out of her head. Her thoughts were bordering on treason. She must remain where she belonged, with the family, the people who had nurtured her. She had a responsibility to her father, to her future husband, and to the important position she would shortly undertake as a weroansqua of her own realm.

Pocahontas had said that she felt her responsibilities strongly and that she was unhappy to have caused trouble. Then she had blurted out that it was impossible for her to marry Kokum.

Powhatan had been astonished. He had said that he could not understand, as it was obvious she had been pleasured well by Kokum. Wasn't she carrying his child now?

Pocahontas had said no, she was not, and tried to explain to her father her ambivalent feelings, her fear of enslavement. Her distress touched her father.

He sat down quietly. After a few moments of thought he said that perhaps she had exaggerated fears about Kokum, but that he would not force her to be with him now. Later she might feel differently about him. Powhatan said he would make a bargain with her. He would find an excuse to send Kokum off on a hunting expedition and then back to the Chickahominies. In return, she must forget about the Tassentasses and stay and collect taxes. He reminded her again that her first duty was to her own people, and that he intended in any case to run the Tassentasses into the sea.

Pocahontas knew that it was a fair bargain. She also knew that her father would forbid her to pay any more visits to the

Tassentasses. But at least now she did not have to worry about Kokum. Even so, she felt guilty for ruining her father's hopes for an easier relationship with the chieftain of the Chickahominies. But how could she help her inner feelings? She knew that she was right about the Tassentasses, but she also knew that her duty was here.

But now her feeling of being torn between conflicting emotions over Kokum had been replaced with conflicting emotions over her regard for Smith and the colonists and her loyalty to her father and to her people.

The past weeks had been difficult but busy. Powhatan had sent her off immediately with some of his older advisers to collect taxes. There was plenty to do, since each subject in the Powhatan Empire had to give to the great chief eighty percent of every commodity made, grown, or acquired. Any oysters, pearls, furs, roanoke—shell beads used as currency—fish, or corn made its way to the treasure houses at Uttamussack.

But in spite of her trips to various towns and the festivities that greeted her, she could not put John Smith and his people out of her mind. She was anguished in her longing to be with him and felt both her loss and her disloyalty to her father. Over and over she had rehearsed in her mind how she could bring the two of them together in a friendly way.

Now, as she heard the ceremonial cry from many throats, she knew it was too late. Smith had been captured. When she had heard about it several suns ago, her emotions had swung between fear and anger. She knew that her father was determined to rid himself of at least one of the leaders of the enemy. There was nothing she could do to change his mind.

She paced the long room, clenching and unclenching her hands at her sides.

CHAPTER
11

Werowocomoco, January 1608

T he great king rhythmically patted the string of pearls on his chest. He stared steadily at Smith who had been left standing for several minutes without receiving a greeting, a demand, or any other acknowledgment. But Smith knew he must not be the first to speak.

There was a low murmur as the courtiers talked among themselves. Smith noticed that all of the women standing proud and beautiful around Powhatan wore ropes of pearls around their necks and wrists, along with copper beaten into decorative shapes suspended on chains. Those nearest to the king wore the largest pearls and the greatest number of necklaces.

The king gave a signal with his hand. He had only to move before several jumped to obey. There was a stir at the foot of the throne and out stepped an imposing woman in her middle years, dressed lavishly in feathers and skins with heavy ropes of jewelry hanging to her waist. She brought a bowl of water to Smith and indicated that he should wash his hands. Moving slowly and with great dignity she gave him a bunch of turkey feathers with which to dry them. A woman of rank, thought Smith, as she gestured to him to follow her.

"Are you a wife of the great king?" Smith whispered in Powhatan.

She turned, startled. "I am his sister, the weroansqua of Apamatuks. Where did you learn our words?"

She is no fool, thought Smith. Do I admit to my lessons with Pocahontas or do I stay silent? The fact that the princess was not there made him wary.

"I have been traveling among the towns of the Powhatan land," Smith replied.

"You are to stay in this spot," said the weroansqua, indicating a position nearer the king. "We are going to have a feast."

Smoke from the torches roiled up to the ceiling and out through the smoke holes, reminding Smith of the older houses in England, before they built chimneys. Serving women, bright in beads and fringed skirts, scurried around bearing finely wrought pottery bowls filled with strips of grilled venison and a stew of corn and poults, along with great platters of golden corn bread. They finished the meal with a delicate doe cheese and dried fruit.

The food was well prepared, and Smith ate steadily. He had not had such delicious fare for a long time. It may be my last meal, he said to himself, but I will savor every mouthful. It was a dangerous moment in his life, but there had been so many that he had learned to take what pleasure he could when it was given to him.

One of the king's advisers stood and started to speak. The room hushed and then became silent. Smith, straining to understand, realized that the speech was a harangue against the foreign invaders and a rallying cry to drive them into the sea. Once or twice he thought he caught the word "Roanoke" and several times he heard "Chesapeake" and "Chickahominy." Then the speaker digressed into a philosophical dissertation on the people of Powhatan. After sitting through speech after speech during his weeks of captivity, Smith knew that the speaker could go on for hours and still keep the attention of his listeners.

Every so often Smith looked around the large room to see if Pocahontas had joined the feast. Her absence seemed ominous, and he hated to look for her and then feel the sinking disappointment. He thought he saw her two brothers, Pamouic and Secotin, but they would never acknowledge any greeting he might make, not here. Smith could imagine the pressure Pocahontas had been subjected to on returning to her father and his kingdom. She was a powerful woman in the Powhatan world, but she was also young and malleable. Still, it was hard for him not to feel abandoned and, worse, disillusioned.

They are going to sacrifice me, thought Smith. There are none of my own kind here to bargain or intercede for me, and there are too many of them for me to overcome. His mind probed every possibility, but he arrived at no solution. He said a few brief prayers. He had always believed that God helped those who helped themselves. Even as he prayed, part of his brain continued desperately to seek an escape from his plight.

Should I speak and to plead my cause? But my grasp of the language is not equal to a formal plea. Besides, they may despise me for not accepting my fate and dying well. He felt truly trapped. He had known the sharp fear of imminent danger many times before, but the sensation had always been accompanied by a surge of excitement, a challenge to overcome his predicament. Now for the first time he experienced the cold wretchedness of despair.

The speaker finally stopped. The king inclined his head, then called to a group of his priests, who moved up to his throne and stood there shaking their rattles. Tonight they did not wear black, but their headdresses were the same tangle of moss-stuffed snakes and weasel skins that Smith had seen on the

191

devillike creatures in Uttamussack. They spoke together in low voices; it was a long consultation. The crowded room remained silent except for an occasional shifting or a muted sigh.

The youngest of the priests signaled to a tall warrior whose face was patterned with the marks of numerous campaigns. He marched to the door and called out a string of commands. The raw night air eddied into the room, bringing welcome relief from the heat that emanated from the press of bodies and the flaming torches. Then several soldiers marched in. Between them they carried two huge stones. They staggered slightly as they maneuvered them into position in the center of the earthen floor. Their furs glistened with raindrops.

Smith watched the preparations. He wished he had a Christian priest to pray with him, to pardon his sins.

Suddenly a platoon of soldiers, bare to the waist, their hair damp and dripping, marched in, each carrying a heavy war club. Their muscles rippled and their skin shone with a mixture of oil and rain as they grouped themselves around the two massive stones and looked toward the prisoner, their faces impassive. Smith stared back angrily. Why don't they look as if they are pleased to club me to death? I know they are. If they are efficient they will stun me with the first blow. But they may prolong the killing and toy with me, he thought, as he looked at their arms and tried to gauge their strength.

Smith turned toward the throne and thought he detected a sardonic smile hovering around Powhatan's lips. Well, thought Smith, he can feel complacent because he is killing us off one by one. He may get his land back, but for how long? The Spanish will be a far rougher crowd to deal with than we have been. God's blood, I wish they would get this over with!

As if in answer to Smith's inner plea, Powhatan stood and raised his arms. There was an instant hush in the long room. The only sound came from the sputtering torches. Smith alone could hear the increased thudding of his heart banging like a drum in his ears.

Powhatan spoke briefly. Smith thought he understood the king to say he would be a sacrifice to the devil god Okeus. And damnation to their devil god! he thought. Reflexively he spat between his fingers. This was not the time to court evil, from any kind of devil.

The crowd gasped. They did not know what to make of Smith's gesture. Was it a threat, an evil spell? Then the soldiers grabbed him by his arms and led him to the two stones, which sloped down toward where they joined, making a rough cradle for his head. At least they were giving him a ceremonial death with suitable respect for his rank, he thought.

Smith was still angry, his stomach tight with fury. He managed to say another prayer, to beg forgiveness for his rage and his sins and to ask God to keep note of the times he had tried to do good.

Two soldiers grabbed him and forced him to his knees. One knee cracked, like a pistol shot echoing around the room. They pressed him forward and down, his face against the winter-cold stone. Smith felt the rough texture against his skin and smelled the mold and dampness of the forest. The sensation was oddly voluptuous, and he was swept with a sense of luxury and security. His eyes closed in a surge of euphoria. He wanted to hold this stone and this feeling to himself forever.

He could hear the soldiers shift as they placed themselves in the best position to swing their war clubs. Dirt flew up from the floor, and he could taste grit in his mouth. He suddenly longed for a familiar scent, a familiar taste, a familiar language. Then anger surged back as he tensed his body, waiting.

He sensed rather than heard a flurry of movement. There was a sudden freshening of the air near his face. Something fell across his back and shoulders. His body arched in surprise. Then he felt

193

light arms encircle his head, a fall of hair brush past his cheek, smooth skin rest against his. He heard the soft familiar voice.

"If they are going to kill you, they must kill me, too."

Pocahontas cradled his head in her arms as she spoke. Then she pressed her face to his. They did not hear the excited babble of voices, the running feet of the guards, nor did they see the consternation on the faces around them. There was nothing but the warmth of their breath intermingling, the light pressure of her breasts on his back. Finally she raised her head to look over her shoulder, past the astonished and hesitating soldiers, to her father sitting grim-faced on his throne.

The great king raised his hand, and the soldiers stepped back. The hushed room watched as the king's favorite child rose from the killing stones. Pocahontas put her right hand out to indicate to Smith that he, too, should rise, and they walked together to stand in front of Powhatan. Curiously, the thunderous expression on his face had disappeared and in its place a play of slight admiration flickered around his mouth, even though his eyes remained stern, even hard.

"Father," Pocahontas began, "I plead with you to spare my life and that of Captain Smith. This man has done us no wrong and indeed only brings, on behalf of his people, goodwill and the desire to trade."

There was not a sound in the room. After a few moments the king said in a quiet voice, "Pocahontas, you were brave to intercede. I will spare the captain." He turned to the guards. "Take him to the great house. I will make arrangements for him later."

The great house stood deep in the forest a mile from Werowocomoco. Smith saw that scalps, hundreds of them, had been hung in neat rows along the walls to create a pattern against the bark. There was no other decoration except for a large mat that fell from the ceiling dividing the house into two rooms. It is not a reassuring sight, thought Smith, but I have gotten this far. Maybe I will make it back to Jamestown. There was no one else in the house, and the scraping of the bare branches against the roof echoed hollowly. He waited dutifully in front of the fire as the soldiers had instructed him to do.

Blessed Pocahontas! He felt joy surge within him. She is a true ally, and more, he thought, and more.

He was dozing when a prolonged sound, the most doleful he had ever heard or imagined, emanated from the next room. As he shook himself awake, the mat was pushed aside and two hundred men, painted and dressed in black, came toward him, wailing softly. Leading them was the great king himself. When Smith started to struggle to his feet, Powhatan motioned for him to remain seated. The black men and the black scalps on the wall had an oppressive effect on Smith.

One of Powhatan's men unfurled a small mat and placed it in front of Smith. The king sat on it and began to speak.

"I have come with my priests and first soldiers. My priests are against what I will say, but my soldiers agree. Time will tell if it is a good policy. My daughter has told me many things about you and your people. She said we should be friends and trade together, and I agreed with her. I intend to send you back to Jamestown in two suns because I would like to have some of your great guns and a grindstone. In exchange I will give you the territory of Capahowosick, and I will forever esteem you as my son by the name of Nantaquond."

Smith was stunned. Could Pocahontas have used her persuasive powers so effectively in the short time between his rescue and this meeting? There could be no other explanation, unless Powhatan had decided, in an abrupt change of mind, that it was to his advantage to acquire the goods he wanted while inducting Smith into his fold. It was a clever strategy. Smith agreed immediately to Powhatan's terms and to the adoption

195

ceremony. But he still feared the powerful priests and what they might plot for the future.

"Pocahontas tells me that your ships were chased to our shores by the men with black beards—the ones you call Spaniards."

Smith nodded.

"You also told her that you and your people will leave after your captain returns from your place across the water."

"Yes, I told her that." Smith recalled that he had tried to placate Pocahontas and her brothers about English intentions months ago, when they had first met.

"I hope that will be soon, for my priests are impatient. After the adoption ceremony you will return to Jamestown. Tonight my men will bring you some supper and a woman to warm your bed."

Smith could not understand why he was being kept isolated, but he did not complain. It was enough that the king's fancy had changed. He thought with sudden hilarity that a scant hour ago he had given himself up for dead and now he was being offered the embodiment of life, a woman. But which woman would they send to his bed? He knew it would not be Pocahontas. He had tried to put his carnal desire for her out of his mind because she was the daughter of a king. But everything had turned from black to white in such a short time—anything could be possible. He wondered how he would feel if she came to him. It was one thing to admire her, to believe and trust in her. It was another to imagine her warm body next to his. Did he have reservations, too, because she was only thirteen or fourteen years old? Some people in England married at that age, even earlier, and they certainly did so in this culture. He sat with crossed legs and stared into the fire.

Pocahontas turned to her father immediately after Smith had been sent off to the great house, the traditional lodging for visitors who were not intimates or relations. She and Powhatan talked intently together, and Pocahontas used every wile to open his mind to her thinking about the Tassentasses. She knew she had to convince her father that the Powhatans needed these men to teach them their great magic. She was convinced that if she could gain time she could persuade her father to get to know the white men. Then he would feel as she did about them. She was careful, however, never to let him know her feelings for the red-haired captain. Powhatan listened to her gravely. He was familiar with her arguments, but the fact that she had risked her life for one of the invaders impressed him strongly. He was more than willing to hear her out. Everyone knew this child of his was exceptional, but facets of her developing character continued to surprise him. She was becoming what she declared she would become, knowledgeable about the Tassentasses. He was still resolved to destroy the invaders, but his daughter was right: first he needed to know how to work their magic.

"Well, daughter, I shall heed your advice. We will trade with the Tassentasses. This is still an experiment, however, I will meet him and discuss our next move. Since you have rescued this man, he becomes your responsibility, so prepare food for him and find him a woman for the night. He is a leader among his people, so she must have a certain rank and be experienced; he is not a boy."

Pocahontas lowered her eyes. It was common courtesy to give a guest someone pretty to sleep with, but was her father exacting a small fee for his compromise? No, he had no idea she cared for Smith. She thought longingly for a moment of slipping into his bed herself, but her father would almost certainly disapprove and rescind all his concessions. She could not risk that. But at the same time she could not choose the woman. Mehta would have to do it for her. It was not fair, she fumed, finally to see him again and then almost immediately have him taken away and joined to another woman. The devil god Okeus must be punishing me for refusing Kokum, she thought. How was she going to sleep tonight when she knew Smith was so near and making love to one of her friends or, even worse, to someone she did not like!

Mehta chose a beautiful ex-wife of the great chief, now married to one of his best soldiers who was away on a hunting foray. There was a great deal of speculation about the Tassentasse that evening among the females of Werowocomoco.

The next morning Mehta grabbed Pocahontas and pushed her along to the early morning bathing spot reserved for the women of the town. They all hurried that winter-bright morning while the sun sparkled so strongly it seemed to give off heat. They could hardly wait to hear about the Tassentasse, that creature some called a monster.

Pocahontas could not make up her mind whether it was worse to hear the story or not to hear it. When the women discarded their clothing to bathe, everyone would covertly inspect the brave's wife who had been with Smith. Would she have love bites on her body and, if so and most important, where? Would her nipples still be rosy? And was there something unusual about this man? Was he covered with hair like a bear? Had he done monstrous things to her?

Pocahontas thought that the woman was being impossibly coy in telling her story. She splashed around in the water, giving every indication that she had been pleasured and pleasured well by the man, monster or otherwise. She didn't say anything, but sported and lolled in the frigid water as if it were the season of hot suns. Pocahontas felt like giving her a good slap. Finally the woman came out of the water and let as many as wanted to watch as she ran the turkey feathers slowly over her voluptuous body. Up to now no one had begrudged her the night with the strange one. After all, her husband had been away for ten nights, and everyone thought it was probably going to be a bizarre experience, anyway. But as the other women could plainly see, it had been very satisfying, and their impatience was building to annoyance when, finally, the wife settled down beside the fire.

She said that from the neck down the Tassentasse was very, very pale. His face was covered with hair like that of a bear, she said. It scratched nicely against her body, she added with a little squirm, but the rest of him was as hairless as her own husband except, of course, for the red-gold curls around his love object. She leaned back and closed her eyes for a moment. She said that that part of his body was quite a beautiful sight, like the sunrise and sunset. But she added archly there was little sunset, for he was quite, quite strong.

Pocahontas felt she couldn't listen any longer when the women gathered in close to hear the finer details. She knew the night would be discussed and dissected for days as the tale became embellished. By the time the woman's husband came home there would be a fantastic story to tell, and the wife would enjoy great status. Then the song makers would take it up. She thought, I will have that stopped. One word from my father . . .

The adoption ceremony was to take place when the sun was as high overhead as it would be during the season of the long nights. The priests were surly and unhappy. They were angry that any concession was being made to the invaders, and they banged their drums with extra force to display their ire.

The townspeople appeared to sanction their king's new policy toward the strange people from over the water, but some had reservations. The priests' obvious disapproval made them uneasy. The priests have insidious ways of showing their displeasure, thought Pocahontas, but I suspect they think as I do. They know that my father is still determined to eliminate the strangers eventually.

When Pocahontas saw Smith before the adoption ceremony, she felt awkward. She knew that when soldiers came home after hunting or battles, they wanted their women and the release of love. Smith, too, would have needed relaxation after the ordeal of his capture and reprieve. Even so, it was hard to think of what he had done with that silly wife of the chief soldier.

Pocahontas tried to hold to her heart the moment of total oneness with Smith, the moment on the killing stones when they were aware of no one in the world but each other. And she knew when he turned his face toward her that he, too, had recognized a special feeling. The god of sky spoke to her through Smith's eyes and she again felt warmth and joy.

She saw also that Smith seemed apprehensive about the adoption ceremony. She reassured him that nothing dangerous or painful would happen. He had only to show filial respect when his finger was cut by a conch shell and his blood mingled with Powhatan's. Smith replied that he considered the adoption a great honor.

Later that day, after the ceremony, Pocahontas was asked to step down from her place near her father and stand next to the captain.

Her father spoke: "We have a custom among the Powhatan people, a custom that has been with us for as long as anyone can remember. When we rescue someone, we are responsible for that person and become his guardian for as long as he lives. Pocahontas, you are now the guardian of Captain Smith. He is your special ward and your lord. Captain Smith will leave now for his camp. Rawhunt, my close confidant, will accompany him. He will return to Werowocomoco with the two demiculverins the captain has agreed to give me. Pocahontas, as part of your new responsibility you will follow shortly with supplies, but you must return to me in a few days' time."

Pocahontas translated quickly so that Smith fully understood her father's wishes. Then she watched as twelve warriors marched away with Smith. They would be with his people by early the next morning.

CHAPTER

Jamestown,
January 1608

C *rash!* Cascades of snow fell to the earth.
    Crack! Great splinters of ice plummeted from the trees and pierced the ground. The world was a maelstrom of snow and ice. The forest floor was strewn with heavy branches, and the noisy crows and sea gulls were silenced.

Smith yelled to Rawhunt and his men to return. When the small cannon had been fired into the trees to demonstrate to the Powhatans how it worked, the noise and havoc had scattered the naturals in a headlong rush for the woods. They dashed for the forest half crazed with fear.

Smith shouted, "Load the demiculverin with more stones, and we will make one more shot. But wait until the natives come back!" Smith was patient. He had returned to the fort from Werowocomoco with the Powhatans scarcely an hour ago, and the sun was just beginning to creep up over the horizon. Now Smith watched as the naturals straggled back, pale and trembling, two of them violently so. The roar of the cannon and the destruction it wrought was completely foreign to them. It overwhelmed them.

Rawhunt put his hand over Smith's. Enough, he signaled, his fingers shaking so that he could hardly guide them. Smith smiled and countermanded his order to fire again. Then, in Powhatan and sign language, Smith asked Rawhunt how he was going to carry the four-thousand-pound cannon back to Werowocomoco and the great king. When he saw that Rawhunt was uncertain and uncomfortable, Smith sent one of his soldiers to the storehouse for several strings of glass beads and copper pieces, which he presented to Rawhunt with a ceremonial flourish. The Powhatans seemed satisfied. They would not return empty-handed to the great king, but returning without the cannon would be a difficult story to relate. Smith did not envy them.

Gabriel Archer, John Martin, and John Ratcliffe stood nearby slapping their sides occasionally to keep warm. As members of the governing council of Jamestown they were anxious to question Smith about his trip to Werowocomoco and find out what happened to Cassen, Robinson, and Emery.

When Rawhunt and his soldiers finally left with their presents and beads, Smith and the three captains sat down to eat together around the fire. Smith tasted the gruel and the coarse corn bread with concealed distaste. I am spoiled by good Indian food, he thought. I must ask Pocahontas to show our people how to prepare decent fare now that we can leave the fort to hunt and fish.

"Smith, you are not listening to me."

The three men were staring at him, their eyes steady and demanding. Ratcliffe, now president of the council, repeated his question. "Where are Cassen, Robinson, and Emery? You walked into the fort at dawn with twelve naturals and gave us no reason for your long absence."

Smith apologized and explained that it had been necessary to dispatch the natives before he could tell his story in detail. He did not want to leave anything out. As he talked he saw that his fellow council members were not sympathetic to his ordeal and their expressions were as frosty as the morning air. He felt that they did not believe that he had done his best and that it was not his fault that Cassen, Robinson, and Emery were ambushed. They felt he should have stayed with them. In the uncertain climate he decided to omit any reference to Uttamusack and the treasure houses. If the council turned on him the riches would be his to explore on his own. But he doubled his efforts to convince them that he had been grieved to lose his men to the Powhatans. He told them that he had prayed for their souls each day as he was moved from village to village during his long march and imprisonment. He also tried to focus their minds on how he had strengthened the colony's situation with the great king, and he pointed out that this last concession had made the trip, even with its trials and sorrow, worthwhile. Now, thanks to Powhatan's support, they could go outside the the fort without fear.

As they finished the meal one of the carpenters ran up to them, his voice hoarse with excitement. The princess Pocahontas had returned, he said. She was at the gates of the fort, and her retinue was carrying provisions.

Smith instantly sprang to his feet and ran toward the palisades. When he caught up with Pocahontas he reached out and grasped her hands. In the cold air her features seemed strongly etched and her eyes luminous. Smith needed to thank her. It had been impossible at Werowocomoco, and there was so much he wanted to say, but she tried to stop his expression of gratitude with her quick smile and a report.

"We saw one of your great canoes—a floating island on the sea."

Smith withdrew his hands from hers in excitement. He yelled the news to the nearest men. They dropped their tools, raced toward the gates, and climbed the towers. Others ran toward the shoreline, jostling one another in their haste. The men strained their eyes, staring off toward the vast mouth of the great bay, their bodies tense. They looked and looked again.

"There are no ships, Captain. The naturals are mistaken." The men were disappointed, their voices rough with anger.

"Captain, tell them it is wrong to deceive us this way, very wrong."

Pocahontas turned toward Smith.

"But we saw a ship. We would not tell you this if it was not true." She called to Pamouic, "Are you sure you saw a canoe?"

"Absolutely," Pamouic said.

"And I am sure, too." Pocahontas was resolute.

The Englishmen searched again, but the horizon dissolved from blue into gray and they still saw nothing. They walked back into the fort grumbling, their chapped lips downturned, their spirits disconsolate.

"Pocahontas, my men are upset," Smith said. "A ship is of paramount importance to us. It is our lifeline to our country. Tell your men this hoax is cruel."

"But my brother would not tell a lie." Pocahontas studied Smith's face solemnly. "Nor would I."

Smith hesitated, but only for a moment "Come, bring your people in. You are always most welcome. And I . . . you know I am your devoted servant always." He bowed deeply. He could not afford any dissension between Pocahontas and his men. She was vital to their existence.

As Smith accompanied Pocahontas to the storerooms, he thought the fort looked less raw and new in the cold air, even though the trees were bare of leaves and there was no other greenery. The wooden buildings had been tempered brown and gray by rain, sleet, and snow, and the fort seemed less of a camp and more like a permanent home. Even the small graveyard added to the atmosphere of a proper settlement.

Smith felt frustrated as he supervised the storing of the corn and game the Powhatans had brought. He wanted to talk privately to Pocahontas, to speak about resuming their lessons together, and to convey to her his gratitude for her steadfast belief in their colony. He thought they might go back to the lessons, but would it be the same? The innocence was gone. There was too much between them now; he could feel it in her responses and the sidelong glances she gave him. Also, there was an intangible quality about her that proclaimed her new womanhood. He wasn't sure how far he wanted their relationship to progress; he wasn't even sure it *could* progress. After all, there was more at stake than just the two of them. The Virginia venture was one consideration, and there was the fact that he was expected to set a good example as a leader to the men. Dallying with the naturals was forbidden unless the women were expressly offered by a chief. Pocahontas was not an ordinary woman, but even so . . . Finally, there was their difference in rank. He gave his head a hard shake. He hated the fact that again he was unsure of himself and again it was because of this young woman.

While Smith and Pocahontas were in the storerooms, Archer, Ratcliffe, and Martin had been talking beneath a large tree in the middle of the fort. The conversation was heated, and Ratcliffe gesticulated, determined to make a particular point.

The workmen began to gather beneath the tree and listen. At a signal from Ratcliffe, Martin left the group and strode unhurriedly, even arrogantly, to the storerooms where Smith was emerging with Pocahontas.

"Smith, Ratcliffe is going to try you for negligence and for the murder of Cassen, Robinson, and Emery. He bases his case on Levitical law."

Smith was thunderstruck. The bastards, he thought. What an injustice! After what I have accomplished for us all. But Ratcliffe is the civil authority of the colony and Archer studied law at Grey's Inn. He can rig a trial exactly as he wants to by invoking a bibical law last used years ago when old King Henry wanted to divorce his queen. Damnation, and to think I longed for my own kind when I was about to be clubbed to death in Werowocomoco just a few days ago! I cannot believe they are serious.

He looked at Pocahontas. Her face had drained of blood and a gray line had appeared around her mouth. She no sooner rescues me from one death sentence than I am faced with another, he thought. But there is nothing she can do here. This is farcical, a joke. He heaved a sigh of anger and frustration and turned to the princess. "Do not stay here. Return to your camp. When this is resolved, I will send for you."

He looked at Pamouic and Secotin and the six soldiers. For a moment he thought of bolting with them. But he would be of no use to Powhatan as a fugitive. There would be no protection anywhere. He would have to stay at the fort and face this charge.

The prosecution, trial, and sentencing took twenty minutes. John Smith was to hang within the hour.

Smith glanced up at one point during the trial and saw that Pocahontas had not left. She stood immobile alongside her retinue throughout the proceedings. When the colonists marched him to the chapel for a service with the Reverend Mr. Hunt, the naturals were still there, silent.

The benches in the chapel were covered with ice, and icicles hung from the rafters. Smith tried to pray. He had said so many prayers recently that he felt drained. But he could not blame the workmen at the trial who showed no loyalty and did not speak up for him. Their position in life was so base that they grasped

210

any opportunity to exercise power. He could understand them, but he despised them. Also, he thought, they blamed me when the naturals falsely reported seeing ships.

He heard Hunt praying for his soul. He was a good man, thought Smith. He had endured the first harsh weeks of attacks from the naturals, the plague that had carried off so many, and the bitter weather. Through it all he had given succor and comfort to his dwindling flock. Now he commends my soul to the Lord, thought Smith. Well, at least this time I am being sent off with the proper ritual instead of the rattles of Powhatan's devil priests.

The Reverend Mr. Hunt said a lengthy prayer for forgiveness. When the workmen finally came for him, they avoided Smith's eyes. Their shame made them treat him with fury and disdain. Although Smith walked proudly with his head up, they pushed and pulled and occasionally kicked him, leaving clumps of icy snow on his hose and doublet. As he was being carried across the frigid ground he could see that Pocahontas and her men were still standing in a cluster in the same place, like colorful statues frozen to the earth.

Under the central tree, he faced his peers. Once again he reminded them of all he had accomplished for the colony, but his fellows on the council stared back, their mouths implacable. No one would would look him directly in the face. Only his staunch friend Percy showed sympathy. Ratcliffe himself took the stout rope that was tossed over the tree limb and checked that the loop was tightly knotted. Then with a casual flick of his wrist he slipped the noose over Smith's head. Smith could smell the raw hemp and it prodded his memory of the dozens of hangings he had witnessed. He thought, I am being strung up like any common thief.

"Wait, Captain!" Pocahontas was walking toward the gathering under the tree. She looked directly at Ratcliffe as he moved a footstool forward and indicated to Smith to stand on it.

"Captain Smith is my special ward," she said in her broken English. "He is also the adopted son of my father, the great chief Powhatan. If he is harmed I cannot answer for what my father will do."

Ratcliffe gave her a hard stare. "Princess Pocahontas, I respectfully say that this matter is none of your business, nor does it concern your father, the king. This man has been fairly tried by our laws and found guilty."

In that instant, there was a great tearing roar from a cannon. The noise reverberated around the walls of the fort like a roll of thunder on a summer day. All forty men stood transfixed. It could mean only one thing: A ship was entering their harbor.

Discipline vanished. All of the workmen tore away toward the shoreline, waving their hats and shouting. In the melee, Pamouic, acting on a glance from Pocahontas and moving quickly, slipped the noose from Smith's neck.

Smith turned triumphantly to Ratcliffe. "The naturals were right. It must be Newport on the *Susan Constant*! The Powhatans sighted a ship almost two hours ago."

"I can't do anything more about you now," Ratcliffe retorted, an angry red flush creeping over his face. "But you have been tried and found guilty. You will hang before the day is finished."

Smith watched Ratcliffe stride toward the riverbank, swinging his arms impatiently. He and Pocahontas followed more slowly. It seemed incredible that the *Susan Constant* would arrive across the vast ocean at precisely the moment that would matter most to him. God must be saving me for a particular reason, he thought, as he offered a quick prayer of thanks.

Again Pocahontas had intervened on his behalf and the few moments she bought had saved him. How could he ever thank her? He wondered again that his destiny could be so profoundly affected by the bravery of this native girl. Although I am not yet reprieved, he thought, at least I have a chance, with Newport back in Virginia.

The riverbank was crowded with men jostling and yelling good-humored obscenities. Their long wait for supplies, for news of home and family and of the rest of the world was over. They hungered for a taste of beer and the sight of a new face.

Newport led the first group of men off the ship, standing tall in the longboat. He waved and stepped ashore as Smith pushed his way ruthlessly and angrily through the men to be the first person to greet the admiral. He knew that Newport liked him. He might think Smith was bumptious and sometimes a rascal, but he also knew he was able and loyal. "I have new colonists and supplies, Smith," Newport called, a wide grin on his face.

He turned and greeted Pocahontas with surprise and pleasure, then put his arm around Smith's shoulders as they walked toward the meetinghouse. Smith wasted no time, his nerves were raw after his ordeal. He wanted Newport to know immediately his story of the past few days. The rest of his report could wait. He had to convince Newport of his innocence before Archer and Ratcliffe had a chance to give their testimony.

Newport heard him out and then said, "Smith, for God's sake, this is ridiculous. All of you are living in isolation under constant pressure. I cannot see that you were guilty of any wrongdoing. I will speak to the other men on the council and get them to rescind the order to have you hanged, then let us put this matter behind us. We have far more important issues before us. At the moment, your men need to unload the supplies. Also, I have a letter for you from Edwin Sandys, but more important, I would like to talk with you about King Powhatan."

Smith sighed. It was all very well for Newport to think the reaction of the men ridiculous, but he had been within a few seconds of losing his life. Constant fear, isolation, and starvation had unhinged the men's minds. Jamestown was a far from healthy dwelling place.

"That will be ten shillings for the lot and I won't take a penny less."

"Why, you bastards!" Smith called out good-naturedly over the water to the sailor on the newly arrived ship. Its sails were furled, and the decks swarmed with workingmen. "I paid for these goods before the *Susan Constant* left for England."

"Well, if you want them now, you will have to pay my price," called the sailor.

"Free enterprise." George Percy smiled ruefully. "We are a captive market. They have us where they want us."

"We have enough new supplies for a year, and the Virginia Company also sent over fifty books, but this cargo will cost us a pretty penny. The crew will be richer than the captains after another few trips," retorted Smith.

"Can't Newport control the prices?"

Smith rubbed his beard. "I am told the merchants in London bypass the captain and deal with a representative on board. He in turn lets certain sailors take their share for protecting the cargo."

"With the prices they ask we will all be impoverished."

"No, Percy, I don't think so. I want to see you after I have a talk with Newport later today. I believe I have found riches at last."

The two men exchanged excited glances. They were so engrossed in their exchange they did not hear Pocahontas approach with her two brothers.

"Captain Smith," she began formally, "a hundred new men have arrived today from your home across the water. My father and I understood that your people were here only for a short

214

time and that as soon as your sick had recovered you would be returning to your home."

Smith's heart dropped. How was he going to explain that he had dissembled for the good of his people?

"Our king in London is so impressed with our stories of the beauty of your father's lands that he wants us to remain, for a while at least," he said.

This was partly true, but it was difficult for Smith to look into Pocahontas's guileless and trusting eyes. He glanced at her brothers. Pamouic and Secotin were not so trusting, he thought, not at all.

"In fact," he went on, "our king has sent special gifts for your father. King James holds him in particular respect. Look, there is one of the gifts."

Smith pointed to the longboat cutting through the water from the *Susan Constant*. In the bow stood two men, and between them was a dog, a rare and elegant white greyhound, its shiny coat silhouetted against the blue of the winter water.

All other thoughts were forgotten as she watched the animal leap gracefully from ship to shore. "Beautiful!" Pocahontas cried in Powhatan.

"My father won't have that animal long. Pocahontas is enchanted with it," Secotin muttered to Pamouic.

"Dear Princess, we will talk later about plans for a delegation to take this lovely animal and our other gifts to your esteemed father," Smith said. He felt that he had saved the situation for the moment. But he would have to have a frank talk with Pocahontas soon. On no account could they afford to lose her faith and support.

That evening Newport invited the council to dine with him on the *Susan Constant*. In the wood-paneled cabin the men's emotions tempered and their tongues loosened over a meal of

215

Powhatan's game, corn, and dried fruit and the Virginia Company's wine. They savored the ruby liquid served in pewter goblets, the first in many months for those who had remained in the colony. The anger and bitterness aroused at the hanging tree that morning disappeared in the candlelit warmth of surroundings that reminded the men of home and loved ones. It was as if the ugly incident had been a nightmare, and in a sense it was, thought Smith. We have done things and probably will do more that are unbalanced as long as we live under these fearful conditions. What we need is more people, and particularly women to civilize us, but all of that is forgotten, thought Smith, at least for the moment.

Newport stood, glass in hand, as the room rang with a toast to King James and the cheers of the men.

"Well, gentlemen," Newport began, "I think you have survived the worst. This colony is on its way to becoming a strong outpost of the kingdom, the beginning of wealth and power for England in the New World. Now I bid you all good night—all of you, that is, except Smith. I want to talk to you."

As the door closed on the departing men, Newport turned to Smith. "First, read the letter from your friend Sir Edwin then give me a full report on the time I have been away."

When Smith finished reading his letter, he gave the wooden stove in the corner a kick to encourage the flames. Then he turned to Newport and gave a full account of the past six months.

"The great king Powhatan wants to trade now," Smith said at last, "but I suspect he plans to drive us out eventually. Also, he has ordered the neighboring tribes to stop harassing us. But, Newport, the most outstanding event has been the emergence of his daughter, his favorite child, as our savior. Pocahontas is truly without parallel." There was a slight gruffness in Smith's voice as he finished.

216

"Yes, I agree with you," Newport replied, "but she is of royal blood, which makes her a superior person. She should be the one to arrange a visit for us with King Powhatan so that we can present our king's gifts and messages of goodwill. Now tell me about life in their towns."

Smith poured another goblet of wine. "The people are in harmony with life and with one another. They live by civilized rules and respect others. They have large towns and small towns, but all are surrounded by farmland rich in vegetables and fruits. They are much stronger, much healthier, than we are; their eyesight and hearing are twice as keen as ours. Their king is a tough, autocratic man, and perhaps his control reinforces their pleasant society. Of course their low-born individuals are as primitive as ours, but the people of rank and distinction are the same here as anywhere I have traveled in the world. They simply are not literate yet or conversant in our ways or our religion. However, neither were some of the princes I observed in Bohemia."

"I look forward to seeing this for myself, Smith. You have read in Sandys's letter that people in London still want to know what happened to our first colony at Raleigh, the one that disappeared in the 1580s. They feel some colonists or their descendants may still be alive. The mystery still disturbs us; I suppose there is a sense of guilt because the old queen was using the fleet against the Spanish at that time and could not spare the ships or supplies to assist the colonists."

"I have a feeling that the great king knows something about the Raleigh mystery," Smith said. "It is just a suspicion, but one of Powhatan's lieutenants mentioned the colony in a speech at Werowocomoco."

"Well, we must try and find out. Meanwhile we must make arrangements to go to Werowocomoco. We are both tired. Good night, Smith, and thank you for your time."

Smith left the cabin, saluted the watch, and clambered over

the side of the ship into the longboat. He thought of the Virginia Company's intention to send over from England a number of able but poor farmers, artisans, and laborers to settle Jamestown— men who had been displaced by the emerging capitalism in England and the demise of feudal society. Well, it is a good plan, thought Smith—a handful of aristocrats and well-born men to run a colony of workers hungry for a chance in life.

In a postscript Sir Edwin sent greetings from the two Reynolds girls who were still unmarried. Smith smiled in the dark as he thought of them.

CHAPTER
~•≫ 13 ≪•~

Werowocomoco,
January 6, 1608

"Pocahontas, I have been patient, fair, and forgiving," Powhatan said. "But now I am angry because I have been deceived about the intentions of the white men. They do not plan to return to their own land. They want to live here permanently." The great chief moved irritably on his couch of furs and clapped his hands together to signal that he wanted water to drink.

"I have only just arrived from my visit to the Tassentasses and I did not sent a messenger from the fort." Pocahontas's brow furrowed. How could he know the settlers meant to stay? she asked herself. "They may be here for a while longer, Father, to collect rare woods and tobacco from us. They want to pay you a visit, and they bear gifts from their king."

"I have no need of their gifts or of their king, but I will see them. I want to ask them myself what their intentions are. I also want more of their guns and machines. So I will trade for a while longer. You may continue as my emissary for that time, because they have faith in you. But, daughter, they have duped you as well as me. The priests have lost their patience and are now demanding a child sacrifice."

"Oh, no, Father!"

"And further, Pocahontas, I want you to reconsider Kokum as a husband. The Monacans are still causing trouble, and Kokum's father has proven a staunch friend and driven them back. I want to keep the Chickahominies firmly on my side. Also, I have looked around and found no other man as suitable as Kokum to be a husband for you."

Pocahontas heard the black wings of the crow beating over her. She felt hollow inside. Had her misjudgment about the Tassentasses brought on the child sacrifice? Guilt made her blood pound against her temples. As atonement she would undoubtedly have to marry Kokum. But how did her father know about the arrival of the new Tassentasses? Her soldiers would never dare send a message without her approval, and Pamouic would never do so without telling her. Secotin? But why would he want to send the news back to her father—unless he wanted to compromise her? These thoughts rushed through her head as she stood before Powhatan. It was only then that she noticed he seemed unusually short-tempered with the people around him. Something had angered him. And where were his wives? He always had a few around to fetch things for him or to be close so that he could pinch them in a desired spot. But Pocahontas made up her mind quickly that this was not the time to talk to her father.

She gave him a tentative smile. "I understand your views, Father, and now I will gather supplies for another trip to the Tassentasses."

The sun was bright when she stepped from the council house out into the cold air. As she took a deep breath to clear her mind she saw her half sister Mehta. "Where are Father's wives?"

"Pocahontas, you have not heard. Sacha strayed."

"Strayed?"

"Took a lover, so now Father is angry at all of his wives. It is a good thing you missed his fury when he found out, three suns ago. The priests told him that his misfortune is due to the presence of the strange ones on our shores."

Pocahontas could recall only one other time when a wife of Powhatan's had taken a lover. "Is Sacha on the rock?" she asked.

"Yes, for three suns and will be there for another four."

Pocahontas turned and walked quickly toward the rock, a wide stone in a central position near the river. Most of the village people had to pass it at least once a day. Before she reached it she could see a band of little boys standing around giggling and lobbing sand at Sacha.

How could Sacha have been so foolhardy? thought Pocahontas, when she found her friend naked, legs spraddled wide as they could stretch, tied to the rock. All the conditioning against extremes of cold and heat, which Powhatan children learned to endure as babies, would not keep Sacha from feeling the cold now. Pocahontas saw that her lips and body were blue. She would have to remain on the rock from dawn until sunset without food or water for a total of seven suns. At night a village elder and his wife, noted for their good works, took her in until the sunrise.

"Oh, Sacha, why did you do it?"

"It was so foolish, Pocahontas, so foolish but I couldn't resist any longer."

Pocahontas knew the lover, a handsome—no, beautiful—soldier, but not one of the leaders. "But Father will send you away!"

Tears started down Sacha's cheek. "Yes, I am to go to a plain Weanoc soldier."

The Weanoc village was not far off, but Sacha might as well have been going to the moon. She would lose her status completely. There was no possibility that Pocahontas would see her again.

223

"Sacha, I feel miserable for you. I know my father is not a young man, but he was so fond of you."

"No, it is not his age, Pocahontas. He pleasures all of his wives equally well. Forgive me, it is just that my heart flew to the soldier and rested with his. He has been sent far away to the north. I know they will put him into every battle with the Monacans until he is dead." Tears coursed down Sacha's cheeks.

Pocahontas wanted to pat Sacha's foot in comfort, but it was forbidden. She could only watch in sympathy as Sacha's pretty, plump body shook with sobs and the cold. In my heart I am as guilty as poor Sacha, she thought. I yearn for the redheaded Tassentasse. If he had given me one signal, I would have been his and thus betrayed not one man but all of my people.

Pocahontas said good-bye to Sacha and turned away sorrowfully. If only my father did not have so many wives, she thought. He is getting older now and they complicate his life too much. She wondered about the Tassentasses. Did they, too, have several wives? Somehow she didn't think so or they would have been sent here on the ship that had just arrived. Then it occurred to her that she had never asked whether John Smith had a wife. Perhaps he is married. That could be the reason he sends me such conflicting signals, she thought. But I must forget about him now, for I must join myself to Kokum. I must do my penance. My friendship for the Tassentasses has brought the wrath of Okeus the devil god down on us, and now we have faithless wives, angry priests, and a child sacrifice to endure. Pocahontas shuddered as she walked back toward the center of town.

Powhatan wasted no time. If the priests decreed there must be a child sacrifice, then sooner was better than later, and a violent event now suited his angry mood. The great chief did not often display his temper, but when he did his empire trembled. Women and children stayed out of his way, taxes were paid quickly, and runners raced through the woods with terse directives to his chieftains. No one petitioned to see him about local grievances until the storm died down. The most anxious of all were his wives. The great chief would surely want a new group of women, fresh and chaste, to seduce him back into an agreeable mood. Already messengers were arriving with information about the most beautiful young women in the realm.

The priests' rattles and chants echoed into the night. Babies cried, and frantic mothers shushed them quiet, whispering into their ears not to call the attentions of the gods upon them. It was a time of terrible dread for the Powhatans. They were strongly familial people who lavished great love and care on their young. Parents agonized over the possibility that their child might be snatched by the priests. Some mothers were even foolish enough to try to hide their young in secret places in the surrounding countryside, but the priests always knew where they were, and the hidden ones were very often the first to be called to the sacrificial altar.

The priests finally settled on a day, and in each of the many towns throughout the kingdom the ritual was the same. The priests, painted black, red, and white, started their dance at sunrise in the ceremonial square. When the townspeople had all gathered—they were quick because any breaching of the rules might provoke the gods—the priests would chant their prayers. Then without a backward glance they would start their walk to the forest, to the clearing where the sacrificial altar stood. The paths to it were not as clean as they were throughout the rest of the woods, for no one would go anywhere near the child sacrifice spot except on the day of the ritual. Families, numb with fear, trailed behind the priests. No one dared to cry or to utter a sound. Even babies were quiet, for their mothers fed them herbs to make them sleepy.

In the clearing the priests lit a fire made of tall logs so that flames shot straight up into the sky. Then they began to chant. They raised their hands in supplication to the devil god, whose white-painted face stared at them from a platform built into a tree trunk in the woods. Then they dropped to their knees and rubbed their foreheads on the ground, a movement calculated to help them choose the right children for Okeus.

Pocahontas stood near her father in the forefront of the crowd, dread enveloping her mind and body. Suddenly she saw Kokum. Father has not wasted any time in getting him here, she thought. As she looked at him she could feel her legs weaken and her stomach turn over. He was standing with Mehta, and for a brief moment she caught her half sister's expression as she gazed at Kokum. Her eyes were wide, her mouth moist. Why, she wants him, thought Pocahontas with surprise. But in that moment the droning of the priests stopped, and a deep sigh swept through the townspeople. Pocahontas found it hard to watch the priests. She saw her brothers out of the corner of her eye; their faces were set and hard.

The priests approached the altar. Pocahontas felt the beginnings of doubt start to nibble at her mind as she compared the Tassentasses and their way of living with her own. The Tassentasses do not make sacrifices of any kind, and yet their canoes, their weapons, their utensils, their knowledge of the stars, and even their magic are bigger and more powerful than ours. The gods seem to favor them, so perhaps the gods prefer them to us.

These thoughts ran through Pocahontas's mind as the priests at the altar turned, their black, red, and white paint glistening in the sun as they threw up their arms to the heavens. One of the priests stepped forward to the sound of loud rattles. He held up his hand. There was silence, and then he called out a name. A woman in the crowd gasped and fell to the ground in a swoon. No! cried Pocahontas to herself. They have chosen a babe that still suckles! The priests usually choose boys between the ages of five and twelve. They are giving us fair warning that the gods are truly angry and the Tassentasses must go. Three more names were announced, and now the crowd moaned softly but constantly.

Pocahontas could not look. She raised her eyes and beseeched the god of sky to forgive her for her cowardice. This was the only ceremony she could not bear, had never been able to bear. She took comfort in the fact that some of the killings were merely symbolic and that boys who survived were spirited off into the forest, where they remained for several months. They then entered a long apprenticeship to become priests. When they had earned their full credentials a year later, they would be sent to a faraway town, away from any relatives. So whether the child was dead or alive, the outcome was the same: The mother never saw her child again.

The baby on the altar wailed until there was a sudden scream. The priests must have pierced his heart instantly, thought Pocahontas. She was trembling from head to foot now. The moans that rose from five hundred throats never stopped. Four more names were called and the ritual proceeded slowly until Pocahontas thought she would collapse from the strain. Although the ceremony had always upset her, she had never reacted so strongly before. I have been weakened by my association with the Tassentasses, she thought. Their ways must be wrong for our people, but their world offers so much. The turmoil over her feelings toward the strange men only added to her distress at the child sacrifice. I will go to them this afternoon. At least while I am with them my thoughts are at ease, she said to herself.

Finally the ceremony ended. The priests marched back to town, and the villagers, some now openly crying, trailed behind. The grieving fathers would cut off all their hair, and the mothers would cover themselves with ashes.

Pocahontas looked for Kokum among the moving throng of people, but he was not there. She wanted to avoid meeting him. She couldn't stand the added strain of his constantly smiling presence and his effect on her mind and body. She decided to take an alternate but slightly longer path back to town.

The trail she chose dipped down toward the river, and when she saw the cold, clear water Pocahontas suddenly wanted a second bath. It would make her feel clean again after the blood and stress of the sacrifices. The river would wash away her revulsion. She would go to the secret place that she and her sisters had sometimes used as children. No one would find her there. She ran the mile to the river and slipped along the bank until she reached the cove. The bushes were still thick here even in winter, and low pine trees clustered close by. She shrugged out of her clothing, waded into the icy water, and scrubbed vigorously with sand and shells until her body was pink and glowing. Finally she dipped her head under the water and pulled her hair back from her face.

As she emerged from the water, she felt a presence. There was no sound, but simply a sense that someone was there. Quietly, quickly, she reached the bank and put on her clothes. Did she hear a rustle? Stealthily she moved from rock to rock along the bank until she was close to a tiny cove. She thought she heard a moan. Maybe someone was mourning and had stumbled across her secret place. Carefully she peered around a tree into the cove, her hand on her knife. Her body tightened in shock. There on the sand lay Mehta, her legs spread wide. And on top of her was Kokum, his body thrusting gently and rhythmically into her. Pocahontas felt paralyzed. She saw Mehta's eyes close in ecstasy, heard an occasional moan escape from her lips. Both of them were far too engrossed to be aware of her presence. She dropped back and silently retraced her steps. When she got to the trail she began to run as hard as she could back to town.

Pocahontas told her brothers she was leaving for the Tassentasses' settlement later that afternoon and ordered the soldiers to collect the necessary supplies. Then she went to see her father in the council house. She found him on his mound of furs, still glum, his hand cupping his chin. Next to him stood Kokum.

Pocahontas needed all of her control to keep her expression composed as she went up to bid her father good-bye.

"Daughter, as you see, Kokum is here, and again he pleads for your hand in marriage."

Pocahontas's eyes flicked over Kokum, and she saw that his expression was sincere and loving; then her eyes focused on his hands. They were well shaped, with long, delicately tapered fingers.

"I am honored, Father," she began politely, "but I am not sure that I am ready for marriage yet. He could marry someone else in the family. Mehta would make him a good wife."

"Kokum says he will wait for you."

"But Kokum is a young man. He needs a woman now."

"Daughter, I am sure Kokum can take care of his needs, and you can't blame him, for you spend all of your time with the Tassentasses. Marriage is a different matter entirely. As my daughter it is a question of alliances and position. I still feel strongly that this union should take place."

Pocahontas felt ill. But she could not argue now. It was hopeless, given her father's present mood. "Father, I take heed of your wishes. But now I must deliver the supplies and fulfill my duty. I will return in a few days." She kept her face expressionless as she said good-bye to them both and left the room.

• • •

As Pocahontas moved through the forest, her manner toward her retinue was unusually brusque. Inwardly she seethed. Of course she could not blame Kokum for taking another woman, or many women, for that matter. She could not really blame Mehta, either. Pocahontas had openly declared her opposition to the marriage. But why, when he still insists he wants me, does Kokum sleep with my sister? It only makes matters more complicated. Worst of all is his duplicity.

She urged her brothers and soldiers into a loping trot. It made her feel that she was running free from her problems. By the time they approached their camp, Pocahontas's mind felt clearer, but she still worried about Secotin. Could he be trusted? Who had relayed the report of the new colonists to her father before she had a chance to tell him? Suddenly Pocahontas felt lonely. Her father was irritated with her, her sister had betrayed her, and she felt unsure of her brother. As for Kokum, Pocahontas shook her head. At least his behavior has delivered me from his hold over my body, she said to herself.

It was unseasonably warm the next morning, and the sun shone as Pocahontas, her brothers, and the soldiers made the short journey to the fort, carrying supplies from Powhatan. The shiny reeds on the thatched roofs within the fort gleamed in the clear air and the lookout gave a cry of welcome as several men at the gates of the fort ran to help the Powhatans with their load. The men laughed with anticipation as they carried bushels of corn and dried foods to the cookhouse and supply rooms. There was never enough food.

As she stepped into the fort Pocahontas felt a surge of relief. She tried to disguise her eagerness as she looked around for Captain Smith. So many new men, she thought, a hundred of them. Most of them were clustered near the chapel, so it must be their special day for the gods, Sunday, she thought. She now knew how to distinguish the working men from the gentlemen. The gentlemen wore bright clothes in shiny satin and taffeta, lavishly embroidered and pinked, and large hats with plumes of feathers—not nearly as grand as the feathers we wear, she said to herself—whereas the workmen wore heavy shoes, plain homespun linen or canvas jerkins with matching breeches, and small flat berets.

The new colonists watched curiously as every courtesy was extended to Pocahontas and her brothers. Word had already spread among them about the princess, the remarkable daughter of the great king Powhatan. There was a festive feeling in the mild air, and the men joked and laughed as they trooped down the path from the church toward the riverbank. The entire population of the fort had been invited to crowd aboard the *Susan Constant* for a meal with wine and rum to celebrate Captain Newport's birthday. They could afford to relax now; their storehouses were full, they could enjoy the fifty books in their library, and relations with the naturals were relatively good. Furthermore, London was patient with their slow progress and confident of the future of their enterprise.

Pocahontas accepted an invitation from Smith and Newport to board the ship with her brothers, although she knew it would be an ordeal. She could never get used to the smell. She had told John Smith once that she would like to send a group of Powhatan women on board to wash the ship clean, but he had laughed. She left her soldiers on shore to wait for them, and the braves stood or sat in a tight little group by the gate.

The sun, warm air, and good food cheered the men. They exchanged stories, and songs rose into the air as tots of rum were passed around. No one noticed a spiral of smoke rising from the vicinity of the cookhouse in the fort, for there was usually smoke wafting up from the chimneys. And for a short but disastrous time no one noticed the flames that shot up behind the smoke.

231

A high keening cry finally pierced the merrymaking. All eyes turned toward shore. Pocahontas's braves were yelling and waving their bows. Behind them the cookhouse was enveloped in flames.

Men rushed down the rope ladders and scrambled into the longboats. Many jumped straight into the water and swam the short distance to the shore.

"The buckets, the buckets," someone yelled as they rowed furiously for the fort.

A human conduit was quickly formed to carry buckets of water from the river to the fire, but they could not douse the flames fed by a gentle wind. The thatched roofs exploded in balls of fire, and most of the timber and mud houses were soon engulfed. The scorching breeze beat back the fire fighters, and flames shot up into the night sky like pennants. "The storehouse! Damp down the storehouse!" yelled Smith as he ran from one site to another directing the water carriers.

"Look, the chapel is going!" Pocahontas was close by his heels, trying to beat out the smaller flames with her mantle. Her brothers and the soldiers used their leather clothing and their feet to stamp out thin tongues of flames as the fire flashed forward.

But the fire was now all around them, hungrily grabbing at each new plank of wood. The glare was like the light of a hundred suns, and the heat burned their skin. The roar of the flames seemed to burst their eardrums while the smoke seared their nostrils.

The wind suddenly shifted and it caught Pocahontas off guard. She stumbled and almost fell trying to escape the fire balls. Smith caught her and pulled her up. For a fleeting moment they looked into each other's eyes, their hearts pounding. They did not see their smoke-grimed faces or torn clothing. Instead they felt again the total unity that had enthralled them at the execution stones in Werowocomoco. As they separated, Pocahontas knew from

Smith's expression that he had made an instant decision. He gave her hand a quick squeeze before he ran back toward the riverbank. It was a new touch. It was possessive.

The colonists fought the flames until stars began to appear in the darkened sky and they were ready to drop from exhaustion. When they finally got the fire under control, the devastation was so widespread that men stood in clumps, tears rolling down their cheeks as they looked at the ruins. All of the supplies were gone, including those brought from England only a few days earlier. The chapel was reduced to a pile of ashes, and the new library had been destroyed. Most houses were smoking ruins. But the graveyard, with its wooden crosses, stood clean and untouched in the smoke-filled air.

As Pocahontas stared in horror at the destruction she heard a voice behind her.

"How do we know one of the naturals didn't start the fire?" called out one of the new arrivals from England.

Every eye turned to Pocahontas's braves as a murmur swept through the weary crowd. The colonists were sullen, their jerkins and doublets streaked with soot and sweat, their hose wet with river water.

"They were the only ones not on board ship with us," another voice yelled.

Some of the men now looked menacing. Pocahontas swiftly joined her brothers and her braves and stood facing the colonists, her bearing regal and protective.

"Don't be fools." Smith strode between the Powhatans and the colonists. "These people brought us food supplies. Are you suggesting that they would give with one hand and take away with the other? They are the emissaries of the great king Powhatan."

There was silence. Smith continued. "Those of you who have newly arrived, remember that Princess Pocahontas is a loyal and true friend of this colony. I am going to accompany her and her men to their camp. We need their food now more than ever."

Pocahontas did not question Smith as they walked through the gates together. He had done more than defuse an ugly moment. She knew that at last he was going to grasp a chance for the two of them to be alone together.

As she walked quickly beside Smith toward the woods, she could feel waves of desire emanate from his body. He did not turn toward her or look at her, but Pocahontas worried that surely her brothers must sense the rank sexuality that enveloped them both. She looked at her siblings, who had walked ahead of her and Smith. Perhaps they were far enough away not to know what was happening to her. Was her body imparting the same energy as John Smith's? Was she, too, giving off an almost tangible animal hunger? She felt alternately hot and cold and found herself panting slightly.

"Go with your brothers." Smith's hand was burning hot as he gave hers a hard squeeze, and his voice was rough as he spoke softly. "When they are asleep, meet me at the old wolves' lair." They did not look at each other or break stride. She did not need to reply.

The Powhatans were exhausted from their struggle with the fire, and they were asleep almost before they dropped to the ground.

Pocahontas quickly dashed water from the drinking gourds over her face and body. She didn't stop to put her doeskins back on but threw her fur mantle over her naked body, the tails swinging against her legs.

Steathily she left camp and ran the half mile to the lair. She couldn't get there fast enough, and her breath came in sobs when she arrived at the hidden place. It was in a hollow with thick bushes and bracken to protect it. The night was dark, almost black, but she could sense Smith immediately. In that instant she felt one of his hands on her wrist and his other arm encircling her. He was rough as his mouth found hers. His beard made an unfamiliar sensation against her skin, and the sharp prickle was a flame to her senses. They rocked unsteadily as hunger enveloped their mouths and bodies.

She moaned as he sank to his knees, pulling her with him. He pushed her flat next to him. The excitement of the dangerous fire and the urgency of the emotions possessing her body combined to give her a fierceness she did not expect, had never known. She wanted to devour him with love. Her body acted as if it was no longer a part of the woman she knew. It moved with a febrile sensuousness, at times frenzied and at times almost still, with only the faintest movement provoking an agony of desire and ecstasy. She felt as if she were part of the man whose body gave her such joy, as if his skin were hers, as if their hearts were one. At other times she felt she was helpless to his slightest whim, that she would swoon with the deliciousness of her captivity. Still she knew that it was her instigation that gave them both this exquisite sensation, that it was her power that reduced them both to helpless joy. Her whole being flooded with euphoria as she gladly gave her body and mind to the man she cherished. The release gave her the strength and abandon to couple again and again. They were still hungry for each other, their passion fierce, nowhere near spent as the first sign of dawn approached and they knew they must part. The force of their need for each other was frightening, and they looked at each other with new awareness, with troubled eyes. Smith groaned. He could not leave her alone. He grabbed her again. His mouth roved her arms, her breasts, her mouth, enflaming her body, and they made love quickly, as if for the first time.

Finally Smith moved away from her. "We must find a safe

place. This lair is too well known. We cannot risk your father separating us."

"I will find a place."

"But now we must hurry. It is getting light. We can talk later. You go first."

Pocahontas gave him a quick look over her shoulder and ran. Her feet were like feathers. She had not slept for twenty-four hours, but she had never felt so fresh, so alive. Every muscle, every pore, every part of her mind, sang with happiness. She was whole; the awakening forest around her was part of her. She was one with the brown earth and the cawing sea gulls. The harmony between her mind and body gave her such joy. No part of her held back. When she drew near the silent, sleeping camp, she dropped to her knees and stretched her arms up toward the sky.

CHAPTER
14

Werowocomoco, February 1608

It had taken five trips between her father the great chief and the colonists at the fort to complete arrangements for a meeting of the leaders of the two groups at Werowocomoco. Smith had been impressed by Pocahontas's skill in negotiating with the seasoned Newport and her difficult father. Talks had dragged on for a full month while Pocahontas made her trips back and forth, bringing food to the bereft English and mediating compromises in both camps. Now a time and place had been agreed upon. The question was who would lead the expedition?

Smith, as an adopted son of Powhatan, thought he should head the first group. But it was finally decided that Newport and Smith, with thirty colonists, would sail the pinnace *Discovery* to Kecoughtan. They would pay their respects to the friendly king Pochins, enjoy his excellent food, and proceed the next day to a landing somewhere close to the great king. From there Smith would lead the advance group into the village to prepare for the meeting between Powhatan and Newport.

Smith invited Pocahontas to sail with them on the *Discovery*, but she said it would be more diplomatic if she stood by her father's side when the English arrived. Smith agreed that this was the wise course, but he had wanted to ask her, to be sure she knew how much he would like to have her with him. He reflected that it would have been wonderful to have her near him during the short voyage, because throughout all her trips back and forth between the fort and Werowocomoco there had been little time for them to be alone together. He had explained to her from the very beginning, on the day after the fire, that they could be severely criticized both at the fort and in England if there was any indication of an intimate tie between them, because he was a commoner and she a royal princess. The situation, he told her, was fraught with peril, since the great king would also disapprove. If he became truly angry, he could lose patience and annihilate the English in one major attack.

Pocahontas had listened carefully and acknowledged the dangers, but pleaded to him. "Let me forget all of that just for the moment, please!"

When he thought of their first night together Smith felt his resolve weaken. He knew that even if the temptation and the opportunity had come a thousand times, he would have succumbed. In a less hurried meeting, later, they had held tight to each other and vowed total discretion. Not only would it be foolhardy to be indiscreet, but their feelings demanded complete privacy. Their need for each other was too profound. They knew they would have to plot their meetings with great care and that they would be few and always dangerous.

Smith found his self-control exercised almost to the breaking point when he had to sit through lengthy meetings and negotiations and watch the movement of her mouth, the thrust of her breasts when she turned, the gravity of her brow as she pondered the colonists' reaction to the latest suggestion of the Powhatans, knowing that he might not be able to be alone with her for days. It was a bittersweet sensation that at times made him spring up and leave the room out of anguish. He had never endured this agony before. He felt baffled, even weakened by the intensity of his hunger for her body. But he was equally fascinated by her personality, which was at the same time simple and pure, complex and subtle.

The day they set sail from Kecoughtan to Werowocomoco was squally, with heavy rain, the kind of rain the English rarely encountered at home. On their islands the rain was so soft, so misty, that it could often be ignored, as if God had gentled his hand as he pushed the winds eastward across the Atlantic. But this downpour came as if buckets of water were being dashed over the countryside. Weather in this New World was always more violent than in Europe, thought Smith. The snow was thicker, the heat hotter, the cold more bitter, and the winds twice as strong. By noon the deluge had abated, the sun came out hard and brilliant over the glistening banks and the *Discovery* dropped anchor in a bay the naturals called Poetan. Waiting for them on shore were two hundred of Powhatan's finest warriors, their furs and feathers bright in the intense light.

Immediately Smith called together the eighteen men they had chosen to make up the advance group in the visit to the great king, while Newport waited on board with a bodyguard of twelve. Smith took with him King James's gifts—the white greyhound, some red woolen cloth, and a sugar-loaf hat such as King James himself wore. As Smith and his men stepped ashore, the warriors' voices rose in a yell of greeting and they thrust their arms up, waving their bows high in the air. Moving quickly, the braves surrounded the colonists and swept them along, chanting as they crossed a series of bridges built for protection against the shifting marshes, and escorted them into the town. Ahead, at Powhatan's lodge, another five hundred men

waited, their weapons at their sides. Along the path, at intervals
of a few feet, were forty huge platters stacked high and spilling
over with fine bread, the crusts brown and firm.

"What a greeting!" Smith called to his men as they entered
the lodge. "Powhatan is leaving us no doubt as to his power
and wealth. They are also extending to us great courtesy."

In a room that was ablaze with color, the great king, eman-
ating majesty, sat on his throne of furs in full ceremonial dress.
Around him his courtiers clustered staring at the newcomers
with avid curiosity. Thirty or more new wives, adorned with
shining copper and glowing pearls, had arranged themselves
decoratively or provocatively, their eyes openly appraising the
English. All of the women wore feather capes in solid colors of
red, purple, green and yellow, so intricately worked they fell
like waterfalls of silk. Smith's men gasped and halted. They had
never seen such an array of colors before. He had to prod them
forward into the long room.

The throne room glittered with light from tall torches. Smith
felt a surge of joy when he saw Pocahontas standing by her father
clothed completely in white with a white cape of swans' feathers.
They gave only minimal recognition to each other. The great king
signaled to Smith and his men to be seated, and the warriors,
who now filled the room, gave great shouts of greeting until it
seemed as if the roof would lift.

The feast began with a variety of delicacies, and Smith's men,
unaccustomed to the ritual of washing their hands before and
after a meal, had to be shown what to do with the proffered
bowls of water and the turkey feathers for drying. Then the
speeches started. The men had been forewarned they would be
long and Smith thought to himself how different this occasion
was from his last visit to Werowocomoco.

The great king did not make an oration, nor did he bother to stand to accept the gifts from King James. Three of his minor kings handled all the courtesies and took the presents, although there was a flicker of pleasure in Powhatan's eyes when the white greyhound was presented. Pocahontas laughed and clapped her hands when she saw the dog again. Smith smiled as he wondered who in the end would be the master of the beautiful animal. During the endless speeches of thanks he found himself glancing at Pocahontas far too often, but she never once looked in his direction. He watched the curve of her high cheekbones and the line of her hand and marveled at her ability to remain still for so long.

The speeches were flowery with profuse expressions of gratitude for the gifts and promises to provide the colonists with ample corn and meat until they could grow their own food. Smith was relieved that King James's gifts had at least secured provisions for their storerooms, but he knew the hardest part of the bargaining was still to come. When the first evening stars began to flicker in the pale sky outside, King Powhatan leaned forward and began to negotiate personally for what he really wanted—the Englishmen's cannon.

"Leave your small arms here in this room," he said. "Look, my warriors do not have their tools of war."

Smith replied, "This is a ceremony our enemies desire, never our friends." But he added quickly, "We put our large guns and our men at your disposal to serve you in any wars against the Monacans."

"I would like some of the large guns for myself." Powhatan gave his slow smile, a smile that rarely reached his eyes.

"We offered guns to your man Rawhunt, but he did not want them."

Powhatan laughed. "They were too heavy to carry, but perhaps you have smaller guns. We will discuss this in the morning."

243

After spending the night in Powhatan's guest lodge, restless with longing for Pocahontas, Smith called his men together and went to fetch Newport from the *Discovery*. Newport left his ship wearing full dress uniform accompanied by the cabin boy Thomas Savage. Both were presented to the great king in ceremonies identical to those of the day before, but when the time came to exchange gifts, Newport gave over young Savage, saying that he was a loan. The boy could learn the ways of the Powhatans and explain them to the English. Powhatan was so enthusiastic about this idea that he offered his tall son Namon to Newport. An exchange of sons, he said.

Newly confident and warmed with the success of the moment, Newport invited Powhatan onto the *Discovery* to look over the goods he had brought for barter. But the great king drew back in surprise. He tapped his fingers against his throne, a scowl on his face.

"It is not agreeable to my greatness to trade for trifles in this petty manner. Lay down your commodities on shore. I will take what I want and pay you what I think is their value."

Pocahontas looked up to Smith in warning. She put her hand gently over her father's and gave Smith a quick nod. The king is getting angry and the trip may be ruined, thought Smith. He turned to Powhatan. "Let me show you some special jewels that only the greatest kings wear," he said. "They are extremely rare, and they are the color of the sky."

Smith hurried to the *Discovery* and returned with a handful of glass-bead necklaces. When he held them up and let them fall over his hand, the flames from the torches sparkled on them and the beauty of the blue glass captured Powhatan completely.

The king turned to Pocahontas. "Let me see the jewels, daughter."

She moved toward Smith and reached for the beads. Their hands touched, and then their eyes locked; their fingers trem-

244

bled, and their breath stopped short. It was only for an instant, but Smith quickly glanced at Powhatan and saw at once that the king had sensed something. God's blood, thought Smith, unless I dissemble, I could ruin everything.

He talked rapidly and at length, extolling the qualities of the beads while he watched Powhatan's face. The king's expression was impassive.

When Smith finished, the great king spoke: "I value these beads highly. I like the boy you gave me, and the other trifles please me well enough. I will give you three hundred bushels of corn, but only on condition that my men can barter further for some of your swords."

Smith heaved a sigh of relief as Newport, thoroughly pleased with the bargain, stepped forward and, through Pocahontas, said, "I would ask one more question of you, Your Majesty."

Powhatan inclined his head.

"We would like to know if you have heard of a group of our people who lived just to the south of your country in a place called Roanoke. They all disappeared some thirty years ago."

The great king did not move or change his expression. He said, "We did hear of some of your people who lived on our shores a long time ago, but we do not know what happened to them. Many, many strangers have visited us from time to time, but they have all left."

With a wave of his hand and a nod the king dismissed the colonists. Newport turned to leave, his walk jaunty, triumph flashing in his smile. He had gotten everything he wanted; the question of the swords could be dealt with later. They would sail for the fort on the next tide.

Still apprehensive, Smith looked over his shoulder as he walked toward the door and saw what he dreaded—Powhatan signaling his daughter to remain with him.

• • •

The great chief waited until all strangers had left the room, then indicated that he wanted to talk to his daughter privately. The warriors and wives retreated to the end of the room.

"Pocahontas, you have gone too far," said the great chief, his voice tight with fury.

Pocahontas had rarely seen her father so angry. She knew there was no use trying to talk to him rationally or deny the incident. She waited, her expression respectful.

"I granted your wish and spared the red-hair's life," Powhatan went on. "You reward me by disobeying the rules of our people, by giving yourself—you the daughter of the ruler—to a stranger. Will he take you as his own in the proper ceremony? No, I can see you don't believe he will. You could now be with his child, an ugly thing."

Pocahontas blanched under her father's verbal onslaught, but still she said nothing.

"You forget that you are the favorite child of the ruling chief," Powhatan said. "You have great station, and heavy responsibilities lie ahead of you. You behave worse than a fisherman's daughter." Powhatan slapped his knee, his face dark with anger. "What is the matter with the women in my land? They behave like the animals in the forest!"

Pocahontas realized that Sacha's infidelity had cut him deeply, and now her behavior with a despised Tassentasse had torn the wound open. Her father had never talked to her so disparagingly. The women in his empire were his riches, his pride, and the wealth of the nation lay in the number of them. Battles were fought and provinces acquired to enrich the empire with women, for it was they who tilled the soil, built the houses, and bore the children. It was through women that the chieftains succeeded to their thrones, and women themselves became chieftains. Pocahontas was amazed that Powhatan had denigrated her sex, even in righteous anger, for women were accorded great respect in his realm. Her father was truly enraged. She put out her hand in a conciliatory gesture.

Powhatan ignored it. "I have had enough, Pocahontas. You are to marry Kokum, and the sooner the better. Then you will continue to collect taxes."

Pocahontas thought for a second that her heart would never start again. "I cannot marry Kokum," she said. "Besides, he pleasures my sister Mehta. He should marry her."

"You refused the man, so he is not to blame for taking Mehta. And who are you to talk, when you lie with one of the dirty ones? Now I have had enough of this. Leave me. I must consult with my wise men."

Pocahontas wanted to flee from the room, but she made herself walk calmly to the door. Once outside, she sank down on a stone. She could not marry Kokum, not after having known John Smith. It was impossible. But what was she to do? Her father was not only furious but adamant. He had given in to her once before, but now he believed she had abused his kindness and betrayed his trust. If she had any possible argument to present he might compromise when his rage had cooled, for he could be practical, particularly with her, but she had broken a basic rule: daughters of the great chief could never give themselves to any other than a chosen consort. They could not even enjoy an evening of pleasure with a homeless traveler, a stranger, as the rest of the women in the realm were allowed to do. She groaned. She would do anything, promise anything, to avoid marrying Kokum.

If only she could get away, but there was no place she could go. She was known everywhere. Would John Smith take her in? No, by going to him she would put his entire colony in jeopardy. She realized that she really did not know what John Smith would do. Their time alone together had been so brief, so precious, so

247

full of hunger for each other that they rarely had said more than a few words. But she had to tell him. She would go to him at once and explain that she might never be able to see him again. As the daughter of a ruler, she knew that anyone in command could not think only of himself and his personal desires.

The tide would not turn for another two hours, and the strangers waited on their big canoe. The women were loading the ship with corn and Pocahontas knew she could mingle with them and pretend to be supervising them, but she would have to take an indirect route down to the water so as not to attract her father's attention.

She ran to her room and quickly discarded her mantle of delicate feathers. She pulled on a doeskin skirt and over it a mantle of marten furs, the soft warmth of the skins a comfort to her body, which felt raw and prickly with anxiety. She whispered prayers to Ahone and to the god of sky as she walked toward the river. If only the gods could tell her what to do!

She slipped into the line of women trailing over the bridges toward the ship, balancing huge baskets of corn on their hips. As they moved close to the ship she saw that Namon, her half brother, was on deck. She signaled to him that she wanted to come on board, then grasped the rope ladder tossed by one of the friendly sailors.

When she saw Smith, he masked his surprise and made his way to her side, his eyes thoughtful. He led her toward the privacy of the bow of the ship. As soon as they were alone she told her story quickly, leaving out any mention of her arranged marriage. She had never told him about Kokum and she was determined she never would.

Smith stared out over the river. She wondered what he was thinking and suddenly began to regret coming to him. What could he do? Telling him of her father's anger would only make him anxious and wary. He had his own people to worry about.

After what seemed an age he finally said, "Your father wants swords badly, Pocahontas. We will take a gamble. He knows how highly we value your ability to negotiate between our two people. We will ask Newport to send your father a message that we are ready to bargain for swords, but we will deal only through Pocahontas, as she had proved so efficient and trustworthy in the past. You must return to your father now. If you travel with us he will only be further enraged."

Pocahontas thought, He doesn't know that I will have to be with Kokum in order to placate and disarm my father. If only I could tell him, but I cannot. I will just have to endure in order to be with him again at the fort.

Pocahontas felt the pressure of Smith's hand on her shoulder as she turned toward the gangway. It was all she could do to keep from throwing her arms around his neck and pleading to be taken away with him this instant. She made the slightest movement with her hand to indicate farewell and walked down the polished wooden deck toward her brother, her heart thudding in her chest. It would be at least two nights before word returned from the English asking for her. Two nights with Kokum!

It was even worse than she had feared. Kokum was as kind and gentle as he had ever been with her. Each night he led her away to bed amid the approving glances of her father and half the town. Each night his practiced touch played over her stiff and unyielding body while her mind was a fury of conflicting thoughts. She beat her fists on his chest in a passion of anger and frustration until her healthy body betrayed her by responding. Each morning she awoke determined to get away and stay away, as soon as Smith sent for her.

But the summons did not come. Powhatan had decided he was tired of answering seemingly endless demands for food.

Instead he would send some of his cleverest warriors to take a few swords rather than barter for them. The soldiers could enter the fort under the pretense of a peaceful visit and then do their deed without arousing suspicion or causing trouble. After all, the king was well within his rights; whatever was on his land was his property.

When Pocahontas heard of the new scheme, she despaired. How was she ever going to get back to the fort? She pestered her father's lieutenants to find out if there had been any messages from the fort. It sickened her to learn there had been one request for her as an intermediary, but the great chief had hardened his mind toward both Pocahontas and the Tassentasses. If one of the strangers had taken his daughter, he could certainly take a few of their swords.

For the first time, Pocahontas was happy to be confined in the women's house. She lingered several days longer than necessary, for she wanted time to think, to formulate some plan, but as much as her mind probed every possibility for escape, she could not come up with a feasible scheme. She could not move until she was requested by the Tassentasses and her father allowed her to go. She was trapped.

For weeks Pocahontas waited. She used the time to be as dutiful a daughter as possible. She loathed duplicity, but she felt she must lull her father into believing in her so that when the opportunity arose he would use her again as an emissary. Her task was made easier because Kokum had to spend a great deal of time away on hunting trips and in forays against the Monacans. She felt absolutely no guilt when she prayed fervently to the god of sky that an enemy arrow would strike him.

A comfort to Pocahontas during these days of trial was the handsome white greyhound. The dog had attached himself to her from the first day. She fed him, and he ran with her in the forest and followed her every movement. People began to know that when they saw the greyhound, Pocahontas would not be far behind.

There was no way she could avoid Kokum when he returned from his hunts and battles. He spent his seed within her at night time and again, seemingly with endless strength. She wondered if he was pleasuring Mehta during the day. The two of them were frequently missing at the same time, but Mehta was always sisterly toward her. Maybe eventually he would turn entirely to Mehta. She prayed each morning to the river goddess Ahone that Kokum would switch his allegiance to her sister. But something within her knew that Kokum enjoyed his life just as it was. His lazy charm and sensitive fingers needed more than one recipient.

She stopped one of her father's runners one day and heard that Newport had sailed away again at the beginning of the season of the new blossoms. Shortly after that, Powhatan's braves made their first attempts to steal the swords and immediately were caught. Word was brought to her father that the red-haired one was furious and had locked up seven braves within the fort. When Powhatan's men tried to release them, there were skirmishes, which the Tassentasses won. The colonists had learned to keep their muskets primed so they could be quick, and their superior firepower worked. It was a great loss of face for Powhatan to have men imprisoned by the Tassentasses. The great chief heard that the red-haired one had ordered the braves beaten and whipped, but they were not killed, as any prisoner of his would have been. Powhatan had lost not only his swords but also seven men, and the loss rankled. In his realm, if a captive was not killed honorably and could not escape, he spent the remainder of his life in ignominy.

Pocahontas could see her father was tense, but she also noticed, when she caught him off guard, that he had begun to watch her reflectively. He was over his anger, and his bevy of fresh new wives kept him mollified and tranquil about the women in his realm. Would he send her to mediate with the strange ones again? She was on her knees to Ahone, Okeus, and the god of sky at least twice a day, praying that he would relent and send her. Several small animals drew their last breath at Okeus's altar in a rush of dawn sacrifices until she realized that the priests might get suspicious if she visited the temple too often. Her life was now so circumscribed that she felt free only when she went to her meadow and talked to the god of sky. It occurred to her more and more often that she had always felt free when she was with the Tassentasses.

Finally, in the full season of the new flowers, Powhatan called Pocahontas to his house of council. "In the past weeks you have been a dutiful daughter and complied with my every wish," he said. "I feel that you have repented your waywardness and come to realize that our way of life and your duties must come first. Therefore I am going to negotiate again with the Tassentasses, with you as my emissary. They send me constant messages that you are the only one with whom they will deal. Pocahontas, you are to go to the Tassentasses and get my men out of their hands. If you accomplish that, I will negotiate further for more weapons. I see that you have been with Kokum constantly when he is here. I take it you realize that he, and not that red-haired stranger, is the man for you. Leave in the morning, but no lingering. I expect you back quickly. I wish you a good journey. You are my finest envoy and I am confident that you will be successful."

Pocahontas was deeply grateful to her father for giving her another chance. She knew he was also testing her, and she was again caught in the old vise of conflicting loyalties. But she steeled herself; she would not waver. "Who will travel with me?" she asked.

"Secotin and Pamouic, of course. They know the route and are accepted at the fort."

Pocahontas dared not ask for substitutes to travel with her, for she did not want to jeopardize the trip, but she had a strong feeling that Secotin would act as their father's eyes on this journey. Still, she felt confident of one thing. No one would ever find the hidden cove, the place she had chosen many weeks before for her meetings with Smith.

Powhatan spoke again: "We have also heard today, daughter, that another floating island has arrived with forty new people and a new captain. It is further proof of the perfidy of these strangers, who told us there would be no more of them arriving on our shores. My priests are impatient. Now go, I will arrange to have presents ready for you to take to the ugly ones."

With Kint, her white greyhound, streaking ahead of her, Pocahontas traveled as fast as she could. She barely hesitated at their campsite by the old wolves' lair, causing her brothers to complain about her haste. Pocahontas did not care. The movement, the fast half-run through the woods toward the strangers' fort, made her feel liberated. It was the softest time of the year, and the forest was a magic carpet of crushed petals, the trees a bower of white blossoms everywhere she looked. She wore her pale, almost white doeskins, her best working clothes. Instead of beads she made a chain of blossoms to wear around her neck and tucked a few flowers in her hair. She and her dog seemed to meld with the flowering trees.

When they reached the gates of the fort, the sentry sent up a shout of welcome. It had been a long time since the colonists had seen the pretty princess, and they were pleased that she had returned.

Almost immediately Smith appeared. Pocahontas could see that he had not changed since the time of the snows except that his darkening color reflected the season of short nights and his red hair had strong touches of gold where it had been burned by the sun. Pocahontas advanced slowly toward Smith. For a moment she thought she would sink to the ground in a surge of emotion when she looked into his eyes and the familiar blue magic enveloped her again. "I have come to speak with you, Captain, on behalf of my father Chief Powhatan," she said.

Smith quickly took her hand and led her toward the rebuilt meetinghouse, but his touch made her tremble so strongly she withdrew it. Her brothers took up their customary stance outside the door of the new building. The rest of the council assembled within minutes when they learned Pocahontas had arrived. She began to speak at once and apologized for her father's men, saying that they had acted impetuously in trying to take the swords and that her father sent his regrets for their behavior. He also entrusted her with conveying his respect and love for his adopted son, Captain Smith.

Smith bowed his head, and when he looked up, he wore a half smile. "Please convey to the great king that I accept his good wishes," he replied. "Tell him I did not kill his men because I hold his daughter in such high esteem. I will release the men to you on the morrow. We thank you for your presents, Princess, and now you will partake of our meal, I hope." He guided her to the table.

When they made love that night, their passion was so intense that Pocahontas thought at times she would faint from joy in his arms. Their hunger for each other was insatiable, the power of it overwhelming. Pocahontas wondered if their fierceness was due to fear that this would be their last meeting, that someone or some event would tear them apart. She wondered if he thought that, too, but she did not ask. She did not want to destroy their precious moments with doubts.

Finally, in the early hours of the morning, they decided that Pocahontas should escort the prisoners to her father immediately. Her early return would reassure Powhatan of her loyalty. Smith told her that the colonists would need her help to barter for the swords her father badly wanted. The negotiations would take time and require a number of trips. Pocahontas agreed with the logic of his scheme. He made it clear to her how important she was to the Tassentasses. It made her feel valuable and vital. She was so happy at the moment that she did not let the worry nibbling at the back of her mind interfere. Would she spend the rest of her life running back and forth between her people and his? Was there any alternative?

The old conflict between her loyalties was still there, but more and more she came to see the virtues of the strange people. She had always believed that the Powhatans and the English could live in harmony. They had much to give each other. In fact, she thought suddenly, that is exactly what I am doing, providing first one then the other with the products of each culture. Yes, she must continue doing this, for it should lead to understanding between them. If only Kokum would disappear. She sighed with frustration. How was she going to handle him? If John Smith knew . . . She started involuntarily with pain. And my father, if he were just a little less difficult, a little less demanding of me . . . But, she thought, I have time on my side. John Smith is determined to establish his people here, and I will help him.

CHAPTER
~*×* 15 *×*~

Jamestown,
September 1608

S mith slapped his fist into his palm as he inwardly exulted. That morning, at a meeting of the council, he had been elected president of the colony. And it was about time, he thought. I am the man to make this enterprise work. I should have been elected in the very beginning. He thought of his old enemy Wingfield, who had been released from imprisonment and sent back to England with Newport in the spring, and again he slapped his fist into his hand with a grin.

During the summer months, Smith had explored far up the Chesapeake Bay, still searching for the route to India. It had been a rough trip. The weather was boiling hot, and on one of the remote outer islands of the bay three of his men had succumbed to spotted fever and died. They had been among the newest arrivals from England. He was thankful that the local Indians had been friendly and had nursed them with herbs and a stay in the sweat house.

He and his men also found evidence that the French had been exploring from the north. This alarmed him and confirmed his conviction that Jamestown must be enlarged.

Their settlement had to be permanent and strong enough to keep the French in the north and the Spanish in the south from seizing the Virginia territory from the English.

He could hardly wait to implement the changes he felt were necessary for the colony. For one, discipline was too lax. The fort should be run on military lines; that would toughen the men, make them better able to withstand hardships. Second, the colonists had been too liberal in dealing with the Powhatans, too free in giving away tools and weapons in exchange for food. And third, he wanted to investigate Powhatan's treasure houses at Uttamussack.

This past summer was the first the colonists had really enjoyed. The great king had sent his warriors to the fort only to trade. Pocahontas's brothers had taught the Englishmen to hunt and fish more proficiently, and Pocahontas had brought women to instruct the men in planting corn and vegetables. The Virginia Company continued to send people out from England. The most recent ship, the *Phoenix*, with Captain Nelson at the helm, had arrived from England on a sparkling day in late spring. The settlers were thrilled to know that ships other than the *Susan Constant* were beginning to make the run to the New World.

Smith had been happy to see several tall men disembark from the *Phoenix*. He and the Jamestown Council had sent a letter to the Virginia Company and Sir Edwin Sandys specifically requesting men who could measure close to the six-foot Powhatans. As he had told Newport, they were tired of being looked down upon, and the Powhatans needed to know that some Englishmen were as tall as they were.

The *Phoenix* had also carried a letter outlining a plan proposed by the Virginia Company to, in a symbolic ceremony, crown Powhatan, king of England.

Smith told Percy, "I cannot believe that London would be so stupid as to think they can coerce a proud man like Powhatan into being crowned king of another country. But King James likes the idea and has got it in his head that it would bring Powhatan closer to the English and make him amenable to accepting more settlers. Newport is expected any day and he is bringing the paraphernalia with him. We will be ordered to proceed with a ceremony soon after he arrives. I can guarantee this project will be a disaster. It might even reverse all the good that Pocahontas has so carefully constructed for us."

It was Pocahontas who had brought prosperity and peace. She had kept Powhatan at bay. She had bought precious time for the colonists. Whenever he spoke of Pocahontas, Smith watched carefully to see if the other Englishmen knew of his closeness to the princess. But there was never any indication that the colonists suspected anything between them.

Newport arrived on the *Merry Margaret*, bringing a richly furnished damask bed with canopy and curtains gorgeously scrolled and tasseled in gold, a bed fit to cradle a crowned head. A scarlet velvet cloak and a crown completed the offering to the great king. The crown was made of copper, the metal most cherished by the Powhatans.

Smith assessed the goods and muttered to Percy, "The whole idea is grotesque. Royal trappings indeed! They will never appease Powhatan. He is too shrewd."

The sentry in one of the fort's towers announced, "The princess Pocahontas."

She might have an idea how to obtain an audience with her father, thought Smith.

He hurried across to her and explained the colonists' need to see her father and arrange a coronation ceremony. She was astonished and then amused. He was already the great chief, she said. But she would arrange a meeting. Smith should plan to leave the fort in three days' time. She would meet him and his men outside the palisades at Werowocomoco and escort them in.

She said her father was on his way home from Uttamussack and was usually in a good mood after seeing his treasures.

Eighty Englishmen volunteered to make the trip to Werowocomoco, and they set off singing with happiness. Any change from the confines and routines of Jamestown was welcome and lifted their morale.

As they turned a bend close to their destination, Pocahontas stood abruptly before them on the road. She signaled to Smith that she had a treat for them and that they were to follow her into an adjoining glen. She danced ahead of them in obvious high spirits and teased and harried the men into a circle around a fire. She told them to sit and close their eyes. Good-naturedly, they agreed.

"I promise you it is safe or you can kill me!" she laughed.

They laid their muskets across their laps and waited while Pocahontas disappeared into the woods. It was a measure of their confidence in her that the men would sit down at all in enemy territory.

Suddenly there was a din of bloodcurdling screams from the forest. The men started to struggle to their feet, muskets at the ready. Was this an ambush?

Out of the woods raced thirty women, their strong young bodies bare except for leaves between their legs. They were painted with intricate scrolls from head to toe in various bright colors—red, blue, green, yellow. Deer antlers, flowers, and other objects adorned their heads. Like Amazons, each carried a weapon—a bow and arrow, a club, a sword. It was a stampede of color and variety as they yelled and sang at the top of their lungs while they danced in a circle around the fire.

The colonists were stunned. They had never seen anything like this display and they looked at Pocahontas in consternation. She laughed at their amazement and called to them to sit down.

A smaller group of girls came from the forest, prancing around carrying rattles, drums, and flutes. They quickly settled down to play their instruments.

The other women now began to dance in earnest, a lascivious ritual that would have enflamed a rock. Their bodies twisted and turned in openly lewd movements, their taut breasts and firm buttocks thrust invitingly first toward the men, then away. The beat started slowly and built up into a ferment of provocation. Bodies trembled, nipples hardened, and gestures left nothing to the imagination.

Smith's face became heavy with disapproval. Discipline among his men had vanished. He looked at Pocahontas whose face was rapt with concentration. Suddenly he wondered, Could this be a trap? Then he realized it was her offering. The men were lonely and sexually starved. This dance was a symbol of her culture and another of her efforts to bring the two people together. Did she see a broader implication? Did she think that if many of her Powhatan maidens formed alliances with the British it would pave the way for her father to accept their own alliance? Smith did not know, but he certainly did not approve. He scowled as he thought, The men are lost to me for the rest of the day. If we are attacked now we will be defeated.

The women stopped their dance as suddenly as they had begun and rushed off into the woods. They returned bearing platters of enticing food. By now the men were in such a state that it took no encouragement to lead them off one by one to the nearby houses of the town.

Smith was sure that Pocahontas would never do anything that was unacceptable to Powhatan. As they stood alone at the town's edge, he asked, "What rank are these women?"

"They are farmers' daughters, right for your workmen and soldiers. This dance is meant to end in lovemaking," she said. "There is nothing furtive about it, and the men will leave on the morrow. It is not a continuing connection, which would be wrong."

Smith decided he would never truly understand these people and he didn't show his displeasure, for he could see Pocahontas was proud of her effort. Danger aside, the men would be grateful for the release. They would have a great tale to tell their envious companions when they returned to the fort.

At midmorning the next day, the great king and an entourage of two hundred warriors traveled downriver by canoe from Uttamussack. Powhatan was in his best mood after counting out the riches in his treasure houses. He smiled benevolently to one and all as he stepped from his forty-man craft and proceeded slowly through the waiting throng to his council house and his eager brides. Smith and his men stood off to the side, but even they received a royal wave and a smile.

"Pocahontas was wise to suggest that we come today. The king is in excellent temper," Smith observed, his voice hopeful.

After a wait of several hours, twelve of Powhatan's tallest men came to summon Smith into the king's presence. Smith was irritated. He was medium height, and whenever he was in Powhatan's territory the great king surrounded him with men who stood six feet four or more. It was one of the many ploys Powhatan used to unnerve him. At least this time I have brought along a few of my own tall men, he thought with satisfaction.

With as much eloquence as he could muster and with the help of the interpreter, Thomas Savage, Smith told Powhatan that his king across the water held him in such esteem and admiration that he would like to crown Powhatan king of England. He then described the ceremony and invited the king to Jamestown for the coronation.

Powhatan sat back on his furs, his wives clustered around him. He looked at Smith coldly with hooded eyes. After a moment he replied, "I also am a king, and this is my land. If your king has sent me presents, eight days only will I wait to receive them. Your Newport is to come to me, not I to him, nor to your fort, neither will I bite at such a bait."

Pocahontas had entered the council room and tried to placate her father. "The Tassentasses desire to do you great honor, Father. It is the custom to go to their fort for the ceremony."

Powhatan was adamant. No pleading by Pocahontas and no fervent speech by Smith could budge him. He would not move from Werowocomoco, and he made it clear that he cared nothing about being crowned king of England. The presents were another matter, however. He would be happy to consider them. Smith and his men retreated from the room as the happy cries of the wives, finally rid of the red-haired one, echoed in their ears.

"There is nothing more we can do here now." Smith stood, his hands on his hips in the warm sun. "Damn London! We will leave immediately for Jamestown and return with the presents and crown. We will have to get that crown on Powhatan's head one way or another to satisfy King James."

Smith then turned to Pocahontas. "Try to convince your father that it is a great privilege to be made a king of England. At least persuade him in some way to go through with the ceremony."

For two months Pocahontas traveled back and forth between her people and Jamestown. Her father stubbornly refused to be crowned until at last a promise of weapons made him say a grudging maybe. The colonists fixed a firm day to travel to Werowocomoco. The coronation, if it did take place, would have to be where Powhatan designated. He had no intention of coming into the despised strangers' camp. The heavy gifts—the great bed, the cloak, the crown—and the agreed-upon weapons were transported on the *Merry Margaret* with Newport by the circuitous river route. Two days later Smith and fifty men traveled overland.

This time there were no beautiful damsels waiting to seduce the English, nor was there even a sizable contingent of courtiers to greet them and escort them into the town. Instead, six men— the shortest men Smith had yet seen among the Powhatans— awaited them. The great king was making plain his contempt for the crowning ceremony. But when the ship sailed into view later in the day, Powhatan sent out a hundred warriors in full regalia to greet the vessel and its cargo of presents and weapons. The great king was intrigued by the huge bed and its rich trappings, which were carried immediately into his living quarters. The royal divan stood high off the ground, and Powhatan confided to Pocahontas that it looked more like a throne than a place to sleep. Several of his wives bounced gingerly on it and wondered among themselves if they would spend half their time falling onto the floor.

The English waited patiently in the large central clearing of the town. They stood in military formation. It was a clear day, warmer than usual for November. Smith and his men had changed into their finest clothing, the gentlemen in velvets and feathered hats, Newport in his uniform of admiral of the fleet. A sailor carried the copper crown, which glowed in the sun as it rested on a velvet cushion. Another man held the velvet cloak, its scarlet splashing vivid color over the scene. The sailors on board ship had been ordered to wear their dress uniforms, as they all hoped the coronation would take place. Newport carried a pistol as well as his sword. He gave orders that at the moment the crown was placed on Powhatan's head, he would fire his side arm and the gunners would then blast a twenty-one gun salute from the *Merry Margaret*. The English were determined to give the ceremony dignity in spite of Powhatan's disdain.

As they waited, Pocahontas, her face happy with her news, approached Smith and Newport and said that the bed was a triumph. Her father was so pleased with it that he would grant the colonists their wish to place an alien crown on his head, but that they would have to get the business over with quickly because he had no time to waste on small matters.

Another hour went by. Suddenly to the noise of banging on a rawhide drum, the great king appeared, his face inscrutable. He was surrounded by his warriors, who laughed and joked while looking curiously at the English. But the braves were heavily armed, just in case there was any sign of treachery.

Pocahontas joined Powhatan's wives on one side of the clearing. They were all sumptuously clothed in furs—soft squirrel, red and silver fox, opossum, glistening mink, marten, and otter. The wives had become more tolerant and sophisticated about the ugly creatures from another land, but the idea that their all-powerful god-king was to be made king of yet another realm amused them and aroused their curiosity.

Newport stepped forward and presented the scarlet cloak in a series of sweeping gestures. Powhatan allowed a warrior to take away his own long rawhide train and let Newport drape the soft velvet across his shoulders. The London tailors had been told that he was over six feet tall, so the folds shimmered to the ground in a spill of blood red. There was a flicker of pleasure across the great king's face, and all the people watching thought how magnificent he looked.

The crowd was silent. The banter had died away. Two gentlemen stepped up and asked Powhatan to bend his knee and incline his head, please. Thomas Savage interpreted.

"I incline my head for no one." The great king was unyielding.

The English were nonplussed. There was not an Englishman tall enough to place the crown on Powhatan's head while he was standing. Consultations followed, then demonstrations. Even Newport got down on one knee and bowed his head to show the king what was needed. The English tried flattery, cajolery, every possible ruse, but the mighty emperor of the Seven Kingdoms was adamant. He would not bend his knee for any mortal.

A thought struck Smith when he looked at Pocahontas standing by her greyhound. He whispered to Newport, who moved with the crown bearer closer to the king. He then spoke a brief word with Pocahontas, who walked over to her father holding her dog Kint by his collar.

Powhatan was fond of the dog and bent down to give it a pat. In that instant Newport grabbed the crown and placed it quickly on the great king's head. Powhatan stood up slowly, a heavy scowl on his face. Would he dash the crown to the ground? Patriotism flooded the English. After all, it was the symbol of their land. A great cheer burst from their throats and tore the pregnant silence. Powhatan stared at them, and then slowly his face relaxed. His expression seemed to say, Let the fools have their fun.

Then Newport cried out, "On behalf of King James of England, I crown you king of England in Virginia!"

He fired his pistol and the Powhatans jumped involuntarily. Immediately the *Merry Margaret* started her salvo of twenty-one guns. A new king had been crowned for England.

The crown stayed but a few moments on Powhatan's head before he handed it to one of his retainers. Smith had no doubt that it would end up in necklaces for his favorite wives. It was plain that the great king's attention was focused on the roar of the cannons. Here was something that had true meaning for Powhatan, and it was easy to see that the avenue to his mind was not through crowns and honors but through weapons and the power that they could give him.

The great king, emperor of the Seven Kingdoms and king of England remembered his manners, however. He took his own heavy train, embroidered with many hundreds of pearls and shells, symbolic of his great wealth, and presented it to Newport.

"For your king," he said. "A gift from Powhatan, ruler of the Seven Kingdoms."

No Englishman failed to notice that he offered his cape but not one of his feathered crowns or other ornaments for the head.

Smith turned over command of his men to one of his lieutenants for their return trip overland to Jamestown. He wanted to sail with Newport to discuss the plans he had for the colony and to have some time to reflect. The overnight sail was ideal for both purposes. But first he wanted to write a letter to King James and the Virginia Company in London telling them that the coronation had taken place. As soon as he was on board he sat down in his cabin and wrote: "Right Honorable Ladies and Gentlemen, I have expressly followed your directions sent by Captain Newport, although I was dead against it. And although I fear it will be a hazard to us all, which is now generally conceded when it is too late, I have crowned Powhatan according to your instructions.

"For the Coronation of Powhatan and toward such ceremony you sent him presents, I give leave to tell you I fear there will be trouble for us all before we hear from you again."

Smith knew it was a rude letter, but he wanted to impress on the people in London that it was next to impossible to dictate policy from several thousand miles away over matters that they knew next to nothing about.

With the letter ready to be sent on the first ship to England, and before he had a talk with Newport, Smith had time to think again about Pocahontas. What she had accomplished for

England and for the colonists was incalculable. Without her the colony would have been wiped out and the investors so discouraged that another attempt would have been impossible for a long while, if ever. The French or the Spanish would then have been able to move in and dominate the Virginia territory and the New World.

She was truly a heroine, thought Smith, although she would be the last to think of herself in that light. She had once told him that she originally only wanted to bring together the two men who meant the most to her, Powhatan and Smith. But her feeling for the English had grown with her knowledge of them and now she wanted to see the people of both worlds live in harmony.

Yes, she is remarkable, Smith thought, but how is she going to fit into my life? She is not only a princess of a foreign land but now a princess of England as well. It is unheard of for someone of my rank to marry a woman so far superior. And what kind of life could I offer her in England? How would she fit in? Would she feel constrained after the freedom of the forest? These were old thoughts that swirled in his head, but they still rankled, unresolved. For his intention was to return to England after he had secured the future of Jamestown.

If only he did not have this passion for her! He got up from the table and walked to the porthole. He thought, A small part of me is impatient and resentful of the time I spend worrying about her and longing for her. It takes me away from my duties, from what I want to accomplish, and that makes me feel guilty. He walked back and slapped the table with his glove in frustration. If only I did not love her! Damn, I have broken my own stringent rule: Never involve yourself seriously with a woman; it only brings trouble. Damn and damn again.

Pocahontas was in Jamestown within five days of Smith's return. She told him that her father did not accept the payment

Smith had offered for more corn and food. She said Powhatan was losing patience with the colonists and was tired of providing them with food from his own stores. They should be growing their own by now. Pocahontas looked apologetic but also worried.

"My father has just had some news about your recent trip up the Chesapeake when three of your men became ill with the fever and spots. We have found out that the entire village suffered from the same malady." She lowered her voice. "Everyone died. Even the priests did not have the magic to make themselves well. It has upset my father very much, and his priests are in a furor. They do not like to think that any of their own are powerless. I tell you this to give you warning. I do not know what my father plans to do."

CHAPTER
~❧ 16 ❧~

Uttamussack,
January 1609

S mith and Percy huddled together under a blanket. They had chosen a deep gully to hide in before they made a reconnaissance of the treasure houses a good four miles farther inland. The two men had told Newport of their plan to raid the great king's riches. All three had agreed that the secret should remain with them. If the rest of the fort knew about the treasure, there would be a stampede.

"I cannot remember how many men guard each of the houses," Smith said, "but it is not important. Once we have set off the fireworks, they will all scatter. These guards have never heard gunshots or fireworks, and the success of our plan depends on that."

Although there was frost on the ground, Smith hardly felt the cold. He was conscious of it, but it did not make him suffer as it would have two years ago. I am getting as tough as the naturals, he thought. He wondered about Percy, though. He was as staunch a friend as a man could find, but not physically strong.

As soon as it was dark, they planned to creep closer to Uttasmussack and set up their powder and paraphernalia. When

275

it blasted with a roar, the native Virginians would run for the woods in panic, convinced that the gods were having their revenge and the world was coming to an end. The risk to the plan was how long it would be before they crept back. Would Smith and Percy have time to assess the treasures? Would they be able to carry off some of the loot?

"We will have just one chance at this," said Percy in a low voice. "The firepower will frighten them the first time only."

The men at Jamestown thought that Smith and Percy were searching for food. God knows we need it, sighed Smith to himself. We have had the worst luck. We laid down a good store, but the rats ate right through it. No one had imagined that the rats would jump ship in such numbers and multiply so quickly.

"There will be precious little mercy if we are caught," retorted Smith. "Since the coronation, Powhatan has been even more arrogant, if that is possible. Not that I am surprised."

"Why hasn't he overrun our settlement?" Percy trembled slightly. He felt the cold as he pulled his jacket around him. They had left their armor behind. "He could muster a force of two or three thousand overnight."

"If you have asked that question once, you have asked it a dozen times." Smith gave a short, low laugh. "I have no answer, except that he refrains from attacking us because of the intercession of his daughter. Look, the light is beginning to fade."

Both men stared out through the forest that spread over the rolling hills. Dusk was beginning to blur the outlines of the trees.

"We will wait another few minutes; then we move," Smith said. "Remember, we will have but a brief time to run for the first treasure house, open it, scoop up as much gold and jewelry as we can carry, and then make our way back to the shallop. No use in trying to keep our muskets primed. It would be too dangerous with our hands so occupied." Smith stood up and stretched. His muscles felt cramped.

The men moved stealthily through the forest. Smith had learned the Indian habit of covering his tracks and moving quietly. Percy was not so proficient, but the two of them made quick progress with their sacks of gunpowder and firing materials.

The light was pretty well gone by the time they had moved as close to the village as they dared. It was going to be a dark night, darker than Smith would have wished, but there was no going back now. In the far distance he heard the yelps and cries of wolves until the chorus died down to mournful howls. His heart started a quick drumbeat in his chest.

Creeping forward, the men could hear the naturals' loud voices as some of them relaxed around a fire, singing songs and telling tales. Smith remembered Pocahontas mentioning that no one had ever dared try to get near the treasure houses. Their awe of their god-king was too profound. In any case, death by days-long torture was certain for anyone who was caught.

Silently, deftly, Smith and Percy emptied their sacks and laid out piles of the fireworks and powder over a space of twenty-five feet, attaching all of it to one line to ensure a series of explosions. Then they edged up even closer to the village. With a quick glance at each other, the sign of the cross, and a clasp of their free hands, they fired the line. Both prayed to themselves as they waited a few seconds for the first explosion.

With a whoosh, the first pile shot flames and thunder high in the silent woods. The forest was as bright as noon in full summer. For a second there was an eerie silence. Then pandemonium broke loose. The noise was deafening. Every creature in the forest joined in the din. As Smith and Percy grabbed their sacks and ran for the treasure houses, they could see the naturals scattering in every direction away from the fireworks. In a trice the village was as empty as a town of the dead.

Running up to the first huge treasure house, the men yanked open the wooden slabs that protected the door and rushed into the long building. They stopped abruptly. Inside on either side of the entrance stood a towering wooden statue, one of a wildcat, the other of a giant lizard. The two menacing sentinels glared down at them. A torch flickered behind each statue, imparting a disturbing half-light.

"God's blood," muttered Percy as he stared up at the chilling creatures.

"Hurry, we must find the gold." Smith yanked at Percy's arm.

The men hurried down the aisles through stacks of furs of every description, piles upon piles of skins, bows and arrows by the thousands, hundreds of mantles thick with embroidery, dozens and dozens of copper artifacts, and caskets of pearls. But no gold, no other jewels.

"Damn, where do they keep their gold? Where are the rubies and diamonds?" Smith rushed impatiently to the end of the building.

Both men pulled up short when they emerged from the stacks of goods at the back entrance of the temple. Again there were two tall wooden statues; this time a man and a bear glowered at them.

"More of their gods," called Smith. "Nothing here, we must try the other temples. Quick!"

They barged out of the storehouse into the deserted town, raced to the second temple, and slammed their shoulders against the wooden barrier at its entrance. They were not surprised this time to see a wooden wildcat and a reptilian monster baring their fangs just inside the doorway. They raced down the length of the eighty-foot building; this treasure house was bursting with food-stuffs: grain, dried venison, fish, nuts, and other foods, mountains of it extorted as taxes from the great king's subjects.

"This third temple has to have the treasure, has to!" Smith shouted at Percy as the two men, running now as if their lungs would burst, reached the last building and broke down the door. They swore in their urgency and impatience as they rushed down the length of the temple. But it was all more of the same. There was not a gold nugget or an emerald in sight.

Under the fierce eye of a wooden bear, its fangs gleaming, the men paused, disappointment heavy on their faces.

"Nothing! Absolutely nothing!" cried Percy.

"We have got to get back into the forest. Quickly! Quickly! The guards will be back any second now," Smith urged as they moved out into the town again.

The village was still empty of people, although the foray had taken longer than they had expected. Both men sprinted for the trees as if all the gods were at their heels. They did not stop running until they had put two miles between them and the town. Finally they collapsed.

"We were lucky," Smith said. "We got out of there in time. But, Percy, it seems incredible that Powhatan has no wealth."

"All those goods are riches to him, John. In his world, which now is ours, he is overpoweringly wealthy."

"Bah!"

"We could keep several towns full of our people alive for a year with the food he has there."

"True, but I had hoped that we would be able to send back to England the same kind of treasure the Spanish have found in the New World."

"They encountered a different civilization to the south of us. I have a feeling that the only way we will find gold and jewels is to pirate them from the Spanish ships off our shores."

"In fact, I have already sent a letter back to London regarding that possibility," retorted Smith blandly.

Suddenly Smith grabbed Percy's arm. "Shh. Do you hear birds?"

"Yes."

"It is the darkest of nights. Those can't be birds!"

Smith moved forward warily, Percy close on his heels. Each faint sound they made on the hard earth was magnified twenty times over in their imagination. Every shape looked menacing.

"We must try to get to the shallop at once. We cannot rest," whispered Smith.

The men moved as silently and quickly as they could. They traveled perhaps another mile and a half. Suddenly there was a trill of birdsong almost in Smith's ear. They're on us, thought Smith, as the hair on the back of his neck prickled. He pulled out his musket and indicated that Percy do the same. God's fishes! and I thought we had got away!

The men moved on through the dead quiet forest. There was another trill of birdsong and answering calls from every direction all around them. They are toying with us, fumed Smith inwardly. If they are going to kill us why don't they get on with it?

It was difficult to see anything in the deep gloom. Smith knew now that they needed a miracle to save them, and he felt unsure that God would provide any more for him.

His shoulder brushed up against a tree, and a twig grabbed the cloth of his doublet. As he turned to free himself he saw that the tree had thick lower branches. He put his hand behind him to catch Percy and put his mouth to Percy's ear.

"The naturals are all around us. If we climb this tree, perhaps we can pick them off from a hidden vantage point."

Smith pulled himself up with Percy following behind. The tree was heavy with branches, and Smith climbed easily, finding one good handhold after the other. The blackness of the night was now intense and he had to feel his way. One last rung—but as he heaved himself up, his hand closed over a living human foot. At the same time he felt a hand grasp his hair.

In that same instant Percy said softly, "They have grabbed my foot."

"They have my hair," replied Smith out loud.

The forest was suddenly busy with voices. Percy and Smith were pulled and pushed out of the tree. It was obvious they were to be taken alive and unhurt, and although the naturals were rough they were not brutal. They want us whole for torture, thought Smith.

As the naturals marched them through the forest Smith understood enough of their conversation to realize that the soldiers knew who he was. When dawn broke, the party of twenty stopped to bathe quickly in the river. Then they ate some corn and dried venison before they embarked in canoes for Werowocomoco. Smith gleaned from their conversation that he and Percy would be turned over to Powhatan himself. He was separated from his friend, so he did not have an opportunity to discuss how they should approach their confrontation with the great king. He was confident, however, that Percy would let him take the lead. Smith slammed his fist into his palm in frustration. He was fed up with being hauled into Werowocomoco for one reason or another, and this time for no reward. All that effort and a whole year of waiting and planning, and there was not a nugget of gold or a single jewel in the treasure houses.

He controlled his surly feelings as he and Percy were reunited in front of the great king. Powhatan, however, did not conceal his anger and disgust. He, too, was exasperated at having to meet once again with the red-haired captain.

He did not bother with preliminary pleasantries, and to be sure he was well understood, he again asked Thomas Savage to interpret, since Pocahontas was nowhere to be seen.

"Just after the big fire," Powhatan said, "my men found the buckle of your shoe in the village of Uttamussack."

"Yes, we had been searching for a village that would barter for food," replied Smith. Percy remained quiet.

"And when you arrive to barter, is it your custom to set off fire magic that makes the night bright as day?"

"My magic went off by mistake. We intended it to go off in the river, to kill fish for our storehouse."

Powhatan pursed his lips in skepticism. "I don't believe you," said the great king. "You people do not speak the truth with me. When your people first came to our shores you said it was only for a short time, that you were escaping from another tribe of warriors, the Spanish, and that you would be leaving soon. That was a long time ago. You are still here and more of you are coming. You are trying to conquer my country for yourselves and your king. I don't like any of you, nor do my priests. I got rid of your kind many years ago to the south, and I do not want you here now. You lie."

The conversation was dangerous. Smith tried to divert it to the subject that interested Powhatan most. "We are still here because your country is so beautiful. We would like to remain on your soil. We are willing to exchange some guns and swords and some of our other magic. We would like to live in peace with you."

A flicker of interest broke the heavy scowl on the great king's face. He still did not have his swords or his demiculverins. Smith fanned his attention and launched into the possibilities of bartering for food. As the two men bargained, Smith felt inwardly relieved that he had steered the conversation away from the colonists' presence on Virginia soil. He was fascinated, however, by Powhatan's admission that he was responsible for the death of other Englishmen to the south. He must mean Raleigh, Smith thought. For the first time the king had openly declared himself to be against the English. This was serious.

After an hour of intense talk, Smith and Percy were taken to the guest house just outside of town. It was dusk now, and the king had come to an agreement with them on the exchange of swords. Smith felt confident that Powhatan had put the matter of their trespassing to the back of his mind. At least it seemed not to concern him heavily.

"I think we got away lightly," Percy said when they were alone.

"I agree, but only for the moment. Now that the king has openly declared his dislike of the English, he will feel he has to act on it. Perhaps the outburst came because of his particular dislike of me. What worries me is that he may regret what he said, and if he does, that makes the two of us expendable."

"What about the agreement on the swords?" Percy asked.

"He can negotiate that with any of the colonists, with Pocahontas's help. I am surprised she was not there."

Both men were tired. They had not slept for twenty-four hours. They quickly ate the meat and cheese left for them and fell into a deep slumber.

Smith felt a soft touch on his shoulder. He sprang to his feet his hand on his scabbard.

"Please, quiet!" Pocahontas's soft voice came out of the dark. "Don't make any noise. I have come to help you."

Smith suppressed the astonishment in his voice as he greeted her. But he touched her arm reassuringly in the dark.

"You must leave," her low voice continued. "My father intends to kill you. An emissary will arrive soon and ask you to come with him to another meeting with my father. Instead you will be taken to the priests and prepared for torture."

Both men remained silent as her voice, barely a whisper, continued.

"I have a canoe waiting in a secret spot beyond the women's bathing place. I will lead you there now. You must go downriver by night and hide during the day until you reach my brother

Pochins at Kecoughtan. From there you can make your way back to the fort."

Smith was not surprised at her news, but he was surprised at the lack of inflection in her voice and the cold matter-of-fact way she had arranged their escape with seemingly no fear for herself.

In the deep gloom of the room she brushed past Smith as they readied to leave. He cupped his hand over her breast and they stood quiet for several seconds. Then she moved and said, "It is the time of the new moon. It will be very dark. We must move touching each other, but silently, please. Every footfall will be dangerous."

The night was colder than the previous one. Smith gave thanks to the Lord that there was no frost yet. They moved slowly from tree to tree. Sometimes they would wait a bit and listen to the distant hoot of an owl or the call of a nightingale. This distracted Smith, who would find himself pressed up hard against Pocahontas next to a tree. She would fling her arm back protectively around him. Smith smiled wryly. In this situation she was totally the master.

They had moved some distance away from the guest house when suddenly Pocahontas stopped, her body tense. She listened. This time she deliberately pressed herself against Smith for a moment as she turned quietly, without a sound, and faced back toward the house. It unnerved Smith that the Indians could hear and see so much more acutely than he did. He could detect a faint rustle now and then in the silent night or the fading hoot of an owl, but there was an extra dimension to the naturals' interpretation of sounds. He knew it would take years for him to learn their lore of the woods.

Pocahontas now put her mouth at his ear and in the barest of whispers said she was returning to the house for a moment. They were to wait for her and not move a muscle.

She slipped quietly away from the men. She was loath to leave them alone, but someone was moving toward the house. She had to know who it was and what he was up to. Anyone this close to them would sense trouble and it would only be a matter of minutes before he raised the alarm. She fingered the dagger at her belt. Smith had given it to her, and she prized it because it was far more effective than her flint knife.

It must be the emissary, she thought, come to fetch the two men. She moved lightly, silently but swiftly now. She had to find the man. Find him before he got away. The air was sharp, but she did not yet detect any scent. It was hard to see, but the ground was so familiar she let her instinct guide her footsteps— a rise here, a pile of leaves there near that small gully. Ah, there it is, the slightly rank smell of man. He is close. I am going to have to kill him, she thought. I have no choice. What if it is someone I know well? She felt her heart squeeze with revulsion. But in the next instant she thrust the feeling from her. I can't think of that. I must save John Smith, she thought. I have made the decision to defy my father for him, and I have to take the consequences.

She crept, as cunning as a cat after its prey, totally focused on her mission. She heard what might have been a footstep. It was so faint it was hard to know, but it was within twenty-five feet of her. His scent escaped her as forest smells intensified in a slight wind—acrid bracken, the mustiness of dead leaves, the damp richness of bark. If only there was a full moon! Her ears strained. There was a footfall on a different surface. The guard or emissary must have entered the house. Or perhaps it is a killer! Yes, my father has sent someone to kill them while he thinks they are still asleep. That would explain how easy it was to get past the usual contingent of guards around the house. They must have been sent away.

Pocahontas dashed the last yards to the house. She had to

gamble that the intruder was inside. At any moment he could emerge, knowing that the prisoners had fled. She flattened herself up against the wall of the house and willed herself to take short, shallow breaths. She could now hear the man moving more boldly. He thought he was alone. But then she heard his footsteps cease suddenly. Had he caught her scent? It would be hard for him to detect her while he was in a room overpowered with diverse smells. But perhaps he had heard her. A keen man might even have heard her breathing, faint as it was. Each of her senses was strained to razor-sharp awareness. Her ears ached with stress. Where was he now? There was no sound; the night was dead quiet. Not even the normal rustling of night animals reached her.

A hand seized her arm; she whirled around. It was Rawhunt, her father's trusted brave, one of his senior advisers, a man she had known all her life.

"Why, Pocahontas? Why are you here?"

With one sure movement, Pocahontas drove her dagger deep into his chest between his ribs. He was killed instantly, a questioning look still on his face as he slid to the ground.

In another quick movement Pocahontas stooped and wiped her knife on his furs and sheathed it at her waist. The confrontation had lasted only a few seconds.

Slipping from tree to tree as fast as she dared, she rejoined the two men. Whispering into their ears, she told them it had been nothing, then led them cautiously on to the cove and the canoe.

She placed her mouth close to Smith's ear: "I have put a little food in the bottom of the canoe. Hug the shoreline for at least an hour. Then cross over to the other side and continue down to Kecoughtan."

She squeezed his hand and brushed her lips across his face. She could barely see him in the dark. Then she left them.

• • •

By dawn Werowocomoco was in an uproar. The great chief had ordered whippings for the delinquent guards who had allowed the dirty Tassentasses to get away and one of his most trusted men, Rawhunt, to be killed. It made no difference that the guards had been ordered to withdraw. They were told that they were lucky not to be tortured to death.

Pocahontas took her early morning bath as usual the next day, after seeing Smith and Percy row away. This time she stayed close to the other women. Her ears were closed to their gossip. It was a tremendous effort for her to do anything. After the two Tassentasses left she had made her way back to town and collapsed near where the sacrificial animals were kept. She had never killed a man, and the memory of Rawhunt's surprised face the night before made her want to retch. It was one thing to kill an animal or even an enemy, but a friend, someone who had always been kind to her! Although she trembled from head to foot she knew that she had to return to her bed, remain quiet, and then turn a calm face to the world in the morning. She was thankful that Kokum was not expected back from hunting until morning. Would her sisters betray her? She didn't know. They were used to her midnight and early morning forays. They might have slept straight through her entrance.

At midmorning the great chief called for his daughter. Pocahontas steeled herself. She knew the meeting would be terrible, but she was not prepared for the thundering rage that her father hurled at her from his new throne, the English state bed piled high with furs.

Her father told her that he was not sure what her role had been in the disappearance of the dirty ones, and he was sure she had nothing to do with the death of his trusted Rawhunt, but he never wanted to see a Tassentasse again. His face turned stone hard as he explicitly forbade her on pain of death ever to

287

see them again. Although it was quite plain for all to see that she was still as flat as a virgin, the marriage with Kokum would take place in the next full moon. She was a rebellious, ungrateful daughter, and he preferred not to see her for a while. He said once more, so that she would understand clearly, "Mark my word, if you go to the Tassentasses or see them again, you will be put to death."

Pocahontas knew her father would make no more concessions. She felt numb. Too much had happened in the past twenty-four hours. She had defied her father. Her lover was lost to her. She had killed a friend, and she was doomed to spend the rest of her life with a man she hated. The wings of the crow thundered in her ears. She could barely move, her limbs felt so heavy.

Somehow she managed to get through the day. She rubbed her body with the ashes of sorrow for Rawhunt, and her escape into mourning for him was a cover for all of her grief. She made herself join the other women wailing over his body while her own heart was torn to pieces over her duplicity. For a while as she swayed in unison with her sisters, her mind became blank. Her guilt, her loss, her torn emotions, the hopelessness of the future swamped her brain, and for an unknown time she moved in a semiconscious trance.

Finally Mehta nudged her sharply. It was turning dusk and the mourners were departing for their houses. She looked at Mehta, who suddenly seemed plumper. Pocahontas wondered dully if she was with seed. Whose seed? She hoped it was Kokum's! But no, that wouldn't make any difference. Whatever the situation, her father would never relent.

That night Kokum led her away and she followed, like a trained dog, she thought bitterly. She had no ally now. She couldn't protest in front of the townspeople and her father. When he had her on the furs and he cupped his hand over her breast, her mind leapt back to the night before, to John Smith's touch. Suddenly she thought, I don't have to accommodate this man now. I don't have to deceive him to get back to the fort. As his face and body neared hers she spat fully in his face.

He wiped the spit away, and when he spoke, his voice was solicitous. "Your grief for Rawhunt must not overwhelm you. My touch will help you to forget."

She looked at him with loathing. With all of her strength she pushed and kicked at him. But he was too strong, and she was too exhausted. With soothing murmurs he entered her again and again during the night. In the end she responded to the now familiar touch. She responded! The horror of it all almost made her lose her mind.

CHAPTER
17

Jamestown,
June 1609

It had been a busy new year and spring. Now that Powhatan refused to give food to the colonists, Smith had been forced to send out groups of his men, almost one hundred in all, to hunt for oysters and catch fish. He commanded them to set up camp in groups of twenty or forty and remain where the food was until he sent word for them to return. He was then able to feed the remaining colonists, who were mainly workmen. They were on meager rations, but still they were able to enlarge the fort and dig a larger and deeper well for water. Smith also sent the men out to clear and plow fields. So that the seasoned settlers could be free to hunt, two captured Powhatans were pressed into teaching the new colonists how to plant corn and, later, pumpkins and beans. When the gentlemen who had arrived on the January ship from England complained about their blisters after their first encounter with manual labor, Smith toughened them and stopped their complaining by having soldiers pour cold water over their wrists. As president of the council, he made everyone work.

During the reconstruction of the fort the naturals were

strangely quiet. Smith had expected the great king to send out war parties to harass the colonists, but the time was actually peaceful. He was unsure how to approach Powhatan again and decided that the best course was to let matters settle for a while, though he desperately wanted to see Pocahontas. He had sent a natural, imprisoned for thievery, back to Werowocomoco with a message for her, but there was no reply. He worried constantly that she had been caught the night they escaped and been punished, even put to death! Each time that thought occurred to him he consoled himself that she was too much her father's favorite to lose her life. But he needed her. He wanted to see her and feel her supple body next to his. How was he to get in touch? How could he meet her? His frustration drove him to work even harder. His only consolation during the trying months was that Jamestown had been strengthened and was ready to receive a large number of new colonists.

On the night that Captain Samuel Argall arrived from London with his crew bruised and battered by a rough crossing on the *Elizabeth Anne*, Smith was happy to be able to sit down at the captain's table and give a decent report of the progress of the colony.

"I have news for you, too, Smith," Argall said. "A new charter has been devised in London for our venture. The administering council is called the Treasurer and Company of Adventurers and Planters of the City of London for the First Colony in Virginia, and it will govern Virginia from London. So the old council is no more. The governor of the colony will be granted a lifetime tenure in office, and Lord De La Warr has been appointed to that position. He arrives here within weeks, along with Gabriel Archer, John Ratcliffe, and nine ships full of new colonists."

The names of Archer and Ratcliffe brought a scowl to Smith's face. Those two bastards, he thought. They did everything they could to blacken my name in London by saying that I was a liability to the colony, but without success. My record has proved them wrong, thank God.

"So in effect I will no longer be president of the council," replied Smith.

"I am afraid not, although everyone now recognizes that you have done a fine job."

Well, that reckons, said Smith to himself. An aristocrat with connections that are stronger than mine is a logical choice as governor for the colony now that it is becoming so large.

"Argall," he said, "I have no stomach for work with Archer and Ratcliffe, or for that matter with De La Warr, although I am sure he is a fine choice. But as you well know, I like to order things in my own way. I am going to hand over the presidency immediately to George Percy, an able man."

Although Samuel Argall argued and protested, Smith would not be budged. He had put his imprint on the colony, he had brought it through the harshest days, and now was the time to relinquish control, well before there could be any power struggle with Archer and Ratcliffe.

Argall then wanted news about Powhatan. He, too, was fascinated to hear that Powhatan had been responsible for the demise of the Raleigh colony. Neither man could understand why he had not attacked Jamestown in the same manner.

"It must be his beautiful daughter who has kept him away from us." There was a gleam in Argall's eye as he spoke. "I confess I find what I hear of her very attractive indeed. She has done an immeasurable service to the colony."

Smith kept his voice bland. "We have not seen her since she rescued me for the third time. I would like to be in communication with her, but so far I have not been successful."

"As soon as De La Warr arrives, we will send a ship and some men to Powhatan to see if we can negotiate for more food," Argall said. "We will need even more supplies now, and we will offer him the swords he wants. Then we will get a message to the princess somehow. I would like to see her myself."

The eagerness in Argall's voice made Smith wonder if the only reason he wanted to meet Pocahontas was for the good of the colony, but he dismissed his jealousy as typical of a frustrated lover. Just speaking of her made his body surge with longing. He got to his feet.

"I will tell Percy of our decision immediately. Now that I am released of my duties I will take Namon and explore down the river again. I have in mind building a house of my own on Pochins's land."

This had only been a half-formed thought, but with a new government coming into control, it suddenly seemed the right solution for his future. Returning to England had become less attractive to him lately. To be independent and seek his own fortune in the New World excited Smith.

Smith and Namon chose a canoe to explore downriver. They stopped first in Kecoughtan and enjoyed several nights of good food and the gentle ministrations of the town's maidens. Instead of dampening his desire for Pocahontas, the nights spent in their soft arms only fueled his longing for her.

During the trip, Smith had made up his mind. He would build his house—he even had a name for it, Nonesuch—and he would try to arrange to marry Pocahontas. He knew it would be an extremely difficult endeavor, as Powhatan would put up every conceivable obstacle, but Smith had no real problems now. The good of the colony no longer depended on him. He would make his own way in Virginia with Pocahontas. He did not have to think any more about the unfamiliar life she would have if she went to England.

He suddenly felt happy and free. All his worries were on their way to being resolved. He had done a good job for the colony, and now he was released from the responsibility. Somehow claiming Pocahontas as his wife did not seem impossible. But how was he to get to her? He was not sure that an open approach through De La Warr and his expedition would be the right method. He would have to arrange a meeting on his own. After he found a place to build his house, Powhatan would see that he had a home planned for Pocahontas and that his intentions were serious. He would try again. He would be patient. It was not easy for him to wait for anything; immediate action had always been his first solution to a situation.

The two men rowed down the wide river on the lazy, warm June days heavy with the scent of honeysuckle. They stopped at various sites as they looked for a possible plantation. He wanted land that sat high off the river with plenty of pasture for the animals that would soon be sent from England, and fields on which to grow tobacco and corn. Smith was convinced that these two crops could be shipped back home profitably. The plantation would be a home base for Smith. He had no intention of stopping his exploring expeditions. He still needed to find the water route to the Indies and all the gold, spices, and jewels that would mean. The riches must be there farther inland; they had to be, and whatever he found he could claim for himself.

In the end he chose a site within ten miles of Kecoughtan. He decided that being near a friendly town had its advantages; it would also be pleasant for Pocahontas, who could visit her friends and relatives there.

He told Namon about his plans for a farm and home and said that he saw Pocahontas there with him. Namon fell silent. Smith thought that meant he approved, and he was encouraged to ask him if he would take a message to Pocahontas to meet him in a secret spot just inside her father's territory. He wanted to discuss the future with her. To Smith's relief, Namon agreed. Smith was overjoyed. He slept that night on the green fields of his own land with the scent of his meadow flowers filling his head, secure in the feeling that his future looked truly promising.

Pocahontas moved like a sleepwalker through the first days after she had killed Rawhunt and rescued Smith and Percy. Rawhunt's last surprised expression kept appearing in front of her at unexpected times. It disturbed her deeply. She would gaze into the fire and there he was, or as she swam in the early morning the water would suddenly reflect his face. She knew perfectly well that if she was faced with the dilemma again she would act the same, but it overwhelmed her to have committed such a final and devastating deed. She prayed fervently to Ahone that she would never have to face such a problem again, and she kept a calm, smiling face in public. She had no moments alone, even at night, for Kokum had an unrelenting sexual hunger for her.

She saw her father only in passing, but he was good-natured with her, and she knew that soon she would be fully reinstated in his affections. She understood his reactions to her deeds and longings, but she shuddered when she thought what he would do if he knew the extent of her disloyalty. This ability to see things from more than one point of view was a way of thinking that she had learned from the Tassentasses. She was not sure if it was a strength. She sighed as she thought. If only I could single-mindedly pursue my only desire. But, she reflected, that was impossible. There was no one in her world she could run to and no place for her to hide. Even Pochins could not protect her from her father. There was no one she could go to at the fort without bringing violence down on everyone's head. At times she felt such despair that she thought of swimming out into the river and down to the sea until she slipped beneath the undertow.

Mehta, definitely showing her seed, was married in three days of feasting and rituals to a young but brave warrior who had proved himself many times over in dangerous forays against the

Monacans. She had been offered the son of a chieftain from the northern section of the Seven Kingdoms once before, but she was adamant about not leaving her father's entourage.

A month later in a quieter ceremony Pocahontas was joined to Kokum. Just before the ritual, the great chief took Kokum aside and according to custom gave him leave to reject Pocahontas, since she was without child. He was relieved to find that Kokum had no intention of backing down and that he was delighted finally to be taken into the great chief's family. Kokum said he was sure there would be plenty of children in due course.

Pocahontas was eager to go out into the kingdom and collect taxes—anything, she thought, just to get away and be busy— but her father wanted her to stay in Werowocomoco.

The great chief smiled at his favorite daughter and said, "I am afraid I have worked you too hard, sending you back and forth so often to the dirty ones. It addled your judgment and tired your body. Look at your sister. She remained quietly at home, and now she is with child. The same will happen to you."

Sometimes Pocahontas thought she would tear her hair out in the middle of the town square from frustration. As time went on she began hunting again. The search, the concentration on her quarry, distracted her. She would spend the day on her quests and return at sundown weary but somewhat at peace. As for the nights, she made a bargain with Kokum. She told him she needed more sleep for her health and that twice at the start of the evening was enough for him until after she had borne a child. He knew it was a reasonable request, since her father was worried that she was not reproducing, but Pocahontas heaved a sigh of relief every time she went to the women's house.

When the sun was riding high and hot in the sky and the nights were short and alive with the chirping of cicadas, Namon returned to visit. He went immediately to pay his respects to the great chief and to give him news of the Tassentasses, but there was not much he could tell him that Powhatan had not already learned from his spies. In any case, after living among the Tassentasses for so long Namon had a sympathy for them and refrained from telling everything he knew. It was a difficult path to walk, but he did as best he could.

Pocahontas saw that Namon watched her from time to time, and she was not surprised when he offered to go with her to the fields while she checked the tobacco crop.

"The Tassentasse chieftain, Smith, would like to see you," he said.

Pocahontas's heart thudded violently as she looked around her. There was no one nearby—only a bogus warrior in the field to scare away the birds. "I am forbidden on pain of death to see him, Namon. Not only would I lose my life, but I know my father would unleash his warriors on the fort. There would be terrible bloodshed."

"But Smith is no longer with his people," Namon said. "He moves alone now. A new great chief will soon appear at the fort along with many more Tassentasses."

Pocahontas's eyes opened wide as she looked at Namon. "If he is alone, I need not fear for my own life, but where can I see him?"

"At a secret spot near the border of Pochins's land. It is safe. He will be there in three suns. I will keep guard when you meet." Namon quickly described the spot and how long it would take to get there.

"Namon, I will try, I will try." Pocahontas's face was suffused with happiness as she walked quickly away. She did not look back to see Namon watching her, concerned.

For the next two days Pocahontas alternated between joy at the thought of seeing John Smith again and despair as to how she would handle the fact that she was now a married woman and belonged to another man. Her body was thrown again into

300

such a feverish pitch of desire that she found her passion was totally out of her control at night and responded to Kokum's onslaughts in a manner that surprised him. It surprised her that he did not like her fervor as much as her usual passivity and reluctance.

On the dawn that she was to meet Smith, she followed her usual routine when she hunted. She left Kint the greyhound with Mehta and collected her bow and arrow. She ran along the river, her feet as fleet as a doe's. The silver-blue of the water danced and sparkled in the sunlight, unraveling ahead of her like a skein at the end of which she would find her lover. She thought she would never reach the place where she was to meet Namon, who would take her to Smith at his hiding spot. The time moved so slowly she wondered at one point if she had over-run the meeting place, but her practiced eye knew the trees and the varying undulations of the ground, and she soon realized that her impatience was playing her tricks.

Suddenly Namon stood in front of her, his long face grave. He signaled to her to follow him. They crept along close to the thicker bushes of the riverbank. Namon moved so slowly that to Pocahontas time stood still. They came to a sudden drop into a deep gully, and there at the entrance to a small cave stood Smith. She broke away from Namon and ran toward him, her arms outstretched. She didn't care what Namon saw; she didn't care about anything but Smith in that moment. All she wanted was his arms around her.

"I want you to come and live with me." Smith's voice was husky with emotion as he clasped her possessively.

As she started to reply, his mouth came down on hers and they were lost in desire and passion as they made love. Pocahontas could neither hear nor see. Her body, a thousand points of sensation and hunger, felt as if it would go through his skin and be one with his. Their passion devoured their senses until Pocahontas

301

was swooning, half animal in her responses. Their carnal rapture was matched by their intense commitment to each other.

It was a long time before they fell apart, exhausted by the ferocity of their emotions.

Again Smith whispered urgently into her ear that she must come with him. He told her he had found a place to build a house. She would be happy there, for it was near Pochins. Smith said he would arrange something with her father somehow.

It was the moment that Pocahontas had dreaded, but he covered her with kisses when she hesitated, and again they lost themselves in passion.

Finally, when they were quiet, she turned to him and said, her eyes full of tears, "My father will never allow me to live with you, and besides . . . "

At that moment Namon called to her from outside the cave: "Hurry, Pocahontas, a hunting party approaches—maybe our brothers!"

Smith gave her a little push. "Meet me here in seven suns, my love. I will take you then."

Pocahontas scrambled back up to the path just in time to see a party of hunters, including her brothers Pamouic and Secotin, coming her way. Had their forward scouts seen anything? She had to hope not. She often hunted alone these days, and her brothers knew it. They would not be suspicious. She waved to them and quickly made her way to the riverbank. She had to slip into the water before the men caught up with her or they would be able to tell immediately that she had been with a man, and one of the dirty ones at that. She was angry that she couldn't walk back holding the scent of her lover on her body until she came to the outskirts of Werowocomoco.

What was she to do? How could she tell her father that she was going to live with the Tassentasse chieftain? For she *was* going to live with him. She *would* meet Smith in seven days' time, but if she spoke about it to her father, he might imprison her. She couldn't take that chance. Pochins's latest wife had run away from her former husband and she wasn't punished. But she had not stepped away from her own people. No, Pocahontas would just run away. Smith was everything to her. She would leave her world and embrace his. Nothing would keep her from him now, nothing.

When Smith returned to Nonesuch, the 150 acres he had purchased from Pochins for ten swords, he found he had a group of visitors from Jamestown on their way back from a hunting trip. They wanted him to return with them to the fort; provisions had arrived from London with De La Warr that would be useful for building his house. Smith calculated that he could pick up his supplies and be back in three or four days, plenty of time before meeting Pocahontas and carrying her back with him to Nonesuch.

The next morning, after an evening of high-spirited celebration while marking out the foundations of the new house, the men prepared to leave for Jamestown by water. Smith agreed to transport the hunters' gunpowder in his canoe. As he picked up two bags of powder to go down the bank toward his craft, the gunpowder caught a spark from the campfire and blew up with a sudden explosion that shattered the calm. A tongue of orange light erupted, followed by a huge bang. Smith seemed to disappear in a cloud of smoke. Men rushed forward frantically trying to see through the acrid cloud, coughing and sputtering. They found Smith unconscious but still breathing. He was badly burned down the right side of his body where he had taken the brunt of the explosion.

When they recovered from their shock the men realized he was near death. Namon, the most powerful of the men with an oar, chose the strongest Englishmen. Together they rushed Smith by canoe to Jamestown, pushing their trembling muscles to exhaustion.

It was three days before Smith regained full consciousness. During those days he called out for Pocahontas time and again in his delirium. A new arrival from London, an expert with leeches who nursed him, could not understand what he was talking about and guessed the strange name he cried was someone he had known in his travels through the Balkans. Namon visited him frequently to check his progress. Appalled to see his strong friend semiconscious and panting with pain, he tried to cool his brow with wet compresses. Finally, on the fourth day, Smith opened his eyes and spoke. Namon could barely hear him but understood that he was saying something about Pocahontas. Did he want her to visit him here?

"Please don't disturb yourself, Captain," pleaded Namon, worried by the terrible weakness of his good friend. "I can try to bring Pocahontas to you, but I don't think our father will let her come to Jamestown."

Smith tried to talk further, but he couldn't control his voice. He had to tell Namon that he would meet Pocahontas at the gully and tell her of his plight. But the pain seared along his side in overwhelming waves, leaving him breathless and swooning after the slightest effort.

On the fifth day a fever and infection coursed through his body. The new onslaught sometimes rendered Smith unconscious and at other times left him trembling violently. A man less strong would have succumbed. Namon became so distressed by Smith's agony that he took matters into his own hands and sent a Powhatan, who was hunting near the fort, to Werowocomoco for special herbs to plaster on the burns.

The first person the hunter saw as he entered the town was Secotin. He told him he did not know which Tassentasse was burned but that his brother Namon needed herbs to heal him. Secotin knew his father would not allow anything to be sent to the Tassentasse camp, so he decided to keep the matter quiet and take the herbs himself. His curiosity was piqued.

Namon was deeply grateful when Secotin arrived at Jamestown. He pounded the herbs into a paste, which he immediately applied to Smith's body. Then he boiled up other herbs and forced the broth down his throat. The colonists were skeptical about these procedures, but they had seen that the bloodletting done a couple of days before had not helped Smith, so Percy had persuaded them that they should at least give the naturals' remedy a try.

Within two days Smith was able to speak haltingly. Both Namon and Secotin visited him and applied still more herbs, and Smith tried to acknowledge them. He asked weakly about Pocahontas.

"She is fine, she has a new husband," replied Secotin as Namon quickly put his hand on his arm as if to stop him.

"Husband?" Smith's voice quavered like an old man's. But he couldn't steady it. In his weakness his face crumpled as if a fresh explosion had torn his body.

"Yes, they were married at the beginning of the season of the new blooms."

That night Smith slipped back into semiconsciousness, and the colonists thought that it would be his last. Namon stayed by his side and persuaded them to help him wrap Smith in an herbal dressing, which they changed three times during the night. By morning there was little improvement and Namon began to despair. Finally that evening the fever broke and Smith's strong constitution began to take over. But it was two more weeks before he could leave his bed and take a few faltering steps.

The seven suns that Pocahontas had to wait before she could meet Smith again seemed interminable. She thought her heart would burst with happiness, and she was constantly afraid that her new mood would show and arouse suspicions. She did not feel like hunting, but she took long runs, with Kint streaking ahead of her, to work off some of her energy. She realized with relief that although she still felt the same sorrow about Rawhunt, she no longer saw his face.

Her only problem was Kokum. She knew that the Tassentasses put high value on having a woman who was theirs alone and who had never known another man. She wished fervently that the Tassentasses thought, like her own people, that an occasional time with another man was not important. Of course Kokum was not an occasional experience, but women did abandon their husbands sometimes, and it must happen in their culture, too, she thought. She knew in her heart that the only important thing was to be in Smith's arms. Then she could explain everything to him.

On one of the waiting days when the thunderclouds hung heavy and black, Mehta gave birth to a baby girl. There were celebrations and gift offerings, and Kokum proved to be an exemplary brother-in-law, showing interest in the child and helping to lead the festival dance in her honor. He even thought of a pretty name for the baby, Leweya, that Mehta and her husband liked.

Pocahontas continued to wait, her patience stretched to the breaking point. Finally the day that she was to meet Smith arrived. Her body trembled in anticipation and she had to pretend to Kokum that she had overtired herself at the festivities the day before. She had bidden her father a particularly affectionate good night the previous evening. She decided to take Kint with her; long before, her father had acknowledged that the greyhound was really her dog, and he certainly would not miss him.

She took a look around her in the clear morning light and realized that there was nothing that she would miss in her father's realm. She could never again truly belong to the life she was leaving behind after all she had learned from the colonists. She had thrown her heart and her mind into a new life. She was not sure that she could wholly belong to the world she was embracing, either, but she wanted and needed the challenge. In any case she would follow Smith into the jaws of the devil god Okeus if he demanded it of her.

She felt as if she walked on clouds of happiness as she followed the path toward the gully and Smith's cave. The trees looked greener, the flowers brighter, and the birdsong echoed the call of her heart. All the misery of the past months had fallen away. When she slipped joyfully down the gully and into the cave she realized that she was early. Smith had not arrived. She made herself a dry spot with leaves and twigs and sat waiting, clutching her knees to her chest and wondering happily what Smith had in mind for their life together. Kint waited patiently at his mistress's feet.

When the sun was overhead she wondered if Smith had gotten lost, but that was impossible, for surely Namon would be with him. She watched the birds darting through the forest during the noon heat while overhead she heard sea gulls cawing as they swooped toward the river. The sun marched relentlessly over and down the sky while Pocahontas became increasingly worried. When the shadows lengthened she knew that she had come on the wrong day. Yes, that must be the reason, she thought. I have miscounted the suns—the days, as the Tassentasses call them. She would return to her people and retrace her steps when it was daylight again.

She went home sorrowfully and returned the next day, and again the third and the fourth. By this time she was wrapped in such gloom she could barely put one foot before the other in her walk back to Werowocomoco. On the fifth morning despair gripped her completely as she went down to bathe. She prayed to the river goddess Ahone to forgive her. Then she prepared to float out to the middle and let the current do what it would with her. But as she stepped into the cool water, Kint's nose touched her hand. The dog had never entered the water before, but during the past days he had never left her side. He seemed to sense her deep distress. Now as she looked down at his fine head, his worried brown eyes seemed to plead with her. She reached down and stroked his ears. Somehow that made her feel better. Perhaps she should not give up so soon. Perhaps Smith would come for her after all. She had waited before; she must try and wait yet again.

At Jamestown, Smith nursed his injuries, but he knew it would be many months before he'd be able to lead an active life again. Certainly he could not build a house, and now that there was no one to share it with, he had lost interest. He did not let himself think about Pocahontas. If anyone but her brother had told him the news he would not have believed it. Her marriage created a wound that had not even begun to heal. To stay alive and regain strength, he clamped his emotions shut to any thought of her. George Percy urged him to go home to England. He needed a good doctor to treat him properly, and he could always return to Virginia when he had recovered.

After some hard thinking, Smith decided to give up his dream of finding a route to the Indies and great riches. He would return to England and take the faithful Namon with him. The two men sailed on the *Falcon* as the leaves on the trees started to turn.

CHAPTER
~•⚜•~ 18 ~•⚜•~

Werowocomoco, September 1609

As Pocahontas walked through the rows of tobacco plants and checked the leaves she noticed that the earth looked tired. The plants were not as healthy as they should have been. It was time to move to Rasawrack for a few seasons and give the earth here a chance to rest. Her father enjoyed his alternate capital, and the change exhilarated him. Rasawrack was close to Uttamussack, and the great chief could spend time there among his treasures.

Yes, she would see her father at sundown, for she had other news as well. It had been two moons since she had been in the women's house. She felt plumper and she was absolutely sure she was carrying John Smith's baby. She did not even entertain the possibility that the child was Kokum's. Her heart knew with total certainty that the last meeting with Smith had given her the child she now bore. She was not sure it was going to be news to her father that she was finally with child. He had spies everywhere, and the attendants at the women's house would have been delighted to gain status by telling him the news of her absence immediately. Certainly her father had been kind and generous lately, even though he had been busy with visiting chieftains, but his mood would not last. Something terrible would happen when she gave birth to a baby with hair the color of the sun. The priests would demand a child sacrifice, and her baby would be chosen for the sacrificial altar. Somehow she must save her child.

She had a plan. She would spend the next few weeks being the mischievous and charming daughter that she used to be, and this would bemuse her father. She would persuade him to send her and Kokum to one of the northern territories for a while, particularly since he was going to his second capital. She wanted to be near Kokum when he went on his sorties against the Monacans. Besides, she had never seen that part of the kingdom.

Powhatan thought it was an excellent idea and approved it the first time she approached him. Her father had another reason for wanting her to be among the Patawomekes along the Potomac River. It would suit him well to have his favorite child there to remind them of their powerful chief. He did not travel that way often enough these days.

Kokum too, was enthusiastic about the trip, although he was surprised to hear that Pocahontas wanted to go north. Mehta did not waste a second getting her father's permission to accompany her sister, who would surely need her during her waiting months. Her husband was on scouting expeditions to the south and would not be able to join her often, but that did not bother her. It would be at least two moons, however, before they would leave.

The rest of Pocahontas's plan was simple. Once she had birthed the child she would cross over the Potomac and throw herself on the mercy of the neighboring Susquehannas. Although seven feet tall, they were not an aggressive people, and since they did not particularly care for the Powhatans they would protect her from them. From that vantage point she could then reason with her father about the red-haired baby she would hold in her arms. Once her father gave his word that the two of them would not be punished, he would never go back on it. It was his first reaction, without time for reflection, that frightened her. It was impossible to go to Jamestown and throw herself and the baby at their mercy, exposing them to her father's full fury. So this plan was the only solution.

From the moment she had given up the idea of drowning herself, Pocahontas was determined to believe that one day Smith would send her a message. She prayed constantly to the god of sky and to Ahone the river goddess to bring them together again. When she had found she was with child she felt her prayers were partially answered, and every day she offered up a small sacrifice in thanks and supplication.

She often thought of sending word about the child to Smith at Jamestown, but she was afraid that he might take action that would harm them all. It would be better to wait until the baby was born and then decide what to do next. She was sure in her heart that Smith would be overjoyed with a child. Even so, she would have liked to consult someone about her problem, but she had no one to confide in. She had heard that there were Englishwomen now in Jamestown, and she thought wistfully that it would be so nice if one of them could become her friend.

Over the past year or more Pocahontas had begun to feel like a stranger among her own people. She knew that this was because she had begun to think like the Tassentasses. Somehow she had created a veil between herself and family and friends. It was not a conscious decision but a natural outcome of her new values and desires. The truth is that I do not belong to either people now, she thought. But as long as I am here, I must try to be more content in my father's world.

One person she saw a lot of was Thomas Savage, the lad close to her own age whom Admiral Newport had left with Powhatan. Thomas was a great success with Powhatan and even ate off the chief's royal plate. The boy had learned the language quickly, but he spoke with Pocahontas almost entirely in English; she wanted to improve her use of the language as much as she could. She in turn took Thomas on hunting forays from time to time, but they were never a success. He was much too clumsy, and as she told him kindly, every step he made awakened the entire forest.

"I am going to Jamestown," Thomas told her one cool morning when the leaves were thick on the ground. "Your father wants me to carry a message to George Percy. He is sending me with turkey, venison, and corn. The settlers are hungry. They cannot hunt or farm because the local chieftains are on the warpath again."

Pocahontas wondered for the hundredth time if she should send a message to Smith. No, better not. She rarely talked to Thomas about the settlers, for she was afraid that some chance comment he might repeat to her father would arouse Powhatan's suspicions. But why was her father suddenly sending all these supplies to the hated Tassentasses? He was certainly responsible for the harassment they were now suffering from the southern flank of the Seven Kingdoms.

"Why are you seeing Percy instead of Smith?" asked Pocahontas.

"Smith left for England almost two months ago with Namon, along with twenty turkeys and two flying squirrels as gifts for King James."

Pocahontas felt as if Thomas Savage had hit her physically in the stomach. For a moment she could not hear his voice. Her face must have revealed her shock, for she felt his hand on her arm and opened her eyes to see him looking at her with concern. "It is nothing," she said. "I felt suddenly faint."

314

Pocahontas knew she was not convincing, but Thomas would take what she said at face value—he was in a hurry. She did feel physically ill, but she would not give in. She needed strength, not only for herself now. But over and over in her mind the same question repeated itself: How could he have left without one word to her? How could he?

"Smith said he might be back next year," continued Thomas. "But as soon as he left, the Chickahominies and the Weanocs attacked the fort."

Of course, thought Pocahontas. The only person my father respected was Smith. He will now use his southern armies to overun the Tassentasses.

"Tell your people to be careful." Pocahontas dared say no more. She went home to bed and turned her face to the wall for the rest of the day. No one disturbed her, for most of the village knew she was pregnant.

Thomas Savage returned a couple of weeks later and told Powhatan that the Tassentasses had accepted the great chief's invitation to come to Werowocomoco to trade for food. They would send a force within the month.

When the time came for them to arrive, Pocahontas wanted badly to see the Tassentasses, watch their movements, and remember the happy times she had spent with them. She could watch their arrival on the way back from one of her hunting expeditions. She made her way through the woods to the town landing later in the day. When she saw the colonists' ships sail up the river, she climbed a tall elm, for she wanted to watch the greeting ceremonies from a discreet distance. No one then could observe her open enjoyment.

Two hundred warriors in fresh paint waited below. The feathered ends of their arrows trembled in a gentle breeze as the braves stood expectant but unspeaking. The ships dropped their last sail, and the well-remembered voices of the Tassentasses echoed across the water as they called commands. The colonists clambered over the sides of the ships and assembled on the dock quickly. Pocahontas could see from her perch in the tree that there were about sixty of them, their armor glinting in the sun.

The Tassentasses stepped forward confidently between the two flanks of Powhatan braves. Pocahontas stared longingly at their faces, trying to see if there was anyone she recognized, and yes, there were several she knew well. She was excited at the thought that later she might be able to talk with them, and she smiled to herself as she waited for the braves to throw their bows high in the air when they greeted their guests with yells of welcome. Instead, the air was suddenly thick with arrows. Their peculiar whining and zinging and the screams of the dying men shattered the forest calm. Within minutes there was not a Tassentasse alive.

Pocahontas could hardly believe her eyes. It had all happened in the time it took to draw a deep breath. The men who writhed on the field below were friends, except for the one she despised, Ratcliffe. As she stared in horror, she almost threw herself down out of the tree to protest the massacre, but reason prevailed. She would only be killed herself, for as her father's daughter she would be committing treason. Conflicting thoughts clashed in her mind. She was shocked at her father's treachery and deeply disturbed that she felt sympathy for both sides in the surprise attack. It was still another symptom of her terrible feeling of ambivalence. She slipped quietly home unobserved.

Two days later the sky at first light was heavy and gray. Thomas Savage left again for Jamestown, accompanied by two warriors to ensure his safety. He promised Powhatan that he would be back within the month. The great chief knew he would return, if only to eat because the English were starving. Powhatan's warriors had successfully besieged the colonists behind their palisades. His spies reported that the dirty ones were depressed and hungry. The massacre had destroyed their morale.

The day became progressively wetter. A wind blew fitfully at first, and then the trees began to sigh and sway. Pocahontas heard the priests' drums as they vibrated ominously and knew that the god of sky was angry. When he was this enraged, whole towns could be flattened and great paths of felled trees would scar the forest. Many of the townspeople hurriedly collected belongings and rushed for nearby caves or gullies that would give them some protection. Pocahontas joined her father who had sent a warrior to fetch her. He had his own underground tunnel that had been there for as long as she could remember. Over the years she had been bundled into its damp safety every time the angry god threatened. This time Kint was allowed in with them, but Pocahontas went reluctantly, as she had been unable to look Powhatan in the eye since the massacre. Where was Mehta? Her nursing servant and her child were with them, but no one had seen her.

The water lashed down in sharp, cold needles. It was late in the season for the god of sky to vent his fury. Generally it was during the warmer times that he streaked the sky with flashes of fire and hurled down great rolls of his voice at the earth. Now when he blew, the towering trees tumbled to the ground like weeds. It was one of the worst demonstrations of his wrath that Pocahontas could remember.

Not until dawn did the townspeople begin to straggle back from their hideaways. Even then, it was only a brave few, for most knew that the deceitful god of sky might suddenly return. Pocahontas slipped out of the tunnel. She loved to walk in the woods when the god was only a little angry, when the noise and the light answered a yearning for excitement in her heart.

The path toward town was strewn with twiglets, broken branches, and here and there an unrooted tree, while the air still felt turbulent and the god of sky made distant noises of displeasure.

There was a sharp sizzling noise. Suddenly Pocahontas felt her breath leave her body in a tremendous rush, and then she knew only complete darkness.

There were waves of pain. Through the grayness that seemed to encompass her like a smothering fur she could hear the priests chanting somewhere nearby. As she tried to open her eyes she glimpsed her old nurse, the faithful Wowoca who had guided her through her childhood. So she was in her own village, in her own bed. But why the agonizing pain? She groaned, and the world went black again.

When she regained consciousness, the pain was gone but she felt unlike herself, wan and weak. She heard her father's voice clearly, but it seemed distant. Yet she could see he was standing by the bed.

"Rest, Pocahontas," he said. "You were struck down by the branch of a tree."

"I do not have the child!" That was the pain, that was her weakness. Pocahontas struggled to sit up.

"No, the child is gone. Now you must do as the priests say so that you will feel better." Powhatan gave her a gourd filled with herbal broth to drink.

Pocahontas felt tears run down her face, but she was too weak to stop them. "How long have I been here?" she asked.

"Two suns," said Powhatan. "The priests say you will feel much better tomorrow."

For the next few days everything possible was done to make

Pocahontas feel comfortable. Many people left offerings at her door, and her father was solicitous in seeing that her every wish was met.

When she was stronger, her father came to see her again. As gently as he knew how, he told her that Kokum had been killed. It had happened in the storm, he said. He did not tell her that some of the townspeople had found him in a cave a good distance from the town when they sought protection there from the lashing rains during the great wrath of the god of sky. Kokum had been struck from behind by an arrow through his heart. They had also found Mehta kneeling over his body wailing in anguish. Since that day Mehta's husband had disappeared, and although no one spoke of it, the villagers knew Mehta's husband had finally discovered that her child was not his and that it was common knowledge. It was generally conceded that he had returned to his people in the north.

Pocahontas did not have the heart to tell her father that she did not miss Kokum at all. She did not let him see the flash of relief that must have shown in her eyes. Powhatan had been good to her despite her disloyalty to him. And she knew as soon as she saw Mehta that the death had somehow occurred because of something that had happened between Mehta and Kokum. She did not mention it to anyone because it did not make any difference to her. She had known from the beginning that Kokum was everything to Mehta. She felt sorry for Mehta, but she was sure there would be someone else in her life soon. Pocahontas's quiet joy at being free of Kokum was swallowed in grief for the loss of her child.

During her illness and recovery, Pocahontas remained deeply disturbed by her father's massacre of the sixty colonists who had come, invited and in good faith, to trade for food. At the time her loyalty had been divided and the horror of the drama

319

unfolding before her had stunned her. So it was only now as she lay recovering that she realized her father's treachery had created subtle doubts about him in her heart and opened her eyes to a different man from the father she had always loved. She needed to live apart from him for a while. She would go someplace where she could be independent of Powhatan and his aggression toward the Tassentasses. Someplace where she could lead a life of her own.

The townspeople arrived in Rasawrack as soon as the harvest was in. When the snows were on the ground, Thomas Savage joined them there from the fort at Jamestown and pleaded with Powhatan to give corn and provisions to his people. "They will not last the winter," he said.

The great chief, however, was adamant. "I am low in supplies for my own people. I have none to spare."

Thomas knew that the treasure houses were bursting with provisions and that the harvest houses were spilling over, but he could not say anything more. His excellent relationship with Powhatan was too valuable to jeopardize, and he needed his special position now more than ever. As he told Pocahontas later, "The colonists are dying in great numbers. They have no courage since the massacre and they have nothing to eat. One man has killed his wife and salted her. The other colonists wondered why he was not getting thin like them, and they found out that he was eating her. They hanged him."

Thomas did not add that shortly afterward when the colonists killed an attacking Weanoc, their morality did not deter them from roasting his body and eating it. Thomas had even feared for his own life because of the resentment the colonists felt toward him for not being able to intercede on their behalf and to persuade the great king to give them provisions.

Pocahontas's heart ached for the people suffering at the fort,

320

but there was nothing she could do for them. Her father was determined to finish off the colonists, and all her past efforts to sustain them seemed to have been for nothing. Powhatan thought her moodiness was due to her lost husband and decided that she should resume her task of collecting taxes. The travel and festivities would lighten her heart, and she would soon find a new husband. He had another alliance in mind with a chieftain's son from one of the northern territories of the Seven Kingdoms, but first she must be diverted from her sorrow.

Pocahontas traveled from Rasawrack for three and four days at a time to collect taxes, then returned to rest for several days. As soon as she felt secure in her new duties she decided she would move away and live on her own. Perhaps she could go to Pochins. In the meantime she dreaded Thomas Savage's occasional trips to Jamestown, for he always brought back increasingly grim news. By the season of the new blooms the population at the fort had dropped from 490 souls to 60. People had died from disease, starvation, the cold, and sneak attacks from the Weanocs and Chickahominies.

One day when it was beginning to be warm, Thomas Savage returned from the fort and took Pocahontas aside. "The colony is no more," he said. "Two new ships arrived, but they were stunned by the great loss of life and decided to abandon the fort. They finished stripping the buildings yesterday and they will sail away today."

Pocahontas looked at him stonily as despair crept over her. It had never occurred to her that the Tassentasses would leave. They were so strong; they had such miraculous equipment with which to work and fight. But, her father had won after all. His way of doing things had proved the most effective in the end.

321

Now John Smith would never return. She had held on to her fragile dream so staunchly, but now that, too, was gone.

London, 1609

In March, John Smith and Sir Edwin Sandys decided to meet in a favorite London tavern, the Cheshire Cheese, halfway between Westminster Palace and the dock near the Tower of London where Smith had his office. He had arrived first, smiled at the sign outside advertising a drink or tobacco for sixpence, then settled himself at a wooden table and ordered two mugs of mulled port wine. Quite a few people in the crowded room were using the new tobacco, he noticed, and clouds of smoke mingled with smoke from the fire. As the weak daylight outside faded, fog rolled in each time the tavern door swung open to admit a new customer, adding to the darkening interior. Smith waved his arm to clear the air around him and wondered if tobacco would be less dear once the trade from Virginia increased.

Outside on busy Fleet Street, the din of hooves clattered against the cobblestones, and Smith distinguished the sound of a horse stopping. That would be his friend Sandys. Sir Edwin's tall figure stooped as he passed under the low lintel of the tavern door.

"Plenty of tobacco here!" Sir Edwin slapped his gloves on the table, sat down, and reached for his mug.

"They are still experimenting in Virginia; this is Tobago stuff. But I can guarantee that once we settle down to farming in Virginia we will take over the market," replied Smith.

"De La Warr decided in the end to postpone his trip to the colony, but Newport and Sir Thomas Gates, the deputy governor, must be there by now. With nine shiploads of new settlers the fort should be strong enough to withstand any difficulties with the Powhatans. We are well placed now to make our effort succeed, Smith," said Sandys.

"My wounds are much better. I thought I would return in about six months' time. I am still keen to find a route to India," Smith replied.

"I hope you will reconsider. We need your help and advice here in London. Tobacco is important, but you cannot build an empire on smoke. We need to settle more townships up the Virginia coast and perhaps make another landing farther north. To beat the Spaniards we need a strong hold on the entire coastline. The glory of England depends on these ventures."

The smoke curled around the men as they bent over their table deep in plans for the New World.

At the Spanish embassy in London, Ambassador Pedro de Zuñiga, splendid in a green velvet doublet, waited for his envoy from King Philip III of Spain. Obeying the king's explicit orders, his London spies over the past few years had taken careful note of every ship that departed for Virginia, their armament, what supplies they carried, and who was aboard. They also recorded what route each ship took. Tonight Zuñiga had good news to relate.

When his countryman had been ushered in and seated and a bottle of sherry had been placed between them, the ambassador spoke: "I must ask you to return immediately to Spain. His Majesty will be delighted to hear that it looks as if the English colony has failed in Virginia. One of our ships arrived this week from Florida with a good wind behind her. It seems the Indians have successfully surrounded and blockaded the English fort. It has been impossible for the colonists to get food, and they are now eating their dead. Their numbers are so depleted that we hear there are only a few left from the hundreds who made up the population last summer. My news is a couple of months old.

They must all be dead now or too weak to put up a fight."

The ambassador stroked his pointed beard. "I do know that nine ships sent out to relieve them a year ago never arrived. If a few ships of ours were sent out now, I believe we could finish off what is left of the colony and start our own settlement along that part of the coast. In my opinion, this is a good time to move up from our southern holdings. We will see all of the New World under Spanish control soon!"

The two men smiled and raised their glasses in a toast.

CHAPTER
~:19:~

Rasawrack,
June 1610

Pasptanze, the tall chieftain of the Patawomekes, had
arching swan's wings perched on his shoulders. He
arrived for a visit two days after Thomas Savage had told
Pocahontas about the departure of the Tassentasses. Pocahontas
felt that the chieftain looked like a man who could be trusted. He
was kindly and his people were famous for their good manners
and gentle ways. They were not particularly strong in warfare,
however, and Powhatan often had to send small armies of young
men up from his southern tribes to protect Pasptanze's village
and the northern border of his kingdom from the mountain
tribes beyond. It also gave Powhatan's young warriors warfare
experience to prepare themselves for border skirmishes against
the Monacans.

Pocahontas had to get away, absolutely had to get away. She
was desperate. When she met Pasptanze she decided instantly
that she would go and live among the Patawomeke. She collected her things and told her father she was leaving with the
chieftain and his party when they returned to their Potomac
river lands. Powhatan did not protest. Pocahontas knew that he

327

was tired of her continual carping over the past moons about his treatment of the Tassentasses and about the opportunities that he had missed in not learning about their tools and weapons. She knew her father thought she was disagreeable and sad because she had lost her husband and her child, and so he forgave her. At the same time he was impatient with her ill temper.

Powhatan did not know that over the last two days Pocahontas had suffered agonies, knowing that the Tassentasses had departed forever. It was so final! She felt moments of sheer panic in her despair. The black wings of the crow seemed to beat on her relentlessly, and her nights had been drenched in the sweat of hopelessness that gaped like a void all around her. She could barely get a morsel of food down, and she knew her face looked stricken, but she couldn't control her mood. Every time she moved out of her house, people were so solicitous they drove her back inside again, for their kindness brought her close to tears.

She tried praying to the god of sky. But when, oh, when would he stop punishing her! Smith was gone, her baby was gone, the Tassentasses were gone. She had paid and paid for her wrongdoing. She did not allow herself to think for a second of her physical passion for Smith; that made her groan aloud in anguish. She grasped for something, anything, that would deliver her from this utter hopelessness. When the Patawomekes arrived it had seemed a signal from the gods for her deliverance.

Powhatan sent her off with her dog, three servants, and Pamouic and Secotin to keep an eye on her. At the last minute Thomas Savage and his friend Harry Spelman, who had remained behind when the other colonists departed, said they wanted to leave with her. They were deeply impressed with the kindness of the chieftain Pasptanze and intrigued by stories of the mountainous countryside in which he lived. They plotted to run away, as they knew Powhatan, who looked on Thomas as his son, would never allow them to leave. Pocahontas was too distracted, too deeply unhappy, to give them any attention, so she fell in with their plan. But five miles along the way, Thomas Savage lost heart and raced back quickly to his safe haven with Powhatan. He had been with him far too long and his loyalties were too entrenched. Harry Spelman remained with Pocahontas and the visiting Patawomekes.

The journey, the few days it took to settle in her new home and the change of scene gave Pocahontas some respite from her despair. Her brothers tried everything they could to cheer her up. And although Pocahontas was still too despondent to give more than a wan smile, she appreciated their efforts. She had duties to perform, however, for her father wanted her to start collecting taxes in the area immediately. No one had worked in the northern territory for a while, and he was concerned that he was not getting his due.

In the beginning, every effort seemed to overwhelm her, but she had to perform in front of the curious Patawomekes who escorted her and watched her every move. During the chores of seeing that the riches of the countryside were collected, her mind dwelled on John Smith.

Although the loss of him was almost impossible to bear, she also suffered from being deprived of exposure to the Tassentasses' way of living, the stimulation that learning about them had given her. Even when she was not able to be with them at their fort, at least she had known it was there. I have seen another world that I like and want to share and I will never see it again, she thought. At times Pocahontas felt that her familiar universe was a deep tunnel with no sunlight at the end. If only she had the child. It would have given her a lasting link with her other life. It would have kept alive the marvels of her times with the Tassentasses.

After a few moons had passed Pocahontas knew that she would somehow be able to live her life. She began to find enjoyment in talking to Harry Spelman. She learned a few more words of English, although she still had to communicate in a mixture of sign language and English or Powhatan. She had begun to hunt occasionally, for she was able now to concentrate on her quarry. And roaming the new countryside with Kint gave her some pleasure. It was far more mountainous than the southern part of the kingdom, and she particularly liked the way the river rushed tumultuously between the cliffs, creating sparkling waterfalls and whitecapped whirlpools. With the beginning of colder weather her appetite improved and her weight returned to normal.

One cool morning when the last of the leaves wafted from the trees and the smoke from the houses curled up into the still air, Thomas Savage arrived, accompanied by two of Powhatan's warriors.

It had been almost six moons since she had last talked to him, in Rasawrack, and Pocahontas, for the first time in a long time, felt happy to see someone. Powhatan's messengers came up regularly by canoe to carry down the taxes collected from his richest subjects. They would then ask questions about Pocahontas's health and well-being, but they never carried gossip and news for her. The long trip up the bay took three suns; it was as far away as Pocahontas could be within her father's realm.

In the excitement of meeting again, Pocahontas and the two boys, Harry and Thomas, talked at once in a babble of English and Powhatan. Secotin and Pamouic joined them around the fire, and she clapped her hands for a servant to bring them an herbal drink. She then asked for news of her people. In English, Thomas told her the town was moving back to Werowocomoco after the next autumn harvest. Mehta had remarried and was

330

expecting again. And Powhatan had lost twenty men in a battle near the fort at Jamestown.

"But I thought my father was at peace in the south and that there were no wars," said Pocahontas.

"He has always fought the English," replied Thomas.

"The English are no longer there," Pocahontas said in a flat voice.

"The English never left—at least not for more than a few hours."

Pocahontas was not sure she had heard correctly and repeated her question in Powhatan.

"The last of the colonists, along with a group that had arrived to join them after being shipwrecked nine months in Bermuda, boarded their ships at Jamestown and sailed off to return to England," Thomas explained. "They dropped anchor the first night at Mulberry Island, just at the mouth of the bay, planning to head into the Atlantic at daylight. The next morning they woke to see three ships beating toward them against the wind. It was Lord De La Warr, bringing men and supplies from London. He turned them right around, and he has been with them at Jamestown ever since. How is that for English luck?"

Pocahontas was stunned into silence while joy and hope radiated through her body. So the English had been there all along! She exulted to herself. John Smith could come back. He might even be back already! Her imagination leapt around in excitement. She only half heard and understood Thomas as he continued.

"De La Warr, as supreme governor of the colony, is doing all sorts of things to make Jamestown a success. You must come and take a look for yourself. Are you able to visit? I heard De La Warr and the captains talking about you. You are famous in England, and the governor wants to meet you."

Pocahontas shook her head as she said no. She had a question she had to ask: "Did any of the first captains return? Newport or Smith?"

"Newport did, but not Smith."

It wasn't important, she said to herself. She had learned to steel herself against bad news and grab at any element that could be promising. It was enough to know that the English were there and that Smith could return at any time. She pressed her hands together in an instinctive gesture of hope.

The English boys chatted on. They decided that when Thomas returned to Jamestown, Harry Spelman would go with him. Thomas said he preferred living with the Powhatans now, but he liked to visit the colonists from time to time. He asked Pocahontas if she planned to live with her father again. When she was silent he had to repeat the question.

Pocahontas jumped, then thought for a moment as she glanced at Secotin sitting impassive next to her. "I like it here among this tribe. It is peaceful. Perhaps I will return later."

As long as my father will not allow me to visit Jamestown, she thought, it is better that I remain here, away from the strife. I cannot stand the continuing warfare and the terrible pressure my father puts on the Tassentasses. One day perhaps my father will relent, stop the warfare, and let me see them again. Then I will return to Werowocomoco, and by then maybe John Smith will be in Jamestown. She hugged herself, trying to hide her hope after hearing Thomas's news.

The seasons slipped by. Her pain had now dulled to an intermittent ache. Pocahontas led a quiet life among the Patowomekes although she was accorded all the deference that the favorite child of the all powerful Powhatan deserved. Every so often her father would send a prospective husband up to meet her, but after a short courtship, she would firmly but kindly refuse the warrior. Her father did not press her, for he remained aware of her lost husband and child. On her part, she would occasionally find out through her contacts in Werowocomoco if her father had a change of heart about her visiting the fort. He remained adamant.

Harry Spelman returned to the north, saying that he had grown to like living among the naturals, but he would visit his own people at Jamestown occasionally and bring back news. Through him, Pocahontas was able to learn of developments in the colony and to hear about the the new governor.

De La Warr was a stern taskmaster. He made the men work a revolutionary six hours a day, in two shifts. They complained at being driven so hard, but the public buildings had been rebuilt and refurbished. On Sundays there were elaborate services in the church, which was now filled with wildflowers at all times. De La Warr presided at the rites from a chair richly embossed in velvet with a red velvet kneeling cushion at his feet. Afterward he would return to his ship, named the *De La Warr*, and entertain the lucky few who were invited to join him.

Pocahontas was fascinated to learn that the governor had abolished communal farming and had given each man his own land to cultivate. The Powhatans had always worked together in harmony to produce crops for everyone to share equally. What would happen when each person farmed for himself? This was another strange idea of the Tassentasses.

Some news was disturbing. Harry had overheard the captains discussing the possibility of abducting Powhatan children and returning them to England unless the great chief ceased his continual warring. She also heard that her aunt, a Weroansqua, had had twenty of her maidens seduce twenty English men and then had the men murdered in their beds. The Tassentasses wreaked revenge by burning her village and starting a town of their own on the ashes called Bermuda Hundred. Pocahontas sighed to herself. Would the warfare never end?

• • •

The Potomac River was so wide in places that it was sometimes difficult for Pocahontas to see to the other bank when she went for her morning bath, but today for the first time since she left her father's seat of power, she saw a ship. Her excitement made her limbs shake. Could John Smith be aboard? Was he coming to look for her? She did not dare hope and forced the thought from her mind. She looked at the ship's sails against the red dawn. It would not arrive at their dock until the sun was higher in the sky, so she would have time to offer a sacrifice to the devil god Okeus. She must run quickly. He must be placated. She must make certain no evil would occur.

By the time she had returned breathless from her sacrifice, Pasptanze, his braves, and Harry Spelman waited on the dock as the ship dropped anchor. Pocahontas's heart swelled with happiness as she caught the first downwind whiff of the Tassentasses, a smell she had not known for such a long time. How she used to hate it! Memory flooded back to her until she felt almost faint with the immediacy the odor evoked. She looked at the men on deck, her eyes searching. She dared not hope Smith was aboard, but she could not help herself. Each time she saw a red head her pulse quickened, but as the men began to walk down the gangway she knew he was not there. She felt a sharp dagger of pain, but it passed quickly. The leader of the men was talking to Pasptanze, using Harry as interpeter. They were all looking at her, so she stepped forward.

"The captain wants to meet you," said Harry. "He has heard a great deal about you. He wants to know why you don't come to Jamestown anymore."

Pocahontas replied in Powhatan. "Tell him my father forbids it, but I would like to send greetings to the people I know at the fort."

"The captain will tell the people in England that he has met

334

you and that I reside here with you. He says the English will be reassured to learn that the mighty king Powhatan's daughter does not wage war, as her father does, but gives shelter to the English. It will encourage people to come to Virginia."

There was feasting that night, and a cool breeze from the mountain blew down the valley. Dancers in brilliant colors twirled and pranced in abandoned relief after a day of burning sun. When the time came for the visitors to retire with the women of their choice, Pocahontas could see that the captain, who called himself Argall, looked at her with longing. Pasptanze noticed, too, and Pocahontas knew that he was waiting for a signal from her. He thought that as a widowed woman she must be hungry for lovemaking and the Tassentasse, although not of her rank, might be an interesting experience. She smiled pleasantly, but slipped away alone. There was only one Tassentasse she could touch.

April 13, 1613

The fair promised to be exciting. Captain Argall returned again on his ship for a visit to Powhatan's northern lands. During the greeting ceremonies he said that he would add some of his own effects to be sold at the festivities.

As Pocahontas walked through the forest toward the displays she suddenly realized that she had been through three seasons of the snow since she had come to the north and first met Argall with his ship the *Patience*. Time slipped by so quickly, but she felt that she had almost healed from her sorrows. Recently for the first time she had begun to wonder what she should do with her life.

Her father had offered to make her a weroansqua with her own territory, since she continued to refuse to marry. She supposed she would have to make a decision soon.

"Pocahontas, you promised to come with me to the fair," said Pasptanze. "Afterward we are invited aboard the great floating canoe!"

Pasptanze had said he would look after her, for her brothers had left that morning, to lead a group of young warriors from the south through their first experience with border warfare. As a matter of protocol Pasptanze often escorted Pocahontas to festivities. She noticed that Pasptanze and Argall had huddled together in deep conversation much of the evening before. It would not be about a war plan, she thought. Pasptanze was a kind man who did not make war unless he was directly commanded to do so by the great chief. No, they were probably planning some form of trade. She smiled as her father's handsome cousin Pasptanze stood before her. He had been the perfect host to her for a long time now.

"Buy my necklace!" someone called from a stand at the fair.

"Three shells will give you the best pair of moccasins in the Seven Kingdoms!"

The sellers' calls could barely be heard above the din of the mingling crowd on the riverbank. Greetings, haggling, and the exuberance born of a good bargain were at full pitch. Children raced around, sometimes snitching a trinket, not caring if they were caught and cuffed around the ears. Young unmarried people wore their finest paints and feathers, for there was more than merchandise on display in the bright sunlight.

Pasptanze was at Pocahontas's elbow, guiding her first to one pile of goods, then to another, solicitous at every turn. He steered her to the finest skins, found the whitest shell necklace, but discarded it quickly when it looked yellow against the flash of her teeth when she smiled. After every merchant's wares had been explored, he piled her bowl high with roast meats, breads, strawberries, gooseberries, and blueberries.

"Now we will go to the ship, Pocahontas. The Englishmen

want to entertain you, for you are the heroine of their fort!"

Pocahontas hesitated. She had not had such an enjoyable time for many, many moons. Surely her father would not mind a quick visit to a floating island. He had never specifically forbidden such an expedition. It would be harmless and a special treat after the pleasant day. "Yes, yes, I will go," she said, "but only for a few moments."

Pasptanze smiled as he held out his hand. With his wife on the other side of Pocahontas they walked to the dock. The chieftain called to the boatswain who waited in the shallop. Pocahontas realized as she watched their movements that the crew must have hoped she would visit them, for the men seemed to be prepared and moved quickly. She was on the deck of the *Patience* in a matter of minutes.

"The Princess Pocahontas!" the watch bellowed.

The captain was at her side almost before she turned around. Samuel Argall had dark hair and a lithe body on a tall frame. He knew he had charm and used it liberally. He quickly ushered the three of them belowdecks to his cabin.

"You do me great honor, Princess," he said as he ushered them to their seats.

The strangeness of the room made her brown eyes snap with excitement. Her curiosity about everything around her, so long subdued, returned almost like a long-lost friend. Her mind felt alive and quick as a hummingbird darting from one thought to another. If only she could speak their tongue fluently, she fumed to herself in frustration. In halting English and sign language, she asked about the fort, about the people she knew, and about Henrico and Bermuda Hundred, the new towns she had heard of. She asked questions about everything she could see—the furniture, the navigational instruments, the charts. She was so engrossed in her questions and Argall's courteous replies that daylight was fading before she realized with a start that she and

337

Argall were alone in the captain's cabin. Where was Pasptanze? She half rose.

"Please be seated, Princess, I believe they have left the ship."

"But I must go, too. How could they leave without me?"

"They did not intend to take you with them."

Pocahontas felt a thrust of fear. She said, "I do not understand."

Argall's face was gentle as he replied, "We intend to keep you with us for a while. A visit, you might say."

"My father will be furious and send his warriors. Don't you understand? He will burn your towns and drive you all into the sea!"

"Dear Princess, our hope is that, because we have you with us, we can persuade your father to cease his attacks altogether."

Fury hit Pocahontas like a blow. Her eyes glittered and narrowed with outrage. With rigid arms she brought her fists down on the table with a crash. In harsh Powhatan she cried, "You have made me a prisoner—a hostage!"

Argall sat back abruptly in surprise. This was not the gentle creature he had heard about. "Please do not be upset," he pleaded. "No one will harm you. You will be given every consideration."

Pocahontas was momentarily speechless. She stood up and began to pace the cabin. How dare they abduct her, the daughter of the most powerful man in the world? She had to get off this ship. She must get a message to Pasptanze. He would send warriors to rescue her immediately. She made a quick move toward the door, but Argall was by her side in one long stride and snatched her hand from the latch. In a lightning-quick movement Pocahontas dealt a blow to the side of his neck. Argall yanked her away from the door and held her firmly in his arms as she struggled to free herself.

"You are wild after all," he said, his mouth just inches from her ear. The scent of him almost made her ill. She went limp, but Argall still held her. "You are a lovely creature. You must not panic; no one will harm you." He put his hand on her smooth black hair and let it rest. It was almost a caress. Then he released her.

Pocahontas stood before him, her hands clenched at her sides, and said in her flawed English, "I am not afraid of you. I want only to speak to the chieftain, Pasptanze."

"I am afraid, Princess, it will do you no good. He is the one who made it possible for us to have you here."

Pocahontas recoiled as if she had been struck. Pasptanze, the kind and loyal chieftain, had betrayed her! She could barely believe her ears. Then she remembered the past evening and the private conversation between the two men. So this was what they had been planning. Anger made every pulse in her body beat like a drum. Had her brothers known about this treachery? They were supposed to keep watch over her. Were they faithless, too? Or had they left for the north with the young recruits not knowing about her plight? Argall stood waiting politely. Then he bowed and said, "May I show you where you will sleep? Tomorrow we sail for Jamestown."

Her mouth was stiff and her voice tight with anger. "What about my clothes and my dog?" she asked.

"They are on their way to the fort with Harry Spelman."

They had thought of everything. This was obviously a carefully structured plan.

Argall struck a brass gong with a mallet. A sailor appeared instantly; he must have been on guard outside the cabin door.

The captain said, "Show Princess Pocahontas to the other cabin. It will be hers for the duration of her stay with us."

Pocahontas swept past the sailor into the adjoining cabin, her eyes smoldering. She looked around her small prison and clutched her arms to herself as her hatred for the strong odors of the men and their ship returned with a vengeance. How would she be able to stand this imprisonment? They were despicable cowards, all of them, her men and the dirty ones, for incarcerating her, a woman of superior rank.

She inspected the bunk where she was supposed to sleep. It was crawling with bugs, so she snatched up the linen and threw it out of the porthole. Until her own things arrived, she would sleep on the wooden deck. She heard a knock at the door.

A sailor with a pleasant face stood in the doorway and said, "The captain would like to know if you will join him at his table for supper."

Pocahontas answered with a brief no. The sailor left, but soon returned with a bowl of something that looked inedible, which he set on the small wooden table under the porthole. The table, a chair, and a chest crowded the small space. Even in her fury, Pocahontas was interested in this furniture. She had not seen any for a long time.

She sniffed the food and immediately called the sailor to remove it. Then she sat on the floor and leaned against the wooden partition separating the two cabins. With her keen ears, she could hear men talking in the captain's cabin, but she was too angry and tried to concentrate on their English words. The day had been exhausting. Later when it was dark the sailor knocked again and entered with a lighted candle, which he put on her table and departed. She got up, went over to the table, and blew it out furiously.

CHAPTER
~•≈ 20 ≈•~

On board the Patience,
April 14, 1613

Pocahontas woke at dawn after a fitful night trying to sleep on the hard floor. It was impossible for her to ignore the smells of the ship.

Breakfast came and again she sent the food away, but the sailor returned almost immediately with some dried fruit. She wondered if it had come from Pasptanze's store of foods. The thought made her push the plate aside.

She felt demeaned, like a pet hare to be bartered for and patronized. She also felt helpless. Her mood swept from anger to sadness and back again, but she was not afraid. She said a quick morning prayer to Ahone and to the god of sky but not to the devil god Okeus. He was now the focal point of her anger, for she felt that he was responsible for her troubles. She felt that nothing more could happen to her except torture and death. The devil god's evil had permeated and destroyed parts of her life, despite all her prayers and sacrifices. If the priests knew how she thought about Okeus, they would denounce her, maybe even sacrifice her, for the priests derived their awesome power from the devil god, and he above all was to be obeyed. No, she would

343

pray only to the god of sky and to Ahone the river goddess.

She could hear the thud of running feet as the ship creaked and groaned into action. In spite of her emotions she felt keen curiosity about what was happening on the ship. She heard an unfamiliar flapping and thought it must be the white banners they put up to catch the wind. Then the ship began to roll gently from side to side. She even felt a slight surge of anticipation as she looked out the porthole and saw the riverbank slip by quickly. She was so high up it was like traveling along in a treetop, and she wondered if any of her people had traveled so high and so fast before. She shivered slightly with the thrill of it.

After a long time the sailor returned and asked her if she would like to go up on deck for some fresh air. She spent the day leaning against the railing of the ship, the soft wind ruffling her hair and the sun slowly melting her anger. It was warm, and the trip down the Potomac River was gentle. Toward nightfall Argall ordered his men to drop anchor before they entered the unpredictable waters of the bay. By the time Pocahontas had shared an evening meal with Argall and two of his officers in the captain's cabin her frame of mind was much improved. She found Argall's courteous manners and readiness to answer her many questions gratifying, and for long stretches of time she almost forgot she was a prisoner. During the day she decided that she was not angry at the Tassentasses but at her own people. The Tassentasses were using her to stop the fighting and establish peace, whereas Pasptanze had betrayed her. For what reason, she could not guess.

When she returned to her cabin she reminded herself that she had wanted to spend time with the English. She had tried through many, many moons to persuade her father to let her go to the fort. This was not the way she would have chosen to be reunited with the people she had grown to admire, but as she had no choice in the matter she should really thank the gods that she was able to be with the Tassentasses for a while. I am certain, she thought, that when my father secures my release he will never allow me to return.

She heard men's voices droning on in the adjoining room as they savored their wine and tobacco. She had ignored the voices in the past; it was too difficult to grasp their strange tongue without being able to see their expressions, but suddenly she heard her father's name mentioned several times.

"Powhatan may not end the war because we have his daughter, but at least he will realize how powerful we are. Now we have extended plans to establish settlements two hundred miles, both north and south of the fort."

"Yes, but we must also make Virginia attractive to more colonists. This destructive war with the great king has to stop."

"It was easy enough to capture the princess. We simply promised Pasptanze that we would be his ally in any battle with Powhatan should the great king retaliate, and we gave him a kettle that he wanted."

Pasptanze betrayed me for a kettle! Pocahontas could hardly believe her ears. "Kettle" was one of the first words John taught me, she recalled, as her mind flashed back to a sunlit meadow and the vitality of the man with red-gold hair. She hugged her arms close to her body as she listened.

"We will keep the princess on board or in Jamestown until we come to terms with her father. That may take a few months."

Pocahontas did not want to hear any more. She was resigned to her fate but not to the fact that Pasptanze had betrayed her for a kettle. She was incensed. It took her a long time to fall asleep, and before she did she wondered how Pasptanze could have treated her so shabbily. There must be someone else behind this plot, she thought. Secotin?

• • •

The thunder of running feet on the deck overhead woke Pocahontas at dawn. There was a different tempo to these steps. They were quicker and harder. She immediately felt a sense of urgency. Then came a sharp rap on the cabin door.

"The captain bids you good morning," said the sailor. "He wants to see you on deck immediately."

It was a pale sunrise, warm but with a good breeze. The small group of men around the captain parted when she approached the bridge. She noticed with surprise that two other ships were also anchored far away in the bay.

"I bid you good morning, Princess," said Argall. "We know that your people have better eyesight than we do. Can you tell us the markings and colors of the flags on those ships on the horizon?"

Pocahontas strained her eyes in the increasing light. The sky was streaked with gold and pink but still gray with the remnants of night. She was able to make out the colors and markings on the larger ship but could see nothing on the smaller one. She described the flags to the captain.

"A Hollander," said one of the officers, "with perhaps a prize ship or a second Hollander."

"Send a longboat over to hail them. We want to be friendly," ordered Argall. "Tell the crew to go alongside the vice admiral's smaller ship, not the admiral's."

By the time the sun was well up, the longboat was alongside the smaller ship, but the men did not disembark. Instead they rested their oars as the officer planted his feet firmly in the rocking boat and hailed the strangers. Those who waited on the *Patience* were startled to see him sit down abruptly and the seamen drop their oars and begin to row furiously toward their own ship. Pistol shots echoed through the air. The water around the longboat spewed up in short, white spray near the hurrying

346

men straining at their oars. The two strange ships had run up their sails and were bearing down on the *Patience*.

"Spaniards!" yelled the officer, as the longboat drew alongside the *Patience*, his vessel splintered by bullets. "No men hurt!"

The men rushed to secure their boat and scrambled furiously up the rope ladders and aboard the ship.

With a shuddering roar, the Spanish ships opened fire against the 160-ton *Patience*. The sea spewed up geysers of water all around them as the shells landed harmlessly in the sea.

"Perfidious Spaniards!" Argall called to his officers. "Hoist the sails!"

"The vice admiral is on our starboard side!" yelled a hand.

"Prime the guns!"

Pocahontas had never heard so many big guns in action. The Spanish broadside stunned her. She did not know that such noise was possible, even from the god of sky. Hands over her ears, she crouched down, forgotten.

"They have twenty-two guns on one ship and sixteen on the other," cried Argall as he rallied his men. "Fire!"

The noise was like the end of the world. Pocahontas could not help allowing a slight cry to escape her lips. She shrank up against the bulkhead. The thought flashed through her mind that perhaps she should go belowdecks, but she dismissed it instantly. She knew she would feel trapped there.

She saw that the *Patience*'s gunfire had struck the smaller ship, tearing gaping holes in its side. The vice admiral's ship veered off and lay dead in the water. The larger ship slowed its advance upon them from windward, took down her Holland flags and ran up the Spanish colors. Both ships had ceased their fire.

She came alongside the *Patience*, and the Spanish captain hailed the English. What was their business and where were they bound? Argall responded that they were en route to their lawful territory in Jamestown and that they were in the King of England's waters. The Spanish ship then claimed that the waters belonged to Spain and demanded that the English strike their sails for King Philip.

"We wish you no harm and we go in peace," called Argall, "but these are English waters and we intend to proceed to our territory in the name of King James."

The English watched as the captain on the other ship disappeared belowdecks with some of his men. Within minutes they reappeared. The Spaniards then opened fire with their heavy guns followed by a volley of small shot. Their men screamed every form of obscenity at the stunned English.

The *Patience* was enveloped in smoke as the two ships raked each other with volleys of gunpowder. Pocahontas for the first time felt fear. She didn't know where to go; there was no sanctuary. She had to endure the fire-raked ship or jump into water churned white by the falling shells. The Spanish ship, with two of its masts broken and tilting crazily, pulled alongside the *Patience* and prepared to grapple. Gunsmoke was so thick that her throat felt raw and she could barely see. The decks were pink with blood and black with gunpowder as the men from both ships swarmed over the railings for hand-to-hand combat. Argall was everywhere, sword in hand, inspiring his men. The battle roiled in fury, but neither side showed an advantage until an Englishman bellowed, "Their captain has fallen. Their captain has fallen!"

The Spaniards retreated to their own ship with the English in pursuit. Pocahontas dared to raise her head and creep out of her corner. Several men lay nearby, twisting in pain. After rushing for a pail of water, she tried to soothe and bind their wounds. She could do little but stanch the flow of blood and rest her hand on a man's brow for a moment of comfort. She was half incapacitated herself, her ears deafened by the guns, her mind swirling with the sights she had just witnessed.

After what seemed an interminable time, the sounds of battle subsided, and the English seamen began to return to the *Patience*.

The smaller Spanish ship, badly holed, had managed to slip away. "We have killed off most of the men on that one," one of the officers called as he sheathed his sword.

"Put the prisoners belowdecks in the admiral's hold. Leave a skeleton crew of ours on board, and we will tow her into Jamestown. There is no treasure, but enough of their own things to give a showing. When we pack these Spaniards off to the West Indies they will have a story to tell about who rules the seas in this part of the world." Argall's voice was triumphant but exhausted.

Suddenly he saw Pocahontas. "God's blood! What are you doing up here? You are supposed to be below."

"I had to help," replied Pocahontas, her face streaked with gunsmoke.

"It is too rough for you here." Argall's tone gentled. "My men will take care of the fallen. We were very lucky. We lost only a few. You are a brave woman, but now please return to your cabin. These are exhausted men and we do not want to have to worry about you now."

A sailor escorted Pocahontas to her cabin, where she slumped to the floor. Her ears rang from the crashing clamor of the cannon, and she felt they would never be the same again. She had witnessed many torturings and sacrifices, but never a battle, and found the latter by far the worse to endure. It was too unpredictable. Anything could happen at any time. How brave the English were! Outnumbered and outgunned, they won with skill, courage, and few losses.

It took two days to repair the damage to the *Patience*. Finally she sailed down the bay before a good wind, towing the Spanish ship. As they prepared to round Point Comfort, toward

Jamestown, the heavier Spanish ship, with a long shudder, settled dangerously low in the water. The crew and prisoners were evacuated quickly. The gold, silver, and jewelry had already been put aboard the *Patience*. Argall, pacing his deck, was furious he could not sail to the fort with his battle trophy. He maneuvered the two ships into the calmer James River and cut the tow line. He decided to send back a ship and crew to see what could be salvaged as soon as they docked.

Their progress was slow, but the blue water sparkled in the sun and sea gulls perched on the ship's rail and swooped along their wake. Pocahontas stood at the bow of the ship eager to catch her first glimpse of the fort. It had been so long. Perhaps John Smith had come back from England! This hope was forever alive within her. If he was not there, she promised herself not to be disappointed and to remember there was always another day. Even so, she knew she would continue to carry an aching emptiness.

As they approached the fort, she was amazed to see what looked like an arrow pointing up into the sky. She clutched an officer's arm as he explained good-humoredly that it was the spire on the new church. The building was enormous. And so many people were scurrying about! The fort now had as many people as Kecoughtan, the largest town in the Seven Kingdoms. The dock was jammed with a jostling crowd as the *Patience* maneuvered into position so that her longboats could guide her up to the pier.

Pocahontas scanned the crowd, searching for the familiar red hair. In her hunt she realized that the faces turned up to them were new. Where were the people she had known? Why, there were women, she noticed, and her eyes quickly took in the strange clothing that they wore.

Suddenly a voice cried out, "Look, it is the princess! It is Powhatan's daughter!"

Pocahontas waved to one of the carpenters she knew from the old days.

He cried, "She brings us good luck! She always brought good luck. Three cheers for the princess!"

They were happy to see her! People who did not know her were waving and cheering even though she was a prisoner. But still it was heartwarming to know that after so long a time the Tassentasses remembered her. Her mind harked back to the many trips she had made through two seasons of the snows bringing supplies and exchanging messages, negotiating, smoothing the way so that the two peoples could live in harmony on the same land. And now, six seasons of the snow later, six years, and her father still waged war against them. She sighed.

Suddenly her eye found Harry Spelman in the shifting crowd of people. He had her dog with him! Their overland trip must have been fast, but they had not been delayed by marauding Spaniards. She felt Captain Argall's hand on her arm as he indicated that they could now leave the ship. He told her as they stepped into the crowd that he was taking her to the deputy governor, Sir Thomas Gates. She would be in his care until her father negotiated for her.

The townspeople pressed around her, gawking with curiosity at the famous Indian princess. Many of them were there because of Pocahontas. The tales they had read and heard about her and her kindness had reassured them about making the dangerous trip to the New World. They touched her skirt and tried to feel her hair before Argall put a stop to that. But Pocahontas was oblivious to it all, for Harry was approaching with her white greyhound. It was hard to tell who was happier to see her, the dog or young Spelman. For the first time in many days, Pocahontas felt like herself again.

Sir Thomas Gates was a spare man, but he managed a wintry

smile when his pretty captive was brought before him. He had been with the colonists since he came to their rescue after the bitter winter of the starving time three years before, and now he had a weapon in the form of the royal princess as a hostage to negotiate an end to the constant battles. He made her welcome.

"Princess," he said, "we will send one of our prisoners, one of your father's men, to the great king to demand the return of our men whom he has taken captive, and the arms and tools that have been stolen over the past months. We will also ask for peace between our peoples. If the great king complies, you will be free."

Sir Thomas watched his prisoner's reactions. He knew she was a skilled negotiator in her own right.

Pocahontas felt on familiar territory. It was a new twist to the old story between the Tassentasses and her own people. "I feel confident that my father will meet your demands," she replied, thinking that Powhatan would accede to all the points except to stop the war. But the colonists would not know that until she was back at Werowocomoco.

Sir Thomas turned to Captain Argall. "I have arranged for Princess Pocahontas to stay with the Reverend Mr. Alexander Whitaker on his farm near Henrico. It is surrounded by four forts, so it is eminently secure. If you will be kind enough to escort her there, she can await her father's summons in the protection of a man of God and his lady."

CHAPTER

Rocke Hall, Henrico,
April 1613

"Repeat after me, Pocahontas: 'Our Father, who art in heaven, hallowed be thy name.' "

She parroted her response with care. The Reverend Mr. Whitaker was relentless about instructing her in Christianity, and Pocahontas found what he had to teach her interesting. But her mind was too full of new experiences to grasp it all.

Pocahontas fingered the dress she wore. She couldn't get used to the material; it was soft, but it had no substance, unlike her skins, which had depth and richness. She felt different wearing a dress, too, more constrained. It was interesting that when she put on her doeskins in the privacy of her room, she returned to her old sense of freedom. Her best dress, the one she was told was for special occasions, made a rustling noise. The swishing sound it made gave her a feeling of importance.

"Thy kingdom come, thy will be done on earth as it is in heaven," the reverend continued.

They pray to their God even more often than we do to ours,

thought Pocahontas, but they offer no sacrifices! She had been able to offer only one toad to the river goddess Ahone in the eight days that she had been with the Whitakers at Rocke Hall, but she felt sure Ahone understood. Pocahontas did not want to offend her hosts, and she remembered vividly the horror the Reverend Mr. Hunt had shown when she offered sacrifices that long-ago spring when the colonists first arrived.

Pocahontas did not tell the Whitakers that it would be easy for her to slip away unseen into the forest at any time, for they and the English soldiers were poor jailers and she was at home in the woods. She stayed because she, too, wanted the warring to end and because she found her new life fascinating. Each day there were many new things to learn.

" 'Give us this day our daily bread and forgive us our trespasses as we forgive those who trespass against us.' "

She enjoyed having her own chair, table, and chest in the small room that was given to her. Her bed was as comfortable as her own couch of furs at home. The food was bad, but she had been helping Mrs. Whitaker, a thin, kind woman, and her maid in the kitchen and they were receptive to some of her suggestions, a few basic steps learned from watching the cooks in Werowocomoco. The tasteless food was not really their fault, for they had never seen tomatoes, potatoes, corn, pumpkin, and turkey before. Mrs. Whitaker said those foods were not available in England.

" 'Lead us not into temptation but deliver us from evil.' "

Pocahontas finished the prayer after her host and waited dutifully for the English lesson that was to follow. This was her favorite time of the day. The minister, whose round cheeks had two permanent pink spots on them, told her she had a special aptitude for the English language, which encouraged her. She was learning her prayers by heart and luxuriated in the challenge of new words, as she had when John Smith was her teacher. She knew that her fluency had increased since she had returned to the colony.

Suddenly she heard horses' hooves prancing to a stop outside the door and a sharp pull on the bell. The maid scurried to pull the door open and found Captain Argall on the doorstep. He strode in with greetings for them both.

"Pocahontas," he said, "we have news from your father. He is deeply grieved that you are our prisoner, and he beseeches us to treat you well. How are you, Princess?"

"Very well, Captain."

"Powhatan has asked me to take my ship into his waters, where he will meet our demands for the return of our men and weapons and give us corn. Once that is done, he expects me to deliver you to him."

Pocahontas nodded in reply.

"If you are ready, Princess, we will leave in the morning."

Pocahontas bowed her head to hide her consternation. So soon! She had just arrived! She had thought her father would take a long time to barter for her return. How would she be able to follow closely the movements of ships and await the possible return of John Smith? The thought struck her that all her life she had been a prisoner to her father's demands and restrictions. She had accepted her duty to her powerful parent, but she realized now that with the English, when she was literally captive, she had more freedom than ever before.

Her face reflected its usual calm as the two men discussed the latest news in the colony and gossip from the letters that had arrived on a ship a few days earlier. The doorbell clanged again.

"Ah, we have John Rolfe to dine."

Mr. Whitaker rose to greet his guest. Pocahontas was too pre-occupied to give him her full attention, but she saw a tall man in his twenties with wavy brown hair and a strong face.

During dinner, when Rolfe was seated next to her, she was pulled from her reverie when he questioned her about tobacco. He was a serious farmer of the crop and wanted to know how often she felt it was necessary let the land lie fallow. She told him of her people's methods, but he questioned them. She found it gripping to debate the merits of his methods of farming tobacco versus her own. She was loath to see him go at the end of the evening and said so, but he reassured her that he often dropped by.

"I am returning to my father in the morning," she replied in a flat voice.

The minister's wife insisted that Pocahontas take her maid, Carrie, as far as Jamestown. It was unseemly, she said, for a royal lady to travel unaccompanied. Pocahontas and Carrie boarded the *Patience* as soon as they arrived at the fort, and Carrie suggested that she change into the rustling taffeta dress for a meeting and dinner with Sir Thomas Gates and Sir Thomas Dale, the acting governor of the colony.

The gown was pale blue, trimmed with white lace. Pocahontas was amused to see that both men's eyes sparkled when they saw her, and each bowed low over her hand. She was glad that she had let the maid dress her heavy hair high and off her face, though she wished she had some of her own pearls to wear.

She was grateful, too, that the minister and his wife had taught her to use cutlery. Although at times she felt awkward, she knew she was making a good impression. The men were intrigued with her now as a person rather than as a pawn in their game with her father. I must remember, she said to herself, how important it is to present myself well and to adopt the customs of my host.

Both knights questioned her in detail about her stay with the Whitakers, and she could not conceal the enthusiasm she felt for her temporary home. Her eyes glowed as she replied that she was just beginning to learn about Christianity and the Scriptures, and she told them how much her vocabulary was improving. She was sure she would learn to speak perfectly if only she could have constant exposure to the English tongue for a few weeks.

The next morning she put on her soft doeskins. By returning to Werowocomoco she knew she was allowing a door to be slammed shut. She could only hope and pray that it would not be closed forever. As she left the tiny cabin and went up on deck, her feet felt as if they were weighted with stone.

"Princess, I have news you may not like." Samuel Argall's face was concerned as he greeted her. He made a movement as if to touch her arm but caught himself. "Sir Thomas Dale decided last night, after a talk with Gates, that it would be unwise for me to take you with me today. We have not finished our negotiations with your father and in order to avoid any misunderstandings or incidents, the other leaders of the colony wish you to remain here for a while longer. They will arrange to send you back to the Whitakers, where they understand you were comfortable."

He did not add that Gates and Dale had been struck by the opportunities that Pocahontas presented. If she became a Christian, what a milestone that could be toward uniting the two people! Her conversion could lead the entire Powhatan nation into Christianity and establish the fact that English Protestants, not Spanish Catholics, had come to Virginia to stay. They had decided that unless the great king met every one of their demands, they would keep Pocahontas. Furthermore, they did not want her to travel with Argall for fear that Powhatan's men might try to recapture her.

Pocahontas was so happy to have a reprieve that she threw herself into her work at the farm in Henrico with fierce enthusiasm. She rushed through her household chores with speed and thoroughness and gladly ran any errand. Within a week she had learned all the household words in English. She pored over the Bible and the catechism with painful intensity, trying to decipher the words and paid careful attention to her twice-daily lessons. Throughout the day she asked question after question.

Mrs. Whitaker was as kind as her husband and as patient. Both realized that their captive guest was exceptional and they gave her as much attention as they would have a daughter. They were both gratified that behind the solemn expression of their charge was an affectionate girl.

It was well into May and the honeysuckle's sweet scent permeated every corner of the house when a messenger arrived with a letter from Argall, which was read to Pocahontas. Her father had returned half the arms and most of his English prisoners but had not produced the stolen tools or the corn. Dale and Gates sent their regrets, but said that under the circumstances it was necessary for Pocahontas to remain in the care of the English for a while longer.

A few days later John Rolfe returned. He was delighted to see Pocahontas again, and they resumed their discussion of tobacco farming and threw themselves with gusto into an argument about the merits and uses of various herbs. When Rolfe returned within a week, he disagreed with her methods for hunting birds and deer. He made a third visit within a couple of days, and they wrangled over the best method for curing skins.

In June the minister decided it was time for Pocahontas to come to church with him and Mrs. Whitaker. She could recite several prayers from memory and would be able to keep up with the congregation. Like most Powhatan women, she had a good singing voice. During the service, the Whitakers were proud to hear her voice raised in song.

John Rolfe, who sat a few pews behind the Whitakers, found that Pocahontas's voice distracted him from his devotions. He was a pious man, and the religious words sung by the exotic young natural created a clashing dichotomy in his heart. He had to admit that he was strongly drawn to the lovely creature from the wild. He made up his mind that when he called on the minister in the future he would help Pocahontas with her Bible study. He would be doing the right thing if he helped her along the road to Christianity.

As her song soared over his head, he tried to pray for the souls of his young wife and newborn baby who were lost near Bermuda when their ship had wrecked during a violent storm while the three of them were en route to Jamestown. The ache of that night three long years ago, when he had held his wife in his arms while her breath died away, had lessened in recent weeks.

He had thought of writing to his family home, Heacham Hall in Norfolk, to ask his father to arrange a suitable bride for him, but somehow he had never gotten around to it. He had the uncomfortable feeling that he was partially blamed for leading his young wife to her untimely death. His grandfather, a rich man, had helped finance new ships for the old queen to defeat the Spanish Armada and could not understand why John had gone off to a strange land when there was plenty to do looking after the family affairs at home. Also whatever bride they picked might not be compatible, and life in the New World was too difficult to risk any added friction. But Rolfe felt he could do good for God and the church and make up for past errors if he devoted some of his spare time to the conversion of a heathen. And the first conversion at that!

Spring passed into summer, summer into autumn. There was not a word from Powhatan. Dale sent messages to Pocahontas in Henrico that kept her advised of her father's silence, but Pocahontas had heard from him on her own. One day when she was alone in the fields near Rocke Hall, she had heard the familiar trill of a bird with a half-note missing—her family's signature call. She had slipped into the woods and met Pamouic.

He had been amazed at her clothes, at how she looked.

"Pocahontas, Father wanted you to understand that he knows you are cared for and in no danger. But he does not intend to make peace with the Tassentasses. He still plans to drive them away. I will tell him that I see you are happy. Please don't tell anyone that I have been here."

Brother and sister exchanged brief messages and gossip, and then Pamouic was gone as quickly as he had appeared.

When the frost turned the leaves to gold, Pocahontas found for the first time that she looked forward to John Rolfe's visits. There was still a dull void in her heart when she thought of John Smith, but her emotions toward him were so intricate and of such depth that every waking moment was interwoven with awareness of him. It was automatic for her to think that he would like this or he wouldn't approve of that. All of her achievements were laid at his feet and each night her prayers in his language united her with him. She listened for news of his arrival, for she knew absolutely that he would return to her one day.

John Rolfe's visits were important to Pocahontas because he brought the Scriptures alive to her. He would read and elucidate to her, and gradually she began to grasp the magnitude and beauty of the story she was studying. Her questions were endless, but Rolfe patiently answered them all. Slowly, through her prayers to her new God, she felt a peace that she had never experienced before. The new God, she felt, was particularly kind, for he had opened his world to her. She told John Rolfe that although she no longer prayed to the god of sky and the river goddess Ahone, she thought that God understood the years that she had worshiped them, for they were really part of the one and true God. John Rolfe smiled at her theory, but he agreed with her completely on the subject of the devil god Okeus: Evil came in many forms.

When the trees had turned to skeletons and snow softened the rough meadows, Pocahontas woke one morning to the familiar smell of corn bread baking. For an instant she thought she was back on her bed of furs in Werowocomoco. She sat up in bed with a start. She lit the logs in the fireplace and knelt down for her morning prayers, then laboriously read a few paragraphs of the Bible. When she had completed her devotions, she sat back on her haunches and deliberated. What was going to happen to her when her father finally settled his feud with the English, either peaceably or by force? She had forced that question to the back of her mind, but now she had to face it. She would have to go back to Werewocomoco, but her life would continue to be guided by the one and true God. Would she be persecuted for this? At best she would be isolated. She could not pray with her people to false gods, she could not enter into sacrifice—a major sin—and she certainly would not pray to the devil in the form of Okeus. Nor could she teach her people to read, although the written word was now her key to so many magic worlds, the source of the energy of her mind. Perhaps she could return as a disciple of Christ, but how long would the priests allow her to teach the new religion? Not even the daughter of the all-powerful Powhatan could survive their anger at her threat to the foundations of their society and the source of their power. For a moment she felt the familiar wings beating over her head. She tried to banish her fear with prayer. After a while she felt strong again and she thought that perhaps she should ask John Rolfe's advice. He was a true friend and might know what she should do.

By the time she and Mrs. Whitaker had returned from paying a call on a friend with a new baby, her spirits had returned to normal. In any case she always felt pleased when John Rolfe came to dinner and he was expected that evening.

• • •

After they finished the reading of the Scriptures after dinner, Pocahontas wondered why she had never before noticed what a fine voice John Rolfe had. She told him about the thoughts that had disturbed her earlier, and as she spoke she saw that his eyes looked first worried and then stricken. They were a clear gray fringed with black lashes. She had never seen eyes that color before.

When she finished talking, he took her hands in his and said, "You must not worry. You have made impressive strides in learning about Christianity, and you can be baptized in a couple of months. Then, dear Pocahontas, you will be a Powhatan princess and a Christian lady as well. You will be one of us. There is no need for you to return to your father if you do not want to."

"But my father may demand my return as part of his peace terms."

John Rolfe thought for a moment, his big shoulders hunched forward. "Will he insist that you stay with him when he knows how you worship and think?"

Pocahontas withdrew her hands and thought, How can I explain my father's strength, my obligation to my people, and my love for my father? I could remain here, but I would be a woman alone. I cannot stay with the Whitakers forever. Her fingers twisted as she thought, I do not truly belong in either world.

"Yes, I suppose I could return." Her voice was barely audible.

After Rolfe left Rocke Hall, he urged his horse into a gallop. He needed to feel the wind hard on his face to damp down his intense desire to hold Pocahontas in his arms. Over the past months he had fallen desperately in love with the Powhatan princess. He had tried to ignore his longing, but he could no longer suppress his intense carnal desire for her. God in heaven knew that he had tried his best to sublimate his longings. God knew, too, that he had been good to her. He had helped her become a Christian and a fine one. He rode into the wind as he spurred his horse on. It is not only her body I crave, he spoke aloud. No, it is also the enchantment of seeing her mind unfold, of leading her down new avenues of learning, of knowing the strength and flexibility of her character. Could she be my wife? Dare I think of her as my helpmeet and soulmate through Christ and in our life together? There is a difference in rank, but is it balanced by the fact that she recently was a heathen outside the church? His voice rose again in the darkness. God must know that my feelings for her are those of an honorable, healthy Christian man. I want this lovely creature by my side, to bear my sons and be blessed in union by the church. He almost reined in his horse as the thought struck him: Will she have me? I know little of her other life. And she is so young; she is but eighteen. Still, he felt reassured as he slowed the horse to a trot.

After a night spent tossing and turning, Rolfe found that his resolve had hardened. He would request permission to marry Pocahontas. Sir Thomas Dale was the man to approach. Rolfe would think about his decision for twenty-four hours and then write to Dale.

CHAPTER
22

Jamestown,
March 1614

Pocahontas had grown pale and thin. A thousand times over the past two months she had gone over and over the various thoughts that churned in her head. When John Rolfe proposed she had been astonished. She had known, of course, that he cared about her, but she had never realized how strongly he felt. She also knew that although she was not in love with him she liked and respected him a great deal. He represented strength and security to her, and most important, he could give her a life she wanted. If she married Rolfe she would really belong to the English. She could not tell him about John Smith, however, could not let him know that her blood, her skin, every part of her, was permeated with the essence of Smith. For many years now he had been her lover in fact and in spirit, and there was the tiny lost baby.

John Rolfe had not wanted to hear about Kokum. That was another life, he said, and whatever happened then had happened to another being. He told her that when she was baptized, all the sins of her past would be wiped away. She would be starting a new life in the eyes of God. Pocahontas was grateful for the magnanimity and forgiveness of the true God. In a way, she felt more privileged than the English who had grown up with Jesus Christ as their Savior. She thought they could not possibly appreciate him as much as someone who had had to sacrifice and pray, trembling with fear, to the devil god Okeus. But it was John Smith and her loyalty to him that left her feeling confused. She knew he would return one day, but would he still want to marry her? Could she marry another man feeling as she did about John Smith? No, she could not. If she married John Rolfe, she would have to put John Smith out of her mind completely. Could she do that after all these years? She concentrated on seeing Rolfe in a different light, as a husband. The more she thought of him in that way, the more she knew that he would be good to her and for her, but Smith remained an aching part of her.

John Rolfe was patient and affectionate through the weeks of her indecision. One day he said, "If you are worrying about how you will get along with the women of Jamestown, you needn't, for they like and respect you very much."

Pocahontas turned to him, both hands outstretched. His thoughtfulness and consideration made her feel even guiltier about Smith. Or was she guilty about Rolfe? Her emotions were in an upheaval.

She prayed fervently and long. Within a few weeks she would be baptized, and she was determined to be received into the church with a clear conscience, her course in life settled.

It was an early spring. The woods around them were a fairyland of white dogwood blossoms. Pocahontas walked into her room on a clear morning and suddenly decided to get out of her muslin dress and into her doeskins. She had not worn them for months. She slipped out of the house and walked swiftly across the fields to a rolling meadow nearby. She sat down, leaned back on her elbows, and gazed up at the sky. It was a serene blue with tiny puffs of white here and there. She prayed as she watched the little clouds drift along, prayed to the true God, but in her heart she knew that he was also the god of sky. As she prayed, her dilemma seemed to drop away. Under the peace and serenity of the blue depths she knew she would marry John Rolfe, and she knew that in doing so her emotions toward John Smith would eventually dim and fade. Smith would always be a part of her, like the rest of her past, but her feelings for him would not intrude on her marriage or lessen her determination to be a fine wife to John Rolfe. It was almost dark when she returned to the house. She had needed a long time in the meadow to express her gratitude to the one God.

When Pocahontas told John Rolfe that she would marry him, he was overjoyed. He told her that as soon as she was received into the Church of England he would publish the banns. In the meantime, he said, he would send off a letter to the governor. With the tension of the past weeks gone, Rolfe's exuberance erupted. He picked Pocahontas up and twirled her around the room until the minister's wife came running in to see what was happening.

Sir Thomas Dale could not believe his good luck when he received John Rolfe's letter requesting permission to marry Pocahontas. He immediately hurried over to consult with Gates. He said, "Somehow I never thought it would be John Rolfe, from an ancient and distinguished family, who would be the first to marry a Powhatan, princess or not. I would have thought him too conventional."

"I agree," Gates said, "but this could not suit our plans better. We must ram this advantage home with King Powhatan. Send a message to Rolfe and tell him we approve wholeheartedly. Then go and see him and the princess to give them your good wishes."

"How do you suggest we negotiate peace?"

"You and the betrothed pair must sail to Werowocomoco and see the great king," Gates explained. "With the princess at your side, and protected by soldiers and extra cannon, demand the return of our imprisoned men and our weapons and tools and present Powhatan with the fact of the impending marriage. I hope fervently that this alliance will give us peace."

"What if the king repudiates our demands and tries to kidnap Pocahontas?"

"I don't think Powhatan will harm his favorite child, his 'delight and darling,' or tear her away from her chosen husband. It is a chance we have to take. This marriage has got to go through, Dale. It will cement once and for all our position in the New World and then we need not worry about the Spaniards again— ever. Virginia, from Florida to Nova Scotia, will be recognized throughout the world as belonging to England."

"The princess has risen to our highest expectations," Dale said, "and the king has played into our hands with his silence. Here, take a glass. Let's drink to her very good health and happiness— and to Rolfe!"

"And most important of all, Dale, to the success of the meeting with Powhatan." They clinked glasses.

Pocahontas, the Whitakers, and John Rolfe journeyed to the impressive new church in Jamestown for the baptism. It was a momentous occasion for the English as well as for Pocahontas. Mrs. Whitaker had given her a white dimity dress to wear, and all of Jamestown was there to witness the solemn event. So many hopes rested on Pocahontas's dark head as she bowed before the priest when she received the sacrament and took the English name of Rebecca. The townspeople prayed that she would be the first of many of her people to embrace their religion. The governing council prayed that her forthcoming marriage would bring peace.

When the ceremony was over, the Reverend Mr. Whitaker smilingly posted the marriage banns. There was a collective gasp throughout the congregation, and a buzz of whispers rose in volume to excited talk as the people streamed out into the brilliant sunshine and gathered in groups. Others pressed around Pocahontas to wish her happiness.

"How can Rolfe, a commoner, marry a royal princess?" one of the soldiers asked.

The people of Jamestown, with the exception of its leaders, were divided in their feeling about the suitability of the match. The broader implications of the marriage did not occur to them. They were concerned that John Rolfe was reaching above himself in choosing the woman he wanted to marry. One did not step out of one's class. Even a man from a fine old family, if he was without a title, should not aspire to marry a princess. Such a union was practically unheard of, and quite a few of the townspeople felt uncomfortable about it.

Jamestown rippled with gossip and discussion, as did the towns of Henrico and Bermuda Hundred. The news spread immediately to the seven forts. Something so pleasurably exciting had not happened for a long time. There was no question of criticizing Pocahontas, for she was popular with everyone. It was John Rolfe who was the center of the little storm, but as he, too, was respected throughout the colony, it was difficult for those who were unhappy about the match to express their views.

While controversy swirled over their heads, the betrothed couple, Pocahontas's maid, Mrs. Whitaker as chaperon, and Dale, and 150 soldiers sailed from Jamestown with Samuel Argall on His Majesty's heavily armed ship, the *Treasurer*, bound for Werowocomoco. A captured Powhatan soldier had been released and sent overland to tell Powhatan of their imminent arrival.

How different her trip on the *Treasurer* was today, compared with her journey in captivity a year ago, thought Pocahontas.

373

She was returning to Werowocomoco for the first time in four years, and she was returning a Christian with her Christian betrothed. She did not know how her father would look upon her and her forthcoming marriage to one of the hated Englishmen. Of only one thing was she sure: He would sense immediately how profoundly she had changed. Neither could have dreamed when she pleaded so many years ago to be allowed to study the Tassentasses that she would become one of them. She put her faith in God that the meeting with Powhatan would go well.

As the *Treasurer* rounded a bend in the river and approached Werowocomoco, Pocahontas eagerly scanned the riverbank and felt a sudden shock. Five hundred of her father's warriors were massed on the bank. In the year she had been away from her people she had forgotten the vibrant colors the Powhatans displayed. The weapons, the multicolored feathers, the intricate headdresses, the swirls of paint, the glistening black hair, formed a panorama that stunned her with the impact of a blow. How beautiful they are, she thought.

The officers on the deck of the *Treasurer* consulted with one another. Powhatan's show of force was formidable.

"Don't worry," said Pocahontas. "My father has sent these men to greet me and escort us to him."

Argall ordered the guns primed, just to be safe. When the ship maneuvered alongside the dock, Pocahontas stepped forward in her blue taffeta dress. She had decided to wear English clothes to reinforce the fact that she was now a Christian. She knew that her father's spies would have brought back the news of her baptism. As she stepped down the gangway followed by the officers and soldiers, the Powhatan warriors threw their weapons in the air with a fierce yell. Pocahontas felt a dart of pride that her powerful father was giving her the kind of welcome usually reserved for his most important chieftains. It was also a fine opportunity to show his great strength, and the English

374

were impressed. Most of them had never before been to the great king's headquarters.

At least a thousand warriors milled around outside the long meetinghouse in Powhatan's village, and others crammed inside. Pocahontas had never seen so many braves, and she realized that many of these men had been sent here by neighboring chieftains.

The chattering stopped and the air was still when she walked the length of the room to greet her father. She saw with a qualm that he had grown much grayer, but she reminded herself that he was a man in his sixty-fifth year. The constant warfare has tired him, she thought. They greeted each other formally, and she presented John Rolfe and Sir Thomas Dale. She noticed that behind Powhatan stood a dozen new wives, more heavily laden with pearls and feathers than any of his previous wives. My father spoils them in his later years, she thought.

The great king put out his hand to his daughter and turned to the Englishmen. "Secotin, my son and trusted lieutenant, will speak to you about your demands. I would now like to speak to my daughter, whom I have not seen for a long time."

The English looked apprehensive, and John Rolfe took a tentative step forward. Warriors quickly signaled him away. Pocahontas gave him a reassuring glance and the room began to empty, leaving her alone with Powhatan. Her father seated her beside him and immediately wanted to know about her life among the English. When she settled her skirts with a rustling flourish she noticed that the departing wives were consumed with curiosity as they glanced back over their shoulders.

She told her father about the past year. "Father, they are very kind to me. I have everything I need, but the important point of my life with them is that I have grown to care for and worship their God. They have only one God, but he is kind and good."

Her father watched her intently. His favorite child was going to leave her people and marry one of the enemy, and furthermore, she preferred their God to the ones she was born to. Pocahontas could see he was bemused.

"Will you come to my wedding, Father?"

"Dear child, my people are negotiating with the English at this moment for the things they want back. I am also considering peace with them. And I am losing my daughter to one of them in marriage. Please do not expect me attend the ceremony gladly!"

Pocahontas smiled at her father's good-humored sarcasm. She understood his ambivalence. She reached out to pat his hand. "Then you are not unhappy that I shall marry one of the strange ones."

"Daughter, I can see you are well suited."

"I will be able to come and visit. And someday you must come and see my house in Jamestown."

Powhatan nodded his head, but she knew that he would never visit her. She would have to come to him. Still, she felt that her father had mellowed. It must be his age, she thought affectionately. We were so angry with each other over the English in years past, but now things have changed between us. We are as we used to be before the Tassentasses came.

The great king declined to see the English again and sent them with Pocahontas back to their ship, with a hundred warriors as escort. It was plain to the English that although Powhatan returned five of their men and some of their tools, he would not concede further on those points. They were relieved and happy, however, that he had given his consent to the marriage between his daughter and John Rolfe.

A day later, as the ship sailed slowly past Point Comfort on its way back to Jamestown, there was a sudden commotion on shore next to a tiny hamlet of half a dozen Powhatan houses.

Warriors brandished their bows and signaled. Pocahontas turned to Dale and said, "They want us to stop. They have a message for us."

While the *Treasurer* dropped anchor, several canoes skimmed out toward the ship like birds, leaving not a ripple behind them. As they drew alongside, a rope ladder was dropped and Secotin and Pamouic grabbed the slippery hemp and climbed nimbly up the side of the ship. The other canoes waited, bobbing gently in the water.

"I have come as my father's emissary." Secotin looked down at Dale from his six-foot-four-inch frame. He wore no headdress or any sign of rank.

Dale invited both men, with Pocahontas as interpreter, to his cabin. Pocahontas watched both of her handsome brothers, so alien in the confined space, but it was Secotin who claimed her close scrutiny. It was obvious that he had achieved the position close to their father that he had always craved. He had taken over the privileged functions that she would have performed as her father's most trusted lieutenant. As she watched him, she wondered if the vital turns in her life, which had cost her such heartache and brought her to Christianity, had been engineered by her ambitious brother. She would never know, but in her heart she was convinced that her instinct was right. It made no difference to her now. Her life was set in a direction that she could not possibly have imagined in the days before the English arrived. She would never relinquish the reservations she had felt about him through the years. Now he could not affect her at all, though he was her father's right-hand man and she owed him her respect. Secotin refused to sit but stood in the cabin and talked briefly to Pocahontas.

She translated for Dale. "My father conveys his good wishes and wants you to know that he is well pleased that your people have made me happy," she said. "He has consulted with his priests and has come to a decision. He feels that the union between his daughter and an Englishman is a symbol. He said that there have been too many of your men and his slain and by his wishes there will never be more warring. He is old now and would gladly end his days in peace. He said that if you attack him, his country is large enough for him to escape from you. He adds that he hopes that this much will satisfy you, his brother."

The Englishmen did not try to hide their jubilation. Dale asked Secotin to convey to the great king his great respect and good wishes. "Tell my brother there will be no war on the part of the English. We will guard the peace jealously." Then Dale asked Secotin to send one of his braves with one of the English soldiers to speed the news to the people at Jamestown that there was peace at last.

On deck, Secotin and Pamouic turned to their sister and embraced her. No one said a word as she held each of them close. They all felt the finality of the moment. She was leaving her life with them forever, but in doing so she had altered the course of their lives as well as her own.

The return to Jamestown was tumultuous. For several miles before the ship arrived at the dock, people ran along the bank waving, cheering and even turning cartwheels. Any doubts about the suitability of Pocahontas's marriage to Rolfe disappeared in the euphoria of celebration. When the couple disembarked they were almost knocked off their feet by the rejoicing crowd.

"It is the marriage that has brought us peace! It is the marriage!" they cried as they bobbed and danced and sang alongside the couple.

As they made their way toward Dale's house, Pocahontas wished that Smith could see the exultation of the crowd. He was the first Englishman who had been able to deal with Powhatan, and she knew that he was the one her father respected most. Smith would have been particularly pleased about today's events. All that he had striven for was now reality. She gave herself a shake as the familiar ache gripped her throat, then said a quick prayer of contrition and took a firmer hold on John Rolfe's arm.

Pocahontas had moved from the Whitakers' house, Rocke Hall, to stay with Sir Thomas Dale near the church and the festivities the people of Jamestown had planned for her and John Rolfe. It was dawn and it was her wedding day. She was out of bed and into the fields. She wanted to pick some wildflowers for the church. Later a dozen women would fill the church with blossoms, but she wanted to offer the first flowers herself, alone in the quiet of the nave. How lovely it is, she thought, that I offer flowers and not a dead creature. As she prayed, she asked God to forgive her that her mind still dwelt on John Smith, but she also thanked God that Smith was less often on her mind these busy days. And she prayed with every ounce of her strength that she would make John Rolfe the best wife he could want.

Pochins was the first to arrive. In deference to Pocahontas's wishes he attired himself modestly to give away the bride, but his warriors—all one hundred of them—were ablaze in feathers and paints. They carried no weapons; these were left stacked outside the fort. Then Secotin and Pamouic, with a smaller contingent from Werowocomoco, arrived and went directly to Sir Thomas Dale's house. They gave Powhatan's gifts to his daughter—the first a magnificent string of pearls, each one the size of an egg, all of them perfectly matched, and the second gift, thousands of acres of land.

By midmorning the meadow not far from the church began to take on the look of a country fair. Venison and turkey roasted on spits, and trestle tables were laden with pies, fruits, and tubs of ale. People from the towns and forts streamed into Jamestown and scrambled to secure a seat in the church well before the ceremony.

When the bride emerged from the governor's house to walk to the church, the crowd was silent. Her dark beauty was framed by a white tunic of the finest muslin and a gown of rich white satin. A little girl born in Jamestown four years earlier held her long veil, which was secured on her head by white blossoms. By her side walked King Pochins, regal and grave.

The ceremony was simple and brief; the bride and groom gave their responses in strong, clear voices. Later, in a house borrowed for the night, Pocahontas told her husband that aside from the religious rites, which touched her at her core, the sight of all the colonists raising their glasses of ale in a toast to them had moved her the most.

In the small hours of the morning Pocahontas eased herself up on her pillow and looked at her sleeping husband. He did not have the devilishly handsome face of John Smith or the perfect symmetry of Kokum, but his good looks, kindness, and generosity inspired deep tenderness in her. Even at the height of his passion this first night together, he had been gentle and giving in a way that she had never experienced before. She repeated her marriage vows fervently, barely whispering as she watched the planes of his face.

CHAPTER
23

London,
May 1614

He gave her firm bottom a light slap. She turned her head on the pillow—eyes fierce, blond hair tumbling—and punched his shoulder. John Smith laughed. He was grateful that at least one of the two Reynolds girls had not married.

"Mary, I am off to see your father this morning. He will probably try to get me to marry you again." Smith sat up in bed, his eyes mischievous.

"Wretch! I wouldn't have you for all the riches of India!" Smith dodged a pillow she threw at him.

"That's what I told him before and shall tell him again."

Smith scrambled out of bed and hopped quickly across the cold floor to gather his clothes. As he glanced back he saw that Mary had pulled the bedclothes up to her chin and was eyeing him with a dangerous glint. He had told her from the beginning that he would never marry. His life as an explorer and adventurer was too precarious to ask a wife to share, but their relationship was so easy, so pleasant that they often teased each other about the subject. He could not add, of course, that once he had wanted to marry.

His mood suddenly changed as he adjusted his hose and buttoned his tunic.

"Another ship has come in from Jamestown," Smith said. "That is why Sir Edwin Sandys has called a meeting of the Virginia Company this morning."

"Are you going back to the colony?"

"Yes, in about a year's time. I plan to travel from Jamestown up the coast as far as Nova Scotia."

"Oh, take me with you! It would be such an adventure!"

Smith smiled as he looked at her sitting up in bed, her arms clasped around her knees. Mary was one of the most pampered women in London. Her slippered toe had never even touched a wet cobblestone.

"Your beauty would be too disruptive for the crew," he said. "The expedition would be in shambles before we would get out of territorial waters."

Mollified, she tipped her fingers and blew him a kiss. He smiled at her from the doorway.

John Smith made his way down Bishopsgate Street, past All Hallows and St. Peter's churches, down to Thames Street and to Paula's Wharf, where Sir Edwin had an office. He had called a meeting there of the officers of the Virginia Company and its parent company, the Somers Company, to consolidate the holdings of the Virginia Company. The Somers Company had been formed to raise money for the enterprise and to keep it solvent. It was up to the merchants of London, a new class, to protect their interests. The king had too many debts to spare money for the New World. Smith was the last to arrive, and Sandys brought him up to date.

"The *Treasurer* has arrived from the colony, and I have had a letter from John Rolfe, our tobacco expert in the New World. He thinks he can finally produce a good mix. He will send a sample of his efforts on the next ship. His wife has helped him a great deal." Sandys signaled to Smith to take a nearby chair.

"I thought Rolfe's wife died in Bermuda." Smith settled himself and crossed his legs.

"She did. He has married Princess Pocahontas. Their union has finally brought the great king to heel. There is peace in Virginia at last."

Smith knew he had gone white at the news. How could Pocahontas have married? She already had a Powhatan husband. Smith shook his head as if to clear it. It had all happened so long ago. He had hardened his heart toward that period of his life. There had been nothing around him on this side of the Atlantic to remind him of the anguish and the loss he had suffered then. At first, when he started to long for her, he had thrust the feeling from him with the iron discipline that had been his strength in life. The long voyage home had begun the healing process and sealed his awareness of the great distance between him and Virginia. The diversions of London and Mary's eager arms had further dulled his grief, but this news was like a fresh slash at his heart. Had he misjudged Pocahontas? Had he been given false news that long-ago day on his sickbed in Jamestown? For a moment his stunned senses conjured Pocahontas as vividly as if she had stepped off the *Treasurer* that day.

Sir Edwin Sandys went on, "We discussed the possibility of voting to pay a stipend to the princess before you got here, Smith. She kept the colony alive during its darkest days and has now secured peace with her father. She is a heroine." Sir Edwin put his quill pen down on the oak table and looked around at the dozen men. "Shall we raise our hands on it?"

The vote was enthusiastic and unanimous.

Sir Edwin said that a lottery held in the courtyard at St.

Paul's last month had raised a considerable sum of money for the Virginia enterprise; it was so successful that an idea had been born of it—to collect more money for a school of religious instruction for both English and Indian children in Jamestown.

"My imaginative friend William Shakespeare has made a suggestion," said the Earl of Southampton. "We should invite the lovely princess, the Lady Rebecca, to visit London with her husband. As a convert to Christianity she could help raise funds for the school."

"Excellent idea." Sir Edwin slapped his knee in his enthusiasm. "She could promote both the school and the entire Virginia project!"

Other members spoke up with suggestions: Lady Rebecca must sit for a formal portrait; Ben Jonson should write a masque; investors could entertain Pocahontas; she might speak to Parliament about her father; the king and queen would want to receive her.

By this time the members were talking simultaneously in their rush of plans for the visit. Only John Smith did not speak. Emotions he had thought long buried had welled up into a tight block in his chest. He had vowed to keep silent about his relationship with Pocahontas, and recent events—her marriage and conversion—only strengthened that resolve. It was imperative that he keep a cool and impartial countenance, no matter how vulnerable he felt.

"Have you nothing to say on this matter, Smith?" Southampton asked.

Smith cleared his throat. "I agree with all the proposals."

Sandys pursed his lips. "I think two of us should ask to be received by the king to advise him of the latest news and to seek his approval. We should also tell Parliament. Smith, will you accompany me?"

Smith nodded. The men concluded their business with generally high expectations.

Sir Edward Sandys and John Smith stood silent and respectful with a group of courtiers in the presence of King James at St. James's Palace. The king spoke.

"Traitor! How could a Briton marry the daughter of an enemy king?"

King James deliberately did not say "Englishman." He knew his privy council hated the words "British" and "Great Britain," terms he had coined to denote the union of Scotland, his birthplace, with England. He sat before them, his weak legs dangling, his suspicious eyes rolling. He knew he cut a sorry figure as king and that he was constantly being compared unfavorably with the true majesty of the old queen, Elizabeth. He mistrusted every last one of the men sitting before him.

"Sire, neither the Princess Pocahontas nor her heirs will inherit any of the Crown's holdings in Virginia," said the Earl of Devon.

"How can we be sure?"

"She has been given enormous amounts of land by her father, King Powhatan. The Rolfes have their house, Varina, on her property and are farming there," replied the Earl of Dorset. "In any case, we have dispatched an edict forbidding any transfer of royal grants to Lady Rebecca."

"I am still outraged that Rolfe would marry one of the enemy," the king said.

"Sire," said one of the courtiers, "may I present Sir Edwin Sandys, who has news of the colony?"

Sir Edwin bowed. He explained that the war between the Indians and the English was over. King Powhatan had agreed to cease hostilities after the union between his daughter and John Rolfe.

"Are we doing anything to cement this peace? We have had cease-fires before," asked the king.

The king was uneasy when dealing with the colony. On the one hand he liked the additional power a position in the New World gave him. On the other, the Spanish were angry that the English had upset their plans to dominate the entire region. James wanted to marry his son Charles to the Infanta of Spain and thus felt constantly ambivalent about the successful adventures of his subjects in Virginia.

Sir Edwin continued, "We feel sure this peace is permanent, Your Majesty, but we intend to beguile the various princes under Powhatan. Sir Thomas Dale is negotiating separate peace treaties with each of them. We want to present them with red coats and pictures of Your Majesty in copper, which they value highly, on chains to hang around their necks. Then we will dub them noblemen of King James." Sir Edwin watched his ruler's reaction.

The king smiled slightly. Smith wondered if he had already taken the first of his many drinks of the day.

"I have received one papal bull after another claiming Virginia for the Spanish." The king's voice was peevish.

John Smith spoke. "If I may say so, Your Majesty, we are certain now that Virginia is yours."

"Yes, yes, well, so be it." The king turned away, his attention exhausted. Smith and Sandys backed out of the audience room.

As they walked out to St. James's Street through the corridors of St. James's Palace, Sir Edwin said, "You can see why we have to work hard to keep enthusiasm keen for the Virginia venture. The king is of two minds. We do not have his full commitment. He is another reason I want to see the Indian princess here in London. I understand she is beautiful as well as charming. She could be invaluable in furthering our cause with the king."

"When do you plan to invite the Rolfes?" Smith asked.

"Not immediately. They are just married. I feel we should wait a year. It will give Lady Rebecca time to become fully educated. I hear she is keen to learn Latin now that she has mastered English. Didn't you know her, Smith? You never mentioned her name, but if I recall correctly you wrote to me about her back in 1608 and '09."

"Yes, I knew her, of course." Smith's voice lowered as sadness engulfed him abruptly.

"Since you are one of the few people who knew her at the beginning of our adventure in Virginia, all of us will want you to be in this country when Pocahontas arrives. It is important to our entire effort, particularly in regard to the crown." Sandys watched Smith as he talked.

"The king is not entirely convinced of the Rolfes' loyalty," Sandys went on. "He has been seeing conspiracy under every bed ever since the Gunpowder Plot in the Parliament almost ten years ago. I think he fears them reigning in their own kingdom and attracting many of our people to their cause. It would be extremely easy for them to do so, of course."

Smith nodded his head.

"The king has been heard to say that the constitution I wrote for the Virginia Company last year is far too democratic," Sandys said. "I am told he imagines the Rolfes using it to set themselves up as king and queen of a separate state in Virginia."

Smith smiled. Pocahontas would make a beautiful queen, but a conspiracy? He shook his head.

The two men emerged from under the portico of the palace and stood in the mud that was the new St. James's Street. As they waited for their horses to be brought up, a group of ragged urchins clustered around hopping, yelling, and begging, with dirty hands outstretched.

"There are homeless children like these all over town. Their farmer fathers are out of work in the countryside. Desperate, they sell the children for a few pence, and the buyers abandon them because they cannot afford to feed them." Sir Edwin threw a few pennies into the air and there was a frantic scramble.

"We should pick out the best children, scrub them, and ship them off to the New World." Smith reached for the reins of his horse.

"We plan to do just that. I will see you later at Westminster Palace."

The committee room in the House of Commons was packed. Every member had turned up for the discussion on the new colony, and a few visitors had been allowed to attend the special session. The thick walls of Westminster Palace were still cool from the winter cold, which was a blessing on this warm May day. Beyond the deep casement windows the Thames flowed invitingly. An occasional riverboat filled with produce or passengers sailed by en route to the village of Chelsea or farther, to Hampton Court.

Sir Edwin repeated his news about the Rolfe marriage and the ensuing peace to his fellow members of Parliament. He regaled them further with the plans for the princess's visit to London. News of the faraway colony seemed almost too exotic for these men, who had spent the day dealing with the enormous debt incurred by squandering money on frivolities that the king and his Danish queen, Anne, had incurred. Their ears pricked up at the news of peace.

"Does this mean there will be no more warfare at all on the part of the savages?" asked a member.

"Why don't we ensure peace once and for all by annihilating the savages?" volunteered another member.

Several others chorused their agreement.

One member asked why the English should bother placating a simple people who interfered with plans to establish a colony.

"They have killed and starved our people for almost ten years now. We need room to expand. We need our people there as a growing market for our goods."

Smith and Sandys argued persuasively for peace. The committee members were divided in their opinions, but they were convinced finally to give the truce a chance. Smith thought, as he left the chamber, The fools have no idea how difficult it is to wage war against the courageous and resourceful Powhatans.

CHAPTER

24

Henrico,
October 1615

Pocahontas looked down at her little son in his cradle. It is true, she thought, he already looks like me and not at all like John. She had decided before he was born that he would be treated like an English baby. During his first months she did not wrap him tightly in skins like a Powhatan child to give them strong, straight backs. And it worked, for the boy was as straight as an arrow anyway. Almost everyone in Jamestown had turned up for the christening, when he was named Thomas after Sir Thomas Dale. Her heart still warmed when she thought of the care and attention everyone gave her child. She knew this was partly because he was the living symbol of harmony between the Powhatans and the English.

What would her other child have looked like? she wondered. Would he also have looked like her or would he have had brilliant hair and eyes the color of the sky? She thought of Smith less often now, and the ache in her heart had dulled, but still she could not guarantee her reaction if he were to walk off a ship one day.

She left the child and walked toward the window. It was a

perfect morning, with the sky an intense blue and trees blazing in red and yellow. The harvest of tobacco had been excellent, and she had stood with pride next to her husband when the bales of leaves were loaded on a ship and sent to London. Her expertise had been essential in growing the new strain. She found now that everyone in the colony came to her for help, not only with agricultural problems but also for hunting and fishing advice. The settlers knew that when she was unsure of an answer she called on her family or other Powhatans for assistance. The doorbell never ceased ringing at Varina. It rang now.

Pochins's wife, Naha, was at the door.

Pocahontas knew as she greeted her friend that Naha would want to slip into her English clothes immediately. She liked to lead an English life when in Jamestown. She copied Pocahontas's own dresses, but she refused to have anything to do with the English God. She was happy with Ahone and even Okeus, and she continued to sacrifice to them. After all, she said, they had given her Pochins.

Naha enjoyed joining Pocahontas when she called on her friends in Henrico or Bermuda Hundred. Pocahontas encouraged her visits because Naha was the only one of her people who came to visit the English for any length of time. Englishmen, on the other hand, often ran away to live permanently with the Powhatans. During her visits, Naha would sit silent and watchful, copying the English mannerisms and trying to understand what was being said.

Pocahontas told her that when her English friends heard they were coming to visit, they competed among themselves for the privilege of receiving them.

"I learned that Englishwomen in their homeland do not have the same amount of freedom we do," Pocahontas told Naha. "Living here they see how independent we are, how much power we can have, how we work alongside our men and even rule

396

them. It makes them like our land and they are beginning to copy us. The men dare not complain, for there are too few women."

Naha noticed that the women also liked to receive Pocahontas because she was a princess. They loved her for her kindness, but she could see that her rank was also important to them.

Every few weeks Pocahontas would ask one of the visitors from Werowocomoco to tell her father that she would like to visit him soon. Her father would send a delegation to call for her, and Pocahontas would slip into her doeskin clothes and go, with her baby, to visit Powhatan for several days. The great chief twirled little Thomas in the air the moment his grandson arrived and did not let him out of his sight for the rest of his stay. He gave the child an Indian name, Pepsiconemeh, for he said the gods would be offended if the boy did not have a proper name in the Powhatan language. The great king told Pocahontas he wondered what would be the outcome of mixing the two bloods. Would it be like blending the salt of the sea with the pure waters of the rivers?

Pocahontas laughed. "Only good will come of it," she replied.

She returned from these visits, running ahead of her escort through the forest, feeling like a young girl again. She would fling open the door at Varina, calling for John Rolfe. Sometimes he would tease her by making her search through the house for him, opening dress cupboards, looking behind doors, and hunting through the stables and grounds. She had grown to love her husband and to love her life with him. He was a gentle, religious man with an inner strength she had learned to rely on and be guided by.

Rolfe had been educated at Cambridge. When he first met Pocahontas three years before he had seen at once that she had an innate gift for language. He was now leading her gently into Latin and Greek, which she studied with such fervor he worried about her eyesight as she pored over her books every night by candlelight and firelight. It intrigued him that she was not particularly interested in history. When he asked her why, she couldn't give him an answer. He thought that perhaps it was too soon for her to relate past events in a culture that was still so fresh to her. And her own people had no tradition of oral or written history.

Pocahontas was proud of her house. Rolfe had built a handsome brick building for his family, and a duplicate of it was constructed for Powhatan in Werowocomoco. Servants sent by her father kept Pocahontas's home spotless. She called them all together this sparkling morning to tell them Sir Thomas Dale was coming to dinner that evening. Every few weeks he left Jamestown and toured the various forts and towns to make sure that the rules he had put into force for the colony were obeyed and that productivity was maintained. Pocahontas enjoyed keeping an open house for all her friends and relatives, but she particularly enjoyed Dale's visits because he often spoke of London. She sighed as she swirled through the house.

"London! I cannot believe a place like London exists!"

At dinner that evening oysters were served with a sauce made of horseradish from their English garden and tomatoes from their Powhatan planting. Crabs followed, caught before their shells had formed, as the Powhatans liked them, and fried delicately.

Sir Thomas Dale turned to his hostess and said, "Princess, you keep the best table in our colony, but then, your people are renowned cooks."

Pocahontas smiled. Sir Thomas never called her Lady Rebecca, as some of the English did, nor did he call her Mrs. Rolfe. "I try to mix my native food with the cooking I have learned from my friends in Henrico," she replied.

"Rolfe, you are lucky to have such a beautiful and gifted wife!"

Roast woodcock with mushrooms, turkey with oyster gravy, and a rare treat—mutton in mint sauce—were served as the main course. Cattle and sheep were new arrivals to the colony and were not butchered until they were ancient so that they reproduced as long as possible. Sweet potatoes, okra, and sea kale accompanied the meat course.

Sir Thomas continued to address Pocahontas. "I, too, would like to have a lovely wife from your people. Now that we are at peace, I have learned over the past months how cheerful, courteous, and dignified the Powhatans are. Most important, I see how compatible and contented you and John Rolfe are. But, alas, I am afraid such a marriage will not happen for me."

Pocahontas and Rolfe looked at each other in surprise.

"You look astonished, but of course you have not heard that I sent an emissary to your father requesting your young half sister Quimca in marriage. But your father refused me."

Pocahontas was more than surprised; she was amazed. She knew that Dale had a wife in England and she knew that Christians never took more than one consort. Were the English beginning to copy the chieftains here? She murmured a vague reply as she occupied herself by cutting a wing off her woodcock.

"Your father said he had arranged Quimca's marriage to a chieftain three days' journey from him. He added that we English already have a daughter as dear to him as his own life. Although he has many children, he delights in none so much as you." Sir Thomas bestowed on Pocahontas one of his rare smiles.

Dale settled back in his chair and rested his elbows on the armrests. "I have had a letter from the Virginia Company. They call themselves the Somers Company these days."

The Rolfes instinctively put down their knives and forks.

"Your friend Sir Edwin Sandys invites you both to travel to

London as guests of the Somers Company. He feels that the great interest Londoners have in Princess Pocahontas will be of inestimable value in promoting Virginia with investors."

There was silence in the room.

"Of course you need not travel until spring when the winter storms are over. I will accompany your party back to England." Dale picked up his knife and fork and ate the last piece of mutton on his plate.

Pocahontas felt a thrill of excitement. London! In almost the same moment she felt a lump in her chest. John Smith! She struggled to control her expression. The conflicting emotions of anticipation and fear stunned her into silence, but she knew she was expected to say something.

"I am honored," she said, her voice barely above a whisper.

"This is very decent of Sandys," Rolfe said. "I think the idea has taken my wife by surprise. Naturally we must give the offer serious consideration. We are both flattered that London should think so highly of us." He looked at his wife with concern. It was obvious the news had made her uneasy.

"Princess," Dale said, "the city will welcome you with open arms. Many celebrations are planned for you. I urge you to think carefully of the good that you will do for your husband and his interests as well as all those of your friends here in the New World."

Dale did not mention that he had written several letters to the monarch over the past year in an attempt to allay King James's ridiculous fear that the princess might establish her own empire with Rolfe and entice the colony to separate itself from England. Sir Thomas was determined to do everything possible to encourage Pocahontas to travel to England and lay that idea to rest once and for all.

Pocahontas tried to concentrate on the pumpkin pudding and a pie made from preserved strawberries, which she and the servants had lovingly prepared. She couldn't eat a mouthful. She replaced her fork and turned to Sir Thomas with a smile. "The proposal is so sudden. I want very much to visit London, but it seems so far away!"

"Well, then, it is settled!" Dale raised his glass to his lips with relief.

But John Rolfe knew it was not at all settled. He signaled to Pocahontas to leave him and Dale to their port and pipes. She left the table gladly and rushed to her son's room to look down at his small sleeping form. She longed to snatch him up into her arms and hold him close to feel the reassurance of his warm body. Her life was so pleasant, so peaceful, so fulfilling, and now this challenge yawned in front of her threateningly. She had never thought she would see wondrous London, the glittering city of her mind. She had never really believed she would be the one to go to where John Smith lived. He was always the one she imagined appearing suddenly off an ocean-borne ship to confront her with her long-buried emotions. But were they buried? She had no idea how she would react to the sight of him. At least in Henrico she could hide behind the full structure of her loving life. She could feel in control. In London I will be lost, she thought. Everything will be so strange, so different. I will not know where to put one foot in front of the other. Weeks of hardship and an ocean will separate me from the comfort and reassurance of the familiar. And he is bound to come into my life there. The fathers of London will recall the early days of the explorers, when Smith was a major figure. "I am so afraid," she whispered, "so afraid that after one look at him I will be tossed into an abyss."

She sank down on her knees by the baby's bed and clasped her hands in prayer, knowing that her new God, the true God, was not tolerant of weaknesses of the flesh, as her old gods had been. She wondered if it was a sin that her heart beat so hard when she thought of John Smith in London. There was no one she could ask.

Later, when she heard her husband's steps on the stairs, she rose and met him in the hall. She felt calmer now. Her prayers had given her strength, and she had recalled her husband's teachings. She must put herself in the hands of God, trust in him to guide her, and do what was expected of her. Linking arms with her husband, she gave him a radiant smile.

There were days when Pocahontas walked through her obligations filled with excitement at the thought of her forthcoming trip to London, but there were other days when a cloud of apprehension fell over her. She steeled herself against her personal worries by reminding herself that she had a duty to perform on the trip. She told her husband, with tears in her eyes, that she would not go to London without Thomas. Rolfe agreed with her and heaved a sigh of relief, believing he had discovered what worried her about the journey.

There was snow on the ground when she paid an overdue visit to her father in Werowocomoco. She reveled in the color and warmth of her people, the songs, the good food, the happy atmosphere. The little tricks Thomas learned this trip seemed particularly attractive. Wanting to feel the security of her childhood life envelop her, she was refreshed by escaping back into an earlier life, when her emotions were simple, unentangled.

She was not surprised to find that the great chief was against the trip entirely. He gave her a long lecture and said that she would be walking into a strange land on the underside of the sea where an enemy lurked behind every tree. His concern touched her heart, and when she and her son said good-bye to Powhatan, they promised faithfully to come back for a visit soon.

When Pocahontas made arrangements to visit her father again four weeks later, however, she received a message from him telling her not to come under any circumstances. As the runner continued his story, Pocahontas's surprise turned to horror. The messenger said that a terrible sickness had swept through several Powhatan towns near the coast, including Werowocomoco. Some adults and most of the children became tired, then turned hot, with red spots appearing all over their bodies. Within a few days many of them had died, including both of her half sister Mehta's children and the lovely Sacha, Powhatan's errant wife, who was found thin and old in exile and was ravished by the fever. The runner reassured Pocahontas that the great chief himself was well. He told her that although the scourge was dreadful, the priests' lack of power to banish the evil sickness had frightened the people as much as the sickness itself. Never in living memory had the priests been unable to apply their magic and medicines successfully. The great chief had forbidden anyone to travel to or from the stricken towns so that at least the evil spirits could not jump from body to body. The runner said the southern section of the Seven Kingdoms was plunged into despair.

When Pocahontas consulted her friends in Henrico, they said their children sometimes had the plague of the red spots, but most of them recovered. They had known of two cases in Jamestown a few weeks before, but the illness had not spread.

Pocahontas watched Thomas protectively for weeks. She bathed him frequently, scrubbing him hard until he yelled in protest. Then she fed him extra food and prayed.

When the first daffodils appeared, preparations for the Rolfes' journey to London intensified, for they would leave in a matter of weeks. Pocahontas planned to take a dozen retainers with her, including Mehta and her husband, Tomoco. When Pocahontas was able to visit her father again, Powhatan said that the journey would distract Mehta from her grief, and a change of scenery might encourage her and her husband to have more children. Pocahontas agreed and said she, too, had one particular request—Pamouic. The great chief acquiesced but pursed his lips with skepticism about the whole idea and held her close to him when they parted.

Pocahontas did not close her eyes during the night before their departure for the Old World. The strange bed in Sir Thomas's house in Jamestown, the excitement, the anticipation, and the faint dread precluded sleep, but when she saw the familiar ship, the *Treasurer*, refurbished and heavily laden with goods for the trip back to England, all her doubts dropped away. The dock was jammed with well-wishers. Everyone who could leave his work was there to cry godspeed to the young princess who once again carried the colony's hopes on her shoulders. Up until the moment the ship slipped her moorings, Pocahontas hoped she might see her father, or at least an emissary, for on her last visit to Werowocomoco he had seemed eager to see her again before she left. Her sharp disappointment was lessened somewhat when she saw Naha and Pochins on the dock. Naha had even toyed with the idea of going to London herself, but Pocahontas knew she could never tear herself away from Pochins for so long.

Samuel Argall captained the ship into the mile-wide river under a light breeze and through calm water. As they turned a bend at the mouth of the river near the bay, a lookout cried, "Small craft!"

Everyone surged to the rails. Ahead of them from bank to bank the river was thick with canoes like a scattering of brilliant flowers. Pocahontas clutched her young son's hand as he squealed with delight when the warriors in full war paint and headdresses roared a sea chant. The great chief had come to see them off. Powhatan would not set foot where the Tassentasses lived, but the river was his, and he refused to let the ship pass until he had said farewell to his daughter and grandson.

After the evening meal on the first night at sea, Dale produced a letter from his tunic. "Sir Edwin Sandys sent a message on the *Treasurer* from London, Princess, to say that your old friend John Smith will write a letter to the palace on your behalf. Sandys is sure the king and queen will want to entertain you."

A wave of anger swept over Pocahontas. I have just begun the journey, she thought, and already I am furious with myself. I cannot let a memory interfere with my life like this! She excused herself from the table, went up to the gently rolling deck, and stood by the rail watching the phosphorescent wake. I cannot feel trapped like an animal, she fumed. I must have more strength!

CHAPTER
25

London,
June 1616

Pocahontas luxuriated in the sunshine that fell across the bed in a warm pool of light. She was exultant over the reception she had received in the streets, in committee rooms, in ballrooms. It seemed astonishing that people could be so fascinated by her. Pocahontas realized that it was not only she who intrigued the various groups that flooded her with invitations but the New World she represented. Even so, it was thrilling to be made to feel so important. She felt a deep satisfaction that she could offer a new life to so many poor and homeless Londoners by promoting the Virginia venture.

It was the morning of her third day in London at the inn provided by the Virginia Company, for the Rolfe family and their retinue. She stretched her arms wide as she thought of how she had been entranced with every aspect of London from the day they had landed. Even the smells did not bother her so much now. They were a small price to pay for the privilege of seeing the towering white buildings crisscrossed in heavy oak, the parks filled to bursting with flowers and birds, and most of all, the people—the babbling, deafening, jostling crowds that squeezed into the narrow streets. She loved the bustle—the rumbling of cart wheels, the yells of the sedan carriers, the lowing of cattle on the way to market, and the shrill cries of hawkers. If at times she felt it was all too exciting to be true, she had only to put her head out of the window of the Belle Sauvage Inn to be drawn into the maelstrom of sound and activity from the streets below. The street scenes were so diverting that she sometimes forgot for hours at a time about the knock on the door she dreaded to hear.

At first the innkeeper had been frightened by the Powhatan servants, who looked so fierce in their native dress and who scrubbed everything in sight with a violence that made him quail at the thought of that energy used in anger. But when the mice and rats disappeared, he decided that there was something to be said for their foreign ways. He told Sir Edwin that he had become so fond of the princess's little boy that their entourage could keep the inn for their exclusive use as long as Sir Edwin cared to pay.

Sir Edwin Sandys had ordered Pocahontas to rest late in the mornings. The round of balls, receptions, fund-raisings, and civic functions in her honor and for the Virginia endeavor would wear her out if she did not pace herself. He did not need to remind her that time, energy, and money had been spent to bring her here to sell Virginia to prospective settlers and investors. She did as she was told, for she had become very fond of her forceful but charming sponsor.

She thought lazily of the swish and crackle of the lavender taffeta ball gown she had worn the previous night and of the announcer who yelled their names at the top of his voice as they entered every room at every function: "Mrs. Rolfe, the princess Pocahontas, and John Rolfe, general of Virginia."

She remembered with pleasure the admiring glances her husband had given her as she executed the intricate steps of the branle faultlessly, her fingers resting on the satin-covered arm of the Prince of Wales. Prince Charles had plied her with question after question about her father and her people. He was enthralled by anything connected with Virginia and furious that he was not allowed to go and see the New World for himself.

"They say it is not safe to travel there yet," he had said, his handsome young face contemptuous of the timidity of his elders.

Pocahontas suddenly sat up in bed and abruptly threw back the covers as the full memory of the evening flooded back. The party had been given by a heavy investor in the Virginia venture, Sir Thomas Legge, in his town house hung with Brussels tapestries. A goodly sum of money had been pledged for Virginia by the enthusiastic guests as they consumed mounds of cold salmon washed down with copious flagons of hock. Pocahontas had enjoyed the strawberries and cream at her host's table while she listened dutifully to the rotund junior minister for foreign affairs on her right.

"You are fortunate in these difficult times in Virginia that you have married one of us. Others of your people may not be so protected." The minister had smiled as he spoke, but there was an edge to his voice that signaled serious intent.

For the rest of the evening as various people were introduced to her, the minister's remark echoed in her head, but when she discussed it later with John Rolfe at the inn he dismissed it as idle chatter. Still, it was not the sort of thing that she could ignore, and she decided she would pursue the subject the next day with Sir Edwin.

During his morning call, however, Sandys was blunt. "I know there is an element in Parliament that feels that the English should secure all the lands along the coast in Virginia and to use force to drive the Powhatans into the interior if necessary."

Pocahontas told John Rolfe that they must do something to stop this thinking immediately. Didn't they realize what the consequences would be if her father unleashed his full power and fury against the settlers?

John Rolfe took her into his arms and spoke with his mouth pressed against her hair. "We have just arrived, so we must be calm about rumors. We will look into this further to satisfy you. If there is a misunderstanding among some hotheaded men, we will work to straighten it out. In the meantime we will keep our ears open to see if there is any real warlike sentiment. I have heard nothing about war from the Virginia venture group."

Momentarily soothed, Pocahontas turned her attention to the activities planned for her and recalled that that afternoon would be a special one—her first visit to the theater. She dressed carefully in forest-green silk, but not the bare-shouldered style that so many of the ladies wore even in daylight. She wished she had emeralds, but she consoled herself with the knowledge that her pearls were widely remarked upon. In any case they suited her complexion, which had been openly admired.

It was daring to go to the theater. Many of the men who backed the Virginia venture were against theaters of any kind. "Morally depraved places," they grumbled. But the king and queen had other ideas. The theaters in the city must continue. The actors needed to sharpen their talents so that they could perform well at court. Pocahontas had pushed hard with Sir Edwin about her desire to go, and her sponsors indulged her whim. Henry Condell, owner of the theater, would be a member of their party. Sandys reminded her that William Shakespeare had been helpful in organizing her trip to London. He had died a few months before. His play, *The Tempest*, which they would see that evening, was based on the shipwreck that John Rolfe had endured in the Bermudas.

Pocahontas gasped as she entered the Globe theater. She had never seen so many people jammed into such a small space. The balconies reached four stories high, almost to the sky! It was a marvel to her that the whole edifice did not crumble under the sheer weight of bodies. Word had preceded them that their party was on its way, and as she was led to her seat in the front of the gallery the entire audience twisted and craned their necks to see the exotic princess.

"But they are so noisy," she protested to Condell as people called and chatted throughout the performance, popping hazelnuts into their mouths and dropping the shells indiscriminately. She recalled the absolute silence among her own people when a dance was being performed or a speech given.

"Theater goers are not a respectful lot in this country or easy to write for," replied Condell with a wry grin.

The excitement of the drama unfolding on the stage, the press of warm bodies seated cheek by jowl, the electric current of raw human emotion, the jewel-colored gowns of the women in the audience, the admiring glances of the men, all gave Pocahontas an enjoyment she did not know she could feel. She leaned back in her seat and gave herself up to the scene around her.

"Not exciting enough!" called a theatergoer in the pit, as a babble of catcalls and suggestions followed.

"I see that at least your husband finds the play absorbing," muttered Condell to Pocahontas.

She glanced at her husband and saw that he was leaning forward with tears in his eyes. Why, he is reliving every minute of the storm in Bermuda, she thought. She felt a pang as she thought of the wife and child who must have been foremost in his mind at that moment.

She started to put her hand on Rolfe's arm when she suddenly realized that these moments were his alone. It was not only the play unfolding before them that affected her husband but the return to London and all the associated memories that must be engulfing him now. She felt a twist of pain as she remembered that he had had a happy life before he met her. Not a marriage like mine to Kokum, she thought. Ah, but what about Smith? a small voice within her whispered. She wondered if going to the theater would always evoke such strong emotions in her. She turned her attention to the drama on the stage.

After returning home from the theater in the late afternoon, she felt strangely shy for the first time with her husband as she hurriedly dressed in a peach satin gown for the evening festivities. She was unsure how to break his silence and decided to let the evening unfold, knowing that once their sedan chairs arrived to carry them to their party, further conversation would be impossible. Not only was she worried about the bearers eavesdropping but each trip was a kaleidoscope of eyes peering into the windows, armies of urchins who followed begging, slippery cobblestones underfoot that caused the sedans to lurch precariously, and a spectrum of odors so strong that she kept a handkerchief soaked in scent pressed to her nose the entire route. Only her eyes were gratified by the view of the elegant churches at every street corner and the grandeur of the buildings and palaces.

At the ball that evening she was delighted that Condell was the first person to sweep her off to dance the courante. She told him that the play had moved them both strongly and that she wanted to see more of Shakespeare's work before they left. He in turn wanted to know about drama in her own country. She laughed as she told him that he would probably enjoy the Powhatan dances more.

"Do the Powhatans move as we do now?"

Pocahontas smiled as she bowed and pointed her toe in the stately dance. "Sometimes, but more often they are much livelier and the best dances are done with no clothes on." She laughed again as her partner's eyes widened with surprise.

When the dance ended, she turned to see John Rolfe weaving his way among the dancers with Sir Edwin in tow.

"Princess," Sandys said, "your husband is concerned about you this evening. He fears you worry about political gossip concerning your father. Would you consider addressing Parliament yourself?"

Pocahontas squeezed her husband's hand in thanks for his thoughtfulness. He appeared to have recovered his spirits. She turned to Sir Edwin. She had thought he would represent the cause for her. Suddenly she felt weary. She had carried messages for so long. Even her trip to London was, after all, just another message. "Would they allow me to talk to them?"

"I am sure the members would be interested in hearing what you have to say. You are here as the representative of their colony and you are the daughter of the king they wish to displace. I think it would be highly suitable for you to tell them about the realities of the New World."

Pocahontas knew that no matter how much she might dread it, she would have to make the speech. She sighed as she gazed at the glittering ballroom. Instead of the cool glasses of hock, the bewigged heads, and the sparkling jewels that surrounded her she could see only the months and years that she had struggled for peace in Virginia, the many miles she had run carrying suggestions, compromises, and directives between the English and the Powhatans. Yes, she would have to be a peacemaker yet again.

She told Sir Edwin she did not want to wait. She wanted to speak to the disgruntled members of Parliament before their opinions hardened, and she knew exactly what she wanted to say. He promised to arrange something within a few weeks.

When Sir Walter Raleigh was allowed out of his prison in

the Tower to visit Pocahontas at the inn—he was only one of many notable men who had requested an opportunity to visit—they had a long conversation about the development of the colony. He listened wistfully, and she could see that he wore the sadness of a man whose destiny remained unfulfilled. Twelve years in the Tower, after being accused of conspiracy with the Spaniards to place Arabella Stuart on the throne, had taken their toll. She told him of her impending speech. He reminded her that the members of the House of Commons came in from the shires of England for only a few months of the year and were under constant pressure to raise money. King James spent hugely to satisfy his expensive tastes. The members of Parliament were good men, he told her, but bored with the tedium of tax problems. Most of them had never been out of England, and the excitement of a faraway war was diverting. "May I advise you, Princess, to keep your talk simple and descriptive?"

When Sir Edwin arrived to take her to Parliament, Pocahontas wore deep red—the color of courage in her country, she told Sandys with a smile. Above her ruff her hair was coiled in a deep bun, and on her hat swirled three gold bands like a coronet.

"No strangers are allowed to speak in the chamber where the members of Parliament sit," advised Sir Edwin. "You have been invited to one of the committee rooms where thirty men await you."

Sir Edwin's coach halted with a jolt in the courtyard of Westminster Palace and he helped her enter the stone archways of the Palace.

The rain slashed against the tall windows framing the gray river beyond. When Pocahontas entered, the room hushed. Her soft slightly accented voice barely carried at first. She told them of her beautiful country, rich in natural resources; then she described her people and their virtues. She spared them no detail of the horrific struggles the English had endured while establishing themselves. She also spoke of the animosity of the natives and of the seven long years it had taken to win confidence and peace between the two peoples. After explaining that her father was a fair man who would not break his word, she added, "But if he were attacked and the peace he has agreed to broken, he would fight. And unlike the past, when he never fully committed himself, he would throw all of his resources into driving the English out, and he has many thousands of men and many of your guns and swords. The English would never be able to keep a steady line of supplies and men coming from faraway England in time to replenish your besieged forts. I beseech you not to think of bringing bloodshed again to two peoples who are now living in hard-earned harmony."

Then Sir Edwin Sandys rose to speak: "What Princess Pocahontas has not told you is that it was she, her father's favorite child, who restrained him from all-out warfare in the early days of the Jamestown settlement. Her love of our countrymen and her diplomacy and skill in negotiation have made a significant English presence in the New World possible."

That night at a banquet given by the lord mayor at the Guild Hall, Sandys told her that during the discussion following her talk, the members of the House of Commons had finally realized the impracticality of their idea. He said her presence as an English wife and the daughter of the Powhatan king had impressed them. Pocahontas felt so relieved and delighted that when she got back to the inn she threw off her yellow ball gown and danced around the room in her most provocative and exuberant Powhatan ritual until John Rolfe finally captured her and covered her with kisses.

417

Hampton Court,
June 1616

Although the weather had turned cool and foggy, the ladies and gentlemen of the court were determined to enjoy their summer pleasures. The bucolic royal picnics often held on the lawns of the palace were simply moved indoors, and the covered tennis court was massed in summer flowers and small trees to bring the outdoors inside. Pocahontas loved it all. Every experience was new, and sometimes she found herself wishing she could spend the rest of her life dallying among the pleasures and basking in the approval of her new English friends.

After her first meeting with the king and queen, she began to like both of them, particularly the ugly little king. When he stopped her in the gardens or along the corridors of rambling Hampton Court palace and engaged her in conversation, Pocahontas realized that he was a highly intelligent man. Each talk was another brick upon which he built his opinion of her, and she felt confident that all was going well and that he liked her. She was gratified when, on the day of the Midsummer Ball, the king suddenly appeared on the garden path before her with his favorite, Lord Buckingham. She told him she was on her way to meet visitors from London who sought advice on Virginia.

"Princess, I have watched you," the king said with a smile. "Each day you keep an appointment. My people make demands on your time, for you are the repository of all the dreams and aspirations of my island-bound but ambitious men—their dreams for England and, I might add, for themselves in the New World. I told Dale that you are a fine embodiment of their hopes."

That evening at the Midsummer Ball the great hall was a blaze of light from hundreds of candles and torches. The chandeliers were waterfalls of flame. The light sparkled off the silver sconces and burnished the rich brocade hangings on the walls. The room was a mass of color with men's clothes vying with the silks and satins of the women, in every shade from palest pinks and yellows to rich purples and blues. In the fashion of the day, the ladies' breasts were fully exposed, the nipples rouged and sometimes surrounded by paste jewelry glued to the white flesh. But these were the only false gems. Rubies, emeralds, and sapphires, garnered from the rich trade with the East Indies, lavishly adorned both men and women. Their wide farthingales swayed dangerously as the ladies moved across the room like small ships on a glittering sea.

The princess hesitated for a moment at the entrance to the hall. She closed her eyes; she had become used to the wave of odors that assailed her. Giving her head a slight shake, she walked in slowly. She was dressed in pale green satin scattered with seed pearls. Her black hair was coiled and dressed high, with the glow and glitter of pearls and diamonds tucked here and there. Around her neck and across her breasts lay a triple strand of pearls, and pearl drops hung from her earlobes. Tucked low between her breasts a small diamond cross glimmered, a gift from the Virginia Company. Behind her walked three of her Virginia servants, now dressed in satin and lace and followed by the faithful Sir David, the courtier assigned to her.

The room grew quiet as all eyes turned to look at the foreign princess. Although she had been visiting at court for a week, there were still many who had not yet seen her. Rumors about her daily baths, her constant walks in all weather, her hold on Charles, the fascinated Prince of Wales, had kept tongues busy. There was even gossip about the talk she had given to Parliament.

419

Her eyes swept the room. It was difficult to see among the jostling crowd, but no face from the past leapt forward. Pocahontas was torn between relief and regret. She smiled gratefully when she saw the king's jester bouncing toward her, cutting a path through the guests, diverting them with cartwheels and grimaces, tweaking a breast here, pulling a beard there. It was still early evening, he could arrive at any time.

The jester bounded in front of her, circled around her, and danced ahead of her, blowing on an imaginary trumpet as she stepped into the crowd.

"Ah, Princess Rebecca!" Sir Edwin Sandys smiled as he bowed over her hand.

She saw him afresh, this tall elegant man with forceful blue eyes and thought again of her gratitude to this remarkable man of vision so widely admired among his peers.

Looking at her, he thought, the queen and her ladies are right: She holds herself more regally than anyone here. She has been a success beyond my wildest expectations. Even His Majesty is impressed and has decreed that she must use her full title.

He noticed that there were tiny lines of strain in the corners of her eyes. "Come," he said. "It will be another hour at least before the king arrives and the dancing starts. Let us sit in one of the adjoining rooms away from the crowd."

They chose one of the queen's small sitting rooms hung in deep red velvet, with oak chairs and a table placed before the large fireplace, in which the fire had been banked low to ward off the evening chill.

"I am sorry to hear that your husband is feeling unwell," Sandys said.

"It is only a cold, but he is susceptible in his chest. He will be with us tomorrow."

As Sir Edwin and Pocahontas talked of their hopes for Virginia, he watched her slow, elegant movements. When she moved there was the faint rustle of her taffeta underskirt and a slight, very faint scent of flowers. It was a fragrance unknown to Sir Edwin. He delighted in her sophistication.

There was a soft knock at the door. Sir David stood in the doorway, his expression reflecting relief when he saw them, but there was a hesitation in his voice. "I have been looking everywhere for you, Princess. I knew you would want me to tell you that Captain John Smith is here and has asked to see you."

Pocahontas half rose from her chair. She looked at Sir Edwin, her chest so tight that her breath came in faint gasps.

"Shall I invite him in, Princess?" asked Sir David.

Sir Edwin saw that her face had gone stark white and yet her eyes glowed strangely. He realized with shock that he had last seen eyes like that when he closed in on a kill in the hunting field.

She nodded almost imperceptibly as apprehension washed over her.

Sir David turned and threw the door open. Smith walked into the room and for a long moment stood staring at Pocahontas. Then he bowed deeply and raised her hand slowly to his lips. If Smith said anything, Pocahontas did not hear him. She was only aware that with his touch everything fell away and when she looked into his eyes, the god of sky was there and the rest of her life meant nothing.

"I could not find you, Pocahontas!"

She opened her mouth to speak, but no words came out.

"Princess, are you all right?" Sir Edwin was at her side.

She struggled to articulate, but still she could not talk.

"I will go and get some hock." Sir David turned quickly and was out the door.

"Come and sit down," Smith said as he and Sir Edwin guided her toward her chair.

The men were gentle. She could hear their worried voices, but although she wanted to speak, she could not. She willed herself to say a word, but not a sound escaped her lips. She knew only that John Smith's eyes and his touch had enveloped her, and nothing else mattered.

CHAPTER
-»⁕ 26 ⁕«-

Hampton Court Palace, July 1616

She sat in the window seat of her bedroom at Hampton Court Palace and stared out at the morning mist rising from the river where one of the royal swans stretched and preened. She had not been able to eat or speak since the night before. It is worse than I even imagined, she thought dully. What am I to do? All through the night she had prayed, but for the first time she was not comforted. She was so new to the Christian religion that there were many things of which she was still unsure, but she knew that what she felt now was a sin, not only in her new faith but among her own people as well. When John Rolfe had tried to tempt her with breakfast this morning her remorse had made her almost faint as he leaned over her, trusting and worried. When he asked her if she would feel happier back at the inn in London, she had nodded quickly. At least the inn is my home in this country and I will feel more in control, she thought. She could escape from the palace and from Smith, but of course he would follow. She remembered the recognition and determination in Smith's eyes. Desire stunned her body again and the hunger made her tremble.

It was not until evening, when Mehta brought little Thomas in to visit her, that the sight of his eager face finally enabled Pocahontas to speak, answering his questions. The Powhatans and the courtiers close to them sighed in relief that the princess could talk again. They said among themselves that perhaps the strain of this visit to England had been too much for her.

The next morning when the entourage climbed into the waiting coaches, for the trip back to the inn in London, everything seemed normal to the waving members of the court, including the Prince of Wales, who had come to see them off. The Rolfes were invited to rejoin the court at a fete to celebrate its return to Windsor in a few weeks' time. Although she was still unable to eat, Pocahontas kept a smile on her face and said a grateful farewell to those who had been hospitable to her and her family.

The next afternoon a note arrived at the inn. Alone, Pocahontas tore it open with shaking hands. It was from Smith. He wanted to call on her that evening. She instructed the bearer to tell him she was not at home. Crushing the note in her hands, she threw it across the desk. She raged around the room, her fists in tight balls, alternately calling on God to banish Smith for ripping her heart apart and beseeching him to guide her, to have mercy on her.

Suddenly she felt an urge to run. If she could just move freely, she would be able to think clearly. She thought longingly of the forests in Virginia. In England women of rank did not travel except in a coach or a sedan, but she could take a walk now, before John returned home from a meeting. She snatched a light hooded wrap to conceal herself and darted out of her room undetected. I can escape for an hour, she thought. Everyone thinks I am resting.

From a doorway across the street John Smith saw her slip out of the inn. He would have recognized her lithe movements in any disguise, he thought, but where was she going without an escort, without transport? He cursed as he followed her up the street. I am like an animal, he thought, blindly pursuing the scent. If I had had any idea that seeing her would reawaken such desire I would never have gone to Hampton Court. My life was pleasant, my memory of her had dimmed, and now I am fired again by my passion for her. I must get my hands in her hair and feel her body against mine. I must know why she married in Virginia. God's fishes, and there is a second husband now, for she is married to Rolfe, a man I respect. As he weaved his way through the traffic, Smith knew that once he had her alone, none of these things would matter. I am stalking her, he thought, as surely as a stag goes after a doe, and the streets of London are my territory. He pulled his hat down farther over his forehead.

A light summer rain gave the cobblestones a polish like pewter and made them slippery. Pocahontas pushed her way among the people bustling off to their various tasks. There were tradesmen and servants, but few women, she noticed, as she threaded her way among the carts, sedans, horsemen, and an occasional coach. It was difficult to walk quickly in the crowded streets, but her mind was diverted from her problems almost at once by the activity, the shouts and calls of hawkers, the cries of children, the beseeching hands of the beggars. She forgot everything as she was carried along, up one street and down another as they curved and twisted, some so narrow that the black-beamed houses plastered together with white daub almost met over- head. She had been gone an hour before she realized that she should have returned to the inn long since. But how to retrace her steps? Suddenly she had no idea where she was. Pocahontas had never been lost in her life, but this was a different world. The signs that she could read to guide her in Virginia did not exist here. Everything is too strange for me still. Then she remembered the river. If she could get to the Thames, she could follow it back to familiar territory. She turned to an old woman selling flowers from a doorway and asked where the river was. The woman gave a toothless grin and waved her down another street, but after a long walk she still had not reached her destination. Her family would be concerned about her now, and she hated the thought of them suffering. The light was beginning to fade and the streets to empty. All decent people would be going to supper. She caught up with three street urchins who were idling near a barrow and asked them for directions.

"The mistress wants the river," said one.

"She ben't no mistress. A stranger woman she is," cried another. He picked up a pebble and lobbed it at Pocahontas's shoe.

"Look 'ow she jumps!" called the third.

As she turned to flee, the boys scooped more stones and rushed after her, chortling and throwing as they ran. In full flight Pocahontas turned a corner, slipped on a wet cobblestone, and fell to her knees. Angry and wet, she felt the sting of the pebbles as they beat against her back and arms. Then she heard a man's voice chasing away the urchins and saw a hand reach out to help her up.

The stranger brushed off her cloak and asked if she was all right. Pocahontas's eyes blazed furiously out of a face splattered with mud. "I was looking for the river."

The man noted her slightly accented voice and her natural demeanor of command. "You have had a shock, and I apologize for the wicked boys. Let me take you to the tavern two doors away where you can wash. You need a drink, too."

She agreed to go with him. She felt filthy and thirsty, and because of his kindness she felt sure he would direct her back to her inn.

Although the public house was crowded from door to wall, Pocahontas could see instantly that the patrons were responsible men of affairs. Her heart warmed, and she sighed with relief as she accepted a pewter mug of wine. Raising the wine to her lips, she felt a strong compulsion to turn around. Coming slowly toward her from the door was John Smith, consternation written on his face. The mug she was holding fell with a crash to the floor.

She didn't remember anything more until she regained consciousness upstairs in a bedroom over the tavern and felt Smith's gentle hands as he alternatively washed the mud from her face and kissed her lips and eyelids. She knew now that she couldn't fight any longer. She would belong to him again and he would answer a need at the very core of her being.

Through his kisses she told him she had to return to her family, for they must be frantic with worry. He replied that a messenger had been sent to say that she was safe, and a sedan had been ordered. Then his hands became urgent and she had no will to stop them. She felt that God had forsaken her. Why else would Smith have been here in this tavern of all the taverns in London? As she responded to his touch she felt the devil must have possessed her, for her body was a wild thing, acting of its own accord once again. He was savage in his need for her, and she welcomed and exulted in the fierce joy that waved rhythmically through her body, reaching a crescendo. They parted, hunger still beating within them.

"I followed you," he said. "I had to remind you of what we are together. I couldn't let you go otherwise."

Pocahantas leaned heavily on his arm as Smith led her down the narrow stairs to the courtyard below and guided her into her sedan. As he walked alongside her in the quiet of the night, their bodies fulfilled with their lovemaking, she asked finally why he had abandoned her that day so long ago. The crossed signals were finally cleared. They could only look into each other's eyes and wonder what their lives would have been had he not been injured, had she not been married to Kokum.

She promised Smith that she would see him again but not often, because there were too many demands on her in London. She did not tell him that she was a prisoner of her own emotions, that he had captured her love at such a formative age that he was an intrinsic part of her, the wellspring of her soul. For it was because of him and through him that her life had evolved as it had. Nor did she say that she was afraid of her feelings.

Life was so busy, so filled with callers, fetes, dinners, and balls, that Pocahontas threw herself into her role as a representative of the New World with intense fervor. She talked, she danced, and at the right moments she sparkled in her old mischievous way as she went from meeting to reception. Her active life kept her from introspection, so that whenever she looked into her husband's eyes she was able to stifle her conscience. And she gained time to conquer her fears.

Smith waited for the next meeting, but he received no word. He sent a discreet note. It was politely acknowledged, but that was all. Then, unexpectedly, they met at a masque. He seated himself next to her, as close to her as he dared. He looked at her high round breasts below her ruff, and it was all he could do to keep from cupping his hands under them and raising them to his mouth. Racked with jealousy, he watched Rolfe and wondered if he, too, knew the wildness that could be found beneath the exterior of this polished woman. It seemed unfair that he had buried the memory of a lovely, savage princess dressed in skins and furs on a far-off shore, only to find her again in London, an acknowledged diplomat and heroine, clothed in satins and jewels, speaking three languages, and in demand everywhere. And she was not available to him.

When the music ceased, he brought her supper. He pleaded for a meeting.

"I am going shortly to my husband's home in Norfolk," she told him. "When we return in several weeks' time I will send you word." There was a dart of pain in Pocahontas's eyes as she turned away.

Rolfe had decided to move them all to Brentford in the autumn after a visit to his family lands. When Pocahontas had lost her voice he worried that the Virginia Company was making her work too hard. In Brentford the air would be clear and they would be a little farther away from the inevitable callers. He wanted a reprieve from London himself for Pocahontas's visit was a success and he was bored with the constant questions about having married so far above himself.

The dust from the road hovered in a permanent cloud over the Rolfe coaches on the week-long journey through the lush greenery to Heacham in Norfolk. Pocahontas thought the journey would never end. Away from the distractions of London she was forced to think about Smith. Their physical attraction to each other had resurfaced as if the years apart had never existed. She was not surprised, for she had always longed for him, but after her happy marriage she was sure her weakness for him would have died if they had not met again. She remembered her first meeting with Kokum at Kecoughtan when her desires were just awakening. When she had danced that warm night poised on the brink of womanhood, she'd had a premonition that she would be a prisoner to her body in life. She was afraid of herself.

She also took advantage of the long, confined hours of travel to pray, although she wondered if God still cared for her now that she was so steeped in sin. She thought of the Virginia Company and her responsibilities to it; if anyone knew she was an adulteress! She shuddered.

She devoted herself extravagantly to her family's needs, lavishing attention on them in an effort to make up for the fact that she yearned for another man.

Whenever the coach stopped and they got out to stretch their legs, she could see that the scenery of the countryside showed an exceptional expanse of blue sky. It was a great comfort to her and she ached to lie in a meadow.

The entire Rolfe family was standing on the steps of Heacham Hall when the coaches finally clattered to a stop. It was a joyful reunion for John Rolfe, and his new family was enveloped in hospitality. From the first evening of long toasts and a sumptuous goose dinner Pocahontas felt as if she had been a member of the family all her life. Their kindness made waves of remorse wash over her as she thought of her duplicity.

As one sunny day led to another, little Thomas enjoyed himself so much that he told his mother and father he never wanted to leave. Uncles, aunts, and grandparents lavished affection on him, and every desire was fulfilled for the exotic young princeling. For the first time Pocahontas was fully aware of her son's English heritage, which stretched back centuries to the Norse invaders. The child was as much a part of England as he was of Virginia. She agreed immediately to sit for a portrait of the two of them. The family would have it as a remembrance until the Rolfes' next trip back from the New World.

Throughout the days Pocahontas watched Thomas with his relatives. She discussed with John Rolfe a plan to leave him behind to be schooled in England. After toying with the idea for a couple of weeks they both decided that his place was in Virginia, to grow and prosper with them in the challenge of a new continent. In the back of her mind she had even considered remaining with Thomas in London for several years, taking just a short time out of her life to live discreetly with Smith. But the more she indulged her heart, the more she knew that her duty lay with John Rolfe in Virginia.

CHAPTER
27

Heacham Hall, Norfolk,
July 1616

T he weeks of Rolfe hospitality seemed to flash by in minutes. Warm sunlit mornings unfolded lazily while the
women of the house visited among themselves in one
room or the other before descending to lunch and heated discussions of politics. Excursions were made down country
lanes thick with flowers for picnics under the trees. Teas followed in the afternoons, with children and laughter on green
lawns. Then came the long twilights that seemed to touch the
dawn, embracing friends and wine. Pocahontas wished these
days would never end. The angles in her figure softened under
the onslaught of the region's rich cream, which seemed to appear
in every dish. But her responsibility to the Virginia Company
could not be ignored, and soon the morning of farewell kisses,
tears, and promises was upon them.

During the weeks that she was cocooned in family affection
she began to think without fear. At first she longed only to return
to John Smith. She made up her mind that the hunger in her body
could not be ignored. It was compounded by the adulation she
had felt for him and by the frustration of their years of separation.

She had to have him, just for a while. The first nights at Heacham Hall were rent by nightmares, and John Rolfe would walk her gently around the bedroom until she stopped trembling.

But the sweet pattern of the country days smoothed the violent swings in her emotions. As the days wore on, she began to see that although most of her adult life had been steeped in passion for John Smith she must somehow make herself renounce him. When she watched her son tumble and play at his father's feet, she knew that deep affection and devotion were strong emotions, too, and were enough for her future life, for she had been happy. She knew also that duty and responsibility were so ingrained within her that if she ignored them, she would eventually destroy herself as surely as if she plunged an arrow through her heart. She knew all of this as she slowly came to her decision . . . but what would she do when she saw Smith?

Brentford was far enough on the outskirts of London, so that the Rolfes could lead a quiet life until their return to London in the late autumn. Even so, callers galloped up hot and dusty to the door of their house almost every day of the week. Rolfe never ceased to be impressed with how Pocahontas used her diplomatic skills in satisfying their queries and concerns about the New World.

Pocahontas had seen Smith once in the distance at a country fair near their village. Her heart thudding, she had pulled a disappointed Thomas away from the jesters who fascinated him and bundled him into their coach. She was sure that Smith had not seen her. It was her recurring fear that she would run into him unexpectedly again when her defenses were down, for then she would be lost.

The king and queen were summering with their court at nearby Windsor Castle. Interested in seeing more of their exotic visitor, they invited her to a ball. The minute Pocahontas glimpsed the royal liveryman bearing the news she knew that a meeting with Smith was not far away. The queen was a thoughtful hostess and was careful to include people who had shared the same experiences.

The Rolfes stayed the night of the ball at an inn in Windsor. Pocahontas dressed carefully, choosing a gown of yellow silk. Her fingers shook as she helped her maid adjust the cool pearls around her throat; she was grateful that her husband was not a particularly observant man. He did not notice that her voice was strained.

The evening was warm enough that she needed only a light wrap for the short walk to the castle. Any other night she would have enjoyed the scene as the chatting guests in their varicolored silks moved like flowers bending in the wind as they approached the courtyard.

Pocahontas saw him immediately when she entered the ballroom. The dancing had already started, and Smith partnered a slender lady whose hair was white-blond. As they swayed through the mannered steps Pocahontas thought she must flee immediately, for he had never appeared so handsome, so desirable. Then their eyes locked. When their hands touched later in the galliard, Pocahontas's mouth was so dry she could not swallow. As the slow dance continued and they were briefly partners again, Smith asked quickly if he could get her some wine. Her nod was enough encouragement so that when he returned he persuaded her to take a tour of the gardens with him. As they walked along a path outside the castle, Pocahontas put her hand up to stop his speech and blurted, her voice hoarse with effort, "I cannot continue to see you. I cannot be your wife, and I cannot deceive my husband again."

Her throat was still so dry that a wave of coughing swept over her. When Smith put his arm around her shoulders the warmth of his body unnerved her almost completely. She moved away quickly and continued.

"You have been a part of me since my childhood, in my blood, my heart, and almost my every thought. I have grown through you, I have struggled for you, and I have killed for you. I have loved you in a way that I will never be able to love another man, but I tell you now that I cannot see you again, ever."

Pocahontas turned, but Smith grasped her and pulled her into his arms. When his face moved toward hers the pain around her heart was so severe she could barely move. She managed to break away from him and hurry back into the castle.

The next morning she did not remember anything that had happened during the remainder of the evening. She knew she must have danced and talked as usual, for her husband was cheerful in his praise of the evening in general and complimentary about her.

As their breakfast was served, he said, "Sandys told me that John Smith spoke to him last night. He has changed his plans and will leave almost immediately for the New World. He wants to explore Virginia between Jamestown and Nova Scotia."

Somehow Pocahontas managed to get through the rest of the month at Brentwood, but when she and Rolfe finally packed for their return to London she knew that she would never be able to hear the name Brentwood again without feeling a wave of melancholy. Not only was her heart lacerated, but Thomas had cut his foot and the wound had become infected. When the physician called and wanted to bleed Thomas, Pocahontas and Mehta had pleaded with Rolfe not to allow it. They said it would drain away his good spirits. The Powhatans had then searched for herbal ingredients at the local market. They had made a plaster of fresh herbs each day and applied it to the child's foot day and night. Before long the healthy little boy had recovered.

When the Rolfes returned to London, Pocahontas threw every ounce of her energy into making speeches and attending dinners. She tried not to turn down any invitation no matter how difficult, for she wanted to be busy. Sir Edwin Sandys gave a ball at Guild Hall for all the merchants and aristocrats who had invested in the Virginia Company and for those who might be future investors as well. Pocahontas created a sensation when she descended the stairs dressed in white velvet, a white ruff, pearls, and diamonds. Later, the king and queen held a masque where the gossips noticed the queen danced every other dance with the Duke of Buckingham, and the Prince of Wales hovered around the exotic foreign princess as she glittered in emerald green.

Ben Jonson came to call at the Belle Sauvage Inn. He wore over his shoulder a copy of Tomoco's bag, which hung from two straps. Made of satin instead of skins it was the current London rage. Pocahontas had heard of Jonson's brilliance, his coffeehouse meeting place, and his ability to sway opinion. He was so fascinated by her that he sat for forty-five minutes without ever taking his eyes off her. As she told Rolfe afterward, "I endured it because of his efforts for the Virginia venture, but where was the famous tongue?"

Pocahontas did not forget her less fortunate friends. She went to the Tower accompanied by Sir Walter Raleigh to visit his fellow prisoner the Earl of Northumberland, Percy's elder brother. Her heart sank when she saw the cold stone room, and she wondered how anyone could exist so cruelly imprisoned year after year without the visiting rights to the outside world that Sir Walter enjoyed.

"I never get used to it, my lady, but the view is diverting," said the aging aristocrat as he waved his hand toward the narrow slit of a window slashed in the fortress walls overlooking the river Thames.

The earl was so touched by her concern that he asked for the pearl earrings she was wearing so that he could fashion silver surrounds for them, using the tools with which he conducted his notable experiments while in the Tower. She returned to visit him three times that winter, and both she and the earl encouraged Sir Walter to make still another voyage of discovery after his imminent release from the fortress. She told the explorer that it would make up for the lost years of imprisonment.

John Rolfe took Pocahontas aside one cold day in December when the fog swirled in off the river and the Powhatans busily stoked the fires in the comfortable rooms at the inn. "It is time we returned to Virginia and our life there," Rolfe said. "Edwin Sandys has told me that our visit here has increased interest in the colony a hundred times over. We must go home and prepare for a wave of immigration."

"I know we have been away from our land long enough, but I am loath to leave this beautiful city!" Pocahontas twisted her hands in her lap as she gazed into the fire.

"I suggest we take passage on the H.M.S. *George,* which leaves in March. If you would prefer to remain for a while longer—"

"Oh, no!" Pocahontas did not want to risk being left alone in a city where she might meet John Smith.

"Jamestown will seem quiet after the excitement of our life here," Rolfe admitted, "but perhaps we will be invited here again in a few years. In any case I will bring you back."

Pocahontas smiled.

The last few weeks of their stay in London sped by. The king received Pocahontas in an audience to discuss his successful colony, and Sir Edwin held a farewell reception for her. Before the guests—London's most successful merchants—Sandys thanked her and her husband for the outstanding effort they had made on behalf of the Virginia Company.

Before she arrived in June, she had never dreamed that she would become so attached to London. She had been curious, of course, and a little frightened; she had come to England to do her duty and endure an ordeal, but her trip had been neither. It had been a turning point in her life, and when she stepped away from English soil she would be leaving behind forever the young girl who had offered up her life and love to John Smith. Someday soon she knew she would be serene. The ache for Smith would cease, and the tenderness and affection she felt for John Rolfe would deepen. There would be other children, for she wanted to have a large family. Now that she knew she would come back to London for visits, she looked forward to returning to her beloved Virginia with her husband and son. There was so much to accomplish, so much still to learn, so much to live for.

CHAPTER
##

Gravesend, England, March 1617

The first crocuses pushed jauntily through the greening grass as Pocahontas, her family, and their servants took coaches to Gravesend, where the *George* awaited the tide and wind for Virginia. The weather was unseasonably mild, and there was not a vestige of the usual turbulence in the air that made March a good month for sailing.

Pocahontas felt a light chill and pulled her coat around her as she greeted the captain. She explained that last-minute business held John Rolfe briefly in London. Then she and the other Powhatans settled themselves on board. Pocahontas liked her quarters, for her bed had a nice porthole view of the sea and sky.

She awoke the next morning coughing and feeling feverish. She asked Mehta for some of her herbal remedies and was strongly dosed with chamomile. By teatime, however, her fever had increased and Mehta asked the captain to send for John Rolfe. Two visitors from the House of Commons who had a last-minute request of the princess were told that she was unwell and were sent away. She ate a light supper and remained in bed.

She clasped Thomas in her arms tenderly but briefly, gave him a good-night kiss, and gloried in his strength and beauty.

The next afternoon Pocahontas had not felt like eating and the fever was still with her. John Rolfe was worried. He sent a messenger to Sandys requesting a physician. The next morning Sir Edwin arrived with the queen's own doctor, but when he wanted to bleed Pocahontas, Mehta resisted strongly.

Pocahontas knew they were worried about her, but she wished they wouldn't be. She would feel better in a day or two and in the meantime it was restful to lie quietly and gaze out of the porthole at the sky and clouds. Not a day had been gray since she arrived at Gravesend. She wondered if her body was betraying her by becoming ill when she was leaving England. The priests in Werowocomoco would have suggested that. She drifted off to sleep, and when she awoke her mouth felt dry. John Rolfe was asking her to drink a little water. He was such a kind and good husband. She felt stronger just by holding his hand. She wished she did not feel so hot; it was like one of the worst summer days in Werowocomoco when one could barely breathe because of the heat.

My father is smiling at me, she thought. He is telling me the heat will go away soon. Why, it was nighttime again. She could hear the sounds of the forest around her, the hoot of an owl, the soft slither of a snake, a field mouse darting under a nearby leaf. She needed to hurry, she had to meet John Smith, she would soon feel his arms around her, but first she would take a cool drink of water, for it was sunlight again and they were talking to her.

John Rolfe's voice is so soft in my ear. I wish I could tell him I am all right and that I can hear them. They are sending for the priests, but the priests do not belong to my life anymore. I am in the hands of the true God and he watches over me. I can feel he is with me now. I must tell my husband not to worry. There,

John is leaning toward me. Is he worried about Thomas? I must tell him, "Do not worry. We have our son."

Pocahontas smiled. They will all feel better and so will I, now that I am lying in my meadow. I can feel the god of sky; he is enfolding me in his arms, my true god. His eyes are so blue. Why, it is John Smith. He is trying to tell me something. I am so happy. The blue is all around me and is one with me.

She reached up her arms to the god of sky.

EPILOGUE

Gravesend, England,
March 1635

The March wind blew the rain around Thomas Rolfe's head as he looked down at the headstone in the small graveyard. He could barely remember that other March so long ago when his mother had left him forever. He remembered how bewildered he had been, but he was so sick himself that it was all a blur. When the ship had reached Portsmouth, his father had been worried about his making the ocean crossing and had sent for a cousin, Sir Lewis Stukley, who took Thomas in and educated him according to his father's wishes. In the years that followed, every ship seemed to carry back from Virginia long and loving instructions from Rolfe, but the letters had stopped after the terrible massacre of 1622. The great king Powhatan had died not long after he heard of the death of his favorite child, and the leadership had passed to his brother Opechancanough, who was determined finally to drive the English into the sea. He failed, but the toll was terrible; hundreds on both sides were slaughtered. Thomas had lost his mother, father, and a grandfather before he was old enough to travel back to Virginia to take up his vast tracts of land and the farm that had been kept for him.

Now he was leaving England; his ship was scheduled to sail the next day. As he stared down at his mother's grave he held in his hand a book he was reading about John Smith's first days in Virginia. He had never heard that his mother had rescued Smith not once but three times. When he had called on Smith, an aging bachelor, he asked him why he had not written about his experiences before 1625. Smith had looked stricken at Thomas, who so strongly resembled his mother and had finally replied that it was difficult for him to recall those first fierce years in the colony.

Thomas knelt in prayer for a long moment by the grave. He wondered if his mother would have preferred to lie in Virginia soil, but he would never know. He stood up and said a few words of farewell. He knew he would never return to England to live. He had made up his mind long ago to grasp the opportunity that his inheritance offered him in the New World. He raised his hand in farewell, then turned and ran eagerly toward the river and his waiting ship.

AFTERWORD

Very soon after Pocahontas's death, John Rolfe returned to Virginia. He wrote regularly to his son, who was in the care of his cousin Sir Lewis Stukley and Rolfe's younger brother, Henry. Rolfe was concerned about Thomas's education and that his inheritance would remain intact. In the latter respect he wrote to his good friend Sir Edwin Sandys asking that the Virginia Company's stipend for Pocahontas be continued for her son's well-being. He also wrote Sir Edwin of the great sorrow and mourning in Virginia when the settlers and the naturals heard of Pocahontas's death. Rolfe traveled inland to tell Powhatan about his daughter, and the old emperor was so distressed that he gave up his throne in favor of his brother Opitchapan and went to live with the Patawomekes, the people farthest away from the English. Even so, he died the following year, in 1618.

Rolfe continued to perfect tobacco growing until it became the colony's main export. He continued a voluminous correspondence with Sir Edwin Sandys, who in turn recruited hundreds of new colonists for the New World.

Opechancanough, who succeeded his brother, Opitchapan,

within four years, was not as wise a ruler as Powhatan. Tension between the English and Powhatans increased, culminating in a bloody uprising and massacre in 1622. Three hundred colonists were killed, including John Rolfe.

Young Thomas Rolfe returned in 1635 to Varina, the house in which he was born. The Powhatans had kept for him the many thousands of acres he had inherited from their royal princess as well as those of his grandfather, King Powhatan. John Rolfe had also secured rights to the lands by taking out a royal patent from the English king for his son. Although Thomas visited the Powhatans from time to time he made his life with the English and married an English girl "of goodly looks," Jane Poythress. From that union descended many generations of statesmen, lawmakers, educators, and ministers, mainly through three distinguished Virginia families—the Randolphs, Bollings, and Blairs.

John Smith returned once to New England to explore in 1619. He then went back to England, where he died in 1631. He never married.